US,
FATEFULLY

TWO SOULS.
FOUR JOURNEYS.
ONE CHANCE TO
CHANGE THEIR FATE.

US, FATEFULLY

KIERSTEN SCHIFFER

Published by Sweet Light Press

ISBN: 979-8-9857701-8-6
e-book ISBN: 979-8-9857701-9-3
Cover Design and Formatting by Damonza

To Andrew, my real-life summer camp romance.
I'm glad I get to spend all of my fractals with you.

Spoilers below!

Only read if you've finished Book One in the Treasured Love series.

Three years after her mom died of cancer, twenty-one-year-old Annie took a summer job as a counselor at Camp Boundless, a camp for children with disabilities.

There she met Theo, a nursing student who she definitely was *not* attracted to for multiple reasons. (He was a younger man, had long hair, and worse yet…he was an optimist!)

As they spent more time together, Theo admitted he had once been a camper at Camp Boundless, having battled childhood leukemia when he was a teenager. Theo also divulged that he had a Near-Death Experience when he was sick and was given the option to return to his life, but with one caveat: he wouldn't live past the age of twenty-one.

When he was in the afterlife, Theo also saw a fractal of his future where he would meet Annie at Camp Boundless. His Angel Guide explained that his and Annie's futures were linked, and that together they could impact not only their own lives but the lives of many others.

What Theo didn't tell Annie was that she was standing beside him in the afterlife and they'd agreed to find their Intertwined Path together. (Annie doesn't remember that part… at least not yet.)

Although she wanted to stay skeptical, Annie had an experience the night her mom died where she passed out on the bathroom floor and felt like she saw her mom in a dream. In that dream, her mom told her, "When he comes, believe him." And because of that vivid directive, Annie can't help but believe Theo's story.

Annie grew more and more attracted to Theo and was just about to admit her feelings to him when she realized their best friend Greta was in love with Theo. With that new knowledge (and the growing pressure of this otherworldly commitment) Annie pushed Theo away.

But when their separation hurt too much, Annie gave in and invited Theo to go home with her for the weekend. At her sister Caroline's house, Theo saw a picture of Annie's mom. Shocked by the image, Theo told Annie that the Angel Guide he saw on the other side was Annie's mom.

He then showed Annie two watercolor postcards that had been sent to him from Montana right before camp started. Theo's postcards matched two similar postcards that Annie's mom had left her in her will.

Tipped off by the return address of Montana they called Annie's Aunt Lydia who explained that right before Annie's mom Grace, died, she put together a final Treasure Hunt for Annie—similar to the ones they used to play together when Annie was a child. The postcards were the first clues to lead them to the treasure.

By this time, Annie sensed an almost otherworldly connection with Theo but tried to deny it. Remembering Greta's love of Theo, she agreed to go on the Treasure Hunt with Theo, but as friends only.

In the final chapter of the book, we flashed to the afterlife once again. There, Annie and Theo's Angel Guide (aka Grace, Annie's mom) informed them there is actually a way to change their fate. They just have to get to a certain point in time, and if they do, they'll be able to jump timelines and Theo will not die young after all.

That exact moment was shown to them as the two of them standing together with Annie wearing a wedding dress.

To make things more of a challenge (and more fun!) the couple agreed to have their memory of the timeline jump erased so neither of them will know that Theo has the possibility of living beyond the age of twenty-one.

Finding that exact point in time will be a long shot. But fortunately, Annie and Theo have a special Angel on their side, and her little game will either push them apart or lead them to the place where their futures will be changed forevermore.

Now, turn the page to see what Fate has in store for our clueless couple as they start out on their first adventure…

PART ONE

CHAPTER ONE

Indiana 1989
ANNIE

"SO YOU GUYS are spending another weekend together, huh?" Greta frowns as she walks to where Theo and I are cramming our bags into the back of his car.

The way she looks at us sends a wave of guilt crashing over me. She's clearly jealous we're leaving together.

Oblivious to the tension in the air, Theo throws an arm around my shoulder and grins big. "Yeah, me and Annie, together again! Some might call us the dynamic duo. But I prefer to call us the 'Wonder Twins'." He motions back and forth between our foreheads. "I think that better explains the weird telepathy we share."

I groan and shove Theo away, once again wishing his enthusiasm had an On and Off switch. When Miles had released us from our jobs as camp counselors for the weekend, I'd tried to sneak to the car so Greta wouldn't see us leaving. Theo was the one who had yelled goodbye to her across the parking lot and blown our cover. Is he really so dense? Can't he see Greta is in love with him?

"Um…Theo's just giving me a ride home," I say, fidgeting with the tangled seat belt strap inside the car so I don't have to look her in the eye. "My car is acting up, so I'm leaving it here this weekend."

Theo stiffens at my lie, but thankfully keeps his mouth shut and plays along.

"Alright, well, you two have fun then!" Greta says in a tight voice. She gives us a limp wave, then stalks to her car. I can tell she doesn't believe my story. Which only makes me feel worse than I already do.

All week, whenever Greta was around, I'd tried to be sensitive and not to talk about how Theo and I had spent last weekend together. But since Theo doesn't know he's her Mystery Man crush, he wasn't so discreet. He'd blabbed on and on at the lunch table about meeting my sister and her husband and playing with their kids. He wouldn't shut up about how much fun we all had together.

At least he hadn't mentioned the Treasure Hunt my mom left behind for me: The mission Theo and I are now on to locate four of her paintings, find their titles, then receive clues to help us track down the mystery treasure she left behind for me three years ago before she died. He'd agreed we could keep that to ourselves. At least for now.

Which is why I can't tell Greta that there's nothing romantic going on between Theo and me. That we're merely on a mission to locate 155 Black Hollow Road, where, hopefully in about an hour, we'll find the first of the four paintings, call my Aunt Lydia with the title so she can send us our clue, and then both go our separate ways for the rest of the weekend.

Theo stays quiet as we pull out of the driveway, like he's waiting for me to explain why I'd lied to Greta. But I can't reveal how I'd figured out that Greta is in love with him, so I just stare out the window and watch the storm clouds gathering over the vast expanse of pastureland, thinking about how their roiling darkness mirrors the trepidation brewing inside my stomach.

Part of me is excited about starting our adventure. Before I'd left my sister Caroline's house last weekend, we'd had fun musing about what might be at the end of the hunt. Would it be my great-grandmother's silver locket we'd yet to locate in mom's belongings? A surprise gift?

Maybe even a wad of cash my mom kept stashed away in one of her strange hiding places?

But another part of me is nervous about what's coming.

"I still say we should have called ahead of time," I shout over the roar of the open car windows. It seems the air conditioning in Theo's rattle trap car doesn't work. Along with the radio and left-hand blinker. Good Lord, I hope we make it to our destination before this little Datsun dissolves into a pile of rust in the middle of the road.

"I think your sister was right," Theo says. "It will be harder for people to tell us 'No' when we're standing right in front of them than if we ask them on the phone."

I turn away so he can't see me roll my eyes. I'm still a little cranky about being out-voted last weekend when everyone chose Caroline's sneak-attack approach over my more measured plan. I can't believe I now have to show up on some stranger's doorstep and ask them to let me into their house so I can paw over their belongings like some beggar off the street. I hate asking people for favors. I hate being at their mercy like that. Although in the case of this painting, my call-ahead argument had been moot. Because there had been no name written on the photograph to look up in the phone book, anyway. Only the strange words Teela Wooket, and an address that was luckily only two towns away.

Theo chatters as he drives, telling funny stories about his campers and speculating about what the what the words Teela Wooket might mean. "I think it's another name for Bigfoot. You know people claim they've seen him in these parts. Maybe we're going to the house where he vacations when he's not scaring people in the woods."

When I only grunt, he presses further. "What do you think Teela Wooket means, Annie?"

"I don't know," I say listlessly. "Maybe, 'all trespassers will be shot on sight'?"

He laughs, then tries some more to get me to talk, to no avail. "You okay?" he finally asks after my twenty-seventh grunt of the trip.

"Yeah, I'm fine." I repeat. But then something urges me to tell him the truth. "Actually, I'm nervous as hell."

"Yeah? About what?"

I hesitate, unsure of how to put my fears into words. "I don't know. I feel like my mom put so much energy into making this Treasure Hunt special for me. It's such a 'once-in-a-lifetime' opportunity that I feel like I have to make this the best experience ever. I have to have fun, and savor it, and learn things, and find all the right pieces. And if I don't have an amazing time, I'll have wasted it all. I'll once again be the ungrateful brat who doesn't deserve all the effort she put into me."

Theo considers my reasoning. "That sounds like you're putting a lot of pressure on yourself."

"I know! And it's stupid, because *I'm* the one making it a big deal. Believe me. I want to have fun and enjoy the last game my dead mom planned for me! But I can't help it. There's something wrong with me. I worry so much about everything. And make things harder than they need to be. And squash all the joy from everything by being too anxious all the time. I feel like I'm constantly trying to figure out how to do things right. Whatever the hell that might be." I shake my head, hoping I'm making sense. "And I can never figure it out. I always end up messing things up and doing everything wrong. I don't want to be this way. But I can't seem to fix it. For some dumb reason, it's just how I am." When I finish, I'm out of breath. And wishing I hadn't revealed how my nonsensical mind really works.

He thinks for a second, then asks, "What if it's okay to feel however you feel right now?"

I scoff. "What do you mean by that?"

"What if you allowed yourself to be worried and anxious without feeling like you need to fix it? What if it you could let it all be okay? How would that make you feel?"

Something swells in my chest, a tickle that works its way up my throat, making a giggle shoot out before I can stop it. "That would feel amazing!" I blurt, then quickly cover my mouth.

He cocks an eyebrow at me, not saying anything more.

"But I can't just do that! I can't just let myself off the hook like that!"

"Why not?"

"Because…because…that would be too easy!"

He shrugs lazily. "Maybe it's okay to let it be easy, Annie."

I roll my eyes at him, pretending that what he's just said is utterly ridiculous. But as I stare out at the grey highway stretching before us, I let his simple words sink in. Could he be right? Could it be okay to feel like I'm enough, that I don't need to change anything at all, only because it makes me feel better right now? Dammit, I don't want to admit it, but I can already tell Theo's going to have me thinking about this conversation long into the night.

CHAPTER TWO

AS WE TURN off the highway onto a smaller road it starts raining; fat drops that pepper the windshield in a rhythmic *rat-a-tat-tat*. Theo turns on the windshield wipers, but true to everything else in the car, they don't work very well. They merely carve a few narrow streaks in the glass, making me wonder how he can even see to drive.

As the rain comes down harder, I start to make a crack about how it feels like our mission is already doomed, but then I remember the phrase Theo's tried so hard to drill into me (*What if the Universe is friendly, Annie?*) and decide maybe it wouldn't hurt to think positive for once.

I focus on picking out the good things currently happening and, surprisingly, it works. I realize I like being chauffeured through the moody landscape by Theo. I like sneaking glances at him in the driver's seat every once in a while, when he's not looking at me. I enjoy how nice he looks in his striped polo and black jeans ('See I can look normal when I want to!' he'd said cheerfully as he'd sauntered out of his cabin this morning.) And I especially like how he has half of his hair pulled up and the rest hanging silky and long, making him look like a goddamn sexy Viking. Yeah, I'm having a really good time. In fact, I don't think there's anywhere I'd rather be than in this car with him right now.

But then we get to an intersection and, after squinting at the green road signs, Theo says the most horrible thing.

"Hmmm…. I think this is the right way to go."

I sit up straighter in my seat. "What do you mean, you *think* this is the right way to go? You were in charge of figuring out how to get to this place."

"Yeah. And I did figure it out…last night."

I let out a heavy breath. "Oh, thank God."

He makes a face. "The only thing is, I forgot the map back at camp."

"What?!"

"Don't worry. I'm pretty sure I can remember how to get there."

My heart revs faster. "Pretty sure?! *Pretty sure?!* You know I don't like pretty sures, Theo!"

He chuckles as he barrels down the road, driving way too fast for someone who has no idea where he's going. "Don't worry, Annie. I'm sure we can figure it out."

I ball my hands into fists at my sides. Most of the time Theo's easy-going nature is an asset. But right now, it's making me want to punch him right in the face.

To make matters worse, the road narrows. Then it turns to gravel beneath the wheels. As the rain comes down even harder, I beg Theo to turn back. But he insists he can get us to where we're going.

When we come to another intersection, he stops and takes a deep breath, looking right and left. We're so far off the main roads there aren't even any road signs here, so I don't know what the hell he's looking for.

Suddenly, he points to the right. "I think it's that way." He confidently accelerates into the turn.

"You think?! You think?!" I rage. "Theo, you're only getting us even more lost!"

"We're fine," he reassures me. "Remember, we're never alone." When he points skyward and gives me a wink, I can't hold back my groan.

At the next intersection, he turns to me. "You pick which way this time."

"You want me to pick?! Theo, this isn't a game!"

"Isn't it?"

"Ugh! Have I ever told you how annoying you are?!"

"Yes. Many, many times." He grins big. "Just take a deep breath and don't think about it. Just trust your gut and point to which way we should go."

"I can't just trust my gut, Theo. My gut doesn't have a fucking map of the backwoods of Indiana printed on it!"

"Just point."

"I can't just—"

"POINT!"

With absolutely no conscious thought, my finger shoots out to the right.

"See?" Theo says smugly. "You *did* know which way to go."

My glare is so vicious it wipes the smile right off his face.

We continue down the maze of back roads and with no other option (since I'm basically a prisoner in the passenger seat) I decide to give up my ranting and go along for the ride. And once again, I'm surprised when I actually start enjoying myself. Theo and I belt out camp songs over the pelting rain, and whenever we get to an intersection he doesn't even have to yell at me anymore. I jump in and point at the next road with absolutely no prompting at all.

Although I don't admit it out loud, Theo is right. Once I quiet my chattering mind, I do get a strong sense of which way to point, almost like a wordless tug in one direction…a guidance not cluttered by any kind of reason. Of course, I'm probably getting us even more hopelessly lost, but with Theo next to me I'm not in a rush to get anywhere other than where I am right now.

∞

All is right with the world. Until the wind picks up even more, buffeting the trees around us like they're made of rubber bands. And Theo's car starts to sputter and lurch. And then, to my horror, dies in the middle of the deserted road with an ominous clunk.

"No…no, no, no," I dig my fingernails into the leather of the seat. "This isn't happening. Tell me you're playing a joke on me. Tell me your car did not just break down a million miles from nowhere."

He furiously turns the key over and over, but the engine only grinds and grinds, never catching. "I'm not sure what's going on. I just had this thing in the shop last week."

His puzzled look only sends my panic rising higher. The trees around us sway and crack, feeling way too close, like a tunnel shrinking tighter and tighter around us, trapping us in their grips. My heart pounds in double time, making it hard to draw a full breath. *No, this can't happen here. I can't have one of my episodes now. Breathe. You have to remember to breathe.*

Theo reaches out and takes my hand. "Annie, it's going to be alright," he says in his soothing voice. The warmth of his skin, the way he looks deep into my eyes, slows the spinning in my head.

"Are you sure?" I squeeze his hand so tight it must hurt, but he doesn't even wince.

"Yes, of course. We're safe inside the car. And someone will come along soon and help us." The concern in his eyes should embarrass me. He must think I'm crazy, gasping and panting like this, but I'm too focused on how to get a full lungful of air to care at the moment.

"It's just, I don't like not knowing what's going to happen," I try to explain.

"I know. I know." He gently runs his thumb over the back of my hand. "It's okay."

"It scares me…the uncertainty…" I blabber on, trying not to think of the reason my fears started. When Mom was in the hospital and I wouldn't know if she was going to have a good day or be in pain. If she was going to be resting comfortably or crying out for the help I couldn't give. I never knew if she was going to make it another twenty-four hours or if today was going to be the day she died. No one could give me any answers back then. And I hated every moment of the not knowing.

"It's going to be okay…I promise." He reaches over the console and pulls me into a hug. The strength of his arms around me steadies me, makes me feel less alone. It's astonishing how much I trust this guy. For some stupid reason, when he says I'm going to be okay, I believe him.

Just then, a flash of headlights reflects off the soaked windshield. Theo and I both whirl to see a car approaching from behind, making its way slowly through the storm.

"See?" Theo says with a bright smile. "We didn't even have to wait that long. Help is already on the way!"

"That is not help!" I snap. "That's a murderer coming to chainsaw us into little pieces!"

Theo blows out an exasperated breath as I wail, "What? You've never seen a horror movie? Stranded motorists are a slasher's bread and butter!"

As the little silver car pulls up beside us, I furiously lock the doors and hiss at Theo scoot way down in the seat like me. That way the killer will think the car is abandoned and continue on his not-so-merry way.

"Just let me handle this," he says, ignoring my theatrics. He rolls down his window and shouts a cheerful hello through the roaring rain. I peek up just enough to see a little grey-haired man at the wheel, a scruffy wire-haired dog furiously wagging its tail in the passenger seat.

"See, it's alright," Theo murmurs to me. "He has a cute little dog."

"Cute little dogs are how they lure you into their death lair!" I whisper. "My God, didn't your mother teach you about stranger danger?!"

Theo explains what happened to the man who quickly replies, "I can call the repair shop for you when I get home. But it might be a while before he gets here. You two might want to come home with me to wait. It's getting awfully bad out here."

As if on cue, a bolt of lightning streaks through the sky, then a boom of thunder rumbles so loud I spring from my hiding place to clutch Theo's arm.

Without a second thought, Theo tells the man, "Sounds like a good idea to me!" and reaches for his door handle.

I tug him back. "Wait a minute! We don't even know this guy." I mutter, while simultaneously fake smiling at the stranger so maybe he'll think we're nice and spare our lives.

"Right," Theo says to me, then shouts out the window at the man. "My friend wants to know if you're a serial killer before she'll go with you!"

The guy chuckles. He's so little it looks like he can barely see over the steering wheel. "That's always a good thing to check on!" He tips forward to look at me. "I used to tell my daughters to be cautious too, so I understand your hesitation. But I promise, old Tully and I," he nods to the excited dog, "We don't have any intentions other than helping out a couple of fellow travelers in need."

Theo whispers to me. "Awww, he called us fellow travelers, Annie. Isn't that sweet?" He's clearly fallen for this stranger's wiles. "And he has a cute dog too! C'mon let's go."

Before I can say "looks can be deceiving" Theo is out of his car and into the old man's front seat with the dog firmly nestled on his lap licking his cheeks. And the only thing left for me to do is follow.

CHAPTER THREE

WHEN CHARLIE (AS the old guy introduces himself) pulls into his driveway, my worries ease. At the end of the dirt path sits a lovely white farmhouse with green shutters and intricate scrollwork along its covered front porch. Brightly colored flower beds surround the foundation and whimsical lawn ornaments sprinkle the grass. Yeah, I guess I can relax. Surely, no mass murderer would live in a storybook cottage like this.

He parks in front of a huge outbuilding a few yards from the house. Then we race through the pouring rain to the side door, laughing raucously as we tumble into the kitchen, soaked to the bone.

Tully, the dog, barks and leaps up on our legs, obviously thrilled to welcome visitors to his home. Charlie pushes past him, nearly stumbling over the whirling ball of fluff to turn on some lights. But when he flicks the switch, nothing happens.

"Looks like the power's out," he says.

Theo glances at me as if he's waiting for me to freak out and start quoting horror movies again, but I just smile. It smells like cinnamon and wood shavings in here, and oddly enough, the strange combination puts me at ease. Not to mention I can now see that the little guy is wearing a plaid short-sleeved shirt with a flat pencil in the pocket and blinking through his rain-soaked wire-rimmed glasses, making him look like a real-life Mr. Magoo. He's so cute it's hard to be afraid of him anymore.

Charlie bustles off down a hall to call his mechanic, coming back a few minutes later with two towels so Theo and I can dry off.

"Because of the storm the mechanic said it's going to be a while before he can get out here," Charlie informs us. "But he'll call and let us know when he leaves the shop."

The delay reminds me of our mission and how it's now in jeopardy; all because Theo forgot the map and has such a stupid, unreliable car. So to punish him, I don't reach out and gently dab off the spot of water he's missed on the column of his neck as he toweled off…even though I really want to.

"How about I make us some tea?" Charlie asks, motioning to the kettle on the gas stove. "Then we can all sit out on the porch and watch the storm pass by."

Theo's face goes dreamy at the suggestion. Of course he's thinking that 'watching the storm pass by' on a porch with a stranger is the perfect way to spend his time. Whereas I'm thinking his time would've been better spent remembering to pack the damn map.

Charlie motions to the living room and tells us to make ourselves at home while he gets our drinks ready. Even though it's the middle of the afternoon, the storm has blotted out most of the light, but I can still make out some details of the cozy space.

There's definitely a feminine touch to the room, with its gauzy white curtains and floral couch. Part of me is waiting for Charlie's wife to come down the stairs and ask her husband why he's brought two vagabonds into their house. But when I stop and try to sense another presence, I only come up with emptiness.

Someone with a keen eye for balance and color clearly curated the room's eclectic design. A beautiful wooden bookshelf sits along one wall, its edges adorned with the same intricate scrollwork as the outside of the house. Carved wooden sculptures and earthy pieces of pottery grace each side of the fireplace. Bright abstract paintings and more subdued watercolors hang artfully clustered around the doorway to the porch. It's definitely not your ordinary farmhouse decor.

"The artwork you have in here is beautiful!" I call out to Charlie as I examine a blocky abstract closer.

"You like those?" Charlie appears in the doorway. The little tuft of hair on top of his head is mussed where he's toweled himself off from the rain. "My wife Sue painted those," he says proudly. "She was the art teacher at the local high school for years. That's where we met."

"So you were a teacher too?" Theo asks, peering at a wooden carving above the fireplace. It's of Cupid, with his chubby arms flexed and a toothpick-thin arrow aimed up to the sky.

"Yeah, I was the woodworking teacher. In fact, what you're looking at there was one of the first gifts I ever made for Sue," he motions to the Cupid, smiling fondly. "I started working on it the day I met her. We hardly knew each other. But it felt like I'd been waiting all of my life to find her. One look, and she'd already pierced my heart," he chuckles.

"Yeah, I know that feeling." Theo cocks an eyebrow at me, as if he's remembering the moment we first met too.

"She's a very talented artist," I tell Charlie, avoiding Theo's stare.

"Yeah, she was." He lets out a heavy sigh, twisting the ring on his finger. "She's been gone five years now, and I still miss her every single day." Theo and I exchange a look but stay quiet.

As if sensing his owner's sadness, Tully jumps at his legs begging for pats. Charlie ruffles the terrier's ears. "Tully misses her too, don't you, Tully? Dad doesn't make you bacon and eggs in the morning like your mom used to, huh?"

Thankfully, the kettle whistles so I don't have to come up with something comforting to say. (And so Theo doesn't make things awkward by telling Charlie that his dead wife is still with him, just not in the same form as she once was.)

Charlie disappears back into the kitchen, shouting over his shoulder for us to head out to the porch and he'll meet us there.

When we get outside, the wind has died down, and the rain has settled to a normal summer shower. The porch is deep and long, with a variety of rockers and plush furniture to choose from. I sit on a little wicker loveseat with cushy floral pillows and try to cover my sigh of relief when Theo joins me, sitting so close his shoulder and leg press against mine. It's getting harder and harder to ignore how much I enjoy touching him. And what a terrible friend to Greta that makes me.

After a while, Charlie toddles out with a tray crammed with a pretty floral teapot, three mismatched china cups and a line of Oreos nearly falling off the edge. He apologizes profusely when he forgets the sugar and can't find the milk pitcher and has to bring out the whole jug. He insists Sue would roll over in her grave if she knew what a poor host he was.

After thanking him again for his hospitality, the three of us begin chatting amiably back and forth. On the way here, Theo had told Charlie about our jobs at Camp Boundless, so he asks us more about working there. Then he inquires about our college majors and what we want to do when we 'grow up', as he puts it.

In turn, we ask Charlie about his family and job at the high school and what he's doing in his retirement. Which turns out to be getting back to the carvings he used to create when he was younger and keeping up the gardens his wife planted over their fifty years of living here.

It's so fascinating hearing about Charlie's life that I completely forget about our mission to find my mom's painting. And that being here is a mistake. And that I'm still supposed to be furious at Theo for messing everything up. Instead, I relax and listen to the patter of the rain on the roof and the low hum of Theo and Charlie talking. I smell the spicy aroma of the tea and the faint tinge of wet dog. And damn if I don't feel myself soaking in the simplicity of this moment, wanting to sear all its nuances into my mind. Theo is right. We only ever have Now, don't we? And this is a Now I already know I'm going to remember forever.

But two cups of tea later I have to pee, so Charlie directs me to the bathroom inside. As I stand to leave, Charlie asks, "So what were you two doing way out here in the boondocks, anyway?"

I laugh, thinking of all our pointless twists and turns. "Oh, we were hopelessly lost."

Charlie nods. "That happens a lot. There aren't many road signs out this way. You've got to kind of know where you're going to have any chance of getting there."

I give Theo a withering look, and he fesses up. "It's my fault. I forgot the map."

"So where were you trying to get to anyway?" Charlie asks. "I know everyone in these parts. Maybe I can help you."

I hesitate, thinking of the weird name my mom had scrawled on the back of the photograph. It's probably futile to even tell Charlie, since I doubt he's going to know what the hell it means. But just as I open my mouth to make up some excuse, my gaze lands on a sign hanging over the doorway that makes me gasp out loud.

"What? What is it?" Theo looks up at where I'm now pointing.

His eyes go wide when he sees the wooden sign above the door. On it are two words painted in white:

Teela Wooket.

CHAPTER FOUR

I DIDN'T THINK a person could pull a muscle from gloating, but Theo is trying his best to prove me wrong.

As soon as he'd read the sign, he'd leapt out of his seat and started dancing around the porch wailing, "See? I told you so! I told you that you knew which way to go!" over and over again.

Now, he stabs a finger at the words Teela Wooket. "You trusted your gut and look? Your intuition led us straight here!"

I'm just as blown away by this seemingly impossible feat as he is. How the heck had I blindly navigated us through multiple twists and turns only to wind up in the path of the exact person we needed to find? The odds of that seem like a million…no, a *billion* to one.

But even though Theo's touting my virtues, that doesn't mean I'm going to give him the satisfaction of admitting he's right.

"Or it could've just been coincidence," I grind out, only because I know it'll drive him crazy. Theo doesn't believe in coincidences. He believes everything happens for a reason. Whether we understand that reason or not.

He ignores me, whooping around the porch some more, making the dog yap and jump with him while I roll my eyes. Poor Charlie just looks back and forth between us, not understanding what the hell is going on.

Theo points at me. "This girl is amazing!" he gushes to Charlie.

"She's brilliant…and knows so much, deep in her heart! She's just too afraid to listen to herself."

"Stop," I warn Theo. I don't like him talking about something so personal in front of a stranger. Even though Charlie doesn't seem like much of a stranger anymore. In fact, I was just about to ask him to be my adoptive Papaw before this melee broke out. Nevertheless, Theo needs to learn how to keep his big mouth shut.

"I'm just saying you're way more connected to your guidance than you realize," Theo says to me.

"Ugh, you're doing it again," I grumble.

"Doing what?"

"Being completely and infuriatingly annoying!" I shout. "Why do you always have to act like you know everything?"

"Well, I *do* know a lot. You've gotta admit that."

I realize he's just teasing. But still, his needling gets to me. "You think you know everything, but you don't."

"Oh, yeah? Like what? What don't I know?" He dances closer to where I'm standing, poking me in the ribs as he taunts.

I slap his hand away, trying to ignore his teasing. But after three more *what don't I know?*s and five more rib jabs, I break down and shout, "Well for one thing you don't know your best friend is in love with you!"

He stops dancing so abruptly it's like someone's just unplugged his power cord. "What did you say?" he asks, looking confused.

"You know what?" Charlie mutters to himself, looking uncomfortable. "I'm just going to clear these dishes here and let you two have a moment to yourselves. Let's go, Tully. You can help your old Pops too." Gathering the tray, he and the dog slip quietly back into the house, leaving Theo and me alone.

"What are you talking about, Annie? Which best friend is in love with me? You?" he says, looking hopeful.

"No, not me!" I throw my hands in the air. "Greta, you dummy! Greta is in love with you!"

He blinks at me, frozen in place like he's trying to process what I've just said. Then all of a sudden, he bursts out laughing. He laughs and laughs, clutching his stomach and shaking his head at me. I didn't think I could get any madder at him, but apparently, I've misjudged myself.

"What? What's so funny?"

He takes a second to catch his breath. "Greta's not in love with me!" he wheezes.

"Yes she is! I saw the two of you whispering at Tim's party. I saw how she looked at you. She told me she has a Mystery Man crush on someone at camp and that someone is *you*!"

He shakes his head, still smiling from ear to ear. "Yes, Greta loves me," he admits. "But she's not *in* love with me. There's a big difference."

"How do you know that for sure? Maybe she just hasn't told you the truth yet."

He lifts a finger in the air. "Ah, but she has told me the truth," he says, looking smug. "I know who her Mystery Man is, and it's not me."

"What? Who the hell is it then?"

He hesitates. "Promise you won't say anything?" When I nod, he goes on. "It's Wendell."

"Wendell?!"

"Yeah. Can't you see it? She's always hanging out at our cabin. Sitting with us at lunch. Following him around."

"Yeah, but I thought she was doing all that to get closer to *you*."

"Nah. She was trying to get closer to Wen."

I cross my arms, embarrassed that once again, I've jumped to the wrong conclusion. God, why hadn't I just asked Greta outright who she liked instead of assuming she had feelings for Theo? I feel so stupid now. But despite that, something's off. I know what I saw at the party.

"But her face…that night when you two were on the couch. She looked so happy. She looked so…so…in love."

"Yeah, probably because she had just confided in me about Wen and I'd told her I thought he liked her too," Theo explains patiently.

"That must have been when you saw her. That's why she looked so happy. She was thinking about him, not me."

What he's saying makes sense. Now that I look back on these past weeks, Greta does spend a lot of time with Wen. But Wen is so quiet, so unassuming…so opposite of Greta, I never considered she might like him that way.

"But what about at the car earlier?" I ask, still trying to piece things together. "She was jealous I was leaving with you. I could tell."

Theo makes a face. "That wasn't jealousy. That was concern. She's protective of me. As her friend. She knows how I feel about you, and she's worried because you've been quite clear about how you feel about relationships."

I wince thinking of how I'm always ranting on about never wanting to be tied down. I make it my mission to let everyone know that I'm not prime girlfriend material. No wonder Greta doesn't want me getting too close to Theo. She's afraid I'm going to break his heart.

He confirms my suspicions. "Greta's worried you're going to hurt me. That's all."

I hold back what I want to say. *I am going to hurt you, Theo. That part is guaranteed.* If I say that, he'll just give me a bunch of reasons why the pain will be worth it for him, and I'll have no good response. I cannot for the life of me understand why he has such a blatant disregard for feeling pain.

"Listen, I understand why you might have been confused," Theo says. "Greta and I are very, very close. And honestly, we do love each other. But we tried dating when we first met. We went out a few times, and I don't know," he shrugs. "It just didn't work out. We didn't like each other that way."

"Alright. Well, I guess that makes sense." I think back on Greta's behavior this summer. "She does hang around Wendell a lot. And she has mentioned a few times she thinks he's cool."

As the implications of this new information slowly sink in, I feel like a weight is lifting off my chest; tiny bubbles of hope filling in where the heaviness once lived.

"Wait a minute," Theo says almost as if he senses my rising emotion. "Is that why you said we could only be friends? Because you didn't want to hurt Greta?"

I look out at the lawn. Then down at my hands. Anywhere except into his eyes. "Maybe."

"Ahhh." He nods, thinking it over. "That was very kind of you. You're a good friend."

"Not really. In case you forgot, I still kissed you the other night."

"Technically, I kissed you, so don't worry. You still qualify as a good friend."

When I finally crack a smile, he narrows the gap between us, standing so close I can feel the heat radiating off his body. "Do you know what this means, Annie?"

A flush runs through me in anticipation of what he's about to say. He holds his arms out from his sides like he's offering himself up to me on a silver platter. "It means you don't have to hold back anymore. You can have me whenever you want me."

He waits, eyebrows raised, a sexy smile spreading across his face. Damn him. He looks so gorgeous it takes every ounce of my willpower to plant my hands on his chest and shove him away. "Stop being such a dork!" He stumbles backwards, laughing hard. But the glint in his eye tells me I'm not fooling him one bit. He knows how much I want him.

I lower my voice, hissing under my breath, "Did you really just proposition me on some sweet old man's porch? While he's ten feet away cleaning up the tea he just served us? Really, Theo, show some restraint!"

"Fine, if that's what you want." I can tell he's trying to be serious, but he can't quite wrench the corners of his mouth down. He looks past me into the house. "I guess we should probably get in there and ask him about the painting now, anyway."

But instead of moving toward the door, he steps closer, lifts one hand and gently grazes his fingertips along the edge of my jaw. "I just have one question first." Sparks fly along my skin where he touches me. "Is the painting the only reason you're here with me right now?" He looks down on me with a gaze so tantalizing it's hard to breathe.

I never knew what swooning felt like, but with his lips hovering only inches away from mine, I think I've just found out.

"Am I sure what is the only reason for *what?*" I mumble nonsensically.

"The painting, Annie. Are you sure you're only here to find the painting?"

Painting? What is a painting?

He dips his head even lower, lips so close…and yet way too far away. "Or are you here because you want to be with me?"

CHAPTER FIVE

I DON'T GIVE in to what I really want. I don't lean in and cover Theo's perfect lips with my own and kiss him until we both faint dead away from lack of oxygen. That would be too irrational. Too indulgent. Too easy.

Instead, I leave him standing there half-dazed on the porch and go to find Charlie.

When I enter the kitchen Charlie is at the sink washing dishes. Seeing me, he dries his hands on a dish towel and cocks an eyebrow, clearly waiting for me to explain our strange outburst on the porch. Luckily, I sense Theo come up behind me. I whirl and give him an imploring look, hoping he'll take the lead and explain why we're here. But he just dips his chin, deferring to me.

So, I give Charlie the bare minimum. I show him the photograph I have stashed in my pocket and say (in a businesslike tone that sounds eerily like Caroline's) that I'm looking for a painting of my mother's because we need some information in order to catalog her work. Charlie's been so sweet to us. But despite how much he's shared about his own life, something keeps me from telling him all the details of our mission.

Theo is clearly baffled as to why I don't share more about our Treasure Hunt with Charlie. But it feels odd to pour out my guts to someone I just met. Besides, Charlie probably doesn't give a shit about some silly game I'm playing with my dead mom. Although he seems awfully excited to hear that the reason we became stranded on the road was because we were looking for him.

"Someone upstairs must have been watching out for you two!" he says, pointing skyward. "My Sue is always helping me out that way. Showing me where to find my lost keys. Helping me pick the right words to say to the kids. Reminding me to take my medicine at night. Sometimes, I swear it's like she hasn't left me at all, her voice is still in my ear so much!"

Theo gives me an 'I-told-you-so' look, which I try to ignore. I'm beginning to realize there are more believers like him in the world than I first thought. Which makes me wonder if converting to his side isn't such an outlandish idea after all.

"So you're Grace Peterson's daughter, huh?" Charlie asks, surveying me closer. "I see the resemblance now."

I startle. "Did you know her?"

"I met her a long time ago. She and my wife took some art classes together at the college years back. They were pals for a while until Sue began teaching and your mom started having kids and life got all hectic and crazy." He chuckles. "But in the best kind of way, of course." He looks wistfully past us into the empty living room and adds, "You complain about the chaos when it's happening, but boy do you miss it when it's gone."

Theo and I catch eyes, neither of us missing the melancholy on Charlie's face. I suddenly don't feel like such an imposition anymore. In fact, I think our unplanned visit might be the highlight of Charlie's day, if not his entire week. Maybe even his year, as sad as that thought might be.

Charlie points to the door. "Let's go take a look at this painting then!"

For a moment I'm confused by why he's asking us to leave, but Charlie quickly explains. "Sue hung the picture in her studio. She liked to use it as an example for her students when she taught watercolor lessons."

He ushers us outside, guiding us down the walkway to the building we parked in front of earlier, which apparently isn't a garage like I first thought, but a studio.

The rain has slowed to a drizzle, leaving a cloudy haze floating around our feet and the smell of clipped grass and damp earth in its wake. Taking in the surrounding view, I think of how nice it's been learning about Charlie and Sue's life; seeing the fruits of their decades-long partnership displayed in the minutiae of their lives. The porcelain cat figurine perched in the flowerbed. The artful curve of the walkway stones they surely placed with their own hands. The worn mat at the doorway reading "Give Peas a Chance," which I suspect Sue picked out before she died.

Suddenly, I get a disorienting wave of nostalgia for a future that hasn't happened yet. A quick flash of a similar life that might be possible with the sweet boy walking beside me…if only our fates could be different.

But our fates can't be different. Or can they?

I shake off the impossible thought and follow Charlie inside the studio. Forgetting there's no power, he tries to switch on the overhead lights, muttering a quiet curse word when he remembers there's an outage. Luckily, the large windows stationed along the back walls provide enough light to see.

Woodworking tools fill the space nearest us. Racks of boards propped up along one side, half-finished carvings clamped to a workbench, piles of sawdust collecting here and there. I suck in a deep breath, enjoying the piney smell I'd whiffed earlier, as Charlie leads us further into the vast room.

There's no divider between Charlie's workshop and Sue's studio space, so I can easily imagine them out here working next to each other, both engrossed in their own work, yet comforted by the presence of the other nearby.

Sue's workspace features multiple easels; their wood spindles splattered with years' worth of paint. Next to the easels are four electric pottery wheels which, according to the spiderwebs lacing their sides, no one has used in a while.

As we marvel at all the equipment, Charlie explains. "Sue used to run classes for kids here in the summertime. We'd have oodles of kids running around here from May to August. You would've thought she'd want a break from the kids, but she just loved sharing her passion for art. She always said the little ones taught her more than she taught them."

He takes a handkerchief from his pants pocket, roughly wipes his nose, and then puts it back, still sniffling.

"Oh, I understand what she meant," I say, thinking of all the things my campers have taught me this summer. "My mom always said to listen to the young ones. They're still fresh. Not so tarnished by the world yet. They still remember how much fun life is supposed to be."

My eyes alight on a fixture in the corner. "You have a kiln too?" I weave through the pottery wheels to check it out. "Oh, my sister would love it here. She's always saying how she wants to get back to throwing on the wheel. She claims it's very therapeutic for her."

"Yeah, lots of people say that," Charlie agrees. "Sue said the focus and repetition helps calm people's nerves. But heck if it wasn't that way for me though. I tried it a few times and it made me so mad I wanted to throw my lump of clay at the wall! But to each his own, right?"

Theo and I laugh as Charlie gestures around the room. "Tell your sister she can come use the equipment any time she wants. It's a shame it's just sitting here, not getting used. And I'd love having the company. I miss the days when this place was so busy and full of life."

My heart pinches at how forlorn he looks remembering his past. As I scan around the studio, I can almost see Caroline sitting at one wheel, little Jack and Emma playing nearby. Excitement rushes through me at the thought. But I get an odd inkling that the emotion hasn't come from me alone.

Charlie points to the wall behind the easels. "So, here's the painting you're looking for." He surveys the scene closer. It depicts an expanse of lake with a beach far off in the distance. "I always liked this one. I was born and raised here in Indiana, and to me it felt like a great homage to the landscape around these parts."

My pulse speeds up as I approach the painting. I always have the same reaction when I look at my mom's work up close. Seeing her brush strokes—her choices of color and shadow—so vivid in front of me makes time collapse in a way that's difficult to explain. It's thrilling to know she actually touched this piece of paper. That she wrote her initials in the corner with the teeny, wispy brush she loved so much. That she picked out the frame and tore the tape that mounted the painting to the mat. It makes it seem like she's still alive. That her essence still lives on in every tiny detail she left behind.

As I stare at the painting, Theo steps close to my side, a wordless offer to steady me if I need him. Oh, how badly I want to lace my fingers in his and hold his hand tight, if only for a few brief seconds just to get my equilibrium back. But instead, I force myself to focus on the business at hand.

"We actually need to see what's written on the back of the piece. Do you mind if we take it down?" I ask tentatively.

Charlie heartily agrees, and Theo takes the painting off the wall and sets it carefully on top of a desk nearby. The painting itself is not big, probably only 8 x 10 without the mat and frame, so it's easy to handle. But when Theo flips it over, I realize we'll have to unscrew the back of the frame in order to find what we're looking for.

I apologize for causing such trouble, but Charlie doesn't seem to mind. In fact, he seems so excited to find the elusive hidden title that he races to his workbench to retrieve a screwdriver.

After removing the various backings of the frame, the three of us lurch over the painting so eagerly we nearly bump heads. But with no overhead light, it's hard to make out any writing.

"Hmmmm…where is it…where is it?" Charlie murmurs to himself. "Shit. Let me get my flashlight."

As he dashes away, Theo and I exchange a wry smile at Charlie's deep involvement in our mission. If the owners of the next three paintings turn out to be as cooperative as he is, then maybe this quest won't be so scary after all.

Charlie returns and points the beam at the textured watercolor paper. Something faint is written in pencil along the very edge, almost hidden under the tape.

"You kids are going to have to read that," Charlie says. "Even with my glasses, my old eyes can't make it out."

I squint at the faint words. "It says...*The View*." I glance up at Theo. "Is that what you see?"

"Yeah. That's what I got too."

Good grief, it's no wonder no one knew my mom gave these paintings titles. If you didn't know to look for it, you'd never even notice the writing was there. It's like even back then, she was already hiding clues for us to find.

I repeat the title aloud a few times to sear it into my brain, even though I know I won't forget. We have to be thorough. With the long turnaround time waiting for Aunt Lydia to send us each clue in the mail (she refuses to read us the clues over the phone, insisting she has to follow Mom's directions to the letter) we can't afford to get a title wrong or it might set our timing back.

I've already worked out our entire schedule. When we started today, there were four paintings to be found and five weeks of summer left. As long as we locate a painting each weekend, and then receive a clue in the mail at Caroline's house the next weekend, we should have all the clues and be ready to search for the treasure by the time camp ends. That means I can fulfill my mysterious intertwined mission with Theo and still be able to end things between us once summer is over.

In other words, if everything goes as planned, I'll have plenty of time to leave him before he dies.

∞

We're hanging the painting back on the wall when the phone rings. It's the mechanic saying he's leaving the shop and will meet us by the car in fifteen minutes.

It sounds like good news, but we're all clearly bummed our time together is over. Even Tully is upset, whining like he knows exactly what's going on when we all pile back in the car to leave.

As I watch the little white farmhouse recede out the back window, Charlie gives Theo his phone number and repeats the invitation he's extended multiple times already.

"Seriously, anytime you kids need a little time away from your bustling college life, you come out for a visit. I'll make you all a cup of tea and we can sit on the porch and talk. Or not say anything if that's what you'd prefer. Me and Tully, we know how to be good company, don't we, Tulls?" He ruffles the dog's ears where he stands on the console wagging his tail.

"Oh don't worry, I'll be back!" Theo says. "That is, if I can ever find your house again!"

They laugh together in the front seat. I can just see the two of them becoming best friends. It would be just like Theo to take the time to develop a relationship with this sweet, and clearly lonely, old man. Me, on the other hand, I'm more the type to let things fade away; to see the futility of investing my emotions in a person I know I'll someday have to grieve.

"And don't forget to tell your sister there's plenty of pottery wheels and a kiln for her to use whenever she wants," Charlie calls back to me. "Bring the kiddos. Or let it be time for herself. Whatever she wants. I'd just love if the space got some use."

I assure him I'll tell Caroline, as I smile out the car window, marveling over how this day has turned out. It started with me being so nervous about what might happen. And so mad at Theo for forgetting the map. And then so scared of getting lost.

But when I'd given in and done what Theo asked—trusted my gut and picked our direction—look what happened? I not only led us right to the painting, but I'd gotten to talk to someone who once knew my mom. Someone who just so happens to have a studio that might be exactly what Caroline needs. Who showed me that slowing down and drinking a cup of tea and listening to the rain for a while might be exactly what I needed too.

Yeah. This was no coincidence.

Today the world was friendly. So friendly I found a single house in the middle of the damn wilderness! How crazy is that?

I guess it's time I admit the truth. Not only was Theo right, but I was right too.

CHAPTER SIX

THEO AND I are back on the road, both of us smiling inanely out the front windshield as we barrel down the highway.

As if accidentally stumbling upon Teela Wooket (which Charlie told us meant "Happy Summer Home" in some Native American language) wasn't astounding enough, when the mechanic had asked Theo to give the engine a try, the car had started right up, like there had been nothing wrong with it in the first place. The stocky guy had poked around under the hood a bit, but he couldn't find anything out of place. It was almost as if someone had wanted the car to stop working at that moment, in that exact spot.

The clouds have now parted, the late afternoon sun illuminating the wet road, making the pavement sparkle like a path out of a fairy tale. My heart is soaring so high that when Theo says, "Hey, look!" and points out at the vista of rolling hills beside us, I know, even before I turn my head, there's a rainbow hanging there beside me.

I get it, Mom. You're here with me, I playfully tease inside my head as I admire the brilliant colors. *You don't have to keep cramming it down my throat.*

Just wanted to make sure, she teases back, exactly like she would've when she was alive. *You always seem to need a lot of proof.*

I startle, realizing how much it sounds like her. Like it's not just my own wishful thinking, but her voice, as clear as if she were sitting next to me. Could I really be doing this? Could I finally be communicating with my mom?

I'm so thrilled by the thought that a laugh escapes my lips before I can hold it back. Theo joins in, laughing like he's heard us teasing back and forth. Which I'm beginning to believe just might be possible. The sound swells louder in my ears, as if another voice has chimed in with us too. And with all the whispers I've been hearing, all the subtle nudges and shots of inspiration I've been feeling lately, I'm finally giving in to the notion that it truly is my mom.

In my joy, I blurt out, "Man, what happened back there at Charlie's…it was so…just so…" Oh hell, I might as well say it. "It was so much fun!"

"It was, wasn't it?" he says. "And I know you were mad at me at first. But we were never really lost, were we?"

"I guess not. Although next time, I'm in charge of bringing the map!"

Theo readily agrees and then launches into an impressive *a cappella* rendition of John Denver's "Take Me Home, Country Roads" as the car skims down the open highway. Everything is so perfect it almost seems like a dream. Until he takes the turn that leads back to camp and my stomach sinks. Dammit. Why did I have to be so insistent about him dropping me off at my car after we found the painting? I don't want this day to end just yet.

I stare out at the passing landscape, desperate to come up with some way to extend our time together. Then I see a road sign that might be my answer.

"Hey, isn't that the town where you grew up?" I motion to a sign approaching on the right.

"Yeah. Why? You want to check it out?" he asks, eyebrows raised high. When I nod, he quickly brakes and yanks the steering wheel so hard we nearly take the turn on two wheels.

As he drives toward his hometown, he chatters excitedly about all the places he wants to show me. His high school, the track where he ran, the local pizza shop where he and his friends used to hang out. Then his eyes go wide. "We could even go to my house and I could introduce you to my mom!"

I must look shocked because he rushes on. "I mean only if you want…you don't have to. If that seems like too much, we can skip that part."

The nagging voice in my head reminds me it's a bad idea to meet Theo's family. To see the house where he grew up. To get even closer to him than I already am. And yet, things have changed recently, haven't they? Theo is not Greta's Mystery Man anymore. So, just as he had offered on the porch, I *could* have him whenever I wanted. Even if it's only for a little while.

I take a deep breath and, for the first time in a long while, forget all practicality and instead say exactly what I want.

"Take me to your house, Theo. I'd love to meet your mom."

∞

Before we get to the center of town, Theo pulls off onto a wide paved road. I think it's a public street until he goes a little further onto the wooded path and stops in front of a gigantic wrought-iron gate.

"What are you doing?" I ask as he leans over and rummages through the glove box. Is he dropping something off at a millionaire's house? I hope there are no security cameras because when this rich guy sees the state of Theo's car, he's definitely going to call the police.

He pulls out what looks like a garage door opener, clicks it and the gates slowly swing open in front of us. Now I'm even more confused. "Wait a minute. Where are we?"

"At my house," he says casually, driving his clunking jalopy through the gate.

"Is this like some kind of private housing division or something?" I scan about looking for other driveways, but we're still surrounded by trees, Theo weaving his way along a curving road that looks like a river of black asphalt pouring down the gentle incline.

"No, it's my driveway," he says like it's nothing. Like everyone in the world has huge electronically controlled gates at the end of their several-mile-long meticulously paved driveway.

"Theo, what's going on?" I ask, internally running through all I know about Theo's family. His dad is a lawyer who moved to Georgia with his girlfriend (now wife) after he divorced his mom. And his older brother, Nate, is married and has three kids. I think his mom may have worked at some point…I'm not sure; we've only ever talked about her in the context of all the years she took care of him when he had cancer. Now I'm mad at myself for not asking for more details.

Theo slows the car, as if he wants to fill me in on something before I see what's at the top of the hill. "Have you ever heard of Beata's Pierogi?"

I think hard. "No. In fact, I'm not even sure what a pierogi is."

He seems surprised but doesn't explain the strange word. Instead, he slips into a television announcer voice. "*The taste of the old country right in your own freezer!* Never heard that on the radio? Or on TV?" When I still shake my head, he goes on. "Well, Beata is my *Babcia*… that's grandma in Polish…and she and my grandpa started a company that makes pierogi a long time ago, and now it's kind of grown into a big thing."

The trees open up around us, revealing an enormous stone and log house perched in the middle of a perfectly landscaped lawn. "Theo!" I gasp. "You're the heir to a vast pierogi fortune and you never mentioned it before?"

He grins over the torn console of the old car he obviously has no business driving. "Not a vast fortune. But yeah, a bit of money. Have I never mentioned that before? Hmmm, must have forgotten." The wink he gives me makes it clear his omission was no mistake.

"Wow, this is crazy," I murmur half to myself, as we park in front of a sprawling four-car garage. Shifting around in the passenger seat, I take in the lavish surroundings. "I don't mean to offend you, but this is not at all what I expected."

"What?" he pats the dusty dashboard. "This baby doesn't scream money to you?"

"Uh, no! In fact," I gesture to the car. His tattered duffel on the backseat. The tennis shoes he's wearing with the treads almost entirely worn off. "Nothing about you screams money, Theo."

"Good. That's the way I like it."

Theo honks the horn merrily before we climb out, and by the time we make it to the edge of the driveway his mom is walking out of the house looking confused. When she sees us, she breaks into an enormous smile and rushes down the walkway, a beautiful Golden Retriever bounding along beside her.

"Oh my gosh! What a wonderful surprise!" she says, clapping her hands excitedly as we approach. At first glance, she reminds me so much of Theo; tall and thin, with a rich tan as if she works outside a lot, with short chestnut brown hair, streaked by the sun, just like her son. The only difference between the two of them is her eyes are dark brown, not pale green like his.

Theo jogs over and wraps her in a big hug while the dog leaps on its hind legs, clawing maniacally at their backs. Mother and son stay that way, holding onto each other, swaying back and forth like they haven't seen each other in ages. Which is true because Theo's been spending most of his time with me lately. A stab of guilt hits me as I think of how my selfishness has robbed her of precious time with her son.

She doesn't seem too mad about it though, because after Theo introduces us, she wraps me in a tight hug. "I'm so happy to finally meet you!" she gushes, telling me to call her Maria instead of Mrs. Teodorczyk after I say a formal hello.

The way she's looking at me so intently—the way she said she was happy to *finally* meet me—makes me think Theo has already told her about me. Of course. Theo said she'd read the note he'd written about me when he came out of his Near-Death Experience. It's no wonder she's staring at me this way. Maria knows I'm the girl with the spun-gold hair he saw on the other side.

She holds me at arm's length, surveying my face, the unspoken truth about my connection with her son hanging heavy in the air between us.

"Your house is beautiful!" I blurt out just to break the awkwardness. Both Theo and his mom turn and blink up at the house as if it's the first time they've really looked at it in a long time.

"Seems a little out of place, doesn't it?" Maria says flatly. I have to admit she's right. The house is a post and beam style, made of a combination of rich mahogany logs and smooth river stone. It looks like it belongs in Aunt Lydia's neighborhood in Montana, not here in the pasturelands of Indiana.

Maria shrugs, turning back to me. "My in-laws had a thing for Westerns."

Theo explains more as he leads us up the flagstone sidewalk to the door. "Watching old cowboy T.V. shows was how my grandparents learned to speak English when they first moved here. My grandpa always dreamed of having a Ponderosa like on *Bonanza*, so this is what they built when the company took off."

I suddenly remember which side of Theo's family is Polish. "So, wait a minute. Beata was your dad's mom?"

As we step inside, I have to crane my head back to take in the two-story great room that greets us. Wide log beams span the vast space, and a huge wrought-iron chandelier hangs from the ceiling. A river rock fireplace soars up through the roof with overstuffed dark leather couches and brightly striped chairs arranged around its raised stone hearth.

All the little touches—from the family snapshots on the wall to the fluffy throw blankets tossed here and there—make the space warm and inviting despite its size. I wish Caroline were here. She would love how they decorated this place. It reminds me of something straight out of one of her design magazines.

Maria picks up on my confusion over which side of the family the house belonged to. "Yeah, my in-laws built the house. But as it turned out, they liked me better than their son."

Both she and Theo huff a matching laugh. "I worked with them for years at the business," she goes on. "And took care of them as they got older. So, when they died, they left the property to me."

I must look baffled because Theo chimes in. "Oh, don't worry, there's no bad blood. My dad was relieved they gave it to her. He never liked living in Indiana, so he was all too happy to get out of here. He still handles the legal business for the company. But he just does it from Georgia now." He leans closer and fake whispers, "In fact he says if he never sees another pierogi for the rest of his life it will be too soon."

I smile, then go back to marveling at the house, ashamed that I'd jumped to the conclusion that Theo was poor. Add that to the list of things I assumed about him that he's since proven wrong.

Maria narrows her eyes at her son. "You look so skinny. Are you sure you're eating enough?"

"Yeah, Mom. I'm fine."

"And getting enough sleep? You know you'll get run down if you don't take care of yourself."

"I'm good." He shoots me an exasperated look, but I can tell by his smile he's not bothered by her fussing. "Don't worry. I'm sleeping and eating and taking my vitamins. I'm a regular picture of health."

Worry creases her face as she continues studying him like she won't be happy until she comes to that conclusion for herself. I can only imagine what it's like to have a child who has battled cancer. All the hours Maria must have spent scrutinizing every detail of Theo, constantly vigilant, searching for any little change that might indicate a threat to his life.

The truth is, I've become vigilant too. Theo told me his cancer started with unexplained bruises on his body. So lately I've found myself scanning his arms and legs for any new bruises that might indicate his cancer has come back. So far, I've found nothing out of the ordinary. But I keep thinking over the phrasing of what his Angels told him on the other side. *I won't live past twenty-one.* At first I thought that meant he'd die sometime *after* he turned twenty-one, but the way they actually stated it makes the timing much more vague. If he won't live *past* twenty-one, doesn't that mean the cancer could return any time before that?

"So, are you two spending the night?" Maria's question snaps me out of my whirling thoughts. "Lord knows we've got plenty of room!"

Theo glances over, trying to keep his expression neutral. But I can tell that, like me, he doesn't want this day to end yet either.

As I start to make an excuse as to why I have to leave, I hear Theo's words from earlier whisper in my ear:

Maybe it's okay to let it be easy, Annie.

I could, couldn't I? I could let whatever this is between us be easy. Lord knows it's what I truly want deep down inside.

"Hmmm. Can we spend the night?" I coyly repeat Maria's invitation. "Well, I guess that depends on one thing…"

"What's that?" Theo jumps in before I've barely finished my sentence.

I turn to Maria. "If I can use your phone to make a collect call to Montana?"

She looks horrified. "Absolutely not!"

Theo's mouth drops open, but luckily Maria goes on, smiling big. "But you can make a *direct* call to Montana if you'd like!"

Theo lets out a heavy breath, muttering, "Oh, thank the Lord."

Maria elbows his side, laughing at her own joke. Following her lead, I elbow his other side and declare triumphantly, "Then it looks like we're spending the night!"

CHAPTER SEVEN

WHILE THEO RETRIEVES his bags from the car, Maria gives me a tour of the rest of the downstairs, which is just as impressive as the living room. The kitchen is huge, with a stove so fancy it looks like it should be in a restaurant and an island made out of a gleaming slab of mottled black marble. The den off the main room is lined with bookshelves packed with the cowboy memorabilia and rare edition western novels that Theo's grandpa—or *Dziadek* as Theo calls him—loved to collect.

After we finish the tour, Theo collects me from Maria to show me where I'll be staying. I follow him up a curving staircase made of logs cut in half, then across an open balcony looking down on the great room that leads to a wing of bedrooms.

He deposits my backpack (which I'm now thankful I threw in his car at the last minute) in a pristine but homey bedroom, then continues down the hallway, stopping two doors down to call out to me, "This is where I'll be staying." He wags his eyebrows suggestively, pointing to his door. "You know, in case you need to find me later."

I roll my eyes, hissing at him to be quiet so his mom doesn't hear him in the kitchen below. But I'm laughing as I retreat into my room under the guise of freshening up. When what I really need is a moment to process all the new information I've learned about Theo in the past few hours.

I grin stupidly at myself in the mirror over the dresser as I brush my hair, thinking of how different Theo seems today. He's much more confident. Not as restrained around me as he usually is. First, there was his playful proposition on Charlie's porch. Then that maddening almost-kiss that completely scrambled not only my brain, but every nerve ending in my body. And now the blatant invitation to his bedroom later. It's almost like he can feel me caving. Like he knows how much I want him and is enjoying this playful back and forth. Taunting me. Teasing me. Savoring the tension between us… just waiting for the moment I finally give in.

When I'm done primping, I find Theo in the kitchen with his mom. He tells me to use the phone in the den to call Aunt Lydia. After I recite the title we found, Lydia whoops loudly, then says she'll put the first clue in the mail tomorrow. I tell her I can't talk more because I'm making a direct call from Theo's mom's house, and she whoops even louder.

"Oh, we're getting awfully chummy with our Treasure Hunt partner now, aren't we?" she teases. "Well, isn't that a surprise?"

"Stop it. This isn't some matchmaking game," I grumble. "It's about something much bigger than that, I'm sure."

"I sure as hell hope so," Lydia deadpans. "What a waste if this whole thing was only about love." She makes a gagging sound. "*Blech*!"

I laugh at her predictable response. My loner aunt has never been the kind of woman to be swept away by the notion of romance. The only time I'd ever heard her wax poetic about a man was when she admitted to looking forward to seeing a particular guy at the feed store. (Which I later found out was only because he so admired her skill backing her trailer up to the loading dock that he gave her free hay bales.)

After hanging up with my aunt, I follow the murmur of voices to find Theo and his mom sitting outside on the deck off the kitchen. Between them, Maria has an array of food set out on a table shaded by a huge striped umbrella. When I was growing up and my mom had friends over, all she ever served was chips, dip, and Cheetos; maybe some homemade party mix if she really wanted to go all out. But Theo's mom has all kinds of exotic cheeses and rolled meats arranged on a wooden board, dishes filled with olives and some kind of green cigar shaped thing that Theo tells me are grape leaves stuffed with rice. Everything seems so fancy, and I don't know… so European. I've never felt so Midwestern in my life.

Maria pours herself and Theo a glass of red wine, and I try not to cringe when she offers me some.

"Actually, red wine makes my skin get all blotchy. I think I'm allergic to it." I don't mention that I hate the taste, smell, and look of the stuff.

"How about a crisp Sauvignon Blanc?" she offers. "That would be nice on a warm night like this."

"Uh yeah. A crisp…uh, whatever you said. That sounds…uh… refreshing."

We all sip our drinks as Theo fills his mom in on the news at camp. When I glance over at him—casually lounging in a chair, swirling his wineglass by the stem, wearing gold aviator sunglasses that he must have found here because I sure as hell have never seen him in them before—I can't believe it, but he almost looks, dare I say, *sophisticated*. Which again, is a new look for him, since he always acts like such a goofball at camp.

I peer at him over my wine glass as heat kindles low in my belly. Good God, when did Theo change like this? He's no longer the dorky teenage boy I'd met at Orientation. Now he's a beautiful grown man. And every inch of my body is telling me, quite loudly, not to forget that fact.

Our cocktail hour unfolds easily, Maria telling funny stories about her grandkids and her plans for a trip back to Greece in the fall. Theo and I volley back and forth like an old married couple, telling raucous stories of our mishaps at camp and an abbreviated version of meeting Charlie. (Again, I don't feel like going into all the details. Although I can tell Theo is dying to say more.)

Just as I'm starting on my second glass of wine, the phone rings. Maria rushes inside to answer it, then reappears a few moments later.

"Your brother is on the phone," she says to Theo. "I told him you were here, so he wants you to come to the factory so he can show you the new automated box-folding machine we got last week."

When I make a face, Maria nods in agreement. "I know, it's weird. But for some reason, Nate's obsessed with this damn piece of equipment." She turns back to Theo. "And apparently he needs to show it to you right this very second."

Theo jumps to his feet, clearly excited to see his brother. His sudden movement makes Ginger, the Golden Retriever, leap from where she was sleeping by his side, knocking into the table and nearly toppling our drinks.

He turns to me. "Do you want to go with me? It's a little hike over that hill." He points off in the distance. "But the view is really pretty along the way."

Theo explained earlier that the factory was on the other side of the property but had its own entrance so the delivery trucks wouldn't spoil his *Babcia's* peace and quiet.

When I glance at Maria, she smiles graciously, retreating into the house to tell Nate we're on our way. I feel bad because I can tell she was enjoying herself and is disappointed our little soirée is over. And truthfully, I'm disappointed too. Theo's mom is hilarious. And so warm and friendly. Even though we just met, I already feel like I've known her my whole life.

So instead of joining him, I shoo Theo away to go see his brother with an excuse about being too tired to hike anywhere. I want to spend more time with Maria. Not only because I like her but because she might give me some more insights about Theo. What better way to get all the juicy details about a boy than from his mother?

∞

Maria comes back outside to find Theo gone and me finishing the last of some kind of thin ham that tastes nothing like the lunchmeat my mom used to serve us.

When she sees me, her face lights up. "Oh, goody!" she squeals like a teenager. "Now I can get some girl time with you! You know, just like a normal mom."

I hide my puzzled expression, wondering why she doesn't consider herself a normal mom. Although I don't have the nerve to ask her outright.

When she generously tops off my wine before she sits, I realize I'm not the only one trying to drum up some juicy details from our conversation. Maria's obviously looking for some intel from me too.

Maria asks about what I want to do when I graduate, and I must be more tipsy than I thought because I actually tell her how I want to one day run a camp for bereaved kids like me. It doesn't escape me that she and her son are the only two people I've ever told about my pipe dream. What is it about this family that makes me want to pour my heart out to them?

Maria gushes about what a great idea it is and how she knows I can do it, which instantly makes me think of my mom. It's exactly what she would say if she were still alive.

As time passes, I become so comfortable (and possibly drunk) that I decide to come right out and ask Maria what I really want to know. "So, do you think Theo is right? About...you know...what he heard on the other side?"

"About the fact that he's going to die young?" she says without skipping a beat. Funny how she doesn't seem thrown off by my question at all. She sighs heavily. "Unfortunately, yes. I do think it's true."

I grip the stem of my glass tighter, realizing how badly I wanted her to say "No". How much I wanted her to look around guiltily, making sure Theo was out of earshot, then quietly confide how she believes Theo has misinterpreted the information he heard. And despite how much he believes he's going to die soon, there's no way it can be true.

But she believes him. Which feels like a kick in the gut.

I wait for her to say more. To explain all the reasons she knows it's true, but she just stares solemnly down into her wine. Something about her resigned expression makes me think of Caroline's reaction when the doctors told us it was time to put my mom into hospice care. I'd been outraged by how the doctors were quitting on her, arguing vehemently that we needed to try other treatments, that we couldn't give up yet. But Caroline told me I had to stop fighting. That I needed to wake up and face the inevitability of what was coming next.

She'd somehow seemed so calm, so accepting of my mom's impending death. But not me. I'd never been able to find that peaceful place like my sister, despite how hard I'd tried. Instead, I'd lived in a state of constant fear for nearly a month, clawing against my complete and utter helplessness until the day my mom died. And that's a feeling I never want to experience again.

"Isn't it hard for you?" I blurt out, thinking back on that time. "Knowing he's going to die soon? Aren't you terrified every single day of your life?" Surely Theo's mom of all people can understand how I'd once felt.

She nods, compassion filling her brown eyes. "It is hard. I won't pretend otherwise. Theo is my baby. I love that child more than life itself." Tears well up, and she swats them away, laughing self-consciously. "Sorry. You'll understand when you have kids of your own. Believe me, if I could trade places with him, I would."

I bite my lip, fighting my own tears. My mom had said the same thing to me so many times. "Oh honey, I'm just glad it's me and not you." I'd never understood why that thought gave her such relief. Maybe Maria is right. Maybe I won't understand that kind of selfless love until I become a mother myself.

She collects herself and goes on. "I went through a period after he got better where I didn't want to let him out of my sight. I held on to him so tightly, worrying about every move he made. Always so scared that something would happen to him. I was so terrified of the cancer coming back that it nearly drove me crazy."

I nod, thinking of Theo describing nearly going crazy himself after he'd gotten better, so consumed by making the right decisions to one day find me, that it nearly paralyzed him.

Maria continues. "I saw myself clutching onto him, stifling his choices. And I remembered all the things I'd dreamed for him when he was sick in that hospital bed. All the things I prayed he'd be able to do when he got better. I wanted him to go to school. To have friends. And play sports. Go to the prom. Drive a car. Maybe even fall in love." She raises an eyebrow at me, and my cheeks flush as I think of how unworthy I am of Theo's precious, possibly once-in-a-lifetime, love.

She laughs, looking up at the darkening sky as she speaks. "I even wanted to have fights with him. I actually dreamed of him being an asshole to me! Can you believe that?" She shakes her head in exasperation. "Oh, I longed for the day when he had enough energy to yell at me and run to his room and slam the door in my face. I wanted to ground him for sneaking vodka from my liquor cabinet and missing curfew because he was having so much fun with his friends. All those everyday things that normal moms complain about. I wanted to have a reason to complain too. I just wanted him to be an ordinary, healthy, infuriating teenage boy."

As she grins, I finally understand why she was so excited about meeting me. Why sitting here having 'girl talk' with someone she believes is Theo's girlfriend (even though I'm technically not) is so thrilling for her. Why she's so eager to do what normal moms do. Because for too long, nothing about her life with Theo had been normal at all.

"I wished for him to have all those big milestones," she says. "And the small ones too. I wanted it all for him. Every up. Every down. I wanted him not only to live, but to have his own life. To make his own choices, have his own success, his own defeats. And I knew that for him to do that, I had to let him go. I had to not only trust that he would be okay no matter what happened, but something much harder." She swallows, voice cracking as she goes on. "I had to trust that *I* would be okay no matter what happened too."

Hearing her poignant words—words that again sound so similar to what my mom might say—makes the lump in my throat swell so big it's hard to talk.

My lips tremble as I fight back the rising emotion. She reaches across the space between us to pat my knee. "I'm sorry, honey. Theo told me what happened to your mom. I know how hard it must have been losing her when you were so young. That really sucks."

I crack up at her choice of words, and she just shrugs and rolls her eyes. I can almost imagine what she looked like as a young girl, so fierce and outspoken, just like Theo has described.

"What? It does suck. Like really hard!" she wails, and I laugh even louder, grateful that she's lightened the mood.

She tips her head at me, voice surprisingly light as she says, "It just so happens in our case, Theo and I have our roles reversed. He's going to die before me, which isn't natural in the order of things. I mean, you want to talk about sucking! That's what really sucks!"

Again, we laugh together. I can't believe we're joking about such a serious issue. But it seems both she and Theo have had enough time to come to terms with their situation that they no longer see any reason to lament their fate.

"It's always been that way between Theo and me," she says. "That blurring of our roles. I've come to believe Theo is here to teach me something, not the other way around. He's always seemed like such an old soul. So wise beyond his years."

"Yeah, he is, isn't he?" I muse. "It's really annoying sometimes. Seriously, how can he always be so damn positive all the time?!"

"Oh, he gets down," she gently corrects me. "He's just good at hiding it. He always felt like such a burden when he was sick." She shakes her head, as if nothing could be further from the truth. "He hated that people had to take care of him. That's why he loves taking care of people now. He knows what it's like to feel helpless. He knows how to soothe people who feel trapped in their circumstances because he's been in their shoes. He knows that people often lose hope, not only because they're sick, but because they feel like they've lost all control of their lives."

Something twangs inside my chest hearing her description. *Helpless.*

Trapped. Lost all control. I may not have ever been in a hospital bed myself, but didn't I feel that same way so often? In fact, aren't those the exact emotions I try so hard to run from now?

I'm glad when Maria interrupts my uneasy thoughts. "Theo loves taking care of people. It truly makes him happy. I have no doubt about that. But sometimes I think he doesn't share how he really feels because he doesn't want anyone to worry about him. Theo has told me that he never wants to be the cause of anyone's pain ever again. So, I think that's why he holds back sometimes. Why he isn't always completely honest about how he feels."

It takes me a second to process what she's saying. Her claims are hard to fathom since Theo is the most open, honest person I've ever met. Or at least I thought he was. It makes me wonder if he's holding something back from me. Something I've been too self-centered to notice before now.

"I know he feels very guilty about the divorce," Maria says. "Which is silly since it would've happened whether or not he got sick. He feels bad about how his treatments and hospitalizations took time away from his brother. But again, Nate doesn't hold any resentment about it. He loves his little brother. He's just glad he's alive." She scoffs sadly. "We tell him none of that is his fault. But he feels so responsible for everything. Like he was such a hardship for us. When really, he's always been our greatest blessing. Still, I'm not sure my words really get through to him." She trails off, lost in thought.

I dig my fingernails into my palms, tortured by the thought of Theo not knowing all the good he brings to the world.

Maria clears her throat, looking a little sheepish. As if she's worried she's said too much. "You can imagine how excited I was that he told you about his experience. That was a big step for him, opening up to you the way he did."

"I was honored he confided in me. I know it's not something he's shared before."

"Thank you for believing him. You don't know how important it was for him to be able to trust you with his story."

"Of course," I murmur, gulping down a big sip of wine so I don't have to say more. Just then the buzzer for the oven rings, and Maria slips into the house to check on dinner, leaving me alone to think of how the boy she's just described seems so different from the Theo I know. The boy who's always lecturing me on how worthy I am just by being born. Could Theo not believe that same thing about himself? It's hard to believe he might struggle with the same problem that I do:

How it's easy for me to show compassion to other people. Yet so much harder to show it to myself.

CHAPTER EIGHT

I PACE AROUND the bedroom, my nerves so tangled up it's pointless to even try to sleep.

The rest of the night had unfurled in the same upbeat, spontaneous way I've come to expect whenever I'm around Theo. He'd returned from the factory with not only his brother Nate, but Nate's wife Sophie and their three little blonde-haired girls in tow.

Theo's older brother was stockier and more clean-cut than Theo, but with the same matching green eyes. And Sophie was kind but harried, eyes constantly darting around as she talked in a desperate attempt to keep track of her rambunctious girls, the youngest of which looks to be about Jack's age. The family made a point of saying they were on their nightly walk before dinnertime. (Apparently, their house is located somewhere on the property too.) But I had the distinct impression they were there to check me out.

My heart nearly burst into a million little pieces by the sweet way Theo introduced me to the rest of his family. He looked so proud to have me by his side, raving on and on about how smart and kind and funny I was. Telling everyone how all the campers loved me and fought for my time and attention…the same way he did too. (He got a laugh with that.) I loved how he stood so close beside me, occasionally resting his hand on the small of my back to guide me to the next person in line for introductions. I loved how natural it felt to be there with him. It's hard to put into words, but it feels like Theo is It. *The One.* The person who is supposed to be by my side for the rest of my life.

But that can't happen, can it?

And yet…don't we still have time?

Inside the bedroom, I make my decision. I'm fed up with over-thinking. I'm fed up with worrying about the future and being so scared all the time. For once, I'm going to go after what I want and worry about the consequences later. Yes, it's time for me to stop being so wishy-washy and instead take the advice of that famous sneaker ad slogan and *just do it!*

Buoyed by my newfound resolve, I burst out of the bedroom and stride down the hallway on a single-minded mission.

We only ever have Now, Annie. Theo's words chant like a mantra in my head as I quietly knock on his door. Well, let's see if Theo is ready for the Now I have in store for him.

Theo swings the door open in a rush, still dressed as he was earlier in his polo and black jeans. But unlike before, his hair is loose, hanging in tangled ribbons like he's been running his hand through it. Interesting. Maybe he's been pacing around his room thinking of me just like I've been thinking about him too.

"Hey there," he says in the low velvet voice that always makes my legs go weak. He doesn't look all that surprised to see me. Of course he's not. He knows me. Knows my thoughts, my emotions, my desires. I was kidding myself to think I could ever shield myself from him. Theo has been woven into my very existence from the moment I first laid eyes on him.

Without another word, he ushers me into his room with a wave of a hand, then closes the door behind me with a loaded click. I can't believe how nervous I am. It's only Theo after all. I've been with him all day. Why am I so jittery around him now? But alone in the dim room, with his tall frame looming so tantalizingly in front of me, I suddenly feel like I can't draw a full breath.

I scan around the cluttered space. "So, this room looks…uh, very lived in." It was supposed to be a joke, but my voice cracks at the end, giving my nerves away.

"Uh, yeah," he says, sounding a bit breathless himself. "I told you my mom never changed it when I moved out."

I smile to myself, liking the fact that he seems nervous too. Looking around, I can see why Maria wanted to keep his bedroom just as he left it. The space is so him. All messy and cluttered, but inviting and warm too. Around the room, he's created little shrines to the things he loves. One wall covered with posters of the 'soft guy' singers he adores: Dan Fogelberg, James Taylor, John Denver. The other with images of distance runners torn out of magazines, with his own ribbons and trophies clustered on the dresser underneath. Near his bed there's a bulletin board tacked with photos of him with his friends, hamming it up in various outrageous poses. And on his nightstand sits a single framed photo…of him and me.

He sees me staring at it. "That was a good night."

I pick it up to look closer, glad to have something to do with my hands. Hands that are itching to touch him.

The picture is from the night of Tim's party. In it, we have our cheeks pressed together, and apparently something really hilarious has just happened because we're both laughing hard, mouths open and eyes scrunched up small. We look ridiculous. And very, very, happy.

"We were drunk," I say, putting it back down, intentionally keeping my back to him.

"You were drunk. I was high," he corrects.

"Ah yes," I say, finally turning around and meeting his eyes. What I see there makes my stomach drop out from under me. "You were such a bad boy that night." I give him a coy smile, enjoying the tension snapping between us, and the memory of the words he'd whispered in my ear back then. The words that shook me to my core.

"Again, I'll tell you what I did that night," he purrs devilishly. "I'm not as good as you think I am." Yet despite his teasing, he doesn't come any closer. Damn him.

He flicks his eyebrow provocatively. "So, you've sought me out in the middle of the night once again. Seems like this is becoming quite a habit of yours."

"Oh, is that a problem?" I take a step toward the door. "Because if it is, I can leave…"

He lurches over to block my path. "No, no…it's not a problem at all! You can come to my bedroom whenever you want! You don't even have to knock!" And just like that, all his bravado is gone, and he's back to being his awkward, lovesick self once again.

"Now that sounds more like it." I give him a playful poke in the ribs.

We both stand there grinning at each other as the silence swells between us. Oh, what the hell. There's no use pussyfooting around this anymore.

I take a deep breath, still not sure how I'm going to say this. Raw honesty is not something I'm all that familiar with.

"So…um…you know that offer you made earlier?" My heartbeat quickens with each honest word. "Back on Charlie's porch?"

"Uh huh." He's frozen in place, not blinking, not smiling…I'm pretty sure not even breathing.

"About how I could have you whenever I wanted?"

"Uh huh." His voice is a mere whisper.

"Does that offer still stand?"

He nods furiously. "Uh huh."

I smile to myself at his sudden muteness. Theo is so rarely at a loss for words. Seeing him this way is kind of fun.

"Uh huh? That's all you have to say?" I narrow my eyes at him. "That doesn't sound very convincing. I mean, if you don't want to—"

He startles back to life, cutting me off. "What I meant to say was hell yes, that offer still stands!" His words tumble out in a rush. "What I meant to say was you can have me every second of every minute of every day that you want me, Annie. What I meant to say was there's no scenario in this whole entire world where I would ever say No to you! *That's* what I meant to say!"

I laugh and poke him in the ribs again. "That's exactly what I hoped you'd say!"

Theo grabs my hands, holding them in his as if we're standing together on an altar. "But before we go on, there's something I've been wanting to tell you," he says seriously. "Something you need to know about how I feel about you."

I touch a finger to his lips, cutting him off before this conversation heads into forbidden territory. "I don't need you to say anything to me, Theo. Other than, *please can you stay?*"

Stepping closer, I ever-so-gently press my body against his. As soon as we make contact, Theo sucks in a sharp breath, his previous platitude forgotten just as I'd hoped. He's so tall I have to crane my head back to see his eyes. Raw desire shines in their mossy depths, a mirror to what I feel simmering in my own.

"Please can you stay?" he whispers, a strand of wavy hair falling across his face as he leans over me. Nodding, I reach up and tuck the errant strand behind his ear, letting my fingertips brush along the skin of his cheek as I bring my hand back down. A tiny moan of pleasure escapes his lips, twisting my insides in such a visceral way. All I can think about is how satisfying it would be to make him moan like that again…and again…and again, until the only sound in my ears is his ecstasy. I want to give him that. And I don't even care what I get in return. That's how much I love him. Even if I can't say it out loud.

But no matter how much I care about him, I'm still going to need an escape clause in the morning.

Just as Theo is lowering his lips to kiss me, I stop him again. "And your other offer? What you said about no strings attached at the end of summer? Does that still apply too?"

He pulls away, disappointment flickering across his handsome features. But he covers it quickly. "Yes. Of course." He musters a forced smile. "No commitment past this summer. If that's what you want."

I nod. Even though that's not what I want. I want him across time and distance, lifetimes and eternities, always together, forevermore. But that's not what either of us can have. So I'll have to stick with what's possible.

"I want this, Theo." I gesture between us. He swallows hard, staring at me with such disbelief that I feel compelled to add more just to make things perfectly clear. "I want *you*."

He shudders as if the three words have physically altered his chemistry. And I hope they have. He deserves to feel as wanted as he makes me feel. He deserves to receive the same love he so freely gives to me.

His eyes dance back and forth between mine, their intensity boring deep into my soul.

"Can you say that last part again?" he whispers, his hooded gaze dropping to my mouth.

I huff a laugh, enjoying watching him unravel. "I want you, Theo." I ever so slowly lick my lips. "Right. Fucking. *Now*."

CHAPTER NINE

THE INVISIBLE WALL that has stood between Theo and me for six long weeks evaporates in an instant, and suddenly we're kissing and clutching and grabbing and rubbing, as if we can't bear to exist with a molecule of space between us anymore.

I want to drown in the rush of this heady excitement. My God, if merely kissing Theo feels this good, how good is it going to feel to do more? Is there a limit to the amount of pleasure I'm able to experience? I can't wait to find out.

Our hands become more and more frantic as they roam over the top of each other's clothes. I would've thought Theo liked his sex slow and deliberate, so he could savor every tiny nuance, like he does with everything else in his life. But damn if he isn't just as frenzied as me.

Just when I'm about to rip off his clothes and wrestle him onto the bed, he breaks away, piercing me with those beautiful green eyes. "Are you good?"

It's hard to think with him looking at me that way. I don't think I've ever wanted anyone as much as I want him right now. "Yes, I'm good," I pant. Then I slow down enough to think about his question. "I mean, I guess I'm a little nervous too," I admit.

"Yeah, I know what you mean. I'm excited. But nervous too," he says. "But nervous is good, right? Nervous means it matters. Nervous means we care."

I nod, thinking over his words. Yes. We care. That's it. That's what feels so different about this. I actually *care* about Theo. Which is a first for me. In the past, all my hookups have held some kind of agenda. Vanity. Avoidance. Selfish release. Yet my relationship with Theo is so pure. So unencumbered. So…dare I say… sweet? This situation I've gotten myself into with him is so foreign I'm not sure how to behave. It's no wonder I'm nervous. Under these new parameters, this might as well be my first time having sex.

I wrench him back to me and kiss him feverishly, overwhelmed by the wild tangle of emotions that have hijacked all my rational thought. My goodness, I don't think I've ever felt so out of control around a man before. And I'm surprised by how much I like it.

I yank Theo's shirt over his head, circle it around in the air like a cowboy's rope and throw it across the room with a loud *yee haw!* just to make him laugh. Once his chest is bare, I'm so overcome by what's about to happen—I'm going to see Theo naked!—I simply stand there taking in his chiseled muscles, the hard plane of his stomach just above the waist of his jeans. I stare for so long he ends up glancing down at himself self-consciously as if he thinks there might be something wrong with his body. Which there most definitely is not.

Almost reverently, I place my palm on the flawless skin just below his throat and slowly caress downward, weaving my hand back and forth so I can take in every ridge and curve of him. God, how long have I dreamed of touching him this way? How long have I yearned to finally know the warm silkiness of his skin? To feel his taut muscles pressed against the palm of my hand? I lean back just enough so I can watch my fingertips circle the lowest part of his stomach, my insides flipping at the sound of the soft groan that escapes his lips.

"God, I love this part of you," I whisper, undoing the top button of his jeans and tugging the waistband open so my fingers can dip even lower. While my fingers work, I kiss slowly down his chest, eventually letting my lips replace my hand in the yawn of his unzipped pants. He laces his fingers in my hair as I bend before him, heaving a shuddering sigh as I lick slowly from the top of one hip bone, all the way across to the other, savoring the sweet taste of his skin.

"My turn," he says thickly, making me stand so he can pull my sundress over my head. He circles the scanty fabric above his head and flings it across the room the same way I just did. But it lands on the lampshade, threatening to topple it over. We gasp as the ceramic base clatters loudly on the nightstand. Once it settles unharmed, we burst out giggling like two school kids caught talking in study hall. Maria's room is at the other end of the hall, but who knows how the sound travels in this gargantuan house.

Theo slips my bra strap off my shoulder, hungrily devouring my breast the second it pops out of the cup. His lips are so warm, his tongue circling and flicking, making my nipple harden in his mouth. He works his way over to give my other breast equal time, and I have to say, both me and my left boob commend him for his sense of fairness.

Feathering kisses along my collarbone, he reaches behind my back to unsnap the clasp of my bra. I let him fumble for a while before I slap his hands away and do it myself, impatiently pulling my underwear down only seconds after my bra drops to the floor.

I stand with my hands held out to my sides, entirely naked now. "Ta Da!" I spin in front of him, knowing he'll appreciate my silliness, as well as a few other things in his line of sight.

His eyes rake down my body and then back up again, drinking in every inch of me; his lips moving faintly as if he's uttering a silent prayer. He struggles for so long I wonder if the sight of me has accidentally broken him. I wonder if I need to give him a whack on the side like a jammed jukebox to get him to play again. Finally, he murmurs to himself, "I've never seen anything so beautiful in my life."

I make a face. "Well, that's a bit dramatic, but I'll take it."

Grabbing my wrist, he pulls me roughly toward him, kissing me deeply, ferociously even, his roughness thrilling me more than I care to admit; the steely bulge now pressed into my stomach thrilling me even more.

Then, for some reason—maybe it was the way he struggled with my bra or the shock on his face when he first saw me naked—a terrible thought pops into my head.

"Wait a minute, Theo," I push against his chest. "You've done this before, right?"

He strains against my hands, claiming my lips again. "Of course." His words come out garbled in my mouth.

"Good. Because being a Mrs. Robinson…deflowering some younger boy?" I shudder. "That is definitely *not* something that turns me on."

He ignores me and starts tantalizing me with little nipple sucks again. Instantly, I relax. Why did I even ask such a stupid question? No one this skilled with his tongue can be a virgin.

I work furiously to get his damn jeans off. Earlier I'd loved their tightness, the way they showed off his perfect ass. But now they've transformed into the last barrier between me and the one thing I so desperately want. Or, to put it more accurately, the one thing I so desperately *need* right now.

Seeing me struggle, Theo enthusiastically comes to the rescue, shucking off his jeans and underwear all in one motion. He stands and says "*Ta Da!*" just like I did. Which turns out to be quite appropriate because what's levitating between his legs definitely qualifies as magical. My mouth, and other parts of me, begin to water at the sight of it.

"I've never seen anything so beautiful in my life," I repeat his line in the same awestruck tone he'd used.

He laughs. Apparently, he thinks I'm joking. Which I most certainly am not.

My insides throb seeing the wetness glistening on the tip of his… um…quite impressive cock. Something primal inside of me makes me drop to my knees in front of him, desperate to taste him. But just as I'm almost zeroed in on my target, Theo catches me by the upper arms and gently pulls me back up.

"I can't believe I'm saying this, but I don't think you should do that," he says, looking pained. "I mean, unless you want this to be over before it even starts."

Begrudgingly, I give in, understanding his plight. I'm so aroused I think one firm brush of his hand in between my legs might end things for me too.

Glancing at his bed beside me, I ask, "Good Grief, why are we still standing up?"

I purposely crawl onto the bed so he can get a good view of my naked ass from behind, then flop back on the pillows with a dramatic sigh.

I open my mouth to seductively ask him to join me, but before I can even get the words out, he pounces on me on all fours, tossing his hair and growling like a lion about to devour its prey. Which is a ridiculous thing to do at a time like this. But it's also such a *Theo* thing to do at a time like this that I can't help but laugh. He cages me under his arms and legs, and bounces me up and down, shaking the bed so wildly I feel like a piece of popcorn in a hot skillet exploding underneath him. He's grinning down at me so happily, and I'm having so much fun that I giggle wildly, then cover my mouth to keep his mom from hearing us. Yes, this is definitely unlike any experience I've ever had in bed with a man before.

Theo goes quiet. Seeing me sprawled underneath him grinning from ear to ear, his expression transforms into something soft and achingly tender. It's an expression I'm not sure someone like me deserves. But right now, I don't feel like questioning anything. Especially myself.

He bends and kisses the column of my throat, then moves down my chest, the tips of his long hair dragging like silky feathers along my electrified skin. My God, I don't think I've ever felt such an erotic sensation as this. The faint tickle of his hair and the firm pressure of his lips combine into such luscious pleasure that I writhe beneath him, all my senses honed to razor sharpness and begging for more. I guess I'm going to have to eat crow. Because this feels so good, I'll never complain about his long hair again.

When he gets to my belly, I pull him back up to me, not sure I can hold out if he goes any lower. I want our first time to be synchronized and equal. Not me selfishly taking and Theo selflessly giving, like always.

Theo lays his weight on top of me and we scissor our legs, grinding rhythmically into each other as we kiss. I really don't want to stoop to begging, but I'm on the verge of doing just that when he dips his hand between my legs. Feeling my wetness, he lets out a deep groan into my open mouth.

He breaks away just long enough to ask, "Uh…should I put on a condom? I mean I don't have to because I'm sterile. But if you want me to, I will."

In that split second everything screeches to a halt. "What?! You're sterile?"

He lifts one shoulder. "Yeah. You know. Because of the chemo." Seeing my horrified expression, he rushes on. "But never mind. I shouldn't have mentioned that right now. I'll just…uh…go get the condom."

I blink at him. "Yeah. You should go get the condom, Theo!" I grind out, trying to force his stunning revelation out of my head as he rolls away from me. The fact that Theo can never have children is definitely not something I want to think about right now. No, we can discuss that little detail at a more opportune time, when we're not two seconds away from having sex.

As he sits on the side of the bed getting himself ready, I run my hand up and down the smooth skin of his back, doing my best to rekindle the flames inside me that have just been so rudely doused. Luckily when he crawls back on top of me—looking a bit sheepish, but also so stunningly sexy too—it's easy to regain my focus.

We kiss for a while longer, building ourselves to the place we'd been before. I spread my legs wider, inviting him to go further…so very much further. We're both breathing hard, my heart nearly pounding out of my chest in anticipation as he positions the tip of his erection at my opening. I'm already dreaming of what it will feel like to have him inside of me, and while most of me is clawing at his hips, barely able to stand the wait, a tiny part of me is scared too. Scared of how much of him there is. Worried about whether or not I can handle all of him.

He gently pushes partway inside of me, and the low *mmmmm* sound he makes when he feels me tight around him nearly sends me over the edge. Again, it surprises me how badly I want to make him feel good. How badly I want him to moan and gasp and shudder all because of me.

"You good?" he whispers in my ear.

"More," is all I can get out in my delirious state. He obliges, gliding a little deeper into me. Then he withdraws, making me whimper, I'm so desperate to feel more of him. He finally thrusts himself all the way inside me, and dammit to hell if I don't cry out, it feels so freaking good. He pumps again, and again, burying himself so deep it feels like my entire body is being reconfigured to match his own. As we move together, I'm not sure I've ever felt pleasure of this magnitude…not sure anyone has ever stretched and filled me this perfectly before. And from the sounds Theo is making above me, he seems to be enjoying himself too.

It feels like I'm hanging onto the precipice of release by a single fingernail. The faint thought that we should go slower in order to savor this more flits through my head. But that logic is clearly not reaching my wildly thrusting hips. I'm completely out of control, and Theo is too because he keeps going faster and faster. And he must be reading my mind because that's exactly what I want him to do.

As we undulate in perfect rhythm, everything begins to warp and blend until I feel connected to him in a way beyond the physical realm. It's like I'm not only feeling my own sensations but his too; as if I'm waffling back and forth between his body and mine…spinning, whirling, blessedly dizzy inside this vortex of conjoined ecstasy.

He tips his head down to watch where we're joined, the motion making his hair brush against my nipples again. And that one whisper-soft touch is all it takes for me to lose my grip and plunge over the edge. Blackness races in from the edges of my vision as I find my release, and all that's left in my entire world is the place where we're merged and the waves of pleasure spasming outward from it, engulfing every inch of my electrified body.

As each contraction rolls in, I gasp and convulse, the sensations somehow intensified by Theo still moving so thick and hard inside of me. My blissful spasms are just beginning to slow when he thrusts deep and lets out a gasping moan that tells me he's falling too. Somehow his completion sends another spike of satisfaction jolting through me as if I'm feeling what he is. As if the two of us are no longer two separate bodies but now one and the same.

Theo collapses on top of me, and we stay that way for a while; panting and gasping, trying to remember who the hell we are and what planet we're on. When I finally settle back into myself, I realize Theo's hair is splayed across my face, nearly suffocating me. I make a big show out of huffing and puffing and trying to blow it away. Giggling at myself because I'm so light and airy, laughter is the only option.

He realizes my dilemma and raises himself up on his arms groggily apologizing. My heart pinches, looking up at his heavy-lidded expression. I don't think anyone has ever gazed at me with such complete and utter adoration in my entire life. And in this moment, I feel perfect. Whole. Complete. It's like Theo's eyes are a mirror, and in them I see a glimpse of not only how he sees me, but who I truly am, deep down inside.

The emotion gushing through me is so strong I do the strangest thing. I reach up, hold his face in both of my hands and kiss him slowly, deeply, with a passion that has nothing to do with sex. He kisses me back, again reflecting all that emotion back down into me. Maybe Theo is even more than a mirror. Maybe he's an amplifier. Taking every quiet little hidden part of me and turning it into so much more. *God, I love this boy with every last inch of my heart. Please.* I beg to whoever might be listening, *Please, don't take him away from me.*

∞

Theo eventually rolls over, flopping like a rag doll beside me. I squeeze my thighs together, already missing the wholeness I felt with him inside me.

"Wow!" he says, grinning up at the ceiling.

"Wow is right," I agree, basking in the warm afterglow.

"Just like…wow!" he says again. "That was the best I've ever felt in my entire life!"

I laugh. I should tell him I feel the same way too. But instead, I measure my words carefully. Hold back a little, like always. "I'm glad you liked it."

I assume he's merely being his over-the-top self again, but when he mutters three more Wows (and appears to be about to add a few more) my heart drops. Uh oh. I think I know what's going on here.

"Theo." I roll on my side and level him under a stern stare. "Don't tell me this was your first time."

"Okay," he says brightly.

Letting out a heavy sigh, I think I'm off the hook. Then I review my exact phrasing. "Wait a minute. Does Okay mean this *wasn't* your first time? Or does it mean that it *was?*"

He shifts his head and shoots me the silliest grin I've ever seen. Which is saying a lot, because the boy has given me a lot of silly grins. "I can't answer that because you told me not to tell you, remember?"

I lurch up on one elbow. "Oh my God, Theo. You were a virgin?!"

He nods cheerfully, not one trace of embarrassment in his expression. "Yup."

"But…but…you lied to me!"

He props himself up so we're face to face. "Technically, I didn't. You asked me if I'd ever done this before when we were kissing. And since I had kissed you before, when I said Yes it was true."

"Are you serious? You're trying to get off on a technicality right now?!" When he merely cocks an eyebrow, I barrel on. "Why didn't you tell me you were a virgin?"

"Because I didn't want you to freak out and make it all awkward. I know how you feel about younger guys. I was afraid you wouldn't want to go through with it if I told you the truth." His cheeks are adorably flushed. Is it just me, or does he suddenly look a lot younger than he did five minutes ago?

I flop on my back with a huff, purposely not responding. Let him squirm for a bit. He needs a little punishment for misleading me, even though I'm glad he didn't tell me the truth. I don't think I would've been able to let myself loose like that if I'd been worried about making his first time perfect. Lucky for us, our first time turned out to be perfect all on its own.

He stares down at me, looking so worried (and so incredibly handsome) I finally give in.

"Just so you know, since you have no frame of reference," I grumble, still pretending to be mad. "That was extremely good sex."

"Really? Was it?" For a split second he looks proud. Then he quickly becomes serious again as he settles next to me. "I mean I know it was good for me. But did you like it too?"

I roll on my side so we're both nose to nose. "Yes. A lot." I reach over and pick up a piece of his hair and twist it around my finger. "How did you know how to do that, anyway?"

He gives a lackadaisical shrug. "I studied."

"You studied?!"

"Yeah. I mean, I read a lot. When I was a teenager and stuck in bed, I used to steal my mom's romance novels. I'd sneak them to my room and pour over them. Man were they ever detailed! Some of them… boy…they pretty much gave you step-by-step instructions of what to do to make a woman happy. Which is exactly what I wanted to learn. I figured if women wrote them, they must be accurate. Since they're the ones who know what they like."

I nod at his impressive logic.

"So, you're saying I did alright?" he asks.

"Oh yeah. You did very, very, alright, Theo." I lean in and give him a little kiss. "Good job on the research, dude. I guess what all those posters in the library said is true. Reading really is fundamental."

We laugh together, then relax into the quiet; breathing shared air, idly grazing our fingertips along each other's skin, basking in just being together. Even though I know I've paddled past the boundary ropes, all the way out to the place marked 'swim at your own risk', I want to stay here and tread water for a bit. This place is new, somewhere I've never been before. Maybe I can let myself enjoy it for a while longer. Surely I'll be strong enough to swim back to the safety of the shore if the waters get too rough.

"So I took your virginity, huh?" I ask.

"Yeah. Are you mad at me for not telling you?"

"I'm still deciding."

"Well, if it helps, just think what a special moment this is for me. I'm going to remember it for the rest of my life."

"That's true." I look over his shoulder, a pleasant pressure building inside my chest. It's stupid, but I somehow feel honored to have been part of this milestone for him. Especially since he might not get many more.

I pretend to deliberate for a while longer, then say, "So I think I've decided how I feel about being the person who 'made you a man'," I air quote myself.

He gives me a sleepy smile. "Yeah? And how's that?"

"Well, let me test it out first. I need to say it out loud before I give you my final verdict."

He looks like he's barely breathing now. "What is it you want to say out loud, Annie?"

I clear my throat ceremonially, then in a bold voice say, "I'm the first girl Theo Teodorczyk ever made love to."

His eyes instantly well up. I knew that description, from me of all people, would dissolve him.

"Yeah," I whisper, brushing another kiss to his precious lips. "I think I like the sound of that."

∞

Satisfied and spent, we doze for a while, Theo's naked body curved around mine in the rumpled bed. It's late, and the house is quiet, the only sounds in the room are the hum of the air conditioner and the faint ticking of the bedside clock.

I force myself to stay awake just so I can listen to him sleep. His breaths come long and slow, blowing gently into my hair. I silently count them, knowing each one for what it truly is: such a precious and finite gift.

It scares me how perfect everything feels right now. The weight of Theo's arm around my ribcage holding me tight. The warmth of his chest pressed into my back. The feeling that I'm exactly where I'm supposed to be. How many nights have I felt so completely untethered, so alone in the world? Not knowing where I would land next, what place I would call home? Now I think I understand why the search seemed so futile…so damn hard all this time. Because the place I was searching for wasn't a place at all. It was this feeling I've just found inside Theo's arms.

I twist inside the circle of his grip, needing to look at his beautiful face. But despite how slowly I shift, Theo's eyes flutter open as soon as I face him.

"Hi," he says in a thick voice.

"Hi." I brush him with a kiss, unable to stop myself. This compulsion to constantly touch him still baffles me. A faint warning tolls in my head, telling me I'm making a big mistake. That I've opened a door I might never get closed again.

"Look at you being all affectionate," Theo says.

"I can't help it." I kiss him again. And again. And again. "It turns out you're irresistible."

He pushes a strand of hair off my face. "Am I?"

Something knives in my chest at the thought that he could even ask such a question. "Yes, you are." I nestle closer, scissoring my leg between his, squeezing him almost ferociously, hoping maybe he'll feel my love without me having to say it out loud.

"In fact, you want to know what Caroline told me you reminded her of the first day she met you?"

He makes a face. "What?"

"A really handsome Muppet."

A smile bursts out on his face. "She said that?" When I nod, he goes on. "Well, I take that as a really huge compliment."

"I knew you would."

We grin at each other with almost sickening adoration as I worm my way even closer to him. And when Theo opens his mouth, I know exactly what's coming.

"Annie, I need to tell you something…"

"Theo, don't!" I reach up to cover his mouth before he tries to tell me he loves me like he did before.

"I was going to say your knee is crushing my balls," he mumbles around my fingers, wincing in pain.

"Oh, sorry." I quickly extract my leg from his crotch.

He scrunches his brow. "Why? What did you think I was going to say?"

"Nothing, nothing," I lie. Then I rush on, this topic of conversation sending my mind reeling back to what happened earlier. "Um… speaking of your balls…."

"Now there's a segue you don't hear often," he says flatly.

I pull myself up on the pillow, needing a little space between us so I can think clearly.

"You can't have children?" My pulse races as I wait for his answer. The idea that Theo of all people—the guy who adores all kids and who all kids adore—can never be a parent is one of the cruelest twists of irony I've ever heard.

"Nope. At least not with those guys," he points to his crotch. "But don't worry…all is not lost."

"It's not?"

"No. Some have been saved."

I huff, irritated. "What the hell are you talking about?"

Chuckling, he scoots up to prop against the headboard too. "My sperm. Right before I started the chemo, they informed us of the side effects, so I banked some healthy swimmers before the rest of them got zapped into oblivion."

"Oh, thank God."

"Yeah. I guess it was a good thing." He looks off into the distance, a shadow passing over his face. Seeing it, I understand why. Even if Theo can physically father a child, he will never live long enough to see that child grow up.

He must notice my stricken expression because he moves on quickly. "Talk about acting horribly. I was so pissed off when they asked me if I wanted to bank my sperm. I mean, can you imagine? I'd just turned sixteen, and my mom was telling me I had to leave a sample in a cup? It was all so embarrassing." He shudders at the thought. "I kept saying no. That I wouldn't do it. But she kept hounding me, telling me I'd be thankful later. Talk about awkward! My own mom was literally begging me to jerk off in a cup! God, it was so humiliating. I finally just did it to get her off my back. I'm telling you, the woman was relentless!"

"Yeah, I'm trying not to think of the visuals there," I tease, and he cringes. "Did she at least bring you one of her romance books to get you hot and bothered?"

His cheeks stain pink. "No! Believe me, the entire experience is something I've tried very hard to forget." A beat later he adds, "Besides, they had movies for me to watch so I didn't need the books."

After we finish laughing I ask, "But don't you think your mom was right? Aren't you thankful you left your uh…*deposit* now?"

He nods. "Yes, she was right. And I've told her that." His smile falters. "Although what does it matter in the end? Because I'll never be able to…"

"I know Theo." I talk over him. "I know." As if stifling the words might somehow soothe the pain of their injustice.

Swallowing around the lump in my throat, all I can think is *Why?* Why has this happened? Why must such a beautiful soul as Theo bear such a heavy burden? I would ask him, but I know he'll only tell me what he always does: that he doesn't consider his fate a burden. That instead he sees his brief life as a gift.

Theo seems eager to change the subject. "Let's not talk about this anymore, okay?"

I can only nod because I know if I try to speak, I'll start crying.

"This is the best day of my life!" he reminds me. Then, in one fluid motion, he pivots and positions himself on top of me again. "And do you want to know why you're lucky to be in bed with a nineteen-year-old, newly deflowered virgin?" He gives me a devilish smile, grinding his growing hardness against me.

"Why?"

"Because I'm ready to go again!"

CHAPTER TEN

"I STILL CAN'T believe you thought Theo was my Mystery Man," Greta scoffs. "What a dummy."

"Do you seriously want to be insulting the person who currently holds your life in her hands?" I tug on the belay rope that runs from the harness around her waist, up through a pulley in the trees, and down to my hands. The same rope that, in about three minutes, will be the only thing keeping her from falling 20 feet to the ground once she gets to the top of the ropes course.

"You would never drop me," she says.

"Keep calling me a dummy, and we'll see if that's true."

She hesitates at the bottom of the rope ladder, checking the carabiner at her waist for the hundredth time. I want to reassure her that everything's in order and she has nothing to worry about, but I know that would only piss her off. Greta would never admit it out loud, but she's scared. Which is why I'd suggested we come here alone.

During orientation, when we'd done our training on the ropes course, I'd helped run the session. As a certified ropes course instructor, I'd taught the new staff safety protocols, how to harness the campers, and belaying techniques. Although the ropes course at Camp Boundless was unlike any I'd ever seen before. It's specially modified so even kids who use wheelchairs can be hoisted in a special rigging and experience the high (both literally and figuratively) of the adventure elements.

The day we'd trained, I'd noticed Greta pacing nervously as she waited. And seen the relief on her face when she found out we'd run out of time, so she wouldn't have to take her turn. Still, I know how much she hates walking away from a challenge, and I could tell not trying it bothered her. Which is why I thought coming here with me today would be the perfect way to help her conquer her fear.

At the base of the tree, she heaves a heavy sigh and glances over her shoulder where I'm anchored a few yards away with my rope, ready to become her human safety net.

"On belay?" she calls out the commands I taught her.

"Belay on," I call back.

She turns back to the rope ladder in front of her and gulps so loudly I can hear all the way back here. "Climbing."

The first few steps up the wobbly ropes are no problem for Greta. She's strong and athletic and should have no problem completing the course. Although she will be at a disadvantage because she can't feel the ropes underneath her rigid prosthetic foot or grip with both hands. But she's so skilled at compensating I won't be surprised if she gets through the course even faster than me. That is, if she'd ever stop looking down.

I'd suggested she use her hook today so she could get better traction than she would with her rubber arm. The prosthetic she's wearing has a silver hook on the end made of two scissor-like pieces she can open and close by shifting her weight against the leather straps attached across her opposite shoulder. It's what she uses when she needs to draw medicine up into a syringe, or open packaging, or take blood pressures. Anything that requires two hands. (Not to mention it's great for scaring the pants off the campers when we tell ghost stories around the campfire at night.)

Watching her, I can tell she's doing well physically. She's finding foot and handholds easily, so that's not a problem. It's more the mental part I'm concerned about. The higher she goes, the more often she stops and looks down. Which is not ideal for someone who's clearly scared of heights.

"I don't think it's that far-fetched that I thought you had the hots for Theo." I pick up our previous conversation, trying to take her mind off her anxiety. "You two are together all the time, and you have to admit, you do love him."

She huffs with disdain. I knew that mushy description would annoy her. "Yeah, but not like *that!*" She peers up at the ropes above her, just as I'd hoped she would. "Just because a girl and a boy enjoy each other's company doesn't mean it has to be romantic, Annie!"

"You guys dated for a while!"

"I know, and that's when we found out that there's a different kind of love. One that's about friendship only. You do know that's possible, right?"

"With a guy?" I argue, mostly just to keep her engaged. "I'm not sure about that."

She's moving faster now and hasn't looked down in a while. It looks like my plan is working.

"Still, can't you see why I got confused?" I ask.

She grunts as she hauls herself up another step. "Yeah, I guess. But you should've just asked me instead of assuming he was off limits."

She's right. I could have simply asked her point-blank about her feelings for Theo. Looking back now, that would've made everything a helluva lot easier. Which is probably why I didn't think of it. Easy really doesn't come naturally to me. "Maybe I was using it as an excuse," I admit.

"What? To torture yourself? It seems like you're awfully good at that."

Her comment takes me aback. Theo has drawn my attention to how hard I am on myself, but I thought that was only because I'd confided so much to him. Greta also mentioning it means I'm not hiding my self-loathing as well as I think I am.

I take up more slack in the rope as Greta falls into an easy rhythm…

hand, hook, foot, foot. "So you're not mad that Theo and I are dating?" I ask.

She's only a few feet away from the first platform attached to the gigantic oak looming over us. I'm being a coward, asking her such a question when she currently has a vested interest in keeping me on her good side. But I haven't had the courage to ask her how she feels about Theo and me being together. When we'd come back to camp four days ago, Theo and I had agreed to keep our new relationship quiet and maintain a strictly professional demeanor toward each other. Which, ironically, is what had given us away.

"Why are you guys acting so weird?" Greta asked in the staff cabin after we'd barely been back for a day. "You two are normally inseparable, and now you hardly look at each other?" She'd studied us closely, and damn if it wasn't me who broke down and blushed. "Oh my God! You did the dirty deed, didn't you?!" Greta bellowed. "You two are getting it on, aren't you?!!"

Theo had just shrugged, looking way too proud of himself. I, on the other hand, had stayed quiet, bracing myself for Greta to rattle off all the ways this was a bad idea. But the barrage never came. She'd just smiled and said, "Good for you guys." Then cuffed Theo upside the head and changed the subject.

Now, as she takes the last step on the rope ladder that is twisting and turning underneath her, she says, "Naw, I'm not mad. It was bound to happen. You two have been obsessed with each other since the day you met. And you both seem really happy, which is all I care about."

"Careful, your sweetness is showing," I tease. It's true, Greta is one of the kindest people I've ever met, even if she does her best to hide it. I've seen how patient she is with the kids, giving them time to try things on their own. Gently encouraging them but not jumping in to help too soon. Like Theo, she understands these campers in a way I probably never will. And yes, she uses jokes as a defense mechanism; always making fun of herself before anyone beats her to it. But I can hardly fault her for that, since I know a thing or two about hiding behind a well-placed sarcastic barb myself.

She hurls herself up onto the platform and I cheer. Risking a quick glance down, she gives me a shaky thumbs up, then scoots across the tiny platform on her butt, turning to wrap her arms around the immense trunk and press her cheek into the bark.

"Have I told you lately that I love you, Mr. Oak Tree?" she croons comically. "How about we stay here together for the rest of our lives? Huh? Wouldn't you like that? I know I would. Don't let that mean lady down there tear us apart."

I giggle, glad she's relaxed enough to make jokes. I tell her to take a minute to catch her breath before she moves on to the next obstacle. It's good we don't have a line of people waiting to go so she can take her time getting through the course.

She gingerly turns around and leans back on the tree with her legs stuck out in front of her. She's still breathing hard, but whether it's from exertion or fear or a combination of both, I'm not sure.

"Keep looking up," I tell her.

"Now you sound like Theo," she grumbles, staring out over the canopy of trees. A childlike sense of wonder lights up her face as she takes in her new vantage point. I know that feeling. It's pretty astonishing to see the forest from a bird's-eye view for the first time.

We both stay quiet, soaking in the peaceful rustling of the wind through the trees, the heated purr of the crickets in the underbrush.

"Theo is the best person I've ever known," Greta mumbles so softly I'm not even sure I'm meant to hear it.

Her rare sincerity startles me so badly it takes a few beats for me to respond.

"Yeah. He's the best person I've ever known, too." I fiddle with the rope at my waist, letting the truth of the words sink into my bones.

She levels me with a threatening stare. "Which is why I'll kill you if you hurt him!"

Her sudden vehemence shocks me, and I stumble backwards a step. She cackles uproariously.

"Oh my God, you should see your face!" Greta wheezes. "You look like you're afraid I'm going to jump right off here like Spiderman and squish you like a bug!"

I roll my eyes. I should've known better than to expect her to stay serious for too long.

Pretending to unhook myself from her belay line, I shout up to her. "You know what? I think I'll just go and let you figure out how to get down from there all by yourself."

"No! Stop! I'll behave now!" she apologizes, and now it's my turn to laugh.

Even though the moment is lighthearted, it reminds me that Greta doesn't know about Theo's destiny. Man, it's going to kill her when he dies. And yet part of me envies her ignorance. Wouldn't I be making different choices if I were oblivious to his eventual fate? Would I still be insisting on upholding our no-strings-attached pact at the end of the summer? Or would I simply be a carefree twenty-one-year-old girl soaking in every nuance of the most amazing person she's ever met with absolutely no fear of tomorrow?

I squeeze my eyes shut tightly, cursing myself for asking such futile questions. If Theo is right about the web of possible paths he was shown on the other side, one connecting to another to another, then there's no use wondering what could have been. Because from what he's told me, once you've picked a path, your destiny is altered forever. Which means that in this game called Life, there are no second chances.

So why do I keep getting this inkling that we still have a chance to change our futures?

Greta eventually hauls herself to her feet, and together we focus on the next element on the course. It's a cable bridge, which isn't all that challenging except for the initial big step down.

"The first step is the hardest," I tell her. "But after that, it gets easier."

As she takes the plunge, I notice she's not as tense as she was before. So I keep on talking.

"Why didn't you tell Wen how you felt that night at the party?"

"It didn't feel right, just blurting it out like that." Her words come haltingly as she focuses on placing each foot just right on the cable. "I figured if it was meant to be, it would be. I didn't feel like I had to force things between us."

I consider that as I keep the rope attaching us together taunt but not too tight. Once again, I'm reminded of my mom's advice of staying open and letting life take you where it wants you to go. Now Greta is basically saying the same thing. Good Grief! Is everyone I know in on this conspiracy to get me to trust in the world's goodness?

Greta pauses in the middle of the bridge to take in the view again. It's amazing how comfortable she is now.

"Why are you so concerned about me hooking up with Wen, anyway?" She cocks her head, making her black helmet shift to the side.

I'm not sure how to answer, so I buy myself some time by instructing her to adjust her helmet and check the chinstrap underneath to make sure it's tight. In truth, I feel terrible about how the boys treated Greta in high school and want her to feel all the love and admiration she deserves. And I think Wen is the perfect person to show her that. But I know she'll think I'm pitying her if I say that. So instead I say, "I just think you two could have a lot of fun together."

She harrumphs, like she knows I'm not telling the entire truth. "He probably doesn't even like me." She starts walking carefully once again.

"Oh, don't worry. He likes you. There's no question about that."

Now that I've pulled my head out of my ass, I've noticed how Wen gravitates to Greta. He always laughs at her jokes. (Under his breath most of the time, but still.) And hangs back to walk with her on the trail. And saves his peanut butter cookie for her at dinner. He's definitely smitten. In his own subtle way.

I tell her all this, but she still doesn't seem all that convinced. "A peanut butter cookie doesn't mean anything."

"Maeve's peanut butter cookies do!" I counter. "You'd have to pry those delectable hunks of yumminess out of my cold, dead hands. I sure as hell would never share mine with you!"

She chuckles and goes to take another step, but her hook gets caught on the handrail. Shifting backwards, she shrugs her shoulders at various angles to get it to open up, making the bridge bounce beneath her. She quickly gets the hook free, but I can tell from her blanched face the snafu has her flustered.

I start to give her one of the pep talks I give my kids, but sensing what's coming, she barrels on with our conversation as if nothing's wrong.

"You know there's more to life than boys, Annie," she says haughtily.

"Of course I know that!" I huff. Wasn't I the one spouting off at the start of the summer about how I had no interest in relationships and instead only saw guys as passing playthings? I'm the world's foremost expert in there being more to life than boys.

She goes on. "My mom taught my brothers and me that life is about balance. That you should have your…whoa…whoa!" The cable wiggles crazily underneath her, making her prosthetic foot slip off. For a split second she panics, then luckily regains her balance once again.

Before I can make the obvious joke she mutters, "And yes, I see the irony that I was talking about *balance* when that happened. So you don't need to point it out."

We grin at each other, and she goes on. "What I was saying was that my mom always said life is about balance. That you have your career, your family, your friends, your relationships. And you should spread out your time and attention among all of those things. That way the weight of your happiness doesn't fall on only one thing or one person. She always encouraged me to have lots of different interests. Not just boys." She stops at the very end of the bridge and leans a little over the side. "And not just sex either!"

We both burst out laughing as she scrambles up onto the next platform. "Oh, your mother told you that, huh?" I shoot back.

"Well, maybe she didn't mention sex directly…but that's what I'm telling you."

"I don't know Greta," I muse coyly. "The sex with Theo was awfully good."

"Stop!" she wails, covering her ears.

"In fact, I'd be pretty happy to put ALL my time and attention on having sex with Theo for a while," I shout. "In fact, I just might make it my exclusive interest for a while."

"Ew…gross! It's like you're talking about my brother!"

I pretend like I'm going to say more and she squeals, "Stop it!" repeatedly until I finally shut up.

Greta completes the next obstacle. And the next. And the next. Her confidence growing with each platform she makes. The last task is the zip line that will bring her to the net at the end of the course. She's so relaxed now that, after launching herself into the air, she lets go of the rope and flaps her arms out to the sides like a bird in flight the entire way down.

I meet her at the bottom of the net. (Which fortunately she'd grabbed with her good arm since the jerk backward might have torn her prosthetic right off.) After I unclip her, we hug and jump around in celebration.

"Man, that was amazing!" she gushes, her smile so bright it nearly blinds me. "After getting through that." She points up at the obstacles in the trees. "I feel like I can take on the world!"

My heart swells, seeing the difference between the shaky girl who started the climb and this badass chick standing in front of me now. This look on her face…*this* is why I chose a career in the outdoors. I don't care if the pay is shit. I want to spend the rest of my life helping people feel this damn good.

As we make our way up the path to where we started, Greta leans on my shoulder, her legs still shaky from all the adrenaline. She chatters almost maniacally as I get her out of her harness, recounting each footstep, each wobble, each recovery while I nod and let her talk.

She's so cute…and so damn proud of herself. I've never seen her so raw, so uninhibited before. And as we settle next to each other on a log, snacking on peanuts and a bottle of Coke, it feels like we've just shared something that will alter our friendship forever.

"Wow. It feels like nothing is off limits now," she muses, still grinning big.

"Nothing, huh? Not even Wendell?"

I brace myself for her to blast me for making it about boys again. But I can't help it. Greta is amazing. And she deserves to have everything she's always wanted. And I know, even if she won't admit it, she wants Wen.

I'm surprised when she doesn't shove me off the log and tell me to shut the fuck up and instead practically shouts, "Yeah! Maybe I should give this thing with Wen a chance after all!"

But then her smile drops. "But how? We never see each other outside of camp. And it's not like this place is all that conducive to romance."

Just then, an idea pops into my head so fully formed it's as if my crackpot team of Angels has sent it from above.

"Don't worry." I give Greta's knee a reassuring pat…and the heavens a little wink. "I think I just might have an idea."

CHAPTER ELEVEN

WHEN WE HEAD out on our Treasure Hunt the next weekend, Annie insists on driving. Which is fine with me, because her silver Mustang is clearly a lot more reliable than my car. It still has all its buttons and cranks. Doesn't clunk when you speed up or screech when you brake. And Annie keeps the interior meticulously clean. She calls it her second home. The only thing that's remained constant in her life for the past three years. Which I find both touching and a little sad all at the same time.

We're in a ritzy neighborhood in Indianapolis, looking for 85 Fox Run Lane, where Richard McMillan, the owner of her mom's watercolor supposedly lives. When I point out the number on the mailbox, Annie stiffens at the sight of the house looming above us. It's huge, with a perfectly manicured yard, a pool in the back, and so many cars parked in the driveway and spilling on the street that there's nowhere for us to park.

She slowly loops around the cul-de-sac half-heartedly looking for a place to leave her car. Her hands are so white on the steering wheel I expect her to keep driving and abort the entire mission. But just as we pass the front of the house again, a car drives off, leaving us the perfect place to pull in. And Annie no excuse to run.

Once parked, she clicks off the ignition and heaves a sigh so heavy it comes out in a puff of white from her lips. (She's got the air conditioning cranked so high you can see your breath. Show off.)

"Maybe we should come back another time. It looks like they're having a party," she says shakily.

"Which makes this the perfect timing," I counter. "We can slip right in and find the painting and they probably won't even notice we're there."

"You want us to crash their party? Theo, that's downright criminal."

"Or downright genius. It all depends on how you look at it." I'm teasing to get her to relax, and it works because she shoves me on the shoulder, letting out a soft laugh.

"It's going to be okay," I say, leaning over the console to offer her a kiss. Surprisingly, she accepts, stopping to look deep into my eyes before pressing her lips to mine. I've noticed her doing that more lately. Locking eyes with me whenever she's nervous, as if whatever she sees there calms her. I hope I have that effect on her. Because I'm going to need to leverage everything I've got in order to convince her she shouldn't break up with me when camp ends.

"Get a room, you two!" Greta shouts from the backseat.

"That's exactly what we're planning to do when we're done here," Annie shoots back, wagging her eyebrows luridly. Greta makes loud gagging noises as Wen looks out the window, wisely not getting involved.

Greta and Wen are with us because Annie's come up with some big plan to get them to admit their feelings for each other. Since the painting we're searching for is here in Indianapolis, where Greta, Wen and I live, Annie decided we'd all carpool home together. First, we're stopping to find the title of the painting, then continuing on to a party I'm apparently throwing at my apartment? I didn't question it. I'm just going along with whatever Annie has planned.

I guess later Annie has it arranged so that all the other counselors we'd 'invited' will conveniently call and cancel at the last-minute, leaving just the four of us alone in our 'little love nest', as she'd put it.

(How she'd managed to simultaneously invite and *un*-invite half the camp, I don't even want to know.)

Now Annie looks physically ill as she takes in the throngs of people milling behind the wrought-iron backyard fence. For someone like her, so averse to flying by the seat of her pants, it's going to take every ounce of courage she can muster just to walk to the front door and knock without knowing what kind of reception we're about to get. It's probably best if I sit quietly and wait for her to make the first move.

Again, her eyes lock on mine, looking for reassurance. "I can do this?" she asks, as if she really wants to know.

"You've done it before," I remind her. We were lucky our experience with Charlie turned out so well. I don't think there could be a better ambassador for a friendly world than that sweet man.

"Yes, that's true," she says with a determined dip of her chin. "I've done it before, and I can do it again." She hesitates, touching my hand. "As long as you're there with me, it'll be okay."

I nod, shooting a stern look over my shoulder, warning Greta not to make fun of Annie's rare admission of weakness. But Greta's already reached up to rub Annie's shoulder in encouragement.

"Someone once told me the first step is the hardest," she tells Annie. "But after that, it gets easier. You just have to keep looking up." I'm not sure what all that means, but it makes Annie laugh. Then she throws open her car door like she's suddenly ready to take on the world.

Greta and Wen wait in the backseat while Annie and I cross the street and head up the sloped driveway. Annie gives me a sideways glance but holds back what I know she's dying to say. "Why the hell didn't you change your clothes?"

I'm still wearing my camp get-up; my green Camp Boundless polo, multi-colored plaid shorts, striped tube socks and red bandana folded up and tied around my head. For some reason, when I'd gone to change after the kids left earlier something had told me to keep it on. I'd listened, although I still have no idea why. This definitely doesn't look like the kind of neighborhood that welcomes shaggy riffraff like me. Which is probably why, after she knocks on the door, Annie tells me to be quiet; she'll do all the talking.

As we wait, the sounds of thundering footsteps and kids screaming reverberate from inside the house. I'd noticed balloons tied to the fence as we got closer, so I have a feeling we're interrupting some kid's birthday party. But I don't dare mention that to Annie, or else she'll surely bolt. She hates imposing on people, even in the smallest ways.

After a few more rounds of loud knocking (Annie refuses to just barge in like I suggest) the door swings open so suddenly we both jump. A harried-looking woman in her thirties with short brown hair and a birthday hat sitting cockeyed on her head blinks at us like she can't quite make sense of what she's seeing. Her expression remains confused as she eyes me up and down, taking in my garish wardrobe. Though I don't turn my head, I feel Annie shooting daggers at me. Yeah, I probably should've changed my clothes.

Annie opens her mouth to start the spiel she's practiced the entire way here. But before she can get a word out, the woman heaves an enormous sigh and says, "Oh thank God." She smiles at me then shouts over her shoulder. "Gary, it's going to be okay! The replacement clown is here!"

Annie's eyes fly to mine as I stifle a laugh. "Don't say it," she grumbles.

I ignore her and whisper it in her ear anyway. "I take that as a really huge compliment!"

Annie's not religious, but I swear I hear her muttering a prayer under her breath.

"Actually, he's not a clown," Annie pipes up, glaring at me. "He only acts like one sometimes."

The woman looks back and forth between us, puzzled.

"What I mean is we're here about a painting that a Richard McMillan owns. It's a watercolor by Grace Peterson," Annie rushes her words together. "We wondered if we could look at it for a quick second.

We need to record some information about it for some research we're doing on her work."

"What?" the woman asks, whirling when a crashing sound comes from the next room. "Benjamin! I told you to keep the Big Wheels outside!" Three kids on plastic bikes whirl by behind her as Annie tries to continue.

"Is this uh…Richard McMillan's house?" She asks between screams from the kitchen.

The woman is so involved in shepherding various factions of kids here and there she's barely listening now. "Uh, yeah. Rich is my dad. I mean…he *was* my dad. He's not with us anymore." She gestures wildly to a man walking by with pool noodles under his arms. "Can you please get them out of here, Gary? Thanks." She turns back to us. "This is my dad's house, but we're selling it. We're only here today because we wanted to use the pool."

"Oh…uh…okay," Annie looks over at me, eyes wide like she has no idea what to say next.

"Listen, I'm sorry," the woman says. "I don't mean to be rude, but this is a really bad time and…oh, oh…get the dog!"

A huge standard poodle explodes around the corner, nails scuffing on the shiny floors as it scrambles directly at where Annie and I stand on the doorstep. I grab the dog's collar and wrestle it back inside while the woman yells for this poor Gary guy to "Come get the goddamn dog already!"

Once the commotion is over, she turns back to us looking sheepish. "Sorry about that. Excuse my language. That was bad. It's just I've got all these kids here for Ben's birthday party and the magician cancelled and I thought they were sending someone over to replace him, but now you're saying you're not a clown…although you kind of look like one." She gestures to me. "And I don't know what the hell I'm going to do with ten five-year-olds for the next two hours. So, forgive me for not being able to help you with whatever research project you've got going on."

Annie's cheeks flush bright red. "I completely understand. I'm so, so sorry we bothered you. We'll just go." With each word, she shrinks even further into herself, like she wishes she could disintegrate right into the lady's front stoop.

Seeing her cower that way, something fierce flares inside me. No, I won't let this end this way. There has to be something we can do to salvage this.

I glance over my shoulder at Greta and Wen waiting in the car, then through the kitchen doors to the melee unfolding in the woman's backyard, an idea forming in my head. I catch Annie's wrist before she dashes away.

"Actually, this might be your lucky day," I tell the woman, suddenly realizing why I'd had the impulse to keep my camp clothes on earlier. "Because it just so happens my friends and I know a thing or two about entertaining kids."

CHAPTER TWELVE

"OH MY GOSH, you guys are the best. You don't know how much I appreciate this. Seriously, I'm not sure what I would've done if you hadn't shown up…" The brown-haired lady, who tells us to call her Lisa, hasn't stopped thanking us since I'd summoned Greta and Wen from the car, told her our qualifications, and explained how the four of us are about to save her ass…for free.

But even after hearing my brilliant plan to take over the party entertainment, Annie still looks doubtful.

"I'm happy to play with the kids," she whispers as Lisa ushers us inside. "But this lady doesn't seem like she wants to help us with the painting. I think this is a dead end."

"Just wait and see," I whisper back. "Once we get everything under control and she relaxes, then you can ask her about the painting again. By that time, she'll be so grateful, she'll have to show it to you." I glance around at the empty rooms and bare walls. "Wherever the heck it might be."

As we pass through the house, Lisa explains that her father died a few months ago. Now, they're preparing the house to be sold, which is why most of the rooms are empty. A situation that might throw a wrench in our plans. Because with all her father's belongings already packed up, Lisa might not even know where the painting is located. But I will not think about that right now. No, right now we need to get these kids under control before they destroy what little is left inside this house.

The four of us huddle in the backyard, quickly trying to come up with a plan, while the kids circle around us and stare. It's no wonder they're captivated. You've got me with the big hair and crazy clothes. Beautiful Greta, with two fake limbs and a voice like a bullhorn. Wen with dark skin they may have never even seen before in this neighborhood. And Annie, who looks like Cinderella come to life. We could probably just sit in chairs and let them gawk at us for the next two hours, and that would be entertainment enough. But we're professionals. We're going to do way better than that.

Annie starts off the festivities by teaching them a bunch of silly songs with hand motions and dances. Then Wen and Greta take over with a series of relay races they've thrown together with various toys scattered around the lawn.

The kids are enthralled. They giggle and laugh and scream, but in a much less blood-curdling way this time. They give us out-of-the-blue hugs and tell us they love us in between activities. And mostly listen to our directions, only interrupting to tell us random stories about how their mom had to flush their goldfish down the toilet because they took it out of the bowl to cuddle it one night. They're so cute I want to scoop every one of them up and give them a big hug. But they're moving too fast for me to catch them.

Everything is going even better than I'd hoped. I'm just about to start my juggling act when I notice Lisa with a group of parents, relaxed and smiling, drinking something out of a plastic cup that I don't think is just Kool-Aid.

Annie stoops down and talks softly to a little blonde girl whose knee got scraped while playing Tag. I come up beside her and tip my head at Lisa. "I think now might be a good time to try talking to her again."

"Really?" Annie glances over, looking worried. She kisses the little girl's knee and guides her back into the action, then returns to me. "I don't know. Lisa's busy with her friends. Maybe I shouldn't bother her."

"But she keeps saying how grateful she is to us. And how she doesn't know how she'll ever repay us," I point out. "Maybe this is something she can do for you."

Annie winces, as if someone doing her a favor physically pains her. She's gotten better at letting me take care of her once in a while, but I know this is a stretch for her. Trust doesn't come easily to her. And with all the things she's lost in her life, I can understand why.

Behind me, Wen announces my apple juggling act (it was all I could find in the house) and the kids start chanting my name. As I back away from Annie, I call out. "Just give it a try. What can it hurt?" Then I take off running before she can list off all the millions of logical answers to that question she keeps locked and loaded inside that beautiful, but stubborn, head of hers.

I toss and whirl and pretend I'm going to drop (but don't actually drop) my apples, watching out of the corner of my eye as Annie approaches Lisa. Only a few moments later, Annie walks away, looking defeated. I have to wait until the children take a break to have birthday cake to ask what happened.

"Oh, she said she remembers the painting. That it's definitely here somewhere. But it's already all wrapped up, so it would be too hard to find it right now." She forces a wan smile. "But she said she'll call and let me know later. Once they get everything moved and unpacked. Whenever that might be." Her bottom lip quivers like she's trying not to cry. The sight of it is like a knife in my gut.

Shit. This ruins everything. Without the title of that painting we won't be able to complete our Treasure Hunt. A task that seems crucial to both of us, even beyond the surface goal of finding the paintings. Though I can't logically explain why. I swallow hard, desperation clutching at my throat, which I try to hide from Annie.

"So you told her about your mom dying? And what she did in her last days of life to put this Treasure Hunt together for you? And what this painting means to you, and she still said no?" I ask incredulously. I mean, yeah, Lisa seemed stressed before. But underneath her harried exterior, she seems like a nice person. I can't imagine how anyone could turn Annie away knowing the real reason she needs to see that painting.

Annie won't look at me. "Well, no. I didn't tell her all that. I just said it was for some research. Like we practiced before."

"Annie..."

"It feels too weird to tell her all that! She doesn't care about my dead mom!"

"Annie," I repeat softly. "People care more than you think they do."

A muscle in her cheek flexes as she grinds her teeth. "I can't just pour my guts out to everyone I meet like you do, Theo! I'm not strong like you!"

I close my eyes as thoughts war inside my head. There are so many misunderstandings I want to point out to her. But then I remember how angry she'd been on Charlie's porch. How she'd accused me of acting like I know everything all the time. Hell, I can't blame her for being pissed. I know how annoying I can be. Sometimes I hate myself for seeing things so differently from other people. After coming back from my NDE, there's been so many times I've felt like an alien living on a completely different planet than everyone else in the world. It's so frustrating sometimes. To have been shown the truth about how much love is here for the taking, then thrown back into a place where no one wants to believe it. Maybe I should listen to Annie and stop being such a know-it-all. Maybe I should just keep my mouth shut and stop trying to give her advice that she never asked for in the first place.

When I open my eyes, she's staring at me. "What? What do you want to say?"

"Nothing. It's nothing."

"It's not nothing. Just say it."

"No. It's your Treasure Hunt. You can do whatever you want." I try to keep my tone gentle. I don't want to sound snide. I truly mean it. She's the one in control.

She takes my hand, and the touch of her skin grounds me; draws me out of my head and back into the moment, with her. She must feel it too, because the furrow in her brow smooths, and when she speaks again, she sounds sincere. "You can tell me. I want to know."

"Are you sure?"

When she nods, I try my best to put my feelings into words. "It's just you said you weren't strong. But I think you might be confused about what real strength is."

"What do you mean by that?"

"It's just that all our lives we've been taught strength looks like being sure and confident. And plowing through things with no fear at all. But I think real strength is allowing yourself to be scared without seeing that as something you have to get rid of. But instead, simply a part of being alive."

She tenses, squeezing my hand almost involuntarily. I can tell she doesn't like the idea of letting herself off the hook so easily. She never does.

I give her hand a little squeeze back. "When I was a fourteen-year-old kid in that hospital bed, getting all kinds of scary procedures and painful treatments I thought I had to be all stoic and strong and hold everything inside so I could be a real man and not a big baby." I laugh at the insult I'd once hurled at myself. "Big Baby. You know, to a teenage boy, that's the worst thing you could ever be called."

She listens intently, expression unreadable, so I go on. "But soon enough the reality of my situation hit me. Once I realized I'd never be able to control my emotions, I stopped fighting them and gave in to how I really felt. I felt scared, hurt, and pissed as hell, and I didn't have the energy to hide it anymore. So I let it all come tumbling out. And you know what? It was a relief. It was such a damn relief. To finally stop pretending to be something I wasn't. To accept exactly who I was at that moment and not condemn myself for any of it or feel like I needed to change. Man, did that ever feel good."

The faintest smile drifts across her face, as if she's felt my relief too. I continue, "So you see, this isn't about being stoic and tough and fearless," I say. "In fact, it's just the opposite. To me, real strength is being soft and tender and open. It's about letting yourself be vulnerable, even if that means you might get hurt in the end."

Her eyes widen, and I wonder if I've said too much. I probably didn't explain it right. But I hope she felt the essence of what I meant. I don't want her to think she's done something wrong. I only want her to let in the possibility that she could open herself up and, no matter what happened afterward, she'd still survive. Just like I did.

Annie opens her mouth to say something, but before she can get it out, the kids at the table start chanting, "Theo! Theo! Theo!" begging me to come juggle again.

I tell them I'll be right there, then turn back to where Annie is still fighting with herself. "But I still don't know what to say to Lisa," she says.

"You will when the time comes. Just do what you did when you got us to Charlie's. Trust your gut and don't think too much. Just go with the first thing that pops into your head."

She looks like she's about to argue more, but the boys yell louder, asking if I can juggle their shoes. And their shorts. And their butts. Boys. You've gotta love 'em.

"Go." Annie pushes me away with a smile I can't quite read. And as I jog to rejoin the kids, I wonder if I've just said the right thing or completely messed everything up.

∞

The next hour passes by in a flash. After I finish my juggling show, Greta boisterously entertains the kids by passing around her prosthetics and letting them touch her residual limbs, while they pepper her with innocent questions about how she ties her shoes, and what happens if her leg falls off when she's running.

Afterwards, Wen gathers the kids around to tell them a story, his soft voice making them settle down as they strain to hear him.

Watching Greta and Wen work side by side, they seem like such opposites. But Annie is right. Together, they make a really great team.

As people trickle away, I realize I haven't seen Annie in a while. Gary—who I've figured out is Lisa's husband—looks lost as he hands out goodie bags asking, "Has anyone seen Lisa?" over and over again. I smile to myself, hoping the reason Lisa has suddenly gone missing is because she's finally decided to show Annie the painting.

Almost all the guests have left by the time Annie bounds out the door to the backyard with a huge smile on her face. "I did it! I got the title!" she yells, waving a piece of paper in the air as she runs to me.

She shows me what she's written down.

"The Struggle," I read aloud, thinking of how the painting depicts an entrance to a dark, foreboding cave nestled deep inside a forest. "Hmmmm. I wonder what that means?" I ask, pointedly not mentioning how appropriate the title is, considering all Annie's just gone through with Lisa.

She throws her hands in the air triumphantly. "Who cares?! All that matters is…I did it!"

Bowled over by her radiant smile, I scoop her up and twirl her around in the air, whooping in celebration.

By the pool Greta and Wen whoop along too. Then, seeing her chance, Greta awkwardly lurches at Wen, wrapping him up in what looks to be a rib-crushing hug. Her odd tackle startles Wen at first, but he eventually relaxes and hugs her back, the two of them smiling at each other in a way that doesn't seem to be only about Annie's victory.

When I set Annie back down, she's so excited she's tripping over her words.

"I did it! I told Lisa all about my mom. And her cancer. And how we used to do treasure hunts when I was a kid. And all about our postcards and everything! And guess what? We found the painting upstairs. In the first place we looked! Can you believe it?!" She stops to catch her breath, grinning big as I smooth the flyaway hairs off her flushed face. "And guess what else?!"

"What else?" It's taking everything I have not to kiss her; she's just so damn gorgeous right now.

"Lisa and Gary are moving to Bloomington. They bought a house in the same neighborhood where Caroline and Jonathan live! Which means Ben will be going to the same school as Jack. Can you believe that? Caroline's been complaining about how she doesn't have any friends. And Lisa's worried about not knowing anyone down there. So I'm going to give them each other's numbers so maybe they can get together. Isn't that wild? I swear, you couldn't have planned this if you tried!"

"That is wild!" I agree. "What a coincidence!"

Annie notices my sarcasm. "I know. I know." She lowers her voice in what I assume is an impression of me. "There are no coincidences. Only perfect synchronicities. But damn. This is all so unbelievable I'm beginning to think you're right!"

As we beam at each other, I have to admit it is amazing how all these puzzle pieces keep falling in place. First, there was Charlie's pottery studio just waiting to be used. Caroline was so thrilled when we'd told her about his invitation that she's already called and set up a time to meet him next week. And now we've stumbled across a woman who has the potential to become Caroline's new best friend. I know Annie feels guilty about her mom organizing this Treasure Hunt only for her. But I'm pretty sure her mom threw in a few treats for Caroline too.

"You were right, Theo," Annie says earnestly. "Lisa did care. Just like you said she would."

"And that doesn't piss you off?" I ask tentatively. "Me being such a know-it-all again?"

"No. I mean, you're not gloating quite as much this time, so that helps." The corners of her mouth quiver like she's fighting back a smile.

She blinks up at me, pure adoration in her eyes. "You're brilliant, you know." She taps my temple.

I smile big. "Oh, nothing I've ever said to you comes from there."

I remove her hand from my head and place it over my heart. "It always comes from here."

She presses her hand harder against my chest bone. As my heart pounds wildly beneath her fingers, a flash of white flares along the edges of my vision, and for an instant it feels as if my heart has fallen forward to rest in the palm of her hand. The symbolism feels poignant. Almost like someone is trying to tell me that Annie holds my life in her hands. But how could that be possible?

Words whisper in my ears, tinny and hollow, as if from far, far away. *You have a chance... You two can change...* Both sentences trail off before I can hear their endings, leaving behind only the faintest residue of hope in their wake.

Annie startles a little, as if something strange just happened to her too. As we've gotten closer these past weeks, our connection has become stronger. Our thoughts sometimes tangling until I'm not sure which ones are hers and which are mine.

She shakes her head hard as if trying to clear her mind, then wraps her arms around my waist and presses her cheek against my chest.

"I still can't believe it," she says, sighing heavily. "I did it."

"Yes, you did."

"And you know what?" She gazes up at me, her blue eyes wide with wonder.

"What?"

"Once I got started, it was easy."

CHAPTER THIRTEEN

ANNIE

"WELL, I'D SAY that was a success," I say as Theo and I watch Greta and Wen walk into the mall the next day.

This morning, when Greta and Wen had woken at Theo's apartment (after sleeping spooned together on the couch) I'd offered to take them each home. But they'd wanted to spend more time together. So apparently, they're now going to shop for new shorts for Wen and underwear for Greta, then get lunch.

"Yeah, they definitely hit it off. And can I just note," Theo says, pointing to my smug smile. "I'm not the only one who knows how to gloat."

I grin bigger on purpose. "It's annoying, isn't it?" I reach across to where he sits in the passenger seat, poking him in the ribs the same way he did to me on Charlie's porch. "So annoying. Isn't it? Isn't it?" He laughs and squirms and tries to slap my hand away.

I merge onto the road that will take us to Caroline's, where Theo and I are about to open our first clue from Aunt Lydia. Glancing over at him, I try to ingrain every nuance of him into my mind. His lovely profile. The shampoo smell of his damp hair. The flawless tan skin on the curve of his shoulder. The flutter of the pulse in his neck.

Something goes cold inside of me watching that flutter. A reminder that too soon that pulse will stop. His heart will cease beating, his blood will stop pumping, and he won't exist in the world anymore. A reality that just seems so damn unfair.

Yesterday at Lisa's, when I pressed my hand against his chest, the strangest sensation had come over me. I saw a flash of white light, and then it felt like I was literally holding Theo's heart in my hands. No, not only his heart but his *entire life* in my hands. And then I'd heard this whisper of what felt like a memory, but not of any experience I've had in this world. It was of my mom telling me something important. Something like *You have a chance... You two can change things if...*

If what, Mom? I now shout inside my head. But despite my desperation (or more likely because of it) no response comes.

I'm not even being selfish in wanting Theo to escape his fate somehow. Because his loss will not only be a travesty to me, but to so many other people too. Watching him with the kids at the party, all I could think of was what a wonderful father he would make one day. It's the one subject that always makes him tear up when we talk about it: how he'll never get to have children of his own. God, he deserves that gift. And his future children deserve it too; to know what it's like to be loved by a man like him. So pure and kind and open-hearted. If only there were a way to make that dream come true...

Theo's head snaps around. "What are you thinking about?" he asks, brows pulled together almost like he's overheard my thoughts.

"Nothing." The quick response sounds suspicious, even to me. So I tell him part of the truth. "I was thinking about how this weekend has been so perfect. I've loved every single second of it."

"Yeah, things just keep getting better and better, don't they?"

I nod, heart aching. It's such a Theo thing to say. His time is running out. And yet he still only sees the bright side of things.

As we get closer to Bloomington, signs for Indiana University begin to dot the highway.

"So where are you looking for jobs when you graduate?" he asks.

"Oh, I'm not sure yet," I say stiffly, hoping he won't press further. The truth is, I should've already sent out my job applications. When

I started college only six months after Mom died, I'd overloaded my schedule hoping that keeping busy would stave off my grief. I'd continued that same strategy for the past three years, which means I'll be graduating a semester early in December. I've always been adamant about wanting to move far away once I finish school. But now that I'm enjoying this rare bout of happiness, I'm starting to rethink whether or not I still want to run away.

A mischievous grin dances on Theo's face. "I bet there are a lot of good jobs in Indianapolis."

"Theo, don't start with this." I try to sound stern, but I can't fight back a smile. He's been good about not talking about what comes after this summer. And I've been good about not thinking about it. But the joy of these past few weeks has started chipping away at my resolve. I never thought I'd ever admit this, but I feel something inside me caving. Do I really have to end things in a few weeks? Why couldn't I stay with Theo for a little while longer?

He cocks an eyebrow at me. "I'm just saying, you would have somewhere to stay if you got a job in Indy. A nice apartment, with a comfortable bed, and a very accommodating roommate who could provide you with a few extra perks, if you know what I mean." He ever so subtly licks his lips, a reminder of the mind-blowing things he did with that tongue last night. Just the sight of it sends heat flickering between my legs. Oh, he's definitely not as innocent as I thought when we first met.

I huff, like his invitation is absurd. Of course it is. Moving in together? Already? Yet, in some strange way, it also feels like the most natural progression in the world. I can almost see us living as a couple. We'd have our little routine. Theo would go to classes and the hospital, and I'd go to work. When I got home at the end of the day, I'd tidy up the apartment, go to the grocery store, and do his laundry. (Is it weird that I would love to do his laundry? That I'd love to have the privilege of folding his shirts with sharp creases and matching his socks…of doing anything to make his life just a little bit easier. Oh man, just the idea of taking care of him makes my heart sing.)

In my fantasy, Theo would cook for me, and make sure my car was filled with gas, and give me massages whenever I asked. We'd kiss as we passed in the hallway. And snuggle on the couch to read. And stay in bed most of the day on Sundays, alternating between making love and dozing until we got so hungry we'd be forced to get up and eat a quick bowl of cereal before dashing back under the covers again. We'd be stupid and silly and drunk on love. At least for a while.

I feel Theo staring at me and realize my beautiful daydream has me grinning from ear to ear.

"It could be exactly like that," he says, once again reading my thoughts.

A knot forms in my throat just thinking of the possibility of such happiness. I risk a quick glance at him. But only for just a second or else I might cry. "It could, couldn't it?" I choke out, forcing my eyes back on the road.

In my periphery I see his determined nod. "Yes. And all you have to do is give in."

CHAPTER FOURTEEN

Somewhere *else*...

ANNIE TURNS IN circles looking for Theo, confused as to why she's now here with me alone.

"Hey, where'd he go? Wasn't he just here a second ago?" she asks, scanning the cluster of mist-shrouded trees we stand inside.

"Time isn't the same here as what you're used to," I say. "So if you try to make this into something linear…well, that's a recipe for a really huge headache."

"Alright," she draws the word out, looking both wary and excited at the same time.

"But yes," I concede. "From your perspective, Theo was just here a second ago."

"Wait a minute. I know why he isn't here." She shakes an accusatory finger at me. "You're throwing another twist into this game, aren't you?"

I nod. "Actually, it's not just me. We're all doing this together. But you won't understand that until later."

Surprisingly, Annie doesn't ask for more explanation. Here, resting in a fuller version of herself, she doesn't feel the need to know everything ahead of time like she does when she's a limited human being.

But I explain anyway. "Theo got some alone time with me, so now it's your turn to get the same."

"That sounds like something you would've said when I was a kid." She smiles big. "You were always so committed to fairness when you were still down there." She motions to our feet even though *up* and *down* is not quite how this works. But I don't correct her.

"And I'm even more fair now, as you can imagine. Pure love never plays favorites."

"I like that, Mom. When I get back I might even put that on a bumper sticker." She sweeps a hand through the air. "*Pure Love Never Plays Favorites*. Maybe with a picture of a rainbow in the background. And a smiley face. And a dog."

"Go for it. It seems like some folks *down there*," I play along. "Need a reminder of that."

She nods in agreement and I motion her closer, so I can look into the beautiful ocean of her eyes. "So do you remember the three things you had to learn in order to have a chance of jumping timelines so Theo doesn't die young?"

"Yes." She's all business now, unfurling her fingers as she answers. "We have to learn to trust ourselves, trust each other, and trust the Universe."

I nod. "And part of that deal was that Theo would remember more about our meeting up here than you would," I reiterate. "At least at first. And because of that, you'd have to learn to trust him."

She picks up where I left off. "And then there was the part of this plan that *neither* of us were going to remember. When we'd have to blindly agree to get married believing Theo's life would be cut short." She scrunches her brow. "So I guess that's the trusting the Universe part, right?"

"Yes. So now we just need to find a way for Theo to learn to trust *you*. And I've got just the thing."

Annie rubs her misty hands together in anticipation. "Oh, I can't wait to hear this."

"How about, to make things fair, we switch up the roles between you and Theo halfway through your adventure?"

Annie looks positively elated. (I mean, even more positively elated than she previously was. Which was already *extremely* positively elated considering her current status as an ephemeral being…but well, you get the picture.)

"Oh, that sounds interesting," she says. "Tell me more."

"We'll make it so that at some point Theo's memories of this place begin to fade, just as your memories get stronger. He'll become more doubtful and afraid. And around the same time, you'll become more sure of yourself. So eventually, it will be *you*, not him, who figures out there actually is a way to change your fates."

"So he won't get to be the know-it-all anymore? He'll have to listen to me instead?" When I nod, she claps her hands excitedly. "Oh, I like that twist!"

"How else will he ever learn to trust you?"

"I've got to hand it to you, Mom. It's the perfect plan."

"Yeah. Perfect is kind of our specialty around here," I gesture to the beautiful forest tableau surrounding us.

Annie looks so happy I kind of hate telling her the rest. "So, um…" I clear my throat, stalling. "There are only a few minor obstacles you have to overcome first. You know, in order for you to get more of your memories back."

She laughs, looking unbothered by my caveat. "I knew there was a catch. There always is."

"Yes, we always throw in a few clauses to make your lives more fun and fulfilling… bursting with love and wonder and appreciation. We're manipulative that way."

"I love it when Angel Guides are sarcastic," she says with a wry smile. "Personally, I consider sarcasm the holiest of humors, don't you agree?"

I merely raise a sardonic eyebrow. Let her interpret that for herself.

Annie throws her arms out to her sides. "Alright, lay it on me. Tell me what I have to do to assume my role as worldly sage to the poor, ignorant Theo?"

"It's not going to be quite like that…"

We crack up again, which makes the circle of cloudy trees we're standing inside dissolve into pure white for a moment. Then, the landscape gradually reforms around us.

I hesitate, curious about how she's going to take this news. "You just have to face a few of your fears, that's all," I sing-song brightly.

"Oh, is that all?!"

"Again, you two were the ones who wanted more of a challenge this time around," I remind her.

"And it will be, considering I'm the world's foremost scaredy cat down there." Again, she points at her feet. And again, I don't correct her misguided sense of direction. There's no way she can fully comprehend how this really works until she leaves all her worldly veils behind.

"It doesn't have to happen all at once," I tell her. "Just baby steps, Buttercup."

Annie rolls her eyes at the babyish nickname. Yep, she's still my daughter; even half-formed like this. We've lived through countless variations of relationships together. But being her mom…that's the role I've always loved the best.

I explain more. "The more you do things that scare you, the more you find out they don't kill you. And the more you find out they don't kill you, the stronger you get. And the stronger you get, the better you'll be able to remember what you've always known deep down inside."

"Which is?"

"That you're loved and supported by a benevolent Universe, and always will be, no matter what happens. See? It's simple."

"Yeah, it feels simple when I'm here," she says. "But when I leave… well, that's a different story."

Her mouth twists as she considers my offer further. "Hey. I've got an idea. Why don't you let me remember that part at least? That this isn't as serious as we all make it out to be."

"I keep trying to get that concept to stick with you. But it's the one message you keep pushing away!"

"Yeah, I'm a bit pig-headed this time around, aren't I?" she muses.

"Just a bit. But it's not all your fault. You humans…you sure do like your drama, that's for sure."

Annie heartily agrees. I pull her close, firming us both up so she can feel the sensation of her head resting beneath the crook of my chin, smell my long-ago perfume, sense the ferocity of my love. This moment will get her through a lot of hard times. I hope she stays open enough to remember it.

"I'll be there to guide you," I remind her, stepping back and grasping her shoulders so I can meet her gaze. "But it's going to be up to you to hear me."

She nods furiously. Then startles, looking down at herself. She's slowly fading away.

I motion her back toward the swirling tunnel of light from where she came. Sensing her reluctance to leave, I give her one last angelic pep talk as I let her go. "You can do this! And don't forget…you always have more choices than you realize."

"I'll try to remember that part," she promises, walking backwards away from me. "But I feel good about this. I think Theo and I can pull this off. If we just stick together."

I give her two thumbs up and a silly grin, which makes her giggle. Good. That's the way I want to send her off. Firmly planted in her most natural self.

"See you on the other side!" she calls out, hooking a thumb behind her, directionally misguided once again.

"Actually, it's not really the *other side* per se," I call out to her fading form. "We're always together; it just *seems* like we're separated, but really…" When she looks back at me confused, I trail off. "You know what?" I wave her onward. "Never mind. You'll figure it out for yourself soon enough."

CHAPTER FIFTEEN

ANNIE

I HOLD THE paper in the air, studying it for what feels like the hundredth time.

"Where do you think she wants us to go?" I ask Theo, wedged in the hammock beside me. We're at The Lookout during our free period, arms and legs wound around each other even though it's one of the hottest days of the summer.

"I don't think we have enough information yet," Theo says, not opening his eyes. "We have to wait to get all the clues before we know what to do. Just like your mom said."

He says it so patiently you'd never know he's already answered that same question from me almost fifty times today.

I let out a heavy sigh, not appeased by his level-headed reasoning. I read the words from our first clue again as if it might make sense this time around.

Find your center star and follow it North, Mom had written in a shaky script.

It was so exciting when we'd opened the envelope at Caroline's four days ago. Exciting, but frustrating too. The damn clue was so vague. I'd wanted landmarks and street names and distances. Not calculating our path off the North Star. Plus, it's aggravating having to wait to get all the clues before we can start. I need to do something. Go somewhere. Make something happen…like *right this very minute.*

It doesn't even matter that I'm currently exhausted. Theo and I both have wheelchair-bound kids this session, which is why we're lying here like zombies, not even making out. Plus, I'd had this really vivid dream last night. So vivid it almost didn't feel like a dream. More of a blip of a flashback, like what you might see in a movie. (Although I know that doesn't make any sense.)

In my dream I was with my mom again, and she was telling me something important I had to remember. And we were laughing, and she hugged me, and I swear it felt so real I had teardrops in my eyes when I woke up in my bunk afterward. But by the time I'd grabbed the pencil on my nightstand, wanting to capture what I could remember from dream, most of the details were already gone. And this morning when I'd looked at the bookmark I'd scribbled on, all I could make out was a few cryptic words:

Me. It's all up to me.

Uh oh. I don't like the sound of that.

Now, I focus back on the clue in my hand. Despite how tired I am, I still want to race to my car and find this place my mom has alluded to. Once I'd read it aloud, Jonathan had slapped a map down on the center of the dining room table. Then the four of us had gathered around trying to figure out exactly where my mom might be sending us.

We'd all agreed that the center Mom mentioned was probably Bloomington. So from there, Jonathan took his trusty protractor (that he just so happened to have in his pocket, the dweeb) and drew various ticks north of there on the map. The most intriguing spot was a state forest that matched the parameters of being centered almost exactly to the north of us. It makes sense that knowing my love of nature, Mom would start my quest there. I'm desperate to find out whether I'm right. But as everyone has so kindly reminded me, that's not how the rules of this game go.

That means I'm now stuck waiting and not knowing. The two things I hate most in the world.

"I think I'm right though," I say into Theo's chest. I'm tucked under his arm with my leg thrown over his, our skin stuck together with sweat. The stickiness doesn't bother me, though. As long as neither of us moves. "The Treasure Hunt has to start in Highwood State Forest."

"Mmmm." His faint response vibrates in my ear.

I lift my head up, ready to rib him for falling asleep and not listening to me. But he looks so peaceful lying there, his features soft and lips slightly parted. I want to kiss him so badly it hurts. But it would be selfish to wake him up. So instead, I stay propped up on my elbow, not minding the cords of the hammock digging into my skin, as I stare at him. I can't believe I've become the person I always made fun of: a girl so hopelessly in love she actually enjoys watching her boyfriend sleep.

I love you. I mouth the words over him like an incantation, half expecting his eyes to fly open at the whisper of my thought. But he just breathes rhythmically, in and out. We've never said the words out loud to each other, but it's almost like we don't have to; we both just know it already. Like how when you wake up in the morning you know the sun will rise. Or when you take a deep breath you know your lungs will fill with air. It's not something you question, or even worry about. You simply take for granted that it's true.

I have no idea why I feel so sure about that. But I do.

I flop back down beside him.

God, I'm in a shitload of trouble.

Nestling my head back on his chest, I savor the faint breeze tickling my skin and sleepily watch a hummingbird flit in the wildflowers along the edge of the platform. It dips its tiny beak in the cups of nectar and drinks and drinks and drinks like it will never get its fill.

The hummingbird lands on a branch only a few feet away, tipping its little head back and forth, its liquid black eyes studying me. I feel it then, the warm presence I don't doubt as much anymore. I feel the happiness radiating from that little beating heart as it watches me and Theo curled there together. Oh, how my mom loved hummingbirds.

"Thank you for this," I say to her in my mind.

Oh, this is all you, Buttercup, she replies. *You were the one who listened.*

"He makes it easy."

Easy is always the way.

I smile. And the hummingbird flies away.

∞

I must fall asleep because the next thing I know I'm being startled awake by a loud noise. My eyes fly open, heart whirling furiously as I try to figure out where I am. I'm almost ready to bolt when I realize the scary sound was just a crow cawing in a nearby tree.

"It's just a bird. You're going to be okay," I tell myself as I snuggle back into Theo, still asleep beside me. But my stupid heart continues to race, mistakenly thinking I'm in some kind of fight or flight danger. I hate this feeling. The pounding and sweating and gasping for air that comes from the adrenaline coursing through my body, completely uninvited. It reminds me of how I feel when…

"No," I say to myself, squeezing my eyes shut tight as I try to will the memories away. "I don't want to think about that."

But a nasty voice taunts in my head. *It's happening again. It's happening again, and you can't stop it.*

There's no warmth in that voice. Not like when I hear my mom speaking to me.

"No. I said I don't want to think about this," I argue back silently.

I chant my familiar mantra—"I will not think about this. I will not think about this."—even though I know it never works.

Don't fool yourself. Your episodes are back. And stronger than ever.

"But I got rid of them. They can't be back."

They're only going to get worse, the nasty voice barrels over me. *All because of* him.

"No. No. No."

Are you forgetting what happened at his mom's house last week?

I cringe as the shame of that night rushes over me. "I told you…I don't want to think about that!"

A harsh laugh cackles inside my skull. *Oh right, you want to run away just like before. Remind me again. How did that work out for you?*

The laughter gets louder and louder. Then it's like someone has kicked open a door inside my mind. And even though I try my best to keep it from escaping, the memory comes pouring out.

∞

It's kind of ironic that what happened that night, right after Theo and I first had sex, was triggered by Maria simply trying to be a normal mom.

When Theo had been off seeing his brother, Maria decided it was her duty as a mom to embarrass her son by showing me his baby pictures.

She'd left me alone in the living room with the thick album while she went to finish dinner, instructing me to check out the ones at the very front because (according to her very un-biased opinion) Theo was the cutest baby ever. And after flipping through a few pages, I had to agree with her. With his riot of silky curls and huge green eyes, Theo looked like he could give the Gerber baby a run for its money. If babies had money, that is.

"I can't believe how fat he is!" I'd called into the kitchen, grinning from ear to ear at the precious little boy smiling up at me through the plastic film.

"I know!" she yelled back. "You wouldn't believe it looking at him now, would you? The gangly lug."

I turned a few more pages, but then the clattering from the kitchen got louder, and I heard Maria uttering a few curse words, so I decided to put the album away and go help her. But just as I was about to slam the book shut, I got the urge to open it to the middle. And what I saw there made my heart catch in my throat.

Staring back at me was a teenage Theo lying in a hospital bed.

Although I wouldn't have recognized him if I hadn't already known about his cancer. In the picture his face was pudgy, but not in the cute baby way like before. Instead, the medication that he'd told me had so many awful side effects, had stretched and bloated it tight. His skin wasn't the rich tan it is now. It was sallow and grey; his head bald except for a few wispy strands around his ears that made him look like an old man.

The only part of him I recognized was his lovely eyes. Although as I looked closer, I realized his beautiful dark eyelashes were gone too. His smile was the same, though. Although a bit more forced than the perpetual one he wears now.

My gaze had strayed to the background of the pictures and suddenly Theo faded away and into sharp focus came the all too familiar nuances of a hospital room. A place I wish I had never gotten to know so well. I saw the needle puncturing the skin on the back of a hand. Heard the relentless alarms of the IV stand next to the bed. Smelled the medicinal tang of disinfection trying in vain to mask the aroma of sickness. Felt the awful sensation of paper-thin skin sliding over the edge of jutting bones.

In Maria's beautiful living room, my heart hammered hard in my chest as I was whisked back to stand next to my mom's hospital bed once again. Seeing it and smelling it and hearing it so vividly in my mind…it was like my body actually believed I was there. Suddenly, I couldn't breathe. My pulse whirled all crazily, and my ears pounded, and my fingertips went cold. And for a second I thought I might faint. Luckily, Maria called out and asked me to bring in the cheese and crackers from the porch, and once I got out into the fresh air, I felt better again.

I'd brushed off the incident as merely a bout of low-blood sugar. Exhaustion after our big day. But that night, after I'd fallen asleep in Theo's bed, I'd had a terrible dream.

In it, I was watching Theo drown. For some reason I was witnessing the scene from up high, as if I was in the nosebleed seats of a stadium, with him a million miles below. He flailed in a dark body of water, desperately calling out to me for help, but I stayed frozen in place as if my feet were trapped in cement.

As I watched him struggle, his head disappeared under the water and never came up again. Panicked and helpless, I fought frantically to get my useless legs to work, to find some way to get down to him, shouting, "Hold on, Theo! I'm coming!" even though I knew I was too far away to save him. Even though I knew there was no way I'd ever reach him in time.

I sat bolt upright in bed, sweaty and gulping for air; my heart once again pounding so wildly I could barely catch my breath. Not wanting Theo to notice, I'd dashed to the bathroom down the hall to get myself together.

Inside the safety of the room's bright lights, I stared at my reflection in the mirror, telling myself over and over that it was all just a dream. Just a horrible, horrible dream.

Or was it a premonition? The nasty voice sounded in my head. *A reminder of how you're going to feel when he gets sick and you can't help him? Just like you couldn't help your mom?*

I angrily pushed the thought out of my head as I paced across the lush bathmats. All too aware of the similarities between the breakdown I was having then and the one I'd had in my own bathroom three years ago, the night my mom died.

A knock had come at the door. The harsh sound making me nearly jump out of my skin.

"Annie, are you alright?" Theo's sleepy voice called through the crack.

"Yeah, yeah, I'm fine," I lied.

"Are you sure? I heard you run out of the room really fast."

I bit my lip, silently willing him to go away. "I said I'm fine. There's nothing to worry about."

"Can I come in?" He rattled the doorknob. I leapt across the room and pressed my back up against the door. No, I could never let him see me this way.

"Please Theo! Just go away!" It had come out harsher than I'd wanted. And even though he'd reluctantly complied, I hated myself for sending him away like that. But I just couldn't let him in.

The next morning I'd refused to let myself think about what had happened. Again, I told myself it was only a dream. That it meant nothing. And after that, I'd fooled myself into thinking I had everything under control.

Now, safe in the swaying hammock, I gingerly prop myself up to study Theo's face again, hoping the sight will soothe me like it usually does. The symmetry of his lovely features makes me feel better, but something still nags at me. A pattern that's getting harder and harder to ignore. It can't be a coincidence that just when I began to admit my feelings for him…just when I began to consider letting our relationship continue past this summer, my episodes started up again. I thought I was all better. That I'd conquered my horrible fear after my mom died. But what if the nasty voice is right? What if the episodes are back for good? And what if it really *is* all Theo's fault?

CHAPTER SIXTEEN

OUR FOOTSTEPS CLANG on the metal rungs of the stairwell as Theo and I climb to the fourth floor.

He gets to the landing first, pausing to look down at me.

"Are you okay? Why are you going so slow?" he asks.

"I'm not going slow. You're going fast." My voice echoes loudly inside the narrow space.

"No, I'm going normal," he says. "You're purposely dragging. What's up?"

In a past life I probably would've deflected his question by childishly dashing up the last three steps and snapping into his face, "There? Is that fast enough for you?!" But today I simply continue my slow tromp up to meet him. There's no use pretending. No matter what defense I throw at Theo, he sees right through me like a pane of glass.

When I get to his side, I confess. "I don't want to get there too early. What if someone's in there crying and wailing and blubbering all over?" I make a face like the thought of such unhinged emotion sickens me. "I don't want to have to hear all of that!"

Theo presses his lips together like he's trying not to laugh. "Annie, we're not walking straight into someone's therapy session. She said there was a waiting room. So you can relax." He lets a grin break free. "Don't worry. You won't have to listen to anyone's *feelings*."

I roll my eyes, trying not to groan out loud. Why the hell does the next painting have to be here of all places?

Last week when we'd looked at the photograph that matched our third sketch, I'd had this really strong urge to do things differently this time.

"I don't care what you all think," I'd said, mostly looking at Caroline. "I'm calling this person ahead of time."

I'm not sure if it was the tone of my voice, or the look on my face, but Caroline hadn't argued. And neither had Theo. In fact, he'd seemed almost proud. As if he'd been waiting for me to finally stand up for myself.

There was a man's name on the back of the snapshot. When I looked him up in the phonebook, it said he was a marriage therapist who had a practice in downtown Bloomington, only minutes away from Caroline's house. For once, finding this clue was going to be easy. Or so I thought. Because when I'd called the number, my hopes were dashed only seconds after the woman on the phone said hello.

"I'm sorry but Paul's retired. He doesn't work here anymore."

"Of course he doesn't," I'd muttered. Then I'd mustered up the courage to ask for his new address. But the lady nicely (and very firmly) told me she couldn't give out that information.

And that's when I'd said a loud curse word into the phone.

Luckily for me, the woman laughed and asked if maybe she could help.

I started to say No, but then I thought back to last weekend. I'd never expected Lisa to help me, but look how that had turned out. So I decided, what the hell. I might as well try playing the old vulnerable card again.

Mind you, I didn't go wild and tell the woman all the details of the Treasure Hunt. But I did tell her I was looking for a painting that meant a lot to me because my mom, who had died of cancer a few years ago, painted it.

"It's still here! It hangs in the waiting room that Paul and I shared!" she'd squealed in a very un-therapist like way.

"What? You mean he didn't take it with him?"

"No. I loved the picture so much that when he was moving, I asked if I could buy it. I just couldn't bear to let it go."

After she introduced herself as Rebecca—also a therapist—she'd invited me to her office, chattering away excitedly, saying she couldn't wait to meet me and learn more about my mom and her artwork.

"I'm jammed packed with clients this Saturday," she said, checking her appointment book. "But I've got half an hour at noon. Thank God you called, or I would've never had time to talk to you."

∞

Now here we are, only one flight away from meeting Rebecca Hill, LCSW. (Whatever the hell those letters mean.) But despite how nice this woman seemed on the phone, I'm still nervous as hell. I didn't have a good experience with the therapist Caroline forced me to see after my mom died. She was an older lady who wore skinny half glasses balanced on the end of her nose and the exhausted air of someone who should've retired years ago.

When I'd given her elusive half-answers or refused to talk at all, she didn't even seem to mind. She just sat there in silence staring at me, probably counting how much money she was making off me with every tick of the clock. Then, after exactly forty-five minutes had elapsed, she'd slapped her hands down on her blank notebook and said, "Well, it looks like you've used up all your time," in an accusatory tone. Like the awkwardness we'd just endured was all my fault.

After that, I'd never gone back. I'd told Caroline I was going to therapy, but really I'd drive laps around town for an hour, then return home with a big smile, pretending to be all better.

Once Theo and I find the office on the fourth floor, we let ourselves into the waiting room just like Rebecca instructed on the phone. The space is compact, with only a couple of chairs and two closed doors on either side of the room.

Theo points to the noise machines humming outside each door. "See? You're safe. You won't be able to hear a thing."

He grins big, meandering around, looking at the artwork on the walls with his arms crossed behind his back like he's visiting a museum. He doesn't seem at all bothered that there are people purging their souls to a virtual stranger only mere feet from where we stand. Unlike me, Theo has a good relationship with his therapist. He started seeing Dr. Arnoff when he was a teenager and still occasionally sees him now. No wonder he's not as neurotic as I am.

"Here it is!" he whispers, pointing to the wall behind me.

I whirl to find my mom's watercolor hanging only inches from my face. The scene depicts a narrow trail cutting through a dense forest. Right in the middle, the path meets a huge silvery birch tree, then splits off into two different directions. The details of the painting are amazing. Each little leaf and curl of bark rendered in soft, but lifelike beauty. I stand there taking it in, almost smelling the loamy earth my mom's painted at the base of the tree, hearing the scared squeak of the tiny chipmunk perched on a rotting log in the foreground, the rustle of wind blowing through the mottled birch branches.

I'm so captivated I don't even realize that I'm saying the words out loud. "It feels so…"

"Familiar," Theo and I say in unison. Then we look at each other and let out a stifled laugh.

I squint at the painting, trying to figure out where I've seen this place before. But just as a wispy memory begins to form, the door to my right swings open.

I turn to see a girl my age coming out, talking animatedly to the woman following her. And the weirdest thing is, the girl is smiling. Her eyes aren't red-rimmed, and she's not blowing her nose or trying to choke back tears for our benefit. She actually looks…*happy*. And so does the woman behind her (who is obviously Rebecca, the therapist).

She chats easily with her client, wishing her good luck on her test and giving her a hug as she says goodbye; not an ounce of awkwardness between them.

I check the name on the door, wondering if I'm in the right place. Therapy isn't supposed to look like this.

Once we're alone, Rebecca addresses me. "You must be Annie! So nice to meet you." She holds out a hand for me to shake, but I'm so flustered I just stand there frozen, staring at her.

Rebecca Hill is not at all what I expected. For one thing, she's young; probably in her early thirties. And she doesn't wear half-glasses or long flowing skirts or turquoise jewelry or anything like that. In fact, she's dressed quite fashionably, in tailored pants and a button-up blouse with a simple gold necklace with a horseshoe pendant peeking out from the neckline. Her blonde hair is styled the same way as mine; half pulled up and half down. Although Rebecca's hair is shorter, falling to a blunt bob just above her shoulders. As she smiles, warmth radiates from her every pore. For some reason I find myself wanting to ask if she'd give me a hug like the one she gave the girl who just left. Hmmm. That's strange.

Rebecca lets out a little laugh, breaking me out of my stupor and making me realize she's still holding out her hand. I grab it, pumping it up and down too hard as I say dumbly, "Yes. It's me, Annie. Meeting you is good too."

I cringe. *Meeting you is good too?* I sound like I barely speak English. Being in a therapist's office always throws me off my game.

Thank God Theo saves the day, reaching around me to introduce himself. "And I'm Theo."

"Great to meet you, Theo," Rebecca says. Then gently inquires, "And you are?"

Oh, right. I didn't mention he was coming on the phone.

Theo and I both speak at once.

"I'm Annie's boyfriend," he says, as I say, "He's my friend."

The two sentences pile on top of each other, making Rebecca

smile knowingly. I'm about to clarify our status, but Rebecca holds up a hand, stopping me. "Oh, don't worry. I'm used to things being complicated." She gestures back and forth between us. "Whatever's going on here…it's nothing new to me."

Theo and I laugh and exchange our own knowing glances. I have the distinct impression he's thinking the same thing I am. That our strange otherworldly connection might be more new to her than she thinks.

"So here it is!" Rebecca points to the painting. "Isn't it beautiful? I really couldn't afford it, but luckily Paul gave me a good deal."

We all stare at the lovely watercolor reverently as Rebecca goes on. "It was kind of my first 'big girl' purchase after my practice started taking off." The way she air quotes herself reminds me of something I would do. "Buying a piece of artwork seems so grown up, doesn't it? I couldn't believe someone like me, who used to have to shovel horse manure just to get by, would ever be in a place to buy a piece like this. But look at me now! The owner of an original piece of artwork. I guess I've finally made it, huh?"

I grin, surprised at how forthright she's being about her past.

She points to the center of the painting. "These two paths always felt very symbolic to me. See? The way one goes off into the darkness and the other into the light?"

I lean closer to see what she's talking about. The sketch Mom left us doesn't have many details filled in. But in the finished work, the difference between shadow and light is quite stark, just as Rebecca pointed out.

She goes on. "It always reminds me of how our minds work… either straying off into scary, fearful thoughts or continuing into the warm, loving ones."

"Wow. That's cool," Theo says over my shoulder. "I didn't notice that before, but you're right. The two paths do seem really symbolic."

Rebecca turns to me, looking sheepish. "But what do I know? You're the expert here. It was your mom who painted it."

"Yeah, she was my mom," I admit. "But the truth is, I've never seen this painting before." When Rebecca looks surprised, I explain how my mom painted this series when she was pregnant with me and sold them when I was just a little girl.

"This must be very moving for you then," Rebecca says gently. "Seeing it for the first time in real life."

I swallow hard, concentrating on the brushstrokes on the tree trunk so I don't have to look at her. "Yeah, it's really cool. When I look at it, I almost feel like I'm back in her studio again. I remember I used to play with my model horses next to her as she painted. I'd take old scraps of mat board and wood to make elaborate arenas with all kinds of obstacles for my horses to jump. And of course, all the competitions ended up with me winning Olympic gold!"

"Of course!" Rebecca agrees, as if she understands exactly what I'm talking about.

"She never talked much when she worked," I say, enjoying the memories of being back in that space again. "But I always remember feeling very peaceful there beside her."

When I glance at Theo, his eyes are trained on me, a serious expression on his face. His gaze darts from me to the painting and then back again, brows furrowed like he's thinking hard about something.

Rebecca heaves a heavy sigh. "She definitely captured that peace in this painting. There's just something about it I can't quite put into words. It makes me so happy every time I look at it. I spent so much time in the woods growing up. I guess it reminds me of those simpler times."

I heartily agree. Then without even thinking, I tell her about how I also grew up playing in the woods and how I'm now turning it into a career. Which leads to talking about Camp Boundless and all Theo and I are doing there this summer.

She gestures for Theo to take the painting down and follow her into her office, but mostly she listens to me as if my story is the most fascinating tale she's heard all day. Which I know it's not. It's just my boring old life. There's nothing special about it. Other than getting myself mixed up with a man who's come back from the dead. I guess that part's kind of interesting. But I keep that tidbit to myself.

Theo sets the painting on Rebecca's desk and whips out a screwdriver from the pocket of his jeans. (We're getting the hang of this clue collection business). As he works to get the back off, I notice a framed photograph on Rebecca's desk of her sitting atop a beautiful chestnut horse.

"So you ride?" I ask, pointing at the picture.

"Yes, ever since I was a little girl," she gushes. "That's Sydney... the love of my life." She smiles fondly at the horse. "I used to compete when I was in high school, but now it's just for fun."

"Oh, having fun is all that matters, right?!" I blurt emphatically, the words not feeling entirely my own. Theo must notice it too, because he stops to give me a look that says, "Where the hell did that come from?"

I shrug, as confused as he is as Rebecca continues. "I've always wanted to use horses in my therapy somehow. They're so intuitive. And they have such a calming effect on people. I think just being around their auras can help soothe so many anxieties. I know it certainly works for me."

"I completely agree." I tell her how working in the stables in high school saved me during some rough times. But I leave it at that. I'm sure she can infer what those rough times were from all I've already revealed.

Theo pipes up, telling her about the therapeutic riding group that works with our kids at camp.

"Oh man, I would love to be a part of that," Rebecca muses wistfully. "I have a dream of developing some sort of equine program for my clients." She waves a hand through the air. "But I'm getting ahead of myself. I've barely got my practice up and running here. I'm probably going to have to wait a while for that!"

Just then, Theo lifts the back of the painting and the three of us gather around to see what's inside. Once again, the penciled words are very faint. But I quickly make them out.

"It says *The Choice*."

"Ahhhhh," we all croon in unison.

"Makes sense," Theo says.

Rebecca agrees. "I have to say, I feel somewhat vindicated. Like I was onto something with my interpretation. You know, the light and the dark. The fear and the love." She touches my arm and says with deep sincerity. "Annie, even though I never met her, I can tell your mom was a very wise woman."

I can only nod because the lump in my throat won't let me speak. I shoot a pointed look at Theo, which he correctly interprets as, "We need to get the hell out of here before I lose it." He replaces the back panel and carefully slings the painting under his arm to carry it back out to the waiting room. But as he's rounding Rebecca's desk, he pauses to take one of her business cards.

"So, Rebecca, what kind of therapy do you do?" He peers down at the words on the card.

As Rebecca draws a breath to answer, I sense what's coming before it happens. Nothing on this quest has been a coincidence. My mom has woven a web of connections whose scope reaches far beyond just these four paintings. What Rebecca is about to say next will be another strand in that web. Of that, I'm sure.

"Oh, the bulk of my practice is working with teenagers and young adults." Rebecca says matter-of-factly, leading us into the next room. "So I mostly deal with issues of depression and anxiety." She stops and looks me directly in the eye. "But my specialty is bereavement."

CHAPTER SEVENTEEN

THEO WISELY DOESN'T say one word about Rebecca's specialty on the way back to Caroline's house. And when I recount our meeting to Caroline and Jonathan, I leave that part out too.

It's not that I wouldn't want to see Rebecca professionally one day. She's cool and easy to talk to and doesn't seem like she'd make me feel even shittier about myself than I already do. Believe me, I'm well aware that I'm still messed up, that I need to face the issues I keep pushing away. But I want to do it on my own terms. Not because my sister, or Theo, or even my well-meaning mom (who apparently is still mothering me from the other side) tells me I have to. I smile at the thought of my mom still being so involved in my life, even from where she is now. Funny, but it's starting to feel like she never left me at all.

As Theo and I unpack the groceries for dinner, Caroline reads off our weekend schedule like a Carnival Cruise director. We're taking the kids to the park, having a cookout dinner, going to the farmers' market Sunday morning, then to Charlie's to make pottery in the afternoon. It sounds like Theo and I are barely going to get any time alone. My sister really needs to make some new friends.

I leave Theo in the kitchen—nodding placidly along to my sister's ranting about the 'absolutely insane' demands of her homeowner's association—and slip away to the den to make my phone call to Aunt Lydia.

Slumped in the overstuffed Lazy-Boy with the phone ringing rhythmically in my ear, I marvel at how everything is running like clockwork.

We've located three paintings and received two clues in the mail. (The latest of which Caroline insists we wait to read until after dinner.) With two more weeks of camp left, our timing will work out perfectly. Next week we'll find the fourth painting and read the third clue that's come in the mail. Then, when camp ends, we'll come to Caroline's, read our very last clue, and hopefully set out to find the treasure right afterwards.

It sounds so simple when I spell it out that way. So why do I still have the nagging feeling there's something about this Treasure Hunt we're missing?

Lydia picks up the phone, but before she can even say hello the sound of a dog barking, a cat screeching, and a string of curse words blasts through the receiver.

"Is everything okay there?" I ask.

"Oh yeah, yeah," she huffs, clearly wrestling with some animal at her feet. "Why does everything have to happen all at once? The postman came, the cat knocked my tea off the table, and you called all at the exact same time. My God, when did my life become so damn hectic?!"

I laugh, imagining her there in her sprawling farmhouse twenty miles away from the nearest town with nothing but open sky and farmlands surrounding her. I guess everyone has their own definition of the word hectic.

"Sorry for interrupting your busy day." I say, sarcasm dripping in my voice.

Lydia good-naturedly laughs at herself. "Oh, honey, don't you apologize. I look forward to your call all week. It's been great getting to hear from you so often now. I've missed you."

"I know. I've missed you too," I admit.

It's not like I'd completely cut my aunt off after my mom died, but I hadn't been great at keeping up with her either. When Mom was still alive, Lydia used to visit Indiana several times a year, and Mom, Caroline and I would travel to Montana for our annual "Wild Women" weekend (as my mom named it) every fall. But after Mom died, it had been too hard for me to continue that tradition. So things have gradually devolved to a few stilted phone conversations between us on holidays; a quick dinner at Caroline's whenever she comes to town. I'm not proud of my behavior, but luckily Lydia has never made me feel guilty about my neglect.

Now, our Treasure Hunt has given us a reason to connect again. It seems Mom is still working her magic…even if she's not physically here to take credit for it.

"Maybe you and Caroline could plan a trip out here sometime soon," Lydia suggests tentatively. "There's still plenty of wildness for us women to make. And I think Grace would love it if we kept whooping it up in her memory."

"I would love that," I tell my aunt, then catch myself. "I mean if I can find the time."

Before she can press me more, I blurt out the title of the painting, then recount the story of how our afternoon with Rebecca had played out. I add in some funny anecdotes about Theo and me at camp this week, not realizing how I'm gushing until I pause for a second to catch my breath and Lydia says, "I'm so happy you're having such fun with him."

I go rigid, hearing her description of me out loud. "Well, it's not like I'm on some kind of vacation," I snap. "I am following my *dead mom's* last wishes after all."

An awkward silence hangs between us, and I silently curse myself for my outburst. Where had that come from?

"No, of course it's not a vacation for you." Lydia sounds a bit hurt. "I'm just glad you and Theo are getting along, that's all. Your mom said once the two of you found each other everything would change for the better."

Her phrasing stops me cold. *Everything will change. Change. Change. You can change things...* Damn, I wish I could remember what those words mean to me.

We chat some more and make plans to talk next Saturday. Just as we're saying goodbye, Lydia says, "Annie, please remember, your mom would never want you to feel bad about anything. Especially about her."

"I know," I say, marveling at how she can pick up on my guilt, even from thousands of miles away.

Lydia goes on. "She was the one who was so adamant about not having regrets, remember? She always used to say." Lydia raises her pitch just slightly, sounding eerily like my mom. "We're all just doing the best that we can. There's no sense in looking back when the only way we can move is forward."

I laugh, enjoying hearing Mom's familiar words again. Lydia's right. She used to say that a lot.

"I'm sorry I snapped earlier," I say, trying to sort out why I'd gotten so defensive. "It doesn't make sense, but I think when you mentioned Theo and me having so much fun together, it made me feel guilty for having such a good time without her."

"But that's what she wanted for you!"

"I know!" I wail. "I know I'm supposed to have a good time, and yet whenever I do have a good time, I feel bad! That's why it doesn't make sense!"

After a pause, she says, "Honey, do you really think how much you grieve equals how much you loved her?"

I ponder her words. "Well yeah. Isn't that how it works? Isn't that how normal people feel?" I don't tell her my suspicions that I'm a sociopath who doesn't feel emotions properly. Better to keep that shameful secret between Theo and me alone.

"But there is no normal way to grieve!" She shouts so loudly I have to pull the receiver away from my ear. "Everyone processes death differently. There is no right way to move on after you've lost someone you love."

I groan, thinking of how much she sounds like Theo. Both of them trying to make me feel better about something that's fundamentally wrong about me.

"Honey, your grief isn't a measure of how much you loved your mom," she says tenderly. "You know that, right?"

"Maybe?" I let out a quivering breath, trying to let her words sink in.

"Besides, who's keeping score?" Lydia says. "Who's measuring out the proper amounts of guilt and grief and time before you're allowed to move on? Your mom sure isn't doing that from where she is. She's got better things to do now. Like meddling in your love life and finding my T.V. remote!"

We both crack up, the lightness sending my heart soaring with hope. It makes me wonder…if Aunt Lydia's simple words can soothe me this much, how might a professional like Rebecca be able to transform my guilt? Maybe it's time I made that phone call after all.

With that thought, a warm wave of relief curls around my body. There's the faintest sense of pressure on the top of my head; what I swear is a whiff of my mom's perfume in my nose. I smile to myself, knowing whose arms are now snuggling me tight.

We say our goodbyes, and I thank Aunt Lydia for making me feel better. But right before she hangs up, she wriggles in one last no-nonsense piece of advice.

"Your mom knew how much you loved her, Annie," she tells me firmly. "So, I'd say it's time you stop trying to prove that to her with your sadness and get on with your damn life!"

CHAPTER EIGHTEEN

I WAS ALREADY in a good mood. But after hearing Aunt Lydia give me permission to let go and enjoy myself, I'm nearly levitating off the ground when I join everyone in the backyard.

At first, no one notices me come outside, so I take a second to soak in the scene. It feels like a dial has been turned up on the world's color knob this afternoon; the sky so neon blue, the grass garishly green, the sun so bright it hurts my eyes.

Under the awning, Jonathan grills steaks in his ratty basketball shorts while Caroline—beautiful in her messy brown ponytail and seersucker shirtdress—chats animatedly to him, holding Emma on her hip and gesturing wildly with her one free hand.

Theo is playing Animal Tag with Jack and doing a helluva impersonation of an ostrich; lurching around, craning his neck as he does a stupid high-legged run, almost but not quite catching Jack by the back of the shirt every few seconds. And Jack is running so fast and giggling so hard I think there's a real chance he might throw up any second.

I don't think I've ever witnessed a more beautiful moment in time than this.

And there's nothing I want more than to throw myself right into the middle of it.

I run out in the yard, crouching down to waddle after Jack like a duck; flapping my arms and quacking loudly, making him nearly choke with laughter. Caroline is probably going to kill me if he pees his pants, but I don't care. We'll deal with real-world problems later. Right now, all I care about is having fun.

The three of us are having a blast and I'm just about to switch to another animal (I hadn't realized how taxing on the thighs being a duck can be) when I realize Theo has stopped and is standing stock still in the middle of the yard staring at me with a dazed expression on his face.

"What? What is it?" I duck walk over to him, wiping sweaty strands of hair off my face, while Jack races circles around us.

Theo is still staring at me oddly as I struggle to my feet in front of him. God, I must look like a mess. That's probably why he's looking at me that way.

A smile slowly grows across his face. "I love you, Annie," he says plainly. "More than anyone I've ever loved before. More than anyone I will ever love again."

Hearing those words makes it feel like the ground has just dropped out from under me. To say I'm shocked is an understatement. His admission is so heart-felt, so sincere…and so out of place amongst the chaos unfolding around us. It's not even the sentiment that feels so surprising. What's surprising is that he's picked this exact moment to finally say the words we've both felt for so long out loud.

"Why would you say such a thing right now?" I glance around, trying to determine if anyone else has heard him.

"It just hit me when I was watching you play and I had to say it."

"You mean when you were watching me waddle and quack like a duck?" I correct.

He huffs a laugh. "Yeah, your waddling and quacking was just so beautiful that—"

"Try to get me! Try to get me!" Jack yells over him.

"—it just hit me so hard," Theo goes on, unperturbed. "I couldn't hold it back anymore. I had to say it. I love you, Annie. So much it hurts sometimes." He slaps a hand over his heart for emphasis.

I blink at him. I don't think there will ever be a day this boy doesn't completely shock me. Oh, how I love the thrill of him.

Theo goes on. "Besides, what's wrong with saying it now?" His last word comes out as a grunt because Jack has just tackled him around the waist…hard. They both tumble to the ground, Theo writhing around tickling Jack, so carefree and unconcerned you'd never know he's just bared his soul to me in the middle of the backyard.

"I don't know…I just thought," I stammer over the whirling mass of arms and legs, not sure Theo can even hear me in the melee. "I thought you'd pick someplace more special to say those words for the first time.

Theo sits up and gestures around the yard. "We're here. Together. Now. What could be more special than this?"

Alright. So I'd had the same thought only minutes ago. But still…

He untangles himself from Jack and gracefully leaps to his feet to stand only inches away from me. Looking up at his out-of-breath, sunlit beauty, I feel my defenses crumble even further away. All I want is to tell him I love him too. But what's the point in saying that when I still haven't decided whether or not I'm going to break up with him next week?

Jack tugs at my arm, begging me to please be a zebra now. I want to hug the little guy because, for once, his nagging has come in handy.

"Listen, Theo…uh…thank you," I blurt out in between Jack's jerks. "You know… for saying…what you just said…but…"

Theo's face falls in disappointment. He wanted me to say it back. But I can't do that. At least not yet.

"But I can't talk about this right now." I motion down to where Jack is now on the verge of dislocating my shoulder he's pulling so hard.

"Oh, right…right…I get it," Theo mumbles, trying not to look hurt. And failing miserably.

Still, he trails after me as I drop into my zebra pose and let out a neigh. "But don't you feel it too?" He looks down at me, not letting the issue drop like I'd hoped. "This thing between us? It feels so special… like…"

How the hell do I end this conversation?

Desperate to escape, I do the only thing I can think of at the moment. I slap him on the leg, shout "Tag! You're IT!" then gallop away on all fours.

∞

After dinner, it's time to open our second clue.

As I struggle to rip the envelope open, Jonathan points to the previous clue, now waiting for its partner in the middle of the patio table. "So, we have *Find your center star and follow it North,*" he recaps. "To which we'll add…"

All eyes land on me as I finally get the page unsheathed. I read the words slowly, savoring the feeling of having a shred of new evidence from my mom. "*Into the dense forest until you can go no more.*" Silence hangs between us as we all ponder the words.

"It sounds like I'm right then," I pipe up. "I bet she's sending us to Highwood State Forest."

"That's a fair guess," Caroline agrees. "Although you won't know for sure until you get the next two clues." She wags a finger at me. "So don't go running off to search before you have all the information, Missy."

"I would never!"

"Right. I know how impatient you are." She turns to Theo, pointing to the glass in front of me. "Have you noticed how she only ever fills her water glass up halfway?"

Theo scrunches up his face. "Now that you mention it, I have noticed that."

Caroline looks triumphant. "That's because she's too impatient to stand at the sink and wait until it's full!"

She barrels on. "And have you ever seen her make a sandwich? She always takes the first bite standing at the counter, only seconds after she puts the last piece of bread on top."

"Hey, now," I protest. "I'm usually starving so—"

"She can't even wait to sit down at the table." Caroline doesn't even acknowledge I've spoken. "She just starts chomping away right then and there."

"Stop making fun of me!" I cry out. "So I don't like to wait for things? What's wrong with that?"

We all laugh at my expense, and I don't even get cranky about it like I usually do. Caroline's right about my impatience. I've always had a problem with wanting to jump in and try to force things to turn out the way I want them, rather than standing back and letting them unfold naturally. I think back to the afternoon at the Cove when Theo had to practically wrestle me into his arms to get me to relax and float in the water. Under his tutelage this summer, I've gotten better at chilling out. But I still have a long way to go before I'm as relaxed as him.

Jonathan skillfully draws Caroline off her assault by asking, "So what do you think the treasure might be?"

I give him a grateful smile before I answer. "Who knows? I haven't really thought about it."

It sounds like I'm trying to evade the question, but it's true. I've been having so much fun going on these mini quests with Theo, meeting new people, and seeing Mom's painting up close, I honestly haven't thought about the final treasure in a while. In fact, it makes me sad to think that we only have one painting left to find. I wish our adventure would never have to end.

"What if it's money?" Jonathan goes on. "What would you do with it?"

I make a face. I doubt it's money, since my mom never put much value in monetary wealth. She believed richness came in how deeply a person enjoyed their life. A philosophy that used to send me into fits of eye rolls, but now makes a lot more sense. And also makes me realize that, under those parameters, she probably left this world feeling like a millionaire.

But since everyone is waiting for an answer, I ponder how I might spend a windfall. In truth, if I did happen to find a wad of cash buried under a tree, I'd use it to finally make a home for myself. A place where I could settle down for more than eight months at a time. Somewhere I could unpack my stuff and decorate the walls the way I liked. Buy those brightly colored dishes from Pier One I've been eyeing for a while now. And finally get mail that wasn't "In care of" someone else.

But I can't say that because it would hurt Caroline. She's tried so hard to make me feel welcome here and, honestly, it's worked. I love spending time here with her and her chaotic life. But that's just it. It's her life, not mine. What I really want is to finally have a life of my own…

…*with Theo.*

As soon as the unbidden words slip into my head my heart begins to whirl erratically.

I reach for my wine glass, trying to cover up the desperation now gripping my chest. *Stop dreaming of things you can't have*, I chastise myself, gulping the tart liquid. *Remember when you hoped and prayed for a miracle before? That only got you passed out on a bathroom floor.*

Upset by where this conversation has led, I blurt out, "I'd probably buy a horse."

That answer seems to appease everyone, and luckily Jonathan changes the subject. But as he and Caroline chatter back and forth, Theo stays quiet, watching me with a solemn expression that speaks volumes. He knows I'm not telling the truth.

CHAPTER NINETEEN

"SO THAT'S IT," Theo says, settling the painting on the hook. "We've officially found them all."

The two of us share a melancholy smile. You'd think we'd be grinning from ear to ear. Celebrating the fact that we've tracked down all four paintings and next weekend, right after camp ends, we'll be searching for the elusive treasure my mom left behind.

But this moment signifies something neither of us feels like celebrating: Our time together is almost over.

"Your mom was always one to think outside the box." Franco, the owner of the painting, says, smiling reverently. "But this Treasure Hunt of hers might be her most creative project yet."

As we'd gathered around the photo album at Caroline's house last Saturday, ready to read the address on the back of the last picture, I'd made a comment about how the hunt seemed to be getting easier; each painting being found closer and closer to home. First, we'd had to go out in the backwoods to Charlie's house. Then to Indy, an hour away. Then to Rebecca's office, right here in downtown Bloomington.

"The way things are going," I'd teased. "Maybe we'll find the last painting hanging in your neighbors' house next door!"

I'd pulled the photograph from its sleeve and flipped it over to find a single word written on the back: *Franco*. Caroline and I had immediately burst out laughing. It may not have been the neighbor next door, but it was pretty much the next best thing.

"What's so funny?" Theo had asked, confused by our outburst. "Who's Franco?"

Once I'd finished high-fiving Caroline, I'd explained that Franco was my mom's best friend. They'd met while getting their Master's in Fine Arts at Indiana University, and the two of them had become so close that Caroline and I grew up calling him and his partner Victor (a sculptor originally from Russia) our Uncles.

Franco and Victor were the primary male figures in our lives after my dad left. In fact, they were so much like family that Franco had escorted me to my sixth-grade father/daughter dance. I remember how lucky I'd felt to be with him that night. With his dashing good looks and Spanish charm, he'd captivated the room. (Especially the blushing moms in charge of the event.) I was so proud that I hadn't even told anyone he wasn't my real dad.

While Mom's career focused on studio work, Franco had become a professor at the university, eventually rising through the ranks to become the Director of Graduate Studies. Although he might have a new title now. I don't know for sure because, like Aunt Lydia, I haven't been great about keeping in touch with him and Victor since my mom died.

Once I found out Franco was the owner of the last painting, I'd been nervous to call him. It was embarrassing to suddenly reach out after turning down so many of his invitations over the past three years. But luckily, he'd held no grudge. In fact, it was quite the opposite. He'd nearly fallen all over himself on the phone telling me how thrilled he was to hear from me again. And when we showed up here at his office an hour ago, he'd hugged me so long and hard that I'd had to make a bad joke about making Theo (my boyfriend!) jealous to get him to let go.

God, it's great seeing him again. I'd forgotten how much fun we'd all had together. Forgotten how well he knows me and—from the way his eyes are glistening—how much he still loves me. When Mom died, I'd thought cutting out the people who brought back too many memories of her would make moving forward easier. But I'm beginning to see that isolating myself has only made everything that much harder.

Now, with the three of us gazing at the painting of a shaded cove at the edge of a still lake titled "The Release", I try to put into words how this last gift from my mom makes me feel. "Yeah, it's crazy all she did to put this treasure hunt together. It's so special, and yet I feel kind of bad she spent so much effort on me. Especially when I didn't do the same for her when things got hard at the end."

After the words are out, I wonder why I just admitted such a thing. I haven't seen Franco since the two of us made stilted small talk at Jack's birthday party last year. Why the hell am I telling him the truth of how I feel? I narrow my eyes at the person responsible for my lapse. Theo looks puzzled by my evil eye, but I don't care. This fountain of honesty I've become over the past few months…it's all his fault.

Franco throws an arm around my shoulder, squeezing me tight. "Aww, don't be so hard on yourself. Every time I came to the hospital, you were there by her side. I'm not sure how much more you could've done for her."

I gaze up at him, stunned. What is he talking about? All I remember from that time is how much I hated visiting my mom. And how I'd abandoned her the night she died. But Franco was there with us those last weeks. He'd witnessed what happened. And I guess he's right…I had been at the hospital a lot. Funny, but all I remember is how useless and angry and unhelpful I was. And how I should've been so much more caring, like Caroline. She was always chattering away with Mom. Putting lotion on her hands. Brushing what was left of her hair. But me? I mostly just sat like a lump by her side, so sad I could barely speak. I'd always just assumed my mute presence those last weeks didn't count for much. But is Franco saying my just *being there* was enough?

Tears spring to my eyes at the thought that I might not be as horrible as I think I am. Seeing my rare emotion, Franco gently grips my shoulders, squaring me in front of him, like he knows if he doesn't hold firm I might try to escape once again.

"Oh, honey. Tell me really. How are you doing?" His brown eyes are so tender, it makes speaking a struggle.

"I'm fine." When he cocks an eyebrow, I let out a little laugh. "Okay. I'm not always fine. It's been hard. These past years…without her. And the Treasure Hunt…it's bringing up a lot of things I've tried not to think about."

"Like what?"

"Like her! I've tried not to think about *her*." It's such a ridiculous strategy, we both burst out laughing.

"And how's that going for you?" he asks. "I mean, your mom was a lot of things. But she sure as hell wasn't someone you could easily forget!"

"I know! See how stupid I am? I don't know what the hell I'm doing!" I angrily swipe at my eyes.

He envelopes me in a big hug, rocking me back and forth with my face pressed so hard against his corduroy jacket I'm sure my cheeks are going to be striped when we're done. But I don't mind. I sway with him, sucking in the turpentine and pipe smoke smell of him that sends me back to when I was a child and everything was so much easier.

Behind us, I hear footsteps moving toward the door. "I'm just going to check out that gallery down the hall," Theo says quietly. He tells me he'll meet me outside when I'm done. I give him a grateful smile as he disappears out the door. Awed once again by how he always knows exactly what I need.

∞

For the next hour, Franco and I talk freely, as if no time has passed between us at all. Although my entire body tenses when he begins telling funny stories about my mom. Talking about her always puts me on high alert, because I'm never sure how my runaway heart is going to react when I let myself think of her for too long. But eventually, I relax enough to listen and even add a few anecdotes of my own.

It's not typical of me to open up that way. But surprisingly, I don't cry the way I might have only a few months ago. In fact, after a while I realize I'm actually enjoying talking about her. Especially when Franco tells stories of her antics from art school, some of which I've never heard before.

Franco nods at the door where Theo just left. "He seems nice," he pulls out the last word to tease me. "And not your type at all."

I grin big, fessing up to my sudden change of taste.

Franco was around during some of my wilder days in high school, when I was drinking too much, using my fake ID to get into college bars and pick up guys way too old for me. As a young bohemian artist, Franco never judged. In fact, he and Victor sometimes bought my roommates and me jugs of vodka, back in the day when they weren't as respectable as they are now.

"Theo's amazing," I admit. "He's helped me so much this summer. Sometimes I think it was Mom who brought us together."

I don't just think, I know it was. I scold myself. *And now I'm going to go against her wishes and end things just when they're getting started?*

Franco nods as if my mom's machinations make perfect sense to him. He tells me of times when he believed she had a hand in his life too. Nudging him into a rest stop on a snowy night, so he ended up missing a six-car pileup. Helping him pick the right fertilizer for his roses. "She was always so good at that, remember? I swear she could make anything grow! I used to tease and call her Mother Nature…she kind of always seemed that way to me."

We both look off wistfully, remembering the time Mom dressed up as Mother Nature for Halloween, wearing a long white robe wound with ivy and fake birds perched on her arms along with a crown of flowers atop her blonde hair. Goodness, no wonder it's been easy for me to accept she's Theo's angel. She practically played one in real life.

When talk turns to what I'm doing after I graduate, I tell Franco

I'm looking at a camp in New York but haven't done much research other than that. I don't mention that moving to New York will put a lot of distance between Theo and me. And how I'm relying on those miles to make forgetting him easier.

"You remember my brother is the Director of the Parks & Recreation Department in Indianapolis, right?" he asks. "I could get you a job up there just like that." He snaps his fingers. "He'd love to hire someone like you."

A chill flitters along my arms. *Ahhhh, now I see why you brought me here, Mom.* I chide in my head. *A job in Indianapolis practically handed to me on a silver platter. Bet that's no coincidence.*

I swear I hear the tinkling of laughter inside my head.

But I'm not ready to give in to her just yet. "I'm not sure if that's exactly where I want to end up," I counter.

Theo's invitation whispers in ear. *I know a place you could live…*

Franco tips his head, waiting for my answer. Oh what the hell. It's always good to have options, right?

"You know what? It wouldn't hurt to hear what's available," I relent, my fantasies about moving in with Theo overwhelming all my good sense. "I'd love to talk to your brother. Who knows, maybe it's my destiny to move there."

Franco plucks a notepad from his desk and scribbles the details. "Well, I don't know about destiny," he mutters, not looking up.

"I meant to say prudent," I say, face flushing in embarrassment. "Maybe moving there will be *prudent* for my career."

Franco hands me his brother's phone number and then grasps my hand, looking me deep in the eyes. "Let me give you a little piece of advice, honey. Never follow prudent. Because prudent only leads to a prudish life. Yuck!" He makes a face. "But passion! Passion will take you places you would've never thought possible!"

My stomach flips hearing his vehement words. *Passion.* Oh, what a word. It sounds like being swept away, your entire body tingling with excitement as you dip and plummet and twist on the runaway rollercoaster ride of life.

It sounds exactly like how I feel when I'm with Theo.

Franco glances at the clock and reluctantly says he has to leave for another appointment. As we head toward the door, I agree to come to dinner at his house when I get back in town for fall semester. "And I won't blow you off this time." I give him another hug. "I'm really going to make it. But only if Victor makes those pelmenis I love." I'd almost forgotten what a great cook Victor is. Man, being a stoic hard-ass has really robbed me of a lot of pleasures in life.

Franco shakes his head in wonder. "What a feat you and Theo have achieved. Finding all five paintings in what? Only a few weeks? That's amazing!"

My stomach lurches. "Five? What do you mean, five? There are only four paintings in the series."

He furrows his brow, thinking hard. "Hmm. I thought there were five. These were the ones she sketched at the retreat she went on when she was pregnant with you, right?"

When I nod, he goes on. "Huh. I thought I remembered seeing them all together and there were five."

"But we only have four sketches. And four pictures of the completed pieces. So I just assumed that was all."

He shrugs, waving a hand through the air. "You're probably right. It was a long time ago. Knowing me, I've probably forgotten the right number by now." He taps his temple, where a splay of grey hairs now creep through the black. "Which unfortunately seems to be happening a lot lately."

We say our goodbyes and I set out to find Theo, brushing off Franco's comment as the ramblings of a well-meaning but absent-minded professor.

CHAPTER TWENTY

THEO

IT'S ALMOST LIKE a dream, looking down and seeing Annie naked, snuggled up against me in my bed. I ever-so-lightly graze my fingertips along her shoulder, down her back, over the curve of her bottom, across the thigh she has slung over my hips. Then I start the slow journey all over again, trying not to spoil the perfection of this moment by thinking of how this is probably the last time I'll ever get to hold her this way.

She lets out a satisfied sigh, gazing up at me in a way that makes my stomach flip. Sometimes I doubt how she feels about me. Then other times she'll look at me like this…so raw and loving… and it's like I can feel everything she can't say out loud.

"What are you thinking?" she asks.

"You know exactly what I'm thinking." I say, kissing the top of her head.

"Yeah, I think I do." She gives me a sleepy grin. "And I like it. Think it some more."

"Okay. Here goes." I squeeze my eyes shut tight, pretending to strain. "There. Can you feel more of it now?" I wish it were possible… to actually infuse my love into her so it would stay and grow and become part of her, even long after I'm gone.

She nestles her head back on my chest and lets out another shuddering breath. "Mmmm, yes. Please don't stop. It feels so good."

We both laugh. "Oh, don't worry. I won't ever stop Annie." I don't say the rest. *I'll never stop loving you. Not in this lifetime or the next.*

We settle back into our comfortable silence, holding each other tightly. After our visit with Franco, we'd stopped by Caroline's to read the third clue from Lydia. But we hadn't stayed long. Instead, we'd begged off to come here to my apartment, both of us wanting to be alone for what I'm assuming (since Annie hasn't corrected me yet) is our last weekend together.

We'd wolfed down a bowl of cereal for dinner then, surprisingly, it was Annie who'd begun ravaging me first. Pressing her body up against my back as I'd washed our bowls in the sink, slipping her hand down the front of my jeans. Stroking me so tantalizingly, making me even more delirious for her than I had been before.

A frantic edge had gripped our lovemaking, again led by Annie. The way she'd dug her fingertips into my skin, kissed me so roughly, pushed me deep inside her like she was trying to fuse our bodies into one. She was so desperate, so greedy. It was like she was clamoring for something she might never find again. Trying to hoard every ounce of our bliss because she knew it would have to last for the rest of her life.

And I was doing the same. Clamoring and hoarding every nuance and sensation and taste of her. Wishing she wasn't making it so obvious that this was the end.

Now in the bed she says, "Pet my other side." She crawls over the top of me and flops down so I can repeat my stroking on her right side. I have to smile at how freely she's accepting my adoration tonight. It's good she's loosening up. She's been so tense lately. I mean, tenser than normal. She's always staring off into the distance, her face scrunched up like she's trying to solve an impossible equation. Which I'm hoping is how she might add me to her life, subtract all the fear of my impending death, and not come up with a negative sum in the end. At least I hope that's the problem she's trying to solve.

She's probably just obsessing over the clues again. She kept repeating the newest one all the way to my apartment as if some great insight might hit her right there in the passenger seat of my car.

"*Dig beneath the hardened heart to find the map at the core.*" She'd chanted her mom's words over and over again, staring out her window, lost in thought.

"I bet we have to look under some tree with a heart shape carving in its trunk or something," she'd said, struggling to pull the strands of wind-whipped hair out of her mouth as she waited for me to respond. I still haven't gotten my car's air-conditioning fixed yet.

"Yeah, maybe," I'd agreed. Even though lately there's been something about the clues that seems suspicious to me. They're all so vague. I wonder if maybe they're not meant to be taken so literally. If instead, they're more metaphorical guidance than concrete directions. But that's probably just me reading too much into things again. I always see symbolism where other people don't. I can't help it. After getting a glimpse of how things work from a heaven's-eye view, it's hard not to see all the patterns of life, hidden, right in plain sight.

A number flips on the clock on my nightstand, reminding me of our time slipping away. Hearing it, Annie goes rigid against me as if she's thinking the same thing I am, about time suddenly moving way too fast.

I work up the nerve to broach the question that's been haunting me all week. "Are we ever going to talk about it?"

A beat passes before she responds. "About what?"

She's playing dumb. Stalling so she has time to think. Heaven forbid she loses control and actually speaks from her heart instead of her head for once.

I pull myself higher on the pillow hoping she'll lift her head and meet my eyes, but she doesn't. Instead, she keeps her cheek firmly planted on my chest as I readjust myself; deliberately hiding her face from me.

"I think we need to talk about what happens when the Treasure Hunt ends," I say.

I'm not sure why I'm asking. Annie has always made the rules of this summer romance (as she calls it) perfectly clear to me: The day we find the treasure is the day we say goodbye.

I'd agreed to her terms weeks ago, so it's not like I can complain. What leverage do I have? I'm merely a dying man with nothing to offer her but guaranteed heartache. Who can blame her for wanting to get the hell away from me?

It's strange to admit, but part of me is rooting for her to get away from me too, just to spare her any more pain than she's already endured. Although it may already be too late. For the past few weeks, she's been crying out in her sleep, waking up terrified from some recurring nightmare she claims she can't remember the details of. But by the way she looks at me afterwards—like she can't believe I'm still breathing—I'm convinced it has something to do with me. She never used to have nightmares like that. But the more time she spends with me, the more frequent they've become.

"Theo, please don't ruin things," she says. "Everything is so good right now."

"I don't want to ruin things." I'm as guilty of avoiding this topic as she is. I want to milk every second of our time together before we have to face reality again. But our avoidance is starting to feel like such an effort. Like we're no longer merely living in the moment, but actively burying our heads in the sand.

"I just think we need to talk about it before the time comes," I say.

What I really want to ask is: *Do I have any reason to hope?*

"You already know what's going to happen."

My stomach lurches sickeningly at the determination in her voice. Again, I don't know why my body's reacting so viscerally. It's not like her sticking with her pre-determined plan is a big surprise. Still, the way she'd just looked at me...I thought maybe...just *maybe* she'd changed her mind.

"I want to hear you say it." I try to sound unbothered, but my voice cracks, betraying my charade.

The next instant she's propped up on one arm staring down at me. "No, what you want is for me to be the villain in all this." Her eyes blaze so hot it almost makes me regret wishing she'd look at me.

"The villain?" I'm so surprised by her vehemence I can barely speak. "Of course I don't want you to be the villain. What are you talking about?"

"You want to make me out to be the bad guy. Make it seem like I'm the one making the decision to leave you when actually *you're* the one leaving me. Have you forgotten that part?"

"But Annie, I don't have a choice," I stammer. "Believe me, if I could stay, I would!"

She cocks her head to the side. "Would you? Because I'm not so sure about that."

My heart is pounding fast now, stomach even sicker than before. "How could you say such a thing? I love you!"

"Right. That's what you say. But that's not how you act. Are you even upset that you're dying?"

"Of course I am!"

"Then why do you always act so happy about it? Why are you so damn accepting of everything? Always going with the flow, believing everything is for the best and the Universe has a plan and everything is going to work out. La la..la…" She grins wildly in what I guess is an impression of me?

The next instant, her face drops. "You say you love me, but if you really loved me why aren't you angrier that we're never going to be together? Why aren't you fighting? Why aren't you raging against God or the Universe or whoever the hell is taking everything you love away from you? Why are you just giving up and accepting your damn fate?!"

I stare wide-eyed at her flushed face, letting her words sink in. Does she really believe I'm unaffected by what's happening to us? That losing her isn't tearing me apart bit by excruciating bit? If so, she's gotten it all wrong.

"I *am* angry, Annie. I hate it! Every day it's like my heart is being ripped out of my chest at the thought of not being with you!"

"Really? Well, you could've fooled me, 'Mr. Nothing-Much-Bothers me'. I want to see you bothered, Theo! I want to see you sad and angry and guilty and fucking pissed as hell like the rest of us mere mortals. Why don't you ever show any of that?"

"Because I don't want to upset you! I don't want to be the reason that you feel worse than you already do!"

She shakes her head, looking offended. "Well, you can stop being the hero now." She gestures back and forth between us. "How about you worry about your emotions and I'll worry about mine, okay? I'm not some fragile flower that's going to fall apart the second you have a bad day. God, Theo!" She rolls her eyes in disgust.

Her face is only inches from mine now and, believe me, there's nothing flower-like about it at all. "I don't think you're fragile. I think you're strong," I say. "But you're always selling yourself short. Always thinking the worst about yourself. I believe you can handle staying with me…at least for a while longer if you would only take a chance and show yourself you can do it."

She sits back, considering my words. "That's what you think, huh?" She seems less blustery now. Almost like she wants to believe what I've said, but won't let herself give in.

A few beats pass and I have to fight to not fill the silence. Or try to soothe her. Or do something, anything, to make her feel better. I guess she's right about me trying to manage her emotions. I had no idea how anxious her pain makes me. I guess she's not the only one who likes to stay in control.

She idly runs her hand across my bare chest, seeming to relax with each stroke of my skin. "You know you've never asked me outright if we could keep dating after camp ended," she whispers.

I blink at her, stunned once again. "My God, I thought it was implied! I told you I loved you!"

"Yeah. I know," she mumbles unconvincingly.

"And I asked you to move in with me," I remind her.

"You weren't serious."

"The hell I wasn't!"

Her eyes dart back and forth between mine as if she's trying to gauge my honesty. Then, subtly, she lets her gaze drift down my naked body and then back up again. This is another thing she's been doing lately. Scanning my body when she thinks I'm not looking as if she's searching for signs the cancer has come back. I used to see only desire in her eyes when she drank me in that way. But now she looks at me like I'm a ticking time bomb.

Knowing she's been caught, her eyes wrench onto mine, searing me with their intensity. "Maybe you haven't fought for us because deep down you don't really want us to stay together. Maybe you think it might be too hard. Not just for me...but for you too."

I swallow hard, surprised that she's read me so well. I thought I'd been doing a good job covering up the heavy cloud that's settled over me these past days. I thought I hadn't let on that something strange is happening to me. It used to be so easy to remember all the warmth and peace I'd felt on the other side. But lately it's like all my sureness, all the trust in the love I'd felt there, is slowly slipping away. And no matter how hard I try, I can't seem to get it back.

"Oh Annie, you've gotten it all wrong," I say. Even though deep down I know she's right. I am taking the coward's way out by letting her be the one to leave me. And a part of me is truly relieved by the thought of not being able to hurt her anymore.

Because isn't she better off without me?

"Oh, I'm wrong again, huh?" she snaps, sitting up beside me. "Here we go. Just like always, I'm wrong and you're right. I don't understand, but you do because you know everything and I don't. I'm sick of hearing that, Theo."

"That's not what I meant. I'm sorry…I misspoke." Frustration courses through me. I never should've opened my big mouth. I never should've cornered her, forced her into making her choice right now. We still have a week together and now I've gone and ruined what little time we have left. Why do we keep misunderstanding each other like this? Lately everything between us has felt so off.

We blink at each other, both dazed by all we've just shared.

"You're right." I touch her cheek. "Everything you've said is right. I don't show how I really feel. I do hold back. Because believe me, I feel every single emotion you mentioned."

I look up at the ceiling, trying to find the words. "And I'm pissed at myself for acting this way with you, because I know better. I know life has its ups and downs and that's just part of it. I know not to fight it. I accept it in every other area of my life. But with you it's just… just…I don't want to dwell on the bad stuff, because it makes me feel like I'm wasting my time with you. I don't want to spend what little time I have left with you being angry and sad and frustrated. Or feeling like a victim and railing against the injustices of life. And because of that, I haven't been totally honest with you about how I feel. I've only shown you one side of me. And that's not being real. I'm sorry."

Her face goes soft. "Well, thanks for admitting that." I expect her to go on, but she waits as if she's asking me for more. So I give it to her, although it's still hard to find the right words.

"I guess I do it because I already feel like such a burden to you."

"Theo, you're not a burden! To me or to anyone else!" She looks horrified. Dammit, I'm fucking it all up again.

"I mean, my *situation* is a burden," I correct, even though that's not entirely how I feel. "You don't think I know how much all of this sucks? You don't think I know what I'm doing to you?"

"You're not doing anything to me. I asked for this."

No, you were forced into this by your dead mom, I think, but I can't say that or else she'll only argue more.

Instead, I try to explain. "I think that's why I hold back. Because

I feel like I'm always trying to make it up to you. To be so positive that it will somehow outweigh all the negatives that come along with being involved with me. So that maybe, in the end when I'm gone, you'll look back and feel like knowing me was worth it."

She opens her mouth to argue, but I lean forward and gently place a finger on her lips to silence her. "Please…just don't, okay?" I can't bear to hear her excuses. I can't listen to her insist that none of this is my fault. I know what this is like for her. I know that deep down I'm her worst nightmare.

She gives me the slightest nod, agreeing not to placate me, and I drop my hand. After a few seconds of gathering her thoughts, she asks, "So are you admitting that you get sad sometimes?"

I huff a laugh. "Oh, all the time. And mad and confused and frustrated. The whole gamut. Just ask my mom. She's seen it all!"

Surprisingly, she looks delighted. "I'd like to see that."

"Really? You actually want to see me act like a dick?"

"I mean, not all the time." She grins coyly. "Just every once in a while. It would make me feel better about myself. To know that you're not perfect either."

"I'm far from perfect. I thought that was obvious!" I point at my face. "Half-blind, with a big nose, and a bit of an issue with putting my clothes away." I wave a hand around my messy room.

She laughs. Then leans over and kisses the tip of my nose, my cheeks, the edge of my eyes, making me shudder with the force of her unspoken emotions. "You're beautiful. In every way," she breathes. Then she pulls back, with a wry smile on her face. "But you are a bit of a slob."

We both crack up and, just like that, the tension between us trickles away.

In the quiet, I think of what she said before, about how I've never officially asked her to stay. It's time I remedy that.

I sit up even straighter on the pillow, hold both of her shoulders in my hands.

"Oh, what's this?" she teases, looking down at my grip. "Theo's about to say something earth-shattering. I'd better get serious now." She furrows her brow trying not to smile.

"I just want to make sure you know that I really, really don't want our relationship to end when summer is over. That if it were up to me, we'd have a fall romance, and a winter romance, and a spring romance, and another summer romance, and another fall romance and…"

She puts a hand over my mouth. "Okay, okay, I get it!"

Once again the beauty of her lit-up face nearly devastates me. She's the girl I've dreamt about for years. The one I've waited to meet for so long. And now, just when I finally have her, I have to say goodbye to her again. This whole situation makes me understand why Annie thinks life is so unfair.

"I want to make sure you know I want you to stay. And that I think you can do this." She shakes her head as if she still doesn't believe me, but I ignore her. "But…here's the disclaimer!" I lift a finger in the air. "If at any time you felt like things were getting too hard and you wanted out, you could still leave, and that would be okay. I would understand. You'd be free to go whenever you felt like it. No questions asked. Just see you later, Theo! Bye bye! And that would be it. I would never force you to stay."

"Oh, Theo," she says, her bottom lip beginning to quiver. "You shouldn't have to offer a disclaimer like that. Not to me. And not to anyone else either."

I brush off her comment, scared I might unravel if I let her implications sink in. "Listen, you don't have to say anything right now." A wave of nausea suddenly hits me. I guess all this talk of our future is making more nervous than I thought. "But whatever you decide, I still believe that no matter what happens, you and me…we'll always be together. Across time and distance, lifetimes and eternities," I pause, hoping she'll fill in the rest. But like always she stays silent, so I finish it for her. "Always together. Forevermore."

She nods, tears spilling over onto her cheeks now. "Are you sure about that?" she chokes out.

I hadn't even noticed my eyes welling too. "I'm sure, Annie."

"No matter what?" She looks relieved. Like our future promise is the perfect escape clause to release her from our impossible now.

I determinedly dip my chin. "No matter what."

With that, she collapses back down onto my chest. "Good." She snuggles her head back under the crook of my arm. "That makes me feel better."

I squeeze her tight, a heavy malaise settling over my body. My God, I don't think I've felt this exhausted, this devoid of hope since I was a kid trapped in a hospital bed slowly wasting away. What the hell is wrong with me?

Maybe it's time I finally give in to all the doubts that have haunted me lately. Because the resignation I just heard in Annie's voice tells me one thing: She's made her decision. And she's not choosing me.

CHAPTER TWENTY-ONE

ANNIE

I'M IN THE early stages of my nightmare—Theo's head still above water, him still calling out my name for help—when I'm startled awake. My heart pounds wildly as my surroundings gradually fill in: the darkness of Theo's bedroom, the empty space in the bed next to me, the ticking of the bedside clock. I let out a huge sigh into the sheets I have clutched in my fists like a life preserver. It wasn't real. Theo is still alive. We still have time.

Our conversation from earlier floods back. Theo's disclaimer. How he gave me permission to walk away when he gets sick again so I won't have to go through what I did with my mom. But I can't forget the haunted look in his eyes as he'd handed me the easy way out.

I hate how appealing I found his offer. Once again, I'd be the coward, abandoning someone I love, right when they really needed me. But it also would mean we could stay together a little while longer and I wouldn't have to end things right away. We could have another year together, maybe even more. And who knows? Maybe by that time I could handle the hard part. Maybe by that time I'll have transformed into the strong girl Theo believes me to be.

The sound of retching comes from the bathroom, followed by the flush of the toilet. I wonder if that's what woke me up in the first place? I throw the covers off and pad to the bathroom, still half asleep. When I get to the doorway, what I see there makes my blood run cold.

Theo sits on the tile floor in only his shorts. He's breathing hard, body leaned back on the bathtub and arms spread wide along its shiny edge making him look like some kind of fallen deity, mounted on porcelain instead of wood. His long hair is disheveled, his skin a deathly shade of pale. And on the counter, next to the sink, sits a bunch of pill bottles.

So many pill bottles.

Like an adding machine, my mind takes in each piece of information and slowly tallies it all up…*tick, tick, tick*…then spits out a summation that makes my knees go weak.

"Oh my God Theo, you're sick." My heart hammers so furiously I can barely get out the words.

He opens his eyes, startling when he sees me there. "Yeah, I'm sick," he says weakly, then closes his eyes again.

"You're sick already?!" My voice rings shrill inside the small space as I realize what he's been hiding from me. "When did this happen? Why didn't you tell me?!"

How the hell could this have snuck up on me? I've been so vigilant, every day looking for signs on his body that would warn me that his cancer is back. I thought he was okay. But obviously I was wrong.

"Tell you? It just started…"

"But…but…you don't even have any bruises!"

"Bruises? What do bruises have to do with—"

"You've known, haven't you?!" I say viciously, a rush of emotions overtaking all my sense of reason. I trusted him. Yet all this time he's been keeping the truth from me. "You've known all summer and you haven't told me!"

"Annie, what are you talking about?"

I bend forward, bracing my hands on my knees and gasping for air. My heart pounds so furiously it feels like it's on the verge of cracking my chest wide open.

"You didn't think I would be with you if I knew, so you kept it from me," I ramble on, my tongue so dried out and sticky it's hard to form words. I'm vaguely aware that nothing I'm saying makes much sense, but it's like an entirely different person has taken over my body. A person who is completely and utterly terrified by what all this means.

"You were tricking me." I stab a finger at him. "Hiding the truth. Waiting until I was in too deep and then you were going to spring it on me when I'd feel too guilty to leave!"

He drops his arms to his sides and sits up straighter, concern lining his face. "Spring what on you? Annie, seriously, I don't know what you're talking about."

"Your cancer. It's back!" I shout through my slowly constricting throat. "You're already sick! But you didn't want me to know!" The effort it takes to yell leaves me light-headed, making the tiny room tilt at odd angles. No. This can't be happening again. I thought I was better. I thought I had my crazy, short-circuiting heart under control. But this feels exactly like the night my mom died. When something went so horribly wrong inside by body that I actually passed out.

"No, no. You've got it all wrong," he says, brows furrowed with concern. "It's just a stomach bug. Two of the kids in my cabin got it at the end of the session. I thought I'd avoided it, but I guess I wasn't so lucky."

"A stomach bug?" I take a step inside the room, just enough to brace one hand on the edge of the sink for support. Which puts me face to face with all those incriminating pill bottles again.

"But what's with all this medicine?" I try to motion to the mess on the counter, but my arm feels cold and weak, like it weighs a million pounds. "It's your chemo, isn't it? You've already started chemo and you didn't even tell me!"

He shakes his head furiously. "No. That's not chemo medicine. I was looking for an antiemetic I used to have…something that keeps you from throwing up. That's why I got those out."

"That's why you got those out?" I repeat in a haze. *Air...I need more air...*

"Yes, of course. I wouldn't keep that from you." He slowly pulls himself up to standing and takes a tentative step toward me, but I cower backwards, accidentally slamming my back into the edge of the door.

"No. No, don't touch me." Blood pounds so loudly in my ears I can barely hear him anymore. "I told you I can't do this, Theo..." A tornado of vicious thoughts grips me. All I can think of is Theo dying. All I can see is him slipping under the water and never coming back up again. Slowly withering away in a hospital bed. Pleading and begging me for help that I can't give. The flurry of horrible images builds and builds, its velocity so powerful that no matter how hard I try, I can't push it away. So much for all my hopes of changing. I'll never be strong enough to overcome a fear as powerful as this.

"It's okay. It's going to be okay," he croons softly, reaching out, gripping my elbow to steady me.

"I thought I'd have more time...you know, to figure this out..." I babble incoherently. "I can't, Theo...it's too much...I just can't...I can't help you."

I vaguely hear him saying my name over and over, but it sounds like he's a million miles away calling out to me through a tunnel that's slowly caving in. His grip tightens on my arm as my vision blurs around the edges and my tingling legs begin to buckle. And I'm scared. I'm so fucking scared.

Theo shakes me hard. "Annie!" He shouts so loudly it somehow shocks me back into the room. "You *can* help me!"

It takes every ounce of effort I have to focus on his face. "What? I can?"

"Yes, go into the kitchen. You know the Lucky Charms cereal we had earlier?"

I blink at him in a stupor. What the hell is he talking about?

He goes on. "Get me as many of the rainbow marshmallows as you can. They always help settle my stomach."

"Lucky Charms? Rainbows? What are you talking—"

"*GO!*"

I'm so stunned by the volume of his voice I turn and blindly stumble into the bedroom, then down the hallway to the kitchen, hoping he's right. Maybe there is some way I can help.

When I get to the kitchen, all the boxes in the cabinet meld into an indistinguishable riot of colors. And my mind feels so full of sludge I have to work hard to remember what he's told me to do.

*Lucky Charms, Lucky Charms…*finally I see the bright red box; numbly pull it out and scatter half the contents over the kitchen island because my hands are shaking so badly there's no way I can pour it out slowly. I grab a bowl and narrow my focus to the shapes on the counter.

*Rainbow…Rainbow…Rainbow…*There's one! Then another. And another. Yes, I'm doing it. I'm finding the rainbows. *Ping. Ping. Ping.* I drop them into the bowl. I'm doing something. I'm helping! I'm going to collect the rainbows and bring them to Theo, and he's going to feel better. All because of me.

When I have enough in the bowl, I hurry to the bathroom, hands still shaking but my trajectory much straighter now.

When I get back to Theo, he's sitting on the closed toilet lid still looking sickly and pale. But he perks up when I hand him the bowl.

"Here you go," I say, surprising myself by smiling. It's stupid to be proud of finding a few measly marshmallows, but damn if that's not how I feel.

He absently takes my offering, surveying my face closely. "Do you feel better now?"

"Me? Feel better?" What is he talking about? He's the one who's sick, not me.

"Yeah. You," he says emphatically. "Has your heart rate slowed? Is your breathing less shallow?"

Again, I have no idea why he's asking about me. But when I take a second to answer his question, I realize I do feel better. My heartbeat has slowed down a lot since earlier. And yeah, now that I notice it... it *is* a lot easier to breathe.

I nod at him, still not understanding what's going on. "Aren't you going to eat those?" I point at the bowl of rainbows. Hey. Look at that. I can actually lift my arm now.

"No," he says, setting them down on the edge of the sink. "They were for you, not me."

"For me?" What? Why would I need a bowl of cereal at a time like this?

"How long have you had them?" Theo asks.

"Had what? Lucky Charms?"

"No, not Lucky Charms," he says exasperated. "The panic attacks."

All I can do is stare at him because the words he's said don't make any sense. "Panic attacks?" I huff indignantly. "I don't have panic attacks!"

His eyebrows shoot up. "Well, whatever just happened looked an awful lot like a panic attack to me."

I huff and sputter some more. "Well, it wasn't! That's just something weird that happens to my heart sometimes." God, I hope he doesn't ask more questions. It's not something I've ever talked about with anyone before.

"What? Like when you have really scary thoughts and your heart races really fast and your fingers go tingly and it's hard to breathe and you feel like you're completely out of control? That kind of weird thing?"

I shake my head at him in disbelief. How does he know exactly how my episodes feel?

As if he's read my mind, he responds. "I know because I've had them too, Annie. Back when I was in the hospital. I used to have panic attacks whenever I thought I might throw up. I developed this fear of getting sick in front of people, and it grew and grew until I'd have full-blown panic attacks because of it." He drops his voice and adds wryly. "Which is kind of a big deal when you're being treated for cancer because…well, you throw up a lot."

My mind reels as I try to take in what he's just said. "You mean what happens to me has a name?" An odd relief floods over me.

"Yeah. It has a name," Theo says gently. "And it has a treatment too."

"What? Something can be done to help me?"

"Yeah. I'm living proof. Look at me…I just threw up and didn't have one. So see? You can get better."

"Wow. I thought it was just something that happened only to me," I murmur.

"It's not just you. A lot of people struggle with anxiety. You're not alone."

His words slam into me with a physical force. *You're not alone.* Just thinking of that possibility makes a warmth cascade down my body.

"When did your panic attacks start?" he asks.

Theo's sincerity softens my tension even more, reminding me that he's not the enemy. In fact, he's the exact opposite. He's someone safe. Someone I can finally be honest with. I swallow hard, surprised by what I'm about to admit for the first time. "They started when I had to be alone with my mom in the hospital."

To my complete surprise, Theo doesn't look at me like a horrible person. In fact, he simply nods as if the awful thing I've admitted makes perfect sense. And because of that, the words come easier.

"Sometimes she'd be in pain and calling out, asking for help. And I'd try to get the nurses, but it would always take so long, and I wouldn't know what to do. I'd be stuck there all alone trying to find some way to comfort her in the meantime. It was so agonizing having to sit there and wait and watch her suffer. I always felt so helpless… so worthless. So trapped. And I hated it. I hated it so, so much. I should've been able to help her. But I couldn't." Tears well in my eyes. "There was nothing I could do."

When I finish I'm out of breath from all I've just revealed.

"So you've been keeping these panic attacks to yourself for over three years?" he asks incredulously.

"Actually, they went away once I didn't have to go to the hospital anymore," I say, thinking back. "I haven't had one in a long time. They only started again when I met…" I stop myself, realizing what I was about to say next.

Pain flashes across his face as he finishes my sentence. "When you met *me.*"

"No, Theo…that's not what I was going to say…"

He holds up a hand, stopping me. I know I should keep trying to convince him otherwise, but it would be futile. He'll know I'm lying.

He's scarily still, eyes distant, as if he's searching back through his memory for evidence of all I've just told him. "So that night at my mom's house when I found you in the bathroom. Were you having a panic attack then?"

I think back to the night when I'd first started having my nightmare. The night I'd barricaded myself in the bathroom and refused to let him in.

When I nod, he looks stricken. "What triggered that one?"

I cringe, not wanting to make him feel worse than he already does. But I can tell from his clenched jaw he's not going to let this drop. "Your mom had shown me pictures of when you were in the hospital." He looks shocked, so I clarify. "She didn't mean to. She was only showing me your baby pictures. I just happened to see the ones from when you were sick."

He blinks slowly, struggling to take it all in. As the silence grows, I'm scared of the conclusions he's drawing.

"Please. You can't blame yourself, Theo," I rush on, desperate to erase the look of agony on his face. "It's my problem, not yours. I don't know what's wrong with me. I just can't stand to see people I love suffer. Especially when I can't do anything about it. I just feel so helpless. It tears me apart."

"Yeah. I know exactly how you feel." His expression is stony as his eyes bore into mine. "I can't stand to see the people I love suffer either."

His unspoken implication hangs like a foreboding cloud between us.

"Seriously, though," I try again. "It's not your fault. You haven't hurt me."

"Yet."

"What?"

"I haven't hurt you *yet*." He looks so damn defeated it kills me.

My pulse quickens again, seeing him this way. But luckily my heart is too spent to rev itself back to its previous level of madness. I've learned that when I make it to the other side of an episode (or panic attack as I guess they're now called) it's impossible for it to return right away. It's like once I've exhausted all its energy, the attack can't hurt me anymore. At least not for a while.

"I understand Annie," he says, looking up at me with his beautiful green eyes. "Really, I do. And truly. This makes a lot of sense. Your panic attacks explain why you're so scared of letting yourself feel too much. Why you always work so hard to keep yourself and everything about your life under control."

"Really? I make sense?" I laugh weakly, trying to bring some levity into the rapidly dimming space. "Because you might be the only person in the world who understands me. Including me."

He smiles, but I can tell it's an effort. He looks like he's getting sicker by the second. And not just because of the stomach bug, either.

He bends forward, rests his elbows on his knees, staring down at the floor for a long time. Finally he says, "I'm going to sleep on the couch tonight."

"No, Theo, please," I take a step toward him, but he holds up a palm, stopping me.

"You shouldn't be near me."

"What?! Don't say that!"

Again, he forces a wan smile. "I mean, so you don't get sick."

"Oh. Just because you're sick." Relief shutters through me. I'm not sure I could stand it if he pushed me away. I stiffen, shocked by my own words. Isn't that exactly what I'm doing to him in a few short days?

Theo works to act normal, but I'm still suspicious. "Are you sure that's the only reason you're sleeping on the couch?"

"Yeah," he says, unconvincingly. "Don't worry. It's all okay. It's just a stomach bug. It'll be over soon. But you need to get away from me now." He gestures to the bedroom, trying to get me to leave.

I can't tell if everything really is okay or if he's trying to make things easy on me again. And from the way he furrows his brows it seems like he's currently asking himself that same question too.

"At least let me sleep on the couch," I say, hating how paltry my offer sounds. "That way you'll be closer to the bathroom."

Surprisingly, he agrees. But I think it's only because he's looking a little green around the gills again and he's desperate to get rid of me.

"You better go," he says, sweat beading on his brow as he slowly stands. "But make sure to come get me if you have another attack, okay? Promise?"

"Yeah, I promise." How is he still able to think of me at a time like this?

I reluctantly leave, grabbing a pillow and heading toward the hallway. My mind whirls, trying to come up with something kind and nurturing to say. But, like always, it comes up empty. Why the hell doesn't compassion come more naturally to me?

But just as I get to the bedroom door, something comes to me and I whirl back to the bathroom to tell him. "And don't forget I'm here too, Theo. Make sure to come and get me if you need any—"

But it's too late. He's already closed the door.

CHAPTER TWENTY-TWO

HAND IN HAND, Theo and I walk to The Lookout for the last time.

Everyone is gone, and we should be too. But after saying farewell to Miles and watching him disappear back into his house, we'd slipped away and found the abandoned path we'd gradually worn back to smooth dirt these past months. There's no way we could leave without saying one last goodbye to the place that has become like a second home to us this summer.

Theo's smile is brighter, more genuine now as he squeezes my hand, looking down on me with unabashed admiration. I know what he's doing. Savoring the damn moment, like always. If I asked him to explain his goofy grin (which I won't because it's not necessary anymore) he'd undoubtable say he's basking in his Now, unwilling to sacrifice our next seconds and minutes and hours together by dwelling on things he can't change.

And the craziest thing is I'm doing the same thing. Three months ago, I wouldn't have believed I could so easily disregard my whirling thoughts for simple, oblivious ignorance like this. But I gotta say, not knowing, or caring what happens in the future (even if it's just for a few short hours) has turned out to be a much better approach to life than I could've ever imagined.

We walk down the shaded path side by side, the bright light just beyond the platform beckoning us forward. As I stare into the glowing sphere outlined in the arch of trees, for a split second the world blurs, turning the scene before me dreamlike, and yet familiar too. A wave of energy rushes at me with such force it's like someone slapping my cheek, telling me to stop and take notice. *Wake up*, it says. *This is important. Not just some everyday déjà vu.*

And in the next instant, the sensation is gone.

I shake my head, trying to rid myself of the strange yet thrilling feeling. What was that? I've walked this trail countless times this summer, but the flash I just saw didn't seem like a recollection of those times. No, it felt more like a deeply buried memory and a joyous premonition all rolled up into one. But how is that possible? The past and the future can't exist simultaneously. That's not how time works.

Theo keeps looking straight ahead, not breaking stride. "You felt it too." He gives my hand a squeeze, and it's only then I notice the sparking sensation prickling between our joined palms.

"Mmmm," I murmur. It's the most noncommittal response I can think of. I don't want to talk to him about what just happened. In fact, the timing of this heart-soaring déjà vu (that supposedly isn't a déjà vu?) kind of pisses me off. The last thing I need is to be handed another bucketful of bliss on the day I'm planning to give it all back.

Please. Don't make this harder on me than it already is, I complain silently to the heavens.

Hey, we're not the ones making things hard, the heavens grumble back. I roll my eyes, resisting the urge to make an obscene gesture at the sky.

Luckily, when we get to the platform the view is stunning enough to make me forget my annoyance at my mom and her meddling friends.

"Just think," I say to Theo, stepping to the edge, being careful not to lean on the rickety railing. "Without you, I would've never known this place existed."

Just like countless other things I wouldn't have known existed if I hadn't met you.

Theo comes to stand beside me, eyes shielded behind the darkened glasses he'd chosen to wear today. "So I guess knowing me turned out to be at least a little worthwhile after all, huh?"

"Just a little," I tease, bumping my shoulder against him. He grins big, looking relieved I've made a joke.

"You know what's weird?" I twirl around, taking in the space that still feels as warm and comfortable as my childhood bedroom, even with our beach chairs and hammocks now gone. "I always felt so happy here."

He makes a face. "Why is it weird? This place is beautiful."

"But it's not just how it looks, though." I try to describe how my chest always swells so pleasantly the moment I arrive at The Lookout. How my spirits soar when I get here, no matter what worries I had the moment before. "It's like this space has a physical impact on me. Like my chemistry changes when I step up on this platform. There must be some kind of positive momentum swirling around this space. Because it feels like it literally whisks me up and makes it impossible for me to stay sad when I'm here."

I should feel embarrassed about making such far-out claims, but I know Theo will understand how I feel.

He furrows his brow. "Now that you mention it, you're right. I feel that way when I'm here too. But that's probably because I'm here with you."

"Well, of course it is. I make everything better," I joke. "But it's more than that…don't you feel it?"

He stares blankly into the shadowed forest behind me, thinking hard. "Yeah, I get what you're saying. But I'm not sure what it is." He shrugs lackadaisically. Oh, how I'm going to miss that shrug. "Maybe this Lookout was some kind of sacred space for Native American celebrations a long time ago. Or the spot where some explorer looked out on his new discovery in sheer wonder, thrilled by all he'd just accomplished. Who knows? Maybe we're picking up on the positive vibes left behind by happy people from the past. I've heard physical spaces can hold onto to energy like that."

I nod, surprised by how easily I accept his explanation. The Annie from a few months ago would've been spitting in disgust if she'd heard that. But now I merely say, "That makes sense."

The bubbly, light sensation around me trills stronger now; like a cat purring louder as it's stroked. As if the space actually likes that we're acknowledging it. Which seems crazy, I know. But I don't even argue with myself about it anymore. I just let it be so.

"I feel it," I say, hoping to please our little sanctuary even more. "There have definitely been some happy people here, that's for sure."

Including us

Theo's gaze flicks to mine, and I know we've shared the same thought. Neither of us speaks it out loud though. What's the point? It's not like our feelings about each other are going to change our fates.

"Darn it," Theo says abruptly, jarring me from my thoughts. "I never got to explore that." He points to a thin deer path that disappears down the steep incline in front of us; its trajectory shrouded by a riot of overgrown shrubs and brambles. In my head I always think of The Lookout as perched on top of a cliff, but it's not. The land actually continues downward, but at such an unforgiving angle only the deer can travel it. And although Theo always claimed he could travel it too, I'd never let him try.

"Yeah, and you're not going to explore it now either," I say sternly. "At least not if I'm around. You're not dying on my watch, Buster."

Once the words are out, they hang awkwardly in the air between us. Why did I have to bring up dying at a time like this?

"Come here," Theo reaches out, blessedly changing the subject. He catches me around the waist and pulls me against his hard body. Running a hand along my cheek, his eyes scan my face like he's trying to soak in every detail of me. Then he bends and gently kisses me. The plushness of his lips, the barely-there pressure of his skin on mine makes my legs go weak with desire.

As his kiss deepens, I reach up on my tiptoes to push my mouth hard into his, questioning my logic once again. Am I really going to give this up? This perfection? This happiness? All to go back to running again?

God, I'm so tired. What would happen if I just stopped and let myself rest for a while? Let myself enjoy the satisfaction that has so graciously been given to me?

Theo's words from weeks ago ring in my ears. *It could be like that. All you have to do is give in.*

I pull away, disturbed by the friction of my jagged thoughts. We need to keep moving. Time is ticking, and we still have a clue to read, and a Treasure Hunt to complete, and a whole handful of seconds, and minutes and hours left together. Everything will go smoother if we stay focused on what we have, rather than what we don't. Some sweet boy told me that once, not very long ago.

We stand side by side staring out over the lake one last time. It's the perfect moment to finally tell Theo I love him. To admit that I heard our voices joined together that day at Caroline's house, promising that across time and distance, lifetimes and eternities we'll always be together. Forevermore.

But that would only make things harder for him. To know how close he came to convincing me to forget all my fears in the name of my love for him. No, it's better if we part with him thinking he tried his best, but there was no way I was ever going to give in.

"So, um…about what happened at my apartment last weekend…" Theo starts.

I reach up and touch his lips with one finger, stopping him from saying more. We never really discussed how seeing him sick had triggered my panic attack. But what's the point in talking about it now? I don't need to face what happened in his bathroom that night. Because it doesn't matter anymore. When Theo's cancer comes back, I'll be long gone.

"Hey, let's not break hundreds of years of tradition here," I say. "How about, just like all those other people from the past, we simply stand here and let ourselves be happy? Just for a little while longer. What do you think about that?"

Theo blinks down at me, looking a bit awed by my new carefree take on life. "I think." He kisses the top of my head, then turns back to the stunning vista before us, squeezing me extra tight. "That, just like everything else in this bonus life I've been given…I would love to do that. With *you*."

CHAPTER TWENTY-THREE

THE FOUR OF us sit around Caroline and Jonathan's backyard table only minutes away from opening our very last clue. It's mid-afternoon, the sky above us scattered with puffy clouds meandering like a herd of white buffalo across a field of blue.

With the long summer days, we still have plenty of time to make it to Highwood Forest—the place I'm now certain is the starting point for our hunt—before the sun goes down. Caroline already has the diaper bag packed for the kids. And Jonathan has a shovel and his metal detector in the back of their van. Now all we have to do is wait for Emma to wake up from her nap. Then we'll read the clue and be on our way.

I glance at Theo sitting beside me, looking mesmerized by a story Jonathan is telling about some Civil War button he once dug up from a cow pasture. I still can't believe that in a few short hours this crazy adventure of ours will be over.

The three clues we already received sit folded in the middle of the glass-top table. I still haven't told Theo about Franco's mention of there being five paintings in Mom's series. It was so long ago that Franco had seen them, I'm sure he was just confused. Plus, Aunt Lydia would've told us if there were more paintings to find, and she'd said nothing. In fact, the last time I talked to her, she was just as excited as we were about the ending being near.

During every phone call, I've tried to pry her for more information about what our directives might mean, but she's been of no help. She swears she knows nothing because Mom sealed the envelopes before she gave them to her. Still, she must know where the treasure is located since she's the one who had to bury it. Mom was so weak when she'd put this game together for me, there's no way she could've done it herself.

Now, I stare at the baby monitor sitting on top of the grill, willing Emma to scream so we can get started.

"Can we just go ahead and open this?" I whine to Caroline, waving the unopened envelope in the air. Earlier she'd insisted we let Emma get a full nap; otherwise we'd have hell to pay with her crankiness. "The stress is too much for me. I can't wait any longer."

"Me either," my sister agrees. "Forget Emma's damn nap. I'll rip that baby from her crib and let her scream all the way to Highwood Forest if I have to. Let's *DO THIS!!*"

We all startle at her uncharacteristic outburst. "Sorry," she says sheepishly. "This is the most excitement I've had in a long time. I'm not quite sure what to do with myself."

My heart warms, seeing the light dancing so brightly in my sister's eyes again. These past weeks of the Treasure Hunt have transformed her. I can tell how much she looks forward to our visits. The silliness Theo always brings with him; our weekly phone calls with Aunt Lydia; all the thrills and speculations that come whenever we open a clue. And our relationship has certainly improved. Caroline doesn't act so much like a wise older sister telling her flighty younger sister what to do anymore. Now it feels like the two of us are equals, playing together on the same team.

"Alright," I say, taking a last steeling breath. "Like the crazy lady in the milk-stained Elmo t-shirt said," I point to Caroline, "Let's *DO THIS!*"

We all cheer loud enough to jar Jack's attention from where he's digging up worms in his mom's flower bed. But only for a split second, then he's back to flinging dirt and crushing marigolds under his little yellow rubber boots once again.

"How about you three each grab a clue," I suggest. "Then we'll go around and read them in order, with me going last reading the new one."

My stomach churns as everyone opens their papers. Except for me. Although I slip the paper out of the envelope, I keep it folded, knowing I won't be able to fight the temptation to read it if I don't.

I can't believe the moment I've been waiting for is finally here. In a few short seconds everything will change. No longer will I have to sit on my ass waiting and worrying and doing nothing. I'll have something to *do*...somewhere to *go*. By the end of this day, I'll finally be able to put to rest all the questions that have been swirling in my head for weeks. I'll finally have all the answers I've been looking for.

The air in the backyard seems to join in our preparation for the big reveal. The breeze settles. The distant traffic noise fades. Even the birds stop their chattering as if they too can't wait to find out what's going to happen next.

"Here goes." Jonathan clears his throat ceremonially and begins reading. "*Find your center star and follow it North.*"

Next comes Caroline. "*Into the dense wooded forest until you can go no more.*"

Theo continues. "*Dig beneath the hardened heart to find the map at the core.*"

All eyes fix on me. Hands shaking, I open the paper that holds our fate. My eyes skim the lines before I read them out loud.

Wait a minute...these words...they don't make sense. My heart hammers hard against my chest bone as I silently read them again.

"What? What is it?" Caroline asks gently. I glance up to see the concern on her face.

"It's just...this can't be right," I murmur.

"Can you just read it?" she snaps impatiently.

Theo places a gentle hand on my back. My eyes fly to his, my heart whirling even faster now. How can this be? He raises his eyebrows, urging me on, and I force myself back to the task at hand.

I read the clue aloud, still not understanding why my mom has put these words in this order.

"There you'll find the Hunt was all a ruse. This adventure was only ever about You and You."

I look up to find Caroline and Jonathan gaping at me.

"Ruse?" They both repeat in unison. I nod dumbly, glad I'm not the only one who doesn't understand what the hell is going on. Although when I glance over at Theo, I notice he doesn't seem quite as surprised as the rest of us.

"Let me see that." Caroline snatches the paper out of my hand, nearly tearing its edge, which pisses me off.

Caroline's eyes fly back and forth over the clue. "What the hell? Was this all some kind of joke?" she mumbles to herself, reading it one more time.

Just then, Emma squawks loudly through the monitor. "Oh great," Caroline grumbles. "Perfect timing as always." She looks at Jonathan. "Can you go get her, please?"

Jonathan dashes into the house, looking grateful for an excuse to get away from us. He's been around my sister and me long enough. He knows a ticking time bomb when he sees one.

Finally, Caroline looks up, still clutching the clue. "So this whole thing…it was all for *nothing*?"

I feel dizzy, like the world I thought I knew has suddenly been turned upside down. How is this possible? We're all packed and ready to go. I've been dreaming about this for weeks. Imagining the search, the digging, the triumphant cheer when our shovel clangs on a box, just like in all those pirate stories I used to love. Now one simple sentence has snatched all of that away from me.

"Yes. This was all for nothing." I grind out, my anger rising faster than any rational thought can temper.

I grab the paper back from Caroline, fighting the urge to rip it into shreds. How could Mom have done this to me? How could she have suddenly changed the rules of the game like this? Treasure Hunts are supposed to follow certain guidelines. You get clues, figure out what they mean, search for where the clues point, and then you find a treasure. You don't just say, "Oh, this time I decided to give you nothing." You don't just quit halfway through and renege on your promise just because you think it might be fun.

"It was all for nothing," I repeat, throwing the paper down on the table. I feel Theo tense beside me, and only then do I realize how I must sound to him. But I'm too mad to even care.

The implications crash down on me. We won't be going anywhere. We won't be finding anything. I won't be getting anything more from my mom. This piece of paper is the end. Talk about disappointment.

"What does '*all about You and You even mean*?" I wail to no one in particular. Jonathan comes back outside with Emma in his arms, hovering near the door in case he needs to clear out of the blast zone quickly.

I rant on. "Does it mean me and me? Or me and you?" I point to Theo. "Or you and you? I have no idea. None of this makes sense!"

Theo stays uncharacteristically quiet. He doesn't chime in with some lofty explanation of a higher purpose for the hunt. Or try to soothe my anger. Or tell me to look on the bright side and think of all the fun we had along the way. No. He just sits there, looking down at his hands clasped tightly on the table, his mouth set in a firm line.

"This is bullshit!" I yell.

My cursing gets Jack's attention, and he mumbles, "Bullshit. Bullshit," as he flings clods of dirt onto the patio.

"Oh, great." Caroline shoots me an evil eye. "Now look what you've done, Annie."

"Oh sorry. My dead mom just pulled a bait and switch on me from her grave, so forgive me for being a little upset right now!"

"Oh, stop acting like such a baby!"

"What?! A baby?! Did you just call me a baby?" Out of the corner of the eye, I see Jonathan slowly backing toward the door.

Caroline takes a deep breath, looking just a bit remorseful. "I only meant you don't have to get so mad."

"I'll get mad if I want to get mad! And you can't stop me!" I snap back childishly. I'll be damned if my sister tries to tell me what to do right now. If she thinks she's making anything better using that condescending tone with me, then she's sadly mistaken.

We both glare at each other across the table. So much for us being a team anymore. Although now that I think about it, maybe Caroline has a point. Why am I getting so angry right now? Wasn't I the one who told Theo the treasure hunts with my mom became more about the fun I had along the way than what she left me at the end? Have I forgotten that part?

Still, it's the principle of the matter that bothers me. And the fact that this surprise has my heart whirling and my breath going shallow and I'm back to feeling out of control once again.

I throw my hands in the air, thoughts running out of my mouth all jumbled up and un-sanitized for consumption.

"It's just…just…I feel so duped. So manipulated by her!" There, I said it. So much for hiding my ungratefulness. It's all out in the open now. "It's like she was trying to make me fall in love with him," I stab a finger at Theo. "Like the whole hunt was just a ruse to make us spend time together. So we could do some kind of mysterious good in the world together, even though no one up there can explain what it is!" I yell up to the heavens.

I'm completely off the rails now. "It's like she did this to force me to be with Theo." I blabber on, talking about him like he's not sitting right there beside me. "But what if I don't want to stay with him? Don't I have a choice in this?" I throw my hands up in frustration. "What if I don't *want* to fall in love with him?!"

I'm breathing hard when I finish. I look around to see everyone, even Jack and Emma, frozen in place, completely stunned by my outburst. It's only then that I turn and see the anguish on Theo's face. Squeezing my eyes shut tight, I wish I could literally pluck out my tongue with the barbecue tongs hanging on the grill. My God, what did I just say? How could I have been so hurtful to the boy that, in the world's worst twist of irony, I already love with all my heart? Despite how I claim otherwise.

"Theo, I'm sorry. I didn't mean…" I say weakly.

But he's not listening anymore. He pushes his chair back with a loud scrape on the concrete, the harsh noise like an audible demarcation of the line I've just crossed. Even through his shaded glasses, it's easy to see the rare anger in his eyes. But when I look closer, I see more. No, he doesn't look only mad; he looks exhausted too. Like he doesn't have to energy to fight with me anymore. Well, I've done it now. I've somehow found a way to push the world's kindest, most patient man too far.

He stands, towering above me, clearly fighting to keep his voice even. "I'm sorry that spending time with me this summer has been such a hardship for you, Annie," he grinds out.

"Theo…I swear, I didn't mean it…"

He refuses to look directly at me. Instead, he focuses on the ground by my feet. "I'm sorry that you had to put up with the horrible annoyance of me loving you."

Tears prick my eyes as I watch everything fall apart by my own hands.

"But you know what? You're right. You shouldn't love me." The saddest smile I've ever seen curves his lips, as he whispers almost to himself, "Because we both know I'm not worth it."

I suck in a sharp breath, his words like a knife in my gut. My mouth flails open and closed as I try to find the words to tell him how wrong he is. But I'm taking too long. He's walking toward the door. And Jonathan is stepping aside to let him pass. And Caroline is staring at me with her *do-something, dammit!* face.

"Theo stop! You *are* worth it!" I rise to my feet, calling breathlessly after him. "You'll always be worth everything to me…you're the only one who…"

But all my desperate ramblings are pointless.

Because Theo is already gone.

CHAPTER TWENTY-FOUR

I STARE AT the doorway where Theo's just disappeared, knowing I should chase after him. But I don't.

Or maybe I should say I can't. Because just like in my nightmare, my feet feel like they're made of cement. And no matter how my heart is yelling for me to *MOVE for God's sake!* my head has taken over and decided that this is for the best. It's better to let Theo go. Even though my words were harsh, they're still true. I'll never be strong enough to watch him die.

I turn to Caroline, bracing myself for her incoming triad. But when our eyes meet, I see only compassion staring back at me.

"Oh, Annie," she whispers. Two paltry words. Yet the understanding in her voice pushes me over the edge. Tears spill freely down my cheeks now.

In an instant she's on her feet, rushing around the table and pulling me into a fierce hug, murmuring gentle shushes into my ear. She rocks me back and forth with the same vice-like grip Mom had when she was alive. It's the kind of hug whose firmness used to help tamp all my raging emotions back down into a more manageable size when I felt like I was losing control. In fact, Caroline's embrace feels so much like Mom's that for a moment I almost forget who's holding me. And as we sway there together, the strangest thing happens.

"Did you start wearing Mom's perfume?" I ask, my voice muffled by Caroline's hair.

"No. Why would you ask that?"

I pull back, wiping my wet cheeks. "Because I smell it. Blue Grass by Elizabeth Arden. She never wore anything else."

Caroline opens her mouth, probably to tell me she's well aware of what perfume Mom wore. But then she gets a funny look on her face. "Oh, wow," she says, sucking in a deep lungful of air. "I smell it too. That's crazy."

We both smile, neither of us needing to voice our conclusion out loud. A warmth blooms in my chest as I stare into my sister's beautiful, wide-open face. And from the way she stares back, I have a feeling she's feeling the same warmth too.

Jonathan comes back outside. He'd followed Theo into the house when he'd stormed off. (Probably apologizing profusely for his rude sister-in-law and getting Theo's phone number so the three of them can still hang out once I go back to school.)

"He's gone?" Caroline asks. Jonathan nods, busying himself with adjusting Emma on his hip so he doesn't have to look me in the eye.

My heart sinks. I imagine Theo driving home to Indianapolis all alone. So angry and hurt. Not even able to say a proper goodbye because of my selfish outburst. It's typical of me to not consider how this has affected him. Have I forgotten he's just had the rug pulled out from under him too?

Caroline claps her hands together in her take-charge-of-the-situation way. "What you need to do now Annie is get your head on straight. This was a lot to take in all at once." She gestures to the papers strewn across the table. "You obviously need some time to think about what this all means. And you don't need us around distracting you. No, you need some time alone." Her brusque tone makes me wonder if I'm not the only one in this yard who needs some time to process what's just happened.

She gives me one last hug, grabs Jonathan, and tugs him roughly into the house.

Alone in the backyard, I'm at a loss for what to do next. What I really want to do is go back and erase the horrible things I said to Theo. But since time travel isn't an option, I do the only other thing I can think of: I start walking.

Caroline's backyard isn't huge, but there are a few trees scattered about and soft grass under my tennis shoes and enough open sky to remind me I still have options, despite my tendency to believe otherwise.

You always have more choices than you realize.

I'm not exactly sure where the words come from, but they soothe me. So I think them some more.

You always have more choices than you realize.

But is that really true? Theo is gone. He's already made the choice for both of us. And there's probably no repairing things after I practically shouted in his face that I don't want to love him. That sounded pretty bad, didn't it? What he doesn't know is, like it or not, I already do love him. And I'm starting to realize that whether he's dead or alive, that's never going to change.

Ugh. This is so impossible! How did I get myself into this mess in the first place? I've spent years avoiding commitment. Yet in just a few short months I've let myself become so enmeshed in a boy I'm not sure what my life will look like without him.

I stomp around the yard, smashing the innocent grass under my feet. I'm so frustrated I'm half tempted to charge through Caroline's flower bed on my next lap simply for the satisfaction of crushing those stinky marigolds to smithereens.

The thought of acting so childishly, just like Jack, makes me laugh. And laughing makes me think of how much fun Theo and I had together on the Treasure Hunt. I can't believe only hours ago I was lamenting about how I didn't want it to end, now here I am complaining because there wasn't an end. That doesn't even make sense! Is that why I'm so angry right now? Not because my mom switched up the rules and didn't hide a treasure, but because I wanted a few more hours of wondering, and dreaming and…oh my gosh, am I really going to admit this?…of *not knowing* what was going to happen next? Have I really become someone who not only tolerates, but actually looks forward to the unknown? It seems impossible, coming from me. But hasn't this hunt already shown me how much I've changed?

I suddenly see my mom's handiwork everywhere.

Before this summer, I would've never dreamed I could find a destination using my gut instincts alone like I did when I found Charlie.

Or that I could connect with a complete stranger by being vulnerable and sharing my story, like I did with Lisa.

Or that I could change my preconceived notions about therapy, like I did with Rebecca.

Or that it might feel good to dive headfirst into memories of my mom, instead of trying to push them away, like I did with Franco.

Before this hunt, I would've never considered that loving someone who was about to die just might be worth it. That grief might not be insurmountable, but simply an emotion like any other. One I'm strong enough to bear.

I stop in my tracks hearing my own optimistic words. My God. I really have changed, haven't I?

When I look up, I realize I'm standing at the base of a gigantic oak tree. Above me, perched in its thick branches sits the remnants of an abandoned treehouse. Jonathan plans to restore it for Jack and Emma when they get older, but so far he's only torn the roof and side walls off, leaving just the platform, which he claims is still in good shape.

I survey the boards nailed to the trunk as a ladder, suddenly desperate to climb up and hide out in the tree's cool embrace. It feels like the perfect spot to figure out what the hell I want to do next.

Unfortunately, as a certified Safety Pup, Jonathan has also removed the bottom two ladder boards so the kids don't have access to the dangerous structure. Which means I have to reach above my head and grab a board almost halfway up the tree, then walk my legs up the trunk with my ass stuck out in the air, like the world's most uncoordinated Spiderman.

Thank goodness my work on the ropes course and lifting campers onto the toilet this summer has built my upper body strength. Still, it's a struggle to haul myself up the boards, which are way too few and far between. (My God, who was this treehouse built for? A giant?) More than once my foot slips off the old mossy planks, leaving me dangling mid-air, held up by only my hands until I regain my footing.

When I get to the top, I heave a leg over the side, my muscles burning. Then—ignoring the splinters nipping at my bare skin—I flop like a dying fish onto the platform, finally coming to rest flat on my stomach with my face pressed into the grooves of the wood, panting hard.

Safely ensconced in the tree, the whole messy shitshow suddenly hits me as funny, and I start laughing at myself. Softly at first. Just a huff. A few *ha ha*'s. A little snort. But the more I imagine how ridiculous I looked getting up here, the harder I laugh. My mirth builds upon itself, sweeping me up in its unexpected joy. I don't even move off my stomach, I just giggle and giggle, my cheek bouncing up and down on the cool wood, my face contorted in hysterics.

Finally, I pull myself up to sitting and scoot across the platform to rest my back against the tree. Eventually my laughter fades away with one last wheeze. But my smile remains.

God, that felt good. My mom used to say, there's nothing better than a good belly laugh to wash all your worries away.

"Well, Mom," I say out loud. "I think my worries have been thoroughly washed away after that. Washed and rinsed and hung out to dry. At least for a little while."

I release a heavy sigh, sweeping my gaze across the scene before me. From this vantage point, Caroline's busy neighborhood looks like the opening shot of a movie set in suburbia. Tastefully colored houses line curved streets. Cars drive by, religiously obeying the speed limit. Kids on swing sets giggle and squeal. Industrious homeowners furiously clip and dig and mow. Birds flit here and there, seeming unperturbed by the commotion. And I sit in the boughs of the tree, watching it all.

I'm not sure if it's because of the remnants of my laughter, or my higher perspective on the world, or the sturdiness of the ancient oak at my back, but I suddenly feel very small. But not in a bad way. No, more in a reassuring way. As if I've relaxed enough to become blended into something much bigger than myself. It's odd, but I can even see myself through the eyes of that something bigger…I guess what Theo would call the friendly Universe. I see how much I struggle. How hard I fight. How I sometimes take things way too seriously. And knowing that, a deep compassion for myself washes over me. A loving amusement at how desperately I try. Suddenly all my struggles seem so unnecessary. And all I can think of is how sweet I am. Stuck here in this crazy, beautiful world, simply doing the best that I can.

Just then, a buzzing sound zips by my ear. I reach up to swat what I assume is a bumblebee away. But the sound darts in front of me. That's when I see a beautiful ruby-throated hummingbird hovering only inches away from my face.

The bird lands on a branch to my right as I sit frozen, staring at the tiny creature, afraid to breathe in case I might scare it away. Its body shines in jewel-toned splendor; greens and golds and purples so bright they look like they've been rendered in iridescent paint. Up close and uncharacteristically still, it looks like a creature from a mythical world. And just like the hummingbird that used to visit Theo and I at The Lookout, this one sits and tips its head back and forth, surveying me sagely with its ink-drop eyes in a way that makes me feel like it's looking deep into my soul.

"I knew you'd be here for me," I say inside my mind.

Like I always am. She says, a smile lighting her voice. *But your laughter made it easier for you to hear me.*

"Yeah, I'm beginning to understand that."

I know logically the bird is simply a messenger. A physical

representation to bolster the part of me that still needs tangible proof before I let myself believe. Nevertheless, having it here to talk to is pretty cool.

"You're too late, you know," I say to the little hummingbird, thinking of the warm sense of love and ease I'd just felt. "I already know what I'm going to do."

I could sense that. Something inside you feels like it's finally come to rest.

I consider her words. Yes, that is what this feels like. A resting. A release. A relaxed stillness I've never really known before.

"Yeah. It came to me all of a sudden, and I just knew."

The dawning had come when I'd looked back over the Treasure Hunt. When I'd finally seen that every single risk I'd taken had paled in comparison to the reward I'd gained in the end. I now realize the risk will be the same with Theo. Yes, losing him one day is going to hurt like hell. But loving him…oh, loving him and supporting him, and getting a second chance to be there when someone I love needs me. The possibility of getting one more second or minute or hour sharing this beautiful world with him? I already know that it will be the greatest gift of my life. And there's no way I'm going to forfeit that treasure just because I'm afraid of being afraid.

I know I don't have to explain any of this to my mom, but I do anyway, continuing our conversation inside my head.

"I thought it was going to be so hard to figure this all out. It seemed so complicated when I tried to sort it out logically. But when the realization hit, everything became so simple."

That's because deep down you already knew what you wanted. You just wouldn't let yourself admit it.

"Yeah, I guess," I huff an exasperated breath. Truly, I'd known the moment Theo walked out the door. Watching him leave, I'd felt a visceral tearing inside my chest, as if he was quite literally taking a part of me with him, leaving behind a hole in my heart that no amount of practical thinking would ever fill.

But even though I'd told her I'd made my decision, I still don't move from my seat against the tree.

"I'm so scared," I murmur softly. "He's going to break my heart, isn't he?"

I can almost feel her stroking my cheek. *He might*, she says. *But so will many other experiences in this world, honey. In this lifetime, your heart will be broken many times over. But it will always break open... letting more and more love flow in.*

I let out a long, ragged breath as her words sink deep into my bones. I know what she's saying is true. Through the cracks Theo's pried open inside me, I already feel that love flowing. And the truth is, even if I could stop it, I don't really want to.

With that realization, a tenderhearted peace settles over me.

"I just wish this wisdom would've hit me a little sooner. Why couldn't I have figured this out before I went and put my foot in my mouth and ruined everything with Theo?" I remember the hurt I'd seen on his face. "I hope he's not too mad. I hope I can figure out a way to regain his trust."

Oh, I have a feeling he'll forgive you. Theo doesn't have it in him to hold a grudge for too long, she says. *And don't worry. This world really is friendly, like Theo says. Everything's going to be okay.*

"No matter what happens next?"

No matter what happens next.

With that, the hummingbird flies away. But I'm not upset it's gone. I don't need a talisman anymore. I've found my mom for good. And I'm never going to lose her again. Of that, I'm sure.

"I love Theo Teodorczyk with all my heart!" I shout up into the trees, basking in how good the words feel leaving my mouth.

So go tell him that, Mom says. *Like right now.*

"Yeah, because we don't have much time left together."

Maybe. Maybe not.

"What?"

I'm just saying that nothing with you two is written in stone. At least not yet.

An unspoken knowing twangs inside my chest hearing those words. "It's not? What do you mean by that?"

By what?

"By what you just said!"

Did I just say something? Hmmm…I forgot, she says coyly.

"Mother! Answer my question. What did you mean by nothing's written in stone?" But despite how I beg, no reply comes. I have the distinct feeling her sudden silence is no accident.

"Fine. Be that way," I say to the rustling leaves above my head. I hope none of the neighbors are looking out their windows watching me argue with this tree. "I'm going now! But can you at least try to put in a good word for me with Theo? Because I have a feeling I'm going to need all the help I can get!"

I wait, but again I'm met with only silence. Goodness. Now I know where I get my stubbornness from.

Grinning big, I scoot toward the edge of the platform. Man, it's crazy how normal that interaction with my mom felt. The banter we'd just shared felt so much like a conversation we would've had in real life. But then again, I guess this is real life. Just one that most people (like the former me) don't realize is possible.

As I scramble and slip back down the ladder, I know what I have to do. I have to find Theo. Right now. Because our time together is limited and I refuse to waste it pretending I don't care.

Of course, when I find him, I have no idea what I'm going to say. For once in my life, I don't have a plan.

And for once in my life, I think I like it that way.

CHAPTER TWENTY-FIVE

ONCE I'M BACK on solid ground, I rush into the house to find Caroline and Jonathan. I need to apologize to them for what I'm about to do next. They've put so much effort into making today special. Getting the kids ready. Packing the car. Planning an elaborate celebration dinner for after we got home with the treasure. (Complete with filet mignon. A luxury for all of us. Even Theo, who's rich.) But I have to tell them I'm ditching them to head off to Indianapolis and find Theo. Where I guess I'll pound on his apartment door and shout apologies through the keyhole and pray to God he'll let me in.

Listen to me, being all dramatic again. It's Theo. Of course, he's going to let me in.

But as I pass through the dining room into the kitchen—where Caroline and Jonathan are talking in hushed tones, most likely about how badly I just fucked up my life—something catches my eye out the front window.

"Why is Theo's car still here?" I ask Jonathan. "I thought you said he left."

Caroline scrunches up her face, confused. "What? Theo's car is still here?" She crosses the room to see where I'm pointing. Only a smidge of Theo's dented front bumper is visible through the window, but it's definitely still there.

"Jonathan!" Caroline gives her husband an incredulous look. "You said he left!"

Jonathan shrugs like he doesn't understand our confusion. "Yeah, because he *did* leave. He went for a run."

Caroline throws her hands in the air. "Honey, when I asked you if he was gone, I meant did he *leave* leave! Like leave to go back to his house! Was that so confusing to you?"

Jonathan tries to defend himself, but I'm too thrilled to listen anymore. Theo hasn't left me. Even after the horrible things I said. Even after the horrible things I've done, I haven't completely driven him away. Maybe things aren't quite as hopeless as I thought.

I wave my hands in front of Jonathan, trying to get his attention. "Which way did he go?"

"Oh, uh…uh," he stammers. "To the right, I think."

"You think? You think? Jonathan, I swear I'm going to…" Caroline's shrill voice fades off into the background as I burst out the front door, running to find Theo as if our lives depend on it. Which, for some odd reason, I think might be true.

Dashing out of the driveway following the way Jonathan directed, I'm determined to find Theo and make things right. I can do this, I tell myself, fists pumping at my sides. I'm going to find Theo and apologize and tell him the truth about how I really feel. And after that, just like my mom said, everything is going to be alright.

But I'm only a few yards down the road when I realize I have a problem. For some stupid reason, Caroline's neighborhood has been modeled after the world's most convoluted maze. Streets branch off here and there all willy-nilly, looping and snaking and dead ending in combinations so endless there's no logical way to figure out which way Theo might have gone. How am I ever going to find him?

As I face my first crossroads, I realize I'm going to have to draw on the lessons I learned on the Treasure Hunt. I'm going to have to channel what I did on those back roads in a torrential thunderstorm and stop thinking with my head and instead follow my gut. Now, jogging in place, staring between Sapphire Drive and Emerald Lane, I close my eyes and imagine Theo running. I feel into the bond between us, letting myself dive heart-first into the connection I've tried to deny for so long. Then I run to the right.

I continue that way for a while, not breaking stride. Not thinking too much. Simply tapping into the wordless twang in my body whenever I have to make a choice of which way to turn. Eventually I abandon the sidewalks crowded with leisurely walkers and moms pushing baby strollers and take to the road, my tennis shoes slapping rhythmically on the asphalt as my mind blurs and my choices become more and more effortless. I have to get to Theo. I can't let him go another minute without knowing the truth of how I feel.

I'm flying high on the adrenaline of my righteous quest. Until I make another turn. Then another. Then another. And I still don't find him. That's when I realize I have another problem:

I'm not a runner.

I ride horses and hike trails and climb rocks. Activities that don't require such a sustained lung capacity as this. I'm not sure how much longer I can keep going at this pace. Plus, with Theo's stamina, he could be miles away right now. On our weekends off, he sometimes used to run through these streets for hours while I slept on the couch. And that was when he was happy and jogging for fun. I can only imagine how much ground he can cover when he's running angry and fast.

I probably shouldn't have acted so rashly. I probably should have calmed down and waited at Caroline's until he came back. (And changed my clothes before I left. Running in August in khakis and a five-year-old bra doesn't make for the most pleasant experience, if you know what I mean.) But sitting still and waiting for him just didn't feel right. And not just because I'm hopelessly impatient. No, it feels important that I make the effort to fix what I've broken. That, for once, I meet Theo where he is, instead of the other way around.

∞

As I push onward—lungs screaming for air and a stitch knifing my side—I silently call on my mom and her band of angelic merrymakers to help me out. *Please tell me where to find him,* I beg. *I'm not picky. I'll take any direction I can get.*

Just then I see a familiar face on a lawn to my right. Lurching up onto the sidewalk, I wave furiously to get her attention.

"Lisa! Lisa! Remember me? It's Annie…from the birthday party," I wheeze. "The one…who was…looking for the painting."

Her eyes widen in recognition. Then her brows furrow as if she's trying to piece together what I'm doing here. And believe me, I'm wondering the same thing about her. But then I remember she told me she was moving to Caroline's neighborhood. That's right. I'd promised to introduce her to my sister so she knew someone in town.

"Oh my gosh, Annie. Yes, I remember," she gushes, coming closer to the white fence that divides us. "How are you?" Although she smiles, she also looks a bit worried as she takes me in. And for good reason. I'm now clutching my side, frantically gasping for air, my face most likely redder than the roses she was just pruning.

"I'm… uh…good," I push out. I need to ask her if she's seen Theo, but I can't seem to find enough air to form the words.

"So you said your sister lives around here, right?" she says. "You'll have to introduce us. The boys are dying to find some playmates in the neighborhood."

I bob my head up and down, trying to be polite. "Yeah…yeah… she's down…on Lovely Street," I attempt to point, but my fingers as so swollen from the blood that's rushed to them on my scorching run, they've hardened into a solid mitt. "She can't wait…to…meet you…too…"

She opens her mouth to say more, but there's no way I can physically keep this conversation going. As great as it is to see Lisa again, I have to get out of here.

"Have you seen Theo?" I blurt. I consider reminding her who Theo is—the tall, goofy guy you mistook for a clown who helped save your son's birthday party—but I realize that would be a waste of precious breath. No one who's ever met Theo has forgotten him.

"Actually, I did!" she says, eyes brightening at the mere thought of him. "He was running so fast! Just zipping along with those long strides, and all that hair blowing back, I told him he looked like—"

"Can you tell me which way he went?" I interrupt, pointing to where two roads converge just past her street.

"Oh yeah," she says, looking a little disappointed that I can't stay and chat longer. "He went that way." She points to the road on the right.

I start running again before she can delay me further. "Thank you, Lisa!" I shout over my shoulder. "I'll be in touch soon!" I feel guilty for my abrupt dismissal, but I'll make it up to her. I'll invite her family down to Caroline's sometime. Jonathan will cook them filet mignon. Theo and I will entertain the kids so she and Caroline can talk. But none of that can happen unless I find Theo first.

"He only passed by a few minutes ago!" Lisa calls after me. "You should be able to catch him!"

"You obviously don't know me very well, Lisa," I grumble to myself as the pain in my side roars back with a vengeance.

Still, the thought that I'm on the right path buoys my spirits. But my spirits alone aren't going to get me to Theo. With the weakness in my legs, the blaze of the sun on my pale head, the burn in my parched throat, I'm not sure how much longer I can keep going. But I have to keep pushing. If this is my penance, then I'll take it. No amount of pain is going to keep me from setting things right with him.

I stumble through the neighborhood, gasping so loudly that people stop working in their yards to stare after me as if they're seriously considering calling an ambulance for help. Normally, my blatant display of weakness would mortify me. But I'm too focused on reaching Theo to care anymore.

I distract myself from my agony by thinking of Theo's crystal green eyes…his beautifully chiseled face. As well as his stupid fashion choices and how much he annoys me. I think of how he makes me want to both slug him and ravage him all at the same time. And how he loves me unconditionally despite all my flaws. And how much I love him despite all his flaws too. Even the one flaw he has no control over. The flaw that will one day take him away from me and break my heart into a million little pieces.

Spurred by a second wind, I sprint around a curve and, in the distance, I glimpse Theo's tall form, running away from me. He's still moving fast, despite having been out here for a while. His strides are smooth and impossibly long, not choppy and desperate like mine. I have a feeling that if by some great miracle I caught up to him, he wouldn't even be breathing hard. Goodness, that boy is amazing. In so many ways.

Realizing the futility in chasing after him, I take a quick turn to my left, hoping to cut him off on his way back around. If he ever comes back around. He may keep going straight…or take a road to the right…there are countless ways he could turn. For some reason, those countless choices available to him materialize in my head as an image: beams of light branching off into the darkness, forming fractals upon fractals of possibilities, like a diamond stretched out before him. No, not only before him. But before me too.

A chill passes over my heated skin at the image of the sparkling geometrical patterns—the patterns which Theo described to me from his NDE but which I've never seen with such clarity myself before. It's probably only oxygen deprivation that has me seeing sparkly stars and beams of light like this. This is what happens right before you pass out from heatstroke, right? But what if this vision is my own memory? What if it's tangible evidence that what Theo told me is true? That I really was there beside him the night my mom died?

Not being able to think straight in my exhausted state, I let the idea go. For now. And instead concentrate on how the hell I'm going to get Theo to make the turn that will lead him back to me.

Turn left, Theo. Left. Left. Left, I chant in time to my feet slapping the road. Then, I imagine an invisible string connecting my heart to his, and I sink my energy down into that enchanted, beating string and tug as hard as I can.

CHAPTER TWENTY-SIX

A FEW MINUTES later I round a corner to find a long stretch of street in front of me. And like a wavering mirage, I can just make out Theo's bobbing head rising over the slope in the distance, running toward me. I nearly collapse from relief at the sight. Although I know finding him is only the first step. Our entire future (or lack thereof) hinges on what I do next.

I can tell the exact moment Theo sees me because he stops dead in his tracks, his arms swinging wildly out to his sides, still caught in the momentum of his run.

I stop too. Not only because I'm on the verge of collapse, but because my heart is in my throat now that our confrontation is imminent. As he walks toward me, I pick up my ragged jog. I feel a crossroads looming right here in the middle of this straight street. I still have no idea what I'm going to say. All I can do is trust that the right words will come when I need them.

He's still far away, walking slowly as if he needs time to gather himself before meeting me. I'm heartened to see he's wearing running shorts and a tank top instead of the garish camp ensemble he'd had on earlier. That means that, unlike me, he was level-headed enough to change his clothes before he started running. So maybe he wasn't as blindly furious with me as I thought when he left the house.

As I get closer and make out his expression, he's clearly shocked to see me out here so far away from Caroline's house. That shock makes me sad. It's like he can't believe I'd make such an effort for him. Like he doesn't believe he deserves it. I swear if I'm lucky enough to convince him to stay, I'm going to devote every minute we have left together finding ways to show him how much he deserves every single good thing in the world.

I try to look strong, jogging up with what I hope is my best running form to where he's stopped in the road. He looks me up and down, face clouded with equal parts disbelief and concern as I come to an abrupt halt in front of him. Instantly I realize my effort to look cool was a poor choice, because a wave of nausea washes over me with such force I have to double over and brace my hands on my knees to get my lurching stomach under control.

"Annie, what are you doing here? Are you alright?" he asks, with what I assume is a worried expression. I don't know for sure because, bent over like this, all I can see is the black asphalt swimming around my feet. Oh God, please don't let me throw up right now. The entire point of this grand gesture will be moot if Theo has to stop and hold my hair back while I puke on his feet.

"Yeah…I just…needed to…tell you…" I pant, holding a shaky finger in the air, asking him to wait.

As I struggle to catch my breath, I concentrate on his orange and aqua running shoes, since they're the only things in my line of sight. He shifts on his feet. Takes a step toward me, then hesitates and steps back. He's definitely worried about me. And nervous too. Amazing how much you can discern about someone just by looking at their feet.

I finally draw myself up to standing, but when I look Theo fully in the face, I suddenly feel faint again. He's not wearing his glasses, and his eyes are so impossibly green illuminated by the sunlight slanting down on them. The corner of his mouth lifts ever so slightly in amusement as he gazes back at me, making my stomach flip again. But not in sickness this time…but in what feels like the vibrant health of my whole soul. And it suddenly hits me, as hard as the blacktop hit my shinbones on my run here, I've never been at the righter place at the righter time than standing here with him right now.

"Are you sure you're okay?" he asks, stepping closer to grip my elbow to steady me. I guess I am swaying a bit. But not for the reason he thinks.

"Yes, I'm very okay," I say, grinning wildly at him. I can only imagine what I must look like, all sweaty and red-faced and woefully out of breath. But none of that matters anymore. "I had to find you. I had to tell you…I couldn't let you go one more minute without knowing the truth…" I still feel light-headed, but it's important I get this out. "You're worth it, Theo! You'll always be worth everything and more to me!"

I don't realize how loudly I've shouted until a woman working in her flower bed stops and looks up. I turn to see a man watering his lawn give us a once-over. Two ladies striding down the sidewalk stop and take swigs of their water bottles, clearly curious about the drama unfolding in the middle of the street.

Theo doesn't seem to notice our audience. He stares down at me, mouth hanging open as if he can't believe what he's just heard.

I barrel madly on, trying not to think, but instead *feel* for my next words. "And I'm so sorry for what I said back there at Caroline's about not wanting to love you. None of that was true. I was just scared and angry and surprised and…I was lashing out. And you got caught in my crosshairs…and you need to know that I didn't mean it…"

He shakes his head hard, as if he doesn't want to let himself believe what I'm saying.

"Annie, you don't have to lie to make me feel better," he says almost bitterly. "All you did was tell the truth back there. I'm the one who won't listen. I'm the one who needs to wake up and face the fact that you don't want me the same way I want you."

"But I do want you! You don't know how much! Please, just listen to me. You need to know the truth. You need to know everything I've held back for way too long!"

Again, I have to stop and catch my breath. As I do I try not to notice how even more people are gathering to gawk at us; some of them whispering behind their hands like they're taking bets on how this soap opera might turn out.

Ignoring them, I go on. "I don't want us to split up. I don't want to say goodbye to you. Even though I know I'll have to one day, whether I like it or not," I blabber, not sure I'm even making any sense. "And I know I need help figuring out how to process all my mixed-up emotions. And I know you need help figuring some things out about yourself too."

He dips his chin in agreement, but stays quiet, letting me go on.

"But I want us to work on all of that figuring out *together*. I don't want to waste any more of the time we have left being apart. I can do this…I know I can. It's going to be hard. And it's going to hurt like hell when you're gone. I mean, you already know that…you saw firsthand in your bathroom the other night how terrified I am of losing you."

When a flicker of pain passes over his face, I wonder if I shouldn't have brought my panic attacks up. But screw it. This is about being honest. I don't want to keep anything from him ever again.

"But that's just it…that's how much you're worth to me. Because I would endure a million of those panic attacks if it meant I could be with you for even a few more minutes of your life. Because as much as I hate to admit it, I know I can survive losing you, Theo. I am strong like you say. And you are too. And any pain we feel will all be worth it, because it will pale in comparison to all the joy we'll feel in the time we have left together. No matter how long or short that time might be."

Tears well in his eyes, but I push on, wanting him to know it all. "I want to be with you across time and distance, lifetimes and eternities, always together, forevermore!"

His mouth drops open. "You heard it that night too," he breathes. "I knew you did."

"Yes, I heard it. But I lied and said I didn't because I was scared of what it might mean for me. But I'm not scared anymore, Theo."

I pause, rethinking my words. "Actually, I am still scared. But that's okay. It's normal. It's not something I have to fix. I can learn how to manage it. Because, just like you said before, I'm not broken. And neither are you."

"Oh, Annie," he reaches for me, but I take a step away from him because I haven't said the most important part yet.

"Wait. Let me say this. You and I have some kind of bond that I don't entirely understand. But you know what? I don't need to understand it. I can let whatever happens next be a mystery. Because I love you, Theo." I harken back to the words he'd told me in the middle of my sister's backyard. "More than anyone I've ever loved before. More than anyone I'll ever love again!"

I heave out a heavy breath, feeling so light and unburdened, I wouldn't be surprised to look down and find that I am literally levitating off the ground.

It feels like the world (and our impromptu audience of nosy onlookers) holds its breath waiting for Theo's response. Waving a hand at the surrounding scene, he says, "Why would you say such a thing right now?" His mouth quirks mischievously. "I thought you'd pick somewhere *way* more special than this to say those words."

I honk a loud laugh. He's repeating my own response from that day in Caroline's yard back to me. Yeah. I deserve that.

"What's wrong with right now?" I take a step closer, placing a hand on his chest right over his heart, repeating his words from that day back to him too. "We're here. Together. Now. What could be more special than this?"

He grabs my hips and pulls me roughly to him. Pressed against him with the electricity coursing between us and him smiling so lovingly down upon me, I'm not sure I've ever felt so happy in my entire life. Talk about worth it. Him. Me. *Us.* It doesn't get any better than this.

He gently brushes a strand of sweaty hair off my cheek, searing me with the force of his gaze. "I love you too, Annie. Always and forevermore." He dips his head as I spring up on my tiptoes and our lips crash together with the force of two people who have finally let go and in doing so, gotten everything they ever wanted.

Applause breaks out around us, and we pull apart, shocked to find a smattering of smiling faces cheering us on from the lawns and sidewalks nearby.

"We love a happy ending!" one of the women shouts.

"Good luck to you, Lovebirds!" another one whoops.

"Yeah, because Lord knows you're going to need it," grumbles the man with the hose. A chorus of outraged ladies scold him loudly.

Theo and I burst out laughing, surprised by the commotion we've caused. We glance at each other, then I lift our clasped hands in triumph.

"I love him!" I shout, making the cheers swell again.

"And I love her too!" Theo pulls my hand down and kisses it with a grand flourish, and the ladies all sigh in unison.

Then—because neither of us can think of an encore for that—we wave goodbye and start winding our way back to Caroline's. (Thank God, at a leisurely pace this time.)

We grin goofily at each other as we stroll down the sidewalk together, Theo's arm slung over my shoulders and my arm looped around his middle. We hold on tight, as if we never want to risk losing each other again. My legs feel like they're made of jelly, my entire body still shaking from the relief of what just transpired between us. I still don't know what the hell is going to happen after today. The only thing I know for sure is, as long as Theo is alive and I have a chance to be near him, I'm going to take it. And after that…well, I'll have the rest of my life to figure that part out.

"So, what just happened back there?" I tease. "I think I might have blacked out. Did I say something to you about liking you or something?"

"Oh, you didn't just say you liked me." He beams down at me. "You confessed your undying love for me. Did you forget that part?"

"Oh. Now I remember! I was trying to get it through your thick skull that," I whirl in front of him so abruptly he almost bumps into me. "You're worth it!"

He nods slowly, struggling to let my words sink in. His eyes dart back and forth between mine. And this time when he speaks, there's a quiet gravity to his voice. "Annie, this life with me…it might get hard. Are you sure you can handle it?"

"No, of course not." I smile up at him, feeling set free by my honesty. "Are you sure *you* can handle it?"

He huffs a laugh. "No, of course not."

I gently reach up to cup his cheek in my hand. "The only thing I'm sure of is I couldn't live with myself knowing I had a chance to spend time with you now and gave it up because I was too afraid of what would happen someday."

He smirks. "So you did listen to me, huh? When I said Now always trumps Someday?"

I pretend to consider for a while. "Hmmm. I guess I did. But don't get too cocky." I give his shoulder a little shove. "Just because I love you doesn't mean I'm always going to let you be right!"

He holds up his palms in surrender. "I'd expect nothing less from you. Things would be boring if you didn't argue with me multiple times a day."

I sketch a mock bow. "I'm glad you appreciate what gifts I bring to this relationship."

He grins, but in the next instant his expression turns serious. "But I want you to know my offer still stands, Annie. If things get too difficult with me, you know…when I get sick…you can leave whenever you want. No strings attached."

I wince, hating that he still doesn't believe he deserves any commitment from me.

"No. I refuse to take that offer." His eyes go wide at the sternness in my voice. "Because I want all of your strings, Theo. I'll take every string you'll give me and then ask for more. Because they are a part of you. Because you deserved to be loved no matter what lies in your future. Because I don't want to take the easy way out this time. I want to be there for you through thick and thin. For better or worse. In sickness and in health. For as long as I possibly can."

Only when I finish, do I hear the vows my words harken to. "I mean figuratively speaking," I rush on, flustered. "Not like…you know…what it sounded like. Sorry. Forget that part." Goodness, I didn't mean I wanted to get married. Or did I?

"I know what you meant," Theo chimes in. "And I appreciate that. I know a commitment like that is a big deal for you. And I can't tell you how much it means to me. But I never expected you to—"

"And that's where you're wrong. It's time you started expecting it, Buster. Because you're about to get everything you deserve. You're not getting rid of me now."

We laugh together, my chest swelling at the thought of what's ahead for us. I can't believe how eager I am about our future. That, for once, I'm not thinking of what can go wrong, but only of what can go right.

"So, what's next for us?" Theo asks.

I mimic one of his carefree shrugs. "I don't know. Probably a little bit of everything. I'd say we're going to mess things up and figure things out. And cry a lot and laugh even more. And make love and make dinner and do everything and nothing at all. We're going to *live,* Theo. For as long as we can. And we're going to do all that living, together."

A smile as bright as the noonday sun erupts over his face. He grabs my cheeks in his two hands and kisses me, claiming me with his ferocity. Committing to me with the force of his unabashed love. Then he breaks away and reaches down and lifts me off the ground, twirling me around as we both giggle like lovesick fools. (Oh man, if only our audience from earlier could see us now. They would've eaten this cheesy shit up.)

Theo finally sets me back down. "That sounds like the best plan you've ever had, Annie."

"Yes, a plan that's not really a plan at all. Pretty strange, coming from me, right?"

He agrees whole-heartedly as we laugh together. Then we link hands again and slowly, peacefully stroll back home. Both of us quiet now, content to simply let the moment be exactly as it is.

When we're a few blocks away from Caroline's, Theo waves a hand to the maze of streets around us. "I still can't believe you found me out here."

"Well, I had a little help." I point skyward.

He nods, understanding, then points to his chest. "Yeah, I felt a strange tugging right here."

"And did you hear this? *Left, left, left?*"

"Yes! I heard that. It was faint, but I thought it sounded like you."

I remember the other help I got. "And Lisa told me which way you'd gone. So that helped too."

"Yeah! Wasn't that crazy seeing her again? Talk about a small world."

"Yeah, a small but friendly world," I bump him with my shoulder.

"Lisa's so nice," Theo muses. "I felt bad I couldn't slow down to talk to her. But I told her I'd come back and see the kids sometime soon."

"Of course you did."

"And as I ran off, she yelled the funniest thing after me. She said I looked like a cross between Steven Tyler and the Road Runner cartoon!" We both chuckle, and he goes on. "And you know what?"

"Yes, I know what, Theo." I snuggle even closer to his shining light. "You took that as a really huge compliment."

PART TWO

CHAPTER TWENTY-SEVEN

ANNIE

"THAT'S THE LAST of it." I walk into Theo's kitchen flapping an empty shopping bag in the air. "I hope you don't mind I put my underwear in the same drawer as yours. I couldn't find space anywhere else, since *someone* feels the need to hoard every t-shirt he's ever owned since he was fourteen years old."

"Hey!" Theo calls from where he's standing at the stove. "Every one of those t-shirts holds a special place in my heart. Races I've run. Places I've been to. Events I've been a part of. I can't give them away. It would hurt their feelings!"

He ignores my eye roll and goes on. "Besides, they like being worn. It makes them feel useful." He winks at me over his shoulder, as if he's well aware of how strange he is, talking about his clothing as if it has feelings.

I pretend to be annoyed, but I actually find it kind of cute how Theo anthropomorphizes inanimate objects. After spending more time with him these past months, I'm getting used to his odd idiosyncrasies. Like how he talks to his favorite spatula, "Ok, ready buddy? Let's show this egg how we flip." And says goodbye to his apartment when he leaves, "You all be good while I'm gone. No throwing parties without me, you hear?" And rotates his beloved T-shirts so they each get equal wearing time, so no one feels slighted. "How about you, Mister Apple

Festival 5K Fun Run? Want to go on some errands with me today? Yeah, I thought you'd be excited about that."

So, I have a boyfriend who's both super-hot and whimsical all at the same time? I'm sure as hell not going to complain about that.

"My drawers are your drawers," he tells me magnanimously, not turning away from the grilled cheeses he's making us for lunch. "Plus, the idea of my underwear rubbing up against yours all day long is about the sexiest thing I can think of. So, no. I don't mind one bit."

Today is the day we're officially moving in together. But it's mostly ceremonial since for the past four months I've been spending all my spare time up here in Indianapolis with him; slowly transferring my belongings from my place to his, one overnight bag at a time. In fact, I'm already so established in this apartment that today I'd only had to unload a duffel of dirty laundry, my sheets, and a bag of goodies I'd bought from Victoria's Secret to commemorate the special occasion. I chalked up the lacy 3 for $20 underwear I bought as a housewarming gift to us both.

I lean on the counter and watch him work, feeling like I need to pinch myself, I'm so happy. I can't believe I'm standing here in Theo's kitchen (correction: *our* kitchen) not counting the hours until I have to leave and go back to school again.

After I'd confessed my love to him in the middle of the street that day in August, we'd celebrated with filet mignons with Caroline and Jonathan just like we'd planned. (Before my mom's little surprise had caused such a hullabaloo.)

We'd even called Aunt Lydia, who seemed just as shocked as us that the whole Treasure Hunt was a ruse to bring Theo and me together. ("I figured Grace had hidden the treasure in the house somewhere…I didn't know!" she'd insisted.) Then via speakerphone we'd all raised a toast to my mom, thanking her for putting together the hunt that had ultimately brought all of us so much closer together over the past months.

But once the party was over, Theo and I had to face a harsh reality:

we would no longer be seeing each other every day. I still had to finish my last semester at Indiana University, and he had to go back to school in Indianapolis, a little over an hour away. Living apart had been hard. Especially with Theo's limited time weighing so heavily on our minds. But my frequent visits, and our busy schedules made the time go fast. And in the end, it hadn't been as difficult as we thought it would be.

Now it's December, and with my diploma in the mail, I'll be starting my position as a Youth Outdoor Program Specialist with the Indianapolis Parks and Recreation Department at the beginning of the year. (A job Franco swears his brother would've hired me for based on my impressive resume, even if he hadn't put in a good word for me.)

So here I am. All grown up. Starting both my new professional job and my new life with Theo. I can't believe I can finally say it out loud: Theo and I live together. God, I love how that sounds. So much so that I may have mentioned it to the cashier at the grocery store as we checked out this morning.

And worked it into the conversation with the guy filling up his car next to us at the gas station.

And made sure the woman from the hospital who called to see if Theo could pick up an extra shift knew exactly who I was. ("Oh, hi! I'm Annie, Theo's girlfriend. We live together now, so you'll probably be talking to me a lot") I'm excited. And proud. And well aware of how lucky I am. What's wrong with wanting to shout that to the world?

∞

One of the best perks of being Theo's new roommate is that I get to stand here and gawk at him like this whenever I want. Today he's wearing silky black sweatpants that show off his perfect backside and muscled thighs with one of his damn worn out t-shirts.

His hair is wavier since he got it trimmed last month. He'd felt bad about reneging on his promise to his younger self when he finally cut it. But I'd told him it was okay since teenage Theo probably never expected his hair to keep on growing…and growing…and growing.

Plus, he didn't cut off much. His signature streaked tendrils are still shaggy. They just hang a bit above his shoulders now instead of below them. Which somehow makes him even sexier than before.

Theo flips our sandwiches onto plates, throws some potato chips on the side, and hands me one with an enthusiastic "Bon Appetite!"

I inspect mine closer. "Oh, bacon…looks yummy."

"With pesto mayonnaise too. But no tomato on yours because it 'makes it too slimy'," he air quotes my familiar complaint with his one free hand. "See? I'm learning your tastes."

I follow him to a tiny table Caroline situated between the kitchen and living room so we'd have somewhere other than the kitchen island to eat. For Theo's twentieth birthday in September, I'd had Caroline decorate the one-bedroom apartment as a surprise, since he'd mentioned multiple times how he wished it had 'more pizzazz'. (Such a Theo thing to say.)

She'd added a lot of color: bright pillows on the couch, a cool tapestry on one wall, and of course a few pieces of her Raku-fired pottery on the bookshelf. As well as an overstuffed chair in the corner, which Theo and I squeeze into sometimes to read or just snuggle and watch the sunset out the sliding glass doors.

The day of his birthday had been so perfect. When he'd come home from class, Caroline and Jonathan and the kids had leapt out from behind the couch and yelled *Surprise!* as he'd blinked around, stunned by our big reveal.

He was so overwhelmed by the gesture he was near tears. He kept repeating, "Wow…I can't believe you guys did this for me," while he took in every new detail. As I stood back and watched him hug my sister and scoop up Emma to look at the pictures of us Caroline had framed for the bookshelf, all I could think of was how close this moment came to not happening. If I hadn't given in and followed my heart, wouldn't we all be living separate lives right now?

After Caroline and her family had left, we'd gone out to celebrate at a bar with Greta and Wen (who are now officially dating) and some of Theo's friends from school. I'd let him guzzle beers while I drank water so I could get him home in one piece. And luckily he was sober enough for me to make love to him, slowly and deliberately bringing him to the pinnacle of pleasure multiple times before he collapsed with the most hilariously satisfied look on his face, muttering "This was the best birthday ever, Annie," as he drifted off to sleep.

The whole night I'd made of point of staying focused on his birthday and how lucky I was to be there to celebrate with him. I hadn't allowed myself to acknowledge what the day meant for our bigger picture: Theo turning twenty meant his time here was dwindling away. And fast.

I won't live past twenty-one. No matter how hard I try to forget those words, their shadow still hangs over every part of our lives.

On the night of his birthday, I'd watched him breathe in and out so rhythmically beside me in bed; the weight of our fate resting like a lead blanket over my chest, making it hard for me to draw a full breath. I tried to think of the fun of the day, the plans we had in the weeks ahead—a trip to his dad's for fall break, a weekend cookout at Charlie's with Caroline and the kids—but the looming eventuality of our end just wouldn't let me sleep.

I finally got up and went out into the living room and curled up on the couch, rubbing the edge of one of the soft blankets Caroline had bought against my cheek to soothe myself. It was probably a good thing I hadn't fallen asleep, I'd reasoned. Although I'd started seeing Rebecca as a therapist a few weeks earlier, we were just starting to peel away the layers of my unprocessed grief. I hadn't yet shared with her about the horrible nightmares I was still having of Theo slipping under the water while I watched from high above, powerless to help him. And with the trigger of his birthday, I knew it was likely the nightmare would return if I'd let myself doze off.

I'd been sitting there for a while, feeling sorry for myself, when I heard footsteps coming down the hall. I looked up to see Theo standing there, bare-chested, his hair messed up, squinting at me in confusion. He looked so beautiful…so real and *alive* in front of me…I suddenly burst into tears.

"What? What's wrong?" he asked, coming to sit beside me, pulling me close.

I pressed my cheek into the bed-warmed skin of the crook of his neck, our connection a balm to my ragged-edged heart. I nestled closer, wishing I could be absorbed into his body, so nothing could ever tear us apart.

"Tell me," he gently prodded.

All I could get out was a strangled, "Time sucks!" before I choked up again.

He blew out a harsh breath. "Yeah. I know." Of course, I didn't have to explain myself to him. I never did. He rocked me back and forth, shushing sweetly into my hair. "I wish it didn't have to be like this," he said, voice hitching on each word. "But I'm sorry, Annie. This is just how it is for us."

He'd pulled away, framing my face in his hands, forcing me to look at him. "But remember. No matter what happens in this life, we'll be together again in the next one. Nothing will ever keep us apart."

I nodded, fighting to make out his face through my blurred vision. "You promise?"

"I promise, Annie."

I wanted to believe him…I really did. But I still questioned how he could be so sure about something neither of us knew for certain.

But his insistence felt so solid, so safe, I gave in and let the tears fall with full force. It's what I was learning with Rebecca. She was teaching me that instead of fighting my feelings, I needed to let them out and allow myself to feel them completely. She said it was okay to let the sadness wash over me like a wave. Because just like a wave, emotions crested and peaked and then floated away. All I needed to do was stay loose and relaxed in their current until they receded enough for me to come up for air again.

So that's what Theo and I did the night he turned twenty years old.

(And what we've done many times since.) We held each other in the dim living room, adorned with all its cheerfully colored accessories, and we let ourselves cry and cry…and then cry some more. We didn't try to look on the bright side. Or talk ourselves out of it. Or distract ourselves from our hurt. We simply felt the impossibility of our situation. And then, when we had emptied ourselves until it felt like there wasn't one drop of moisture left in our bodies, we watched as the wave retreated back into its ocean of emotion, leaving us both alive and well, still sitting together, breathing air on his overstuffed couch.

And with one last shuddering sigh I'd lifted my head to meet Theo's red-rimmed eyes and said, "I'm hungry."

And he'd looked back at me and said, "I could eat."

∞

Now, on our official move-in day, we sit at our tiny table eating our grilled cheeses with the Christmas music we both love lilting cheerfully in the background. Next to the couch sits a fake silver tree my mom used to display in her studio at Christmastime…the one Caroline deemed so tacky and hideous that she couldn't wait for me to get it out of her house.

We'll be splitting our time over the holidays between my family and Theo's family, so the little tree is enough for us now. Next year we're going to get a real one. We've already got it all planned out. We'll go to a farm and cut one down ourselves and tie it on top of Theo's rattletrap car. Then we'll bring it home and decorate it while playing Sleigh Ride (our favorite Christmas song) and drinking hot chocolate laced with peppermint schnapps all night long.

That is, if Theo is still alive for Christmas next year.

The thought makes my stomach turn, my sandwich becoming like glue in my mouth. Depressing thoughts like that still pop into my head all the time. Rebecca says it's normal, so there's no use in fighting them. The best I can do is simply watch them come…then watch them go again.

So that's what I do now. I remind myself to loosen my jaw and let out a long, slow exhale. I look across the table at Theo, always my anchor, and let his nearness soothe me again. He reads his Chemistry textbook while he eats. He's been cramming for a big exam on Monday, so I stay quiet and let him concentrate. I pretend to sort through the mail piled next to me, but really I sneak covert glances at him, feeling my pulse slow as I watch the adorable way his brows furrow as he reads; how he sometimes mumbles words—*Anabolic, Glycolysis, Tertiary Structure*—because he claims hearing it out loud helps him remember the information better.

I smile to myself, enjoying how easily I sink into this quiet moment. We both agree that ever since I committed to being with him, we've felt an overwhelming sense of peace…like we're on the right path, whatever that path may be. Still, our lives feel so ordinary, so blessedly unremarkable that I have no idea how us being together for the next year or so before Theo dies is going to "affect many others." (Words that lately I've begun to hear vividly inside my own head, not just repeated secondhand through Theo's stories.)

Sometimes, just before I drift off to sleep at night, I get a flash of one particular image that feels so important. It's of the two of us facing each other with a blue sky behind us… and I think both of us are wearing white? With maybe flowers in the background? I'm not exactly sure. But when I describe it to Theo, he doesn't know what I'm talking about. It's funny, but it's almost like his memory of our time in the afterlife is fading while mine is becoming stronger. I keep hearing snippets of our conversation with my mom, seeing momentary clips of us standing with her…stepping out into the darkness…her showing us something…something we're excited about. Something that's important, the details of which still seem so fuzzy to me.

I've stopped asking Theo about it because he gets agitated when he tries to bring it back and can't. (I want to say, See? Isn't it annoying when someone remembers something that you don't?) I laugh thinking about how I kind of like this role reversal. Although I'm still not sure

I want the pressure of being in charge of decisions that are beginning to feel a lot like life or death.

Hearing my laugh, Theo looks up and smiles. "What's so funny?"

"Nothing," I say, focusing back on all the good of this day. "You're just cute when you're memorizing things…and chewing…and breathing…and pretty much doing anything at all."

He gives me a suspicious look. Even after all these months, he's not used to me being so affectionate with him. But that's okay. I'll wear him down soon enough. I'll soak him in so much love he'll start expecting it, instead of always being so surprised by my appreciation like he is now.

"Hey, would you do me a favor and quiz me on this?" he asks, pointing at his textbook.

I nod, eager to do anything I can to help him. And as I twirl the book around and question him on facts he'll most likely never get to use, all I can think is, "Yes, Theo. For as long as I'm allowed to, I will do you every favor in the world."

CHAPTER TWENTY-EIGHT

THEO

AS I RISE out of sleep, my first thought is, "I can't feel my left arm."

And my second thought is, "Now I know how Greta feels."

Opening my eyes, I smile up at the bedroom ceiling. I'll have to tell Greta about this when we have brunch with her and Wen later. She'll think it's hilarious…me getting a glimpse into how it feels to be armless like her. For two damn seconds. Oh man, will she ever give me hell.

Looking over, I realize what's causing my problem. Annie lies sprawled on top of my arm, her shoulder pressing against my brachial artery; clearly causing a loss of blood flow to my lower extremity.

Listen to me. I sound like such a nurse. I know some people might think it's strange that I stayed in school considering my situation. But I've learned so much. And helped so many kids. Returning the kindness I received as a child was always my goal when I decided to become a nurse. Truthfully, it was the nurses, not the doctors who saved me during that dark time. And if I can give back just a minuscule portion of the kindness they gave me, then I'll consider my time in school and working at the hospital well spent.

I gingerly wiggle my limp arm out from under Annie, trying my best not to wake her. She sleeps so fitfully—sometimes calling out my name in the middle of the night like she's terrified—I hate to disturb her rare peace.

She finally told me more about her recurring nightmare. In it, she's watching me drown, but she can't find a way to save me. God, I can only imagine how awful it must be for her, feeling so helpless like that. Every time I hear her cry out, I curse myself for what I'm putting her through. Though she swears she wants to be with me, no matter what. I've been working on my guilt issues with my therapist and making good headway. But it's still hard to see Annie struggle without feeling like I'm to blame.

Lately I've been even more worried about her. I keep catching her staring at me with her brows all scrunched up like she's trying to sort out some really hard problem. The other day when I asked what was bothering her, she said, "It's just…I feel like there's some way we can change things. That there's something we can do…some decision we can make that will alter our fate and you won't have to die young. Do you ever feel that way too?"

I'd hated how disappointed she'd looked when I said that I didn't. It's odd how lately she's been talking more about our time together in my NDE…mentioning details even I don't remember. Honestly, I've been having trouble remembering many details of that time at all. Which is strange because it all used to be so vivid to me. But now when I try to draw it back, it feels like I'm slogging through a headful of sludge. I don't know what's wrong with me. I don't like feeling so lost…so rudderless. But I guess I'm going to have to take my own advice and trust that the friendly Universe will take care of us. Even if I don't know exactly how yet.

I scoot up on my pillow and shake my arm, trying to get the feeling back. As pins and needles prick along my skin, I smile down at Annie, curved against me in the tousled sheets. She's so beautiful this way… her blonde hair strung across her face and mouth hanging open as she softly breathes in and out.

It's springtime now and we've been living together for four months.

But I swear, every day I wake up next to her I feel like I have to pinch myself, I'm so happy. It's times like these I wish I'd driven a harder bargain with my Angels. Why did I give in so easily to their offer of a few measly years? I should have fought for more time.

I guess I'd accepted their deal so readily because I didn't have all the information I have now. Back then, I couldn't imagine any place could be better than the pure bliss of the afterlife. But when I made that decision, I hadn't met Annie yet. I hadn't known a love like this could exist here in the physical realm. And now that I do know that love…well, I'm not sure even heaven can get better than this.

I stare up at the ceiling, pondering my poor bargaining skills for a while. Until I get the sensation that I'm being watched. Glancing down, I see Annie's wide blue eyes blinking up at me.

"Awfully serious this morning," she says, voice husky with sleep. "What world problem are you currently solving today, Mr. Brilliant?"

I smile. She's always calling me sweet names like that. Mr. Sexy. Mr. Amazing. Mr. Perfect. (And still sometimes Buster when I annoy her.) And I have to say, her flattery is starting to sink in.

I reach down and brush her hair away from her face, stalling for time. We've made a promise to always be honest with each other. But this moment is so perfect I don't want to ruin it by bringing up a subject that's futile to debate. So instead, I recount my story about feeling like I didn't have an arm when I woke up and how Greta is going to think my whining is hilarious.

"That's all I was thinking of," I fib. She gives me a suspicious look, like she knows there's something I'm not telling her, but she doesn't press me for more. It's another thing we've learned over these past months: to give each other space when we need it. She's much better at it than I am. Because when I see Annie in pain, all I can think is, "How can I make it stop?"

"Actually, I've been thinking about something myself," she says.

"Really?" I make a face. "How long have you been awake?"

"Longer than you realized. I've been creeping on you for a while now."

I shrug, not surprised by her claim. Annie says I tend to space out every once in a while. But luckily, she thinks it's cute. Unless we're talking about something serious. And then she tells me I'm being *avoidant.* Yeah. We've both spent a lot of time in therapy lately.

"So what have you been thinking about?" I wag my eyebrows provocatively as she pushes up to sit cross-legged beside me. Usually when we have a lazy morning like this, we end up making love for a while before we get up. So I assume her comment is the start of our foreplay. But when I study her expression closer, I'm surprised to see she almost looks nervous.

"You know what? I don't think there's any right way to say this," she says ominously, biting her bottom lip. My stomach drops looking at her. Why would she ever be nervous around me?

"So I'm just going to dive right in." With that, she heaves herself on top of me, legs straddling both my sides.

"Ooof," I grunt. She's landed right on my stomach.

"Sorry…sorry." She scoots down and positions herself against my hips. She's smiling now and, goodness, it's hard to concentrate with her on top of me like this. She's wearing one of my old t-shirts (which she complains endlessly about, but seems to wear more than I do) and her cheeks are flushed pink either from sleep or nerves, I'm not sure which. It's all I can do not to grab her hips and grind my growing hardness into the middle of her splayed thighs. But I can tell she's trying to be serious. And that whatever she has to say is important.

No, this definitely is not about sex.

"Ok. Here goes." She takes a deep breath, steeling herself, then blurts out, "I want to have your baby."

It takes me a long time to make sense of her words.

"What?!" I explode after a few incredulous beats. Surely I haven't heard her right?

"Now listen. Just hear me out," she rushes on. "Wouldn't it be wonderful? Haven't you always wanted to have a baby? You would be such a good father. And I would be such a good mother. And we would both be such good parents together. We both love kids so much. Right? Right?" She doesn't wait for me to answer. "And you've said it before…how you've always dreamed of having a child of your own. Remember? You said that. I heard you say that. More than once."

I sputter underneath her, stunned by this idea that seems to have come out of nowhere. "I…I…of course I've said that…but…but…" I can't even form a coherent sentence, I'm so stupefied by her offer.

"Think about it. Our baby would be a part of you and a part of me. Wouldn't that be amazing? We love each other so much, Theo," she pleads, pressing her hands into my bare chest. "Just think about how much we would love our baby!"

A hint of desperation tinges her voice now, her eyes almost wild as she begs. Then it hits me… the real reason she wants this.

"Annie," I reach up and gently stroke a hand down her arm. "But I could never do that to you. I wouldn't be around long enough to help you raise the baby. And that wouldn't be fair to you."

"Oh, don't worry about me!" She waves a hand through the air, dismissing me. "I can do it. And I want this. So, so much! Please. Just listen to me."

I open my mouth to argue, but she cuts me off. "You always say you don't want to make decisions based on what you know about your future. That you want to behave normally…the same way you would if you didn't know you were going to die."

"Yeah…but…"

"So the only reason you're saying no is because you know your future already. I know how you feel about me, Theo. And I know how much you want to be a father. In a normal world, you would want this as much as I do!"

"Of course I would. But in a normal world, would we really be talking about having a baby when we're twenty and twenty-two years old? I don't think so! So what we know of our future affects your idea too."

She considers this, frowning. "Well, maybe that's true," she admits. "But a lot of people have babies when they're young. You know. If they're really religious. Or have an accident."

Ignoring my huff of exasperation, she barrels on. "Of course, you and I can't have a simple accident. Because we actually have to make an appointment at the bank and schedule a withdrawal and then do whatever we have to do to get your healthy swimmers up in there." She gestures to her crotch. "We have to follow all the procedures and processes…you know, all the romantic stuff like that."

She gives me a wink, and I can tell she's doing everything she can to loosen me up to the idea.

"How long have you been thinking about this?" How could I have missed something that's obviously been weighing on her mind for a while now?

She tips her head back and forth. "I don't know. I guess since Christmas. Seeing you with your nieces. And with Jack and Emma. It just got me thinking. And once I started imagining it, I haven't been able to stop."

"Ahhh," I think back to Christmas morning at Nate's house. I'd been playing with my niece, Mandy and the new Barbie Dream House Santa had brought her when I'd looked up to find my mom and Annie linked arm in arm, staring at me with the same expression: 75% love laced with 25% sadness.

But even though I understand where Annie's coming from, she obviously hasn't thought this all the way through.

"But having a child is such an enormous responsibility, Annie. How could I put that all on you alone? Along with everything else I'm asking of you?"

"But I wouldn't be alone," she pushes on, even more determined now. "I'd have Caroline and Jonathan and your mom and all your family. And you're loaded! So the baby and I would never have to worry about money. You've got plenty of cash to take care of us for the rest of our lives."

I blink up at her. Alright, so maybe she has thought this through. God, I love her determination. I don't know why I worry about her. Nothing in life is ever going to stand in her way.

"Oh, I see why you're doing this now," I tease. "You're trying to get my money. That's your real motivation."

"Yes, that's right," she plays along. "I'm a gold digger. I'm only after your money. So now will you please impregnate me so I can get my greedy hands on your fortune?"

We both break out laughing at that. If Annie were greedy, she certainly wouldn't have pursued a career that barely cracks minimum wage.

She stares down at me, eyebrows raised in hope. Seeing her this way makes me stop and, for the first time, let what she's suggesting sink in. Could we really do this? Is it possible that I might get to experience what it's like to be a father before I go? With that thought, a surge of intense emotion rushes over me, catching me by surprise. I have to turn my head away and press my cheek into the pillow to fight back the tears. Oh, if Annie only knew how much I want to give in. Having a baby with her would be the greatest blessing of my short life. But wouldn't it be selfish of me? And wouldn't it only make things even harder? To eventually have to leave behind two pieces of my heart instead of just one when I die?

I feel Annie lean closer, hair tickling my cheek as she whispers, "Please, just think about it, Theo. You don't know what it would mean to me, to still have a part of you with me when you're gone." Her voice hitches. She takes a moment to gather herself before she speaks again. "And think of your mom…your family. It wouldn't be selfish or irresponsible for you to leave a baby behind for all of us to love and cherish forever. It would be the most generous gift you could give us."

I squeeze my eyes shut, but the tears spill through onto the pillowcase anyway. I can almost imagine it… holding a tiny baby in my arms. A baby so pure…so perfect…so much a part of Annie and me. A blended physical incarnation of this otherworldly, eternal love the two of us share. My God, just the thought of it is almost more than I can bear.

I work to collect myself, and when I'm finally able to open my eyes again and look at her, tears spill down her face too. For some reason we both crack up, laughing at our theatrics, as we have many times before. Laughing seems like a strange reaction, considering the impossible predicament we're in. And yet that joyous release always feels like the closest representation of heaven I've ever felt here on Earth.

She wipes the tears off my cheek and I reach up and do the same to her, both of us smiling big as we devolve into more laughter, lightly slapping each other's cheeks, than smacking each other's faces harder and harder, until I end up pulling her down to me and smothering her in giggling kisses. One thing's for sure. If, for some crazy reason, I ever *did* get to live a long life, I would never, ever, get bored with this beautiful woman by my side.

She sits up, pushing her mussed up hair off her face. "So will you at least think about having a baby with me?"

I dip my chin decisively. "Yes, Annie. I will think about having a baby with you."

Her face lights with hope as, unbeknownst to her, I finish the rest of my sentence inside my head:

"There's just one thing I need to do first."

CHAPTER TWENTY-NINE

A FEW WEEKS later, I get a surprise phone call from Maeve.

"Maeve! How's life treating you?!" I shout after hearing her Irish brogue greet me through the receiver.

We've only talked a few times since camp ended, but whenever we reconnect it's like we're back in the empty dining hall again, drinking tea and solving the great mysteries of life. (All while eating our weight in oatmeal cookies.)

"Well, life was treating me a little rough for a while there," she confesses.

"Uh oh. What happened?" The last time I'd heard from her, she was working at a bakery during the day and taking cooking classes at night.

She tells me how she'd had to drop out of classes for a while because she wasn't making enough money at the bakery to cover both rent and tuition.

Before I can even offer any sympathy, she barrels on. "But you'll never guess where I'm working now. Camp Boundless! Miles just hired me as the full-time cook a few weeks ago. So I'll be taking care of the guests during the off season as well as at summer camp. And it comes with free housing, so I'll be able to save up and get back to school eventually."

"That's amazing!" I say, thinking of how lucky she is to be back at camp. "In fact, I'm kind of jealous. You know how I love that place."

"Of course I do. That's why I wanted to invite you and Theo to come out to visit me this Saturday."

I heartily accept, but only for myself. "Theo usually works on Saturdays, so I don't think he'll be able to make it."

"Oh, don't worry. He'll make it," she says confidently. Then she laughs, almost as if she's in on some kind of private joke.

"Wait? Have you already talked to him?"

"Oh…uh…no. I just meant," she stammers. "If he hears there's a chance to see me and Ewan, I'm sure he'll find a way to make it happen."

I tell her not to get her hopes up, but she rushes on as if she hasn't heard me, giving me a time and place for us to meet her at camp. After we hang up, I worry she's going to be disappointed when I show up alone. Theo's been talking about how busy he's been at the hospital lately. And how they're cracking down on people switching shifts.

But the strange thing is, when I mention Maeve's invitation later, he just shrugs and tells me it's not a problem. He's already taken that day off.

∞

I glance over at Theo, walking down the trail beside me. We're at camp, meeting Maeve at the waterfront because apparently she and Ewan already have a routine where they row around the lake at the same time every afternoon.

"And Ewan doesn't allow any variation in that schedule," Maeve had informed me on the phone. "So if you guys get here early, you're just going to have to wait. When you have your own kid, you'll understand."

I'd laughed, but the mention of having kids made my stomach flip. Even though Theo and I haven't talked about my baby proposition since that day two weeks ago, the idea still lumbers everywhere with us, like a little pink and blue elephant that won't leave the room. Theo hasn't said Yes yet. But he hasn't said No either. He's clearly thinking about it. So I'm still holding out hope he's eventually going to give in to my plan.

"Man, it's good to be back here again," I say, gazing around at the springtime forest. "Especially when it's not ninety degrees out and my clothes aren't plastered to my body like I'm sweating Elmer's glue."

He nods his agreement but doesn't say more. Being at Camp Boundless when there's a refreshing breeze, a lingering nip in the air, isn't as novel for Theo as it is for me. Unlike me (with my crazy weekend schedule) Theo has been back to camp several times since we left last summer. Once for an Alumni work weekend in the fall, and a few more times this spring to see his old buddy, maintenance man Tim.

Apparently, Tim and the other full-time maintenance man, Rick, are restoring an old cabin damaged by fire several years ago. A cabin that just so happens to be the same one Theo stayed in as a kid and still holds a special place in his heart. (Although what *doesn't* hold a special place in Theo's heart? I can't think of much.) So Theo comes out here and helps them fix the cabin up when he can. But only when I'm working. When we both have the same days off, we always like to spend our free time together.

We'd gotten here a little early so we could stop and catch up with Tim and Rick. Or more like, so *I* could catch up with Tim and Rick. As we'd chatted by Tim's garage, Theo mostly just stood there like a statue, staring off into the distance like his mind was a million miles away. Which is so unlike him. Even now, he's still acting strangely. He's walking kind of stiff and robotic, almost like he's nervous for some reason. And ever since we got here, he keeps checking and rechecking the backpack he brought. Like it holds a fortune and not just the sunglasses, water bottle, and tattered paperback of Richard Bach's "Bridge Across Forever" I saw him stuff inside just before we left.

I don't know what the hell is wrong with him. Maybe this baby thing has scrambled his brain or something. Or maybe...just maybe...

it could be something even better than that. Maybe the real reason he's acting so strangely is because he's made his decision. Yes! That could be it! I bet Theo is nervous because he's about to tell me he wants to have a baby with me.

CHAPTER THIRTY

MAEVE IS JUST pulling the little silver rowboat up to the shore when we get to the lake.

Seeing her, I break into a run, waving my hands wildly and shouting to get her attention.

Ewan is already climbing out of the boat when we reach them. He rushes past us as if we're not even there, shucking off his orange life jacket and plopping down on his knees in front of a pile of construction trucks waiting in the sand. His shock of red hair and the freckles smattering his nose are the same. But he looks more grown up than he did last summer; his limbs lankier and his cheeks not so plump anymore.

Maeve rushes toward me with open arms, locking me in a fierce embrace the second we meet. She smells more like the mildewed life jacket she's wearing than her normal cinnamon and sugar scent. But the warmth emanating from her soft curves is as comforting as those nights I sought refuge in her kitchen, desperate for the mere whiff of a mother's love.

As Theo finishes docking the rowboat, Maeve catches me up on her new life at Camp Boundless. "I have to make proper food now and not just the sweets I love," she says, hooking a strand of black hair behind her ear. "But I enjoy taking care of the guests. And we get to live here at camp, which you can tell," she gestures to Ewan, now smashing two dump trucks together on the beach, "is the perfect situation for him."

"It sounds like it was meant to be," I say, noticing how happy she looks as she watches Ewan play.

"Yeah, so it might take me longer to get my certificate?" she says. "That's okay. I mean, why do I need to rush when I get to live here?" She nods to the glistening lake, the gently rustling forest around us. "This place is like paradise."

"I totally agree," Theo says, walking up from the water.

Maeve's face lights up as she greets Theo for the first time. Theo sweeps her up in one of his all-encompassing hugs as she gushes a muffled, "Oh, how I've missed you, dearie!" into his shirtsleeve.

Theo rocks her back and forth, not letting her go for a long while. I smile, watching them. I know what it feels like to be hugged by Theo. He holds you really tightly and lingers, somehow physically pouring appreciation from his body into yours through some kind of magical transfiguration. In fact, his hugs are so amazing that if I didn't know I could get one whenever I wanted, I might even be a bit jealous of Maeve right now.

When they finally break apart, Theo heads over to Ewan's construction site and crouches down beside him. "Hey Ewan. Do you remember me? From last summer?"

Ewan glances up for a split second. Then says matter-of-factly, "Yeah. You're the one with the angels all around you." He goes back to driving a little yellow bulldozer through the dirt.

Theo and I lock eyes. His mouth crooks up in a knowing smile. "Yeah, that's me, Buddy," he says to Ewan.

"Oh, never mind him," Maeve says, swiping a hand through the air. "He's always saying stuff like that. Telling me about the people he sees at the dinner table. How my Granddad comes and sits on his bed and tells him stories at night. The other day he was talking to someone during his nap, and when I asked what he was doing, he said he was telling Midnight to quiet down because he was purring too loudly."

She waits a beat and then adds, "Midnight is our cat who died six months ago."

It's funny, but stories like Maeve's don't seem so outlandish to me anymore. Still, I've never thought of actually being able to see my angels. Does that mean I still might be able to see Theo after he's gone? If so, I want Ewan to teach me how to do that.

"That's just how kids are," Maeve says. "My Nana said little ones are closer to the other side. They don't have as many veils as we have yet. That's why they can see all they do. It's pretty cool. Most of the time. Other times, it can get a little creepy, you know…when he's looking over your shoulder like there's someone lurking behind you."

"I can imagine." I narrow my eyes at the space around Theo, trying to see his angels too. But my veils must still be too thick because all I see is the lake behind him.

Ewan wails that he's thirsty, and Maeve trots back to the boat to retrieve his water cup. Theo and Ewan are *vrooming* little cars around in the sand when Ewan says seriously, "My angels tell me not to be scared when it happens." He glances up at Theo. "Because you'll be there to help me."

Everything inside me goes cold. Ewan's words sound so ominous. Like a portent of something foreboding to come.

When I look at Theo, he seems just as surprised as I am.

"Yes, of course I'll be there to help you, Buddy," Theo says gently. "You never have to be afraid if I'm around."

Ewan doesn't acknowledge him, just keeps plowing his cars up and down the mounds of damp sand.

I'm barely breathing now. What did he mean by 'when it happens'? When *what* happens? When he *dies*? I'm just about to question Ewan further when Maeve returns.

Theo and I must still look a little flustered because she looks back and forth between us, scrunching up her brow. "What's wrong? What did he say now?"

"Nothing, nothing." Theo waves her off as I force a smile. Theo stands and comes over to me, lacing a hand around my waist and snugging me up against him as if he knows I need the support.

Maeve smiles, taking us in. "Look at you two. I'm so glad you stayed together. You make such a beautiful couple."

"We do, don't we?" I make exaggerated googly-eyes at Theo, and they both laugh.

Smiling big, Maeve adds, "And you two would make beautiful babies too."

I tense at her comment. I doubt she knows what a sensitive topic she's hit upon.

Theo scoffs loudly. "Well, I don't know about *that*!"

Hearing the dismissive tone in his voice, my hopes from earlier plummet right into the sand. Maybe I jumped to the wrong conclusion about Theo's odd mood. Maybe having a baby with me is the furthest thing from his mind. In fact, what if he's acting strangely because he's about to break it to me that he *doesn't* want to have a baby with me? Why didn't I consider that?

As I fight to cover my disappointment, I vaguely sense Theo take a step behind me. Maeve's eyes dart up to look at him over the top of my head. She startles. "Oh, I almost forgot," she blurts, her round cheeks going pink. I whirl around to see what Theo's done to make her so discombobulated. But he's just staring straight ahead with a blank look on his face.

"I uh…I uh," Maeve goes on, "I saw an egret's nest on the other side of the lake when Ewan and I were rowing around. Can you believe that, Annie? An egret!"

My brain is so muddled up that it takes a second to decipher what she's just said. But when I do, my spirits lift just a bit. "An egret's nest? Really? Like with eggs and everything?"

My goodness, I've seen plenty of blue herons around the lakes of Indiana, but Great Egrets are much more elusive. And to see the nest of an egret—which are usually so camouflaged in undergrowth or high in the branches of a tree they're hard to spot—man, that would be an even greater rarity. The conservation guy at work would go nuts if what Maeve is saying is true.

"Can we go check it out?" I ask Theo.

He shrugs as if he couldn't care less. "I guess. If you want. Doesn't matter to me."

I make a face at him. Why is he acting so weird?

"Are you alright?" I ask.

"I'm fine."

"He looks fine to me," Maeve chimes in. "Totally and completely *fine*."

"See, I'm fine," Theo repeats. "Besides, we should get going if we want to see this eagle." He takes off toward the boat.

"Egret!" I call after him, but he doesn't seem to be listening.

The poor guy must really be torn up about having to disappoint me. He didn't even say goodbye to Maeve and Ewan before dashing off. If I were a nicer person, I'd let him off the hook. Tell him I've changed my mind and I don't want to get pregnant anymore. But that would be lying. And when we committed to being together, we promised to always be honest with each other, no matter how hard the truth might be to hear.

I apologize to Maeve as she collects Ewan's cars to leave, telling her we'll drop by the kitchen later to say a proper goodbye. I wait until they disappear up the trail to join Theo at the boat.

"What's wrong with you?" I hiss at him. Maybe he'll just tell me I can't have his baby now and get it over with. Then I can drown my sorrows on this wild-egret chase and forget I ever hoped for having a piece of him to cherish after he's gone.

"Nothing." He throws his backpack inside, making a point of not meeting my eyes.

Then it dawns on me what else could be bothering him.

I catch Theo's hand, give it a little tug to make him stop and look at me. He turns so we're facing each other.

"Are you upset about what Ewan said about his angels telling him not to be afraid… that you'd be there 'when it happens'?" I air quote the little boy's words.

He scrunches up his face, like he'd forgotten all about it. "No."

"Really? It seemed like a strange thing to say to me."

Theo waves me off. "I'm sure it doesn't mean anything. He's probably talking about a time when he has to come to the children's hospital and he sees me there. That's all."

"Yeah, but what if he's talking about when you're an angel too?" I'm surprised Theo hasn't considered this. "What if he's saying you're going to be there when he *dies*?" I lower my voice even though Maeve is long gone. "Could it mean that Ewan is going to die soon?"

The instant I finish my sentence, my stomach burns. I can't fathom something happening to that innocent little boy who was just playing so happily with his cars. It almost feels like tempting fate for me to say those words out loud.

Theo blows out a heavy breath. "No, I'm sure that's not what it means. Besides, even if he is talking about when he dies, time isn't the same in the other realm as it is here. His angels could be speaking of a time many, many years from now. Telling him I'm going to be there as a familiar face from his childhood to greet him when he comes home."

I must look unconvinced because Theo goes on. "I told you I saw all kinds of people I hadn't seen since I was a little boy when I died. In fact, I saw some people who I'd never met at all, but who still somehow seemed really familiar and connected to me. Just because Ewan's been shown something…whether it's some run-of-the-mill accident that sends him to the hospital or the moment he finally dies… either way, it doesn't mean it's going to happen anytime soon."

I nod, letting his words soak in. They make sense. I can't fully grasp how things work in the afterlife, having never been there myself like Theo has, so I guess he knows what he's talking about.

Theo touches my arm. "You good?"

"Yeah, I'm good," I say. But as I climb into the boat, I wonder if I've just unwittingly lied to him.

Because as Theo launches us out into the lake, I can't shake the nagging sensation there's something in Ewan's comment that's more important than Theo realizes. Ewan's words have triggered a memory (or is it a premonition?) that now bobs right along the edge of my mind…floating just out of reach. But hell if I know what I'm supposed to remember. Is it a decision? A question? A choice? I'm not quite sure. All I know is, it feels like there's a clue hidden inside the little boy's cryptic words. A clue that just might change all of our lives.

CHAPTER THIRTY-ONE

ALTHOUGH MY THOUGHTS had been racing when I got into the boat, it's impossible for me to stay agitated now that I'm being rowed across a shimmering lake on a perfect spring day by the sweetest, most beautiful man I've ever met.

Theo smiles at me as he languidly strokes us further and further from shore. Thanks to him, I don't miss a second of the surrounding splendor: The water hitting the sides of the metal boat, tolling a hollow knell. The scent of the blooming honeysuckle wafting through the air. The caw of a gaggle of red-winged blackbirds serenading us from the cloudless blue sky. Not one detail slips by me unnoticed.

He rows us along the edge of the cove, where it feels like a lifetime ago I fought against letting him hold me in the water. It was the place he finally talked me into giving in to him, if only for the briefest of moments. It was then I first learned that letting go wasn't falling, but floating. That I was safe resting with his hands underneath me. That I could always trust him to support me. That he would never let me drift away.

Theo stops rowing, allowing the boat to sway in the gently rippling water. I can tell by the wistful look on his face that he's thinking of that day too. The sun beats pleasantly down on my bare arms, the sweater I had on earlier now abandoned on the floor of the boat.

"I thought I'd bring you back to the place where you first fell in love with me," Theo says with a crooked grin.

I remember the argument we'd had on the rowboat that day. When we gotten into a splash fight over whether or not I liked Theo. Just one of the hundreds of beautiful memories we'd created that summer.

"All I said was you had nice arms, and you blew it all out of proportion." I pretend to be irritated, but I can't quite wrench down the corners of my mouth.

"You acted like it was nothing. But deep down I knew you loved me," he taunts, the same way he did that day.

I roll my eyes, playing along. "Okay, I probably did. I just hadn't realized it yet."

"I had already realized I loved you," he says. "From the very first moment I laid eyes on you. Technically, even before that."

I think of the note he'd written in the moments after his NDE. When he'd described each feature he'd remembered about me from our time together in the afterlife. He'd dreamt about me for so long, yet never lost hope that one day he'd find me. Goodness, I still don't know how any of this is even possible. But luckily, I'm not so hung up on understanding *how* we're connected anymore. Now, all I care about is being grateful that we are.

"Are you glad you finally gave in to me?" he asks, giving the oar a stroke so we don't drift into shore.

I nod. "Giving in to you…questioning everything I once believed was possible…that was the best decision I ever made."

I laugh at how easily I bare my soul to him now. The old me would've rather choked on the pile of dead leaves floating by this boat than ever admit to such tender emotions.

"What was I thinking back then, anyway?" I tease. "Why was I so set on only dating old dudes? When you young bucks have so much more stamina in bed."

He flicks a devilish eyebrow. "I'm glad I stand up to your rigorous testing."

We laugh together, the sound bouncing off the shiny surface of the lake.

"And was I worth all the trouble?" I ask.

He shakes his head. "You were never any trouble."

"What? With all my fibbing and lying and denying how I really felt? I kind of made things difficult for you."

"We both withheld information from each other last summer. So I'd say we're even. Besides, we're always going to have our issues. That's a normal part of being a couple." He leans toward me, lowering his voice conspiratorially. "And it's also what makes being together such an adventure."

I smile thinking of how aptly he's described our partnership. Being with Theo has always felt like an adventure, hasn't it? From the discovery of getting to know him. To the pilgrimage of the Treasure Hunt. To getting stuck in the trenches and almost giving up and saying goodbye. To the triumph of moving on as a committed team. We're so good together now, I wish our journey never had to end. If only there were a way for us to find a different path…

All of the sudden, Theo shades his eyes, squinting at something off in the distance. "Hey. Is that the egret's nest over there?" He points over my shoulder.

I turn to look where he's pointing. It's hard to tell if the clusters in the trees are nests because we're kind of far away. But as I focus closer, it eventually becomes clear that the clumps in the branches are squirrel and not egret nests. The whole time I'm investigating, I'm vaguely aware of the boat shifting from side to side, the sound of a zipper opening and then closing back up quickly.

When I turn back around, Theo has moved forward in the boat to sit on the bench right next to mine. He's bent over, shoving his backpack under his feet. And when he straightens, he looks almost guilty, like I've caught him red-handed at something, which is odd.

Before I can ask him what's up, he levels me under a serious stare.

"You know there's nothing you could ever say that would make me stop loving you, right?"

The rare gravity in his voice surprises me. "Of course," I chirp back. "For some reason you're freakin' nuts about me."

"Yes, I am," he agrees, remaining serious. "I just want you to feel like you can always be honest with me. That you don't have to do anything…or say anything just to make me happy."

I make a face. "Where is this coming from?"

He fidgets in his seat, moving his hands from the bench to his lap, then back again like he doesn't quite know where to rest them. Oh God, is he going to bring up the baby thing right now? I was really enjoying myself. I'm not ready for him to dash my hopes quite yet.

"It's nothing," he says. "I just wanted to make sure you knew how I felt. That's all."

His eyes suddenly go big. "Oh, my God! Is that the egret?" he points over my shoulder again. "Right there. Taking off out of the water?"

"Where?!" I whirl around fast, hoping to glimpse the elusive bird before it disappears. Great Egrets are big and easy to spot once they're airborne. So hopefully Theo has really seen one this time, and this isn't a false alarm again. But even though I scan both the edge of the lake and the sky, I can't make out any movement at all. Except for in this boat, which for some reason is now sloshing wildly from side to side.

"Why are you rocking the boat so much?" I turn to Theo. "Are you trying to dump me in the—"

The words die on my lips when I see what's before me: Theo kneeling on one knee, holding up an open velvet box with a glittering ring inside.

I never thought I was one of those kinds of girls, but Lord help me, I gasp out loud, then cover my mouth with both hands before I can even think. I guess it's simply the body's reaction when someone shocks you this way.

"Annie, I know I don't have a lot of time to offer you," Theo's voice shakes as he stares into my eyes with such raw sincerity it's hard to draw a full breath. "But I promise with the time I do have left, I will love you with all my heart…with all my soul…with every fiber of my being until you know without a doubt how beautiful and special and brilliant you are. I promise to make your life better every day… in every way I can. And I promise to love you across time and distance, for lifetimes and eternities. And most of all, I promise that you and I will always be together. Forevermore." His eyes well up as he chokes out his ultimate question. "Annie Peterson…will you marry me?"

He waits, his expression so open, so loving, I'm not sure I could speak even if I had the words. And that's the problem. I don't have the words. Because I have no idea how I'm going to answer his question.

∞

How had I not seen this coming? Of course Theo, raised so traditionally Catholic, would want to get married before having a family. But how could he ask this of me when he knows how I feel about marriage?

A memory flashes into my head, unbidden. Of Mom, Caroline, and me, waiting in the dressing room of the church only minutes before Caroline was supposed to walk down the aisle to marry Jonathan:

Mom clutches Caroline's shoulders. "You don't have to do this, you know," she says with a firm set in her jaw. "You can still get out of it. Marriage is not the answer to all your problems. In fact, it's usually just the start of them."

"Oh God, not this again," Caroline says, sounding exhausted. She catches my eye, but I only shrug, not knowing what to say. Even though Mom loves Jonathan, this isn't the first time she's tried to talk Caroline out of marrying him. And the truth is I kind of agree with my mother's reasoning. Why would anyone want to get married when you could keep your options open in case something better comes along?

"How would you even know about what problems marriage causes, Mom?" Caroline says. "You've never been married!"

"That's right. Because I value my freedom. And you should too," Mom

says haughtily. "Why do you want a man to take over your life and tell you what to do? Women can get along just fine on their own without being trapped with one person for the rest of their lives."

Caroline heaves a heavy sigh. "Mom, have you ever been in love?"

Mom huffs and sputters for a few moments, unable to form a response.

"Yeah," Caroline says with a kind smile. "That's what I thought."

With that, Caroline snatches her bouquet off the table and strides confidently out the door to her waiting groom, leaving Mom and I blinking at each other in confusion.

Theo clears his throat, snapping me back to the lake and him in the boat kneeling before me, looking like he's on the verge of throwing up.

Why is he doing this when I'd told him that story about Caroline's wedding day only a few weeks after we first met? At the time I said I believed what my mom did…that getting married was an archaic tradition created to limit a woman's freedom. I'd been adamant that I never wanted to get married. He knew that. That's why I never expected him to ask this of me.

"Annie…what do you think?"

"What do I think?" I repeat, stalling for time.

My mind races. What do I think? That's a fantastic question. What do *I* think? Not what my mom thinks. Not what I've been told. Not what the former Annie thought before her entire world got turned upside down last summer.

I stare down into the face of the person who has split my heart open and filled me up and kept me safe and given me all of himself, then promised me even more. And suddenly, I understand what made Caroline walk so confidently out of that room on her wedding day.

Because, like her, I know something my mom never did. That real freedom doesn't come from protecting yourself from being hurt. It comes from being strong enough to throw your arms wide open to the world and let yourself love.

And there's no one I love more than Theo. He will always be the one and only option for me.

I take a deep breath and speak from the only place I can. My own vulnerable heart.

"Yes Theo. Yes! Yes!" I clutch his cheeks in my hands and plant a kiss on his quivering lips. "There's nothing I want more in this world than to marry you!"

And I swear as we fall into each other's arms, I hear my Angel Mom squeal with delight.

CHAPTER THIRTY-TWO

THEO

"SO THERE NEVER was a Great Egret?" Annie asks, now sitting beside me in the boat.

"No. I mean, I guess there could've been. Who knows? But Maeve never saw it. It was just a way to get you onto the boat."

"I can't believe she was in on your plan. That's why she called me out of the blue the other day."

"Yeah. And Tim and Rick were in on it too. Everyone's really excited. In fact, they're waiting at the beach to take a picture of us when we get back."

She crinkles her brow. "But what if I'd said No?"

"Oh, we had a signal for that," I say brightly. "If I was openly sobbing when we got to shore, they'd know that no pictures would be needed."

She laughs loudly, tipping her head up to the sky.

After she quiets, she holds her left hand out in front of her, wriggling her fingers so the sun glances off the green stone. "I can't believe you remembered what I liked."

Another notch of nerves releases in my chest, seeing how pleased she is with my choice. "How could I forget? You said you never wanted to get married…but *if,* for some crazy reason, you did happen to get married, you wouldn't want a diamond because diamonds are too cliché." I cock an eyebrow for confirmation, and she nods. "You said you wanted an emerald because green is your favorite color. But," I lift a finger in the air, "it couldn't just be any old ring from a store. You wanted a ring that meant something. A ring that had some kind of history. A story behind it that made it extra, super-duper, special."

She laughs at herself, still not tearing her gaze from the ring. "Yeah, I was awfully specific for someone who never wanted to get married, wasn't I?"

"Oddly so," I agree. "Do you really like it?"

It's silly of me to ask since she'd openly wept when I'd revealed the history of my *Babcia*'s ring. I'd told her of how, when my grandma and grandpa had gotten married in Poland, my *Dziadek* could only afford a tiny little chip of a diamond. Since he'd always hated that he couldn't give the love of his life something more extravagant, the first thing he did when the pierogi company took off was buy *Babcia* this beautiful emerald ring.

"So, did I surprise you?" I'd done a lot of sneaking around these past weeks. I'd hoped she hadn't noticed my odd behavior.

"Uh, yeah!" she says. "I never even considered you'd propose to me. Especially after I told you I never wanted to get married."

"Yeah. It was a pretty big gamble. But I figured, what the hell." I lift one shoulder. "What do I have to lose? The worst you could say was No."

She touches my cheek. "Well, guess what? I learned something today."

"Yeah? What's that?"

"That I never want to say No to you."

I swallow hard, overcome by her tenderness. "Still, I was so nervous," I croak. "I didn't hide it very well, did I?"

"No, you did not." She gestures back to the beach. "On the trail down here, we passed two wooly bear caterpillars and a black squirrel, and you didn't stop and *ooh* and *ahh* over any of them. So I knew something was up." She elbows my side playfully. "Although I don't know why I didn't see it coming. I should've known you'd want to get married before having a baby."

The word *baby* reverberates loudly between us. It's the first time we've spoken the word out loud since Annie proposed the idea of having one a couple of weeks ago. But that doesn't mean I haven't thought about it night and day ever since then. The possibility that I could become a father in the time I had left here? Man, that idea always felt even farther fetched than getting married. But now, all of that has changed.

As the boat rocks gently in the water, a silence settles over us. Annie looks off in the distance, a faint sadness etching her features. Oh shit. She thinks I don't want to have a baby with her.

"Yes!" I shout abruptly.

Her eyes go wide. "Yes?!"

We both know what we're talking about. There's no need for further explanation.

I dip my chin. "You said Yes to me and now I'm saying Yes to you." A knot forms in my throat, but I push my words past it. "But to be clear, I would have said Yes to you no matter what your answer to me had been today."

"Really?"

"Really. I can feel it, Annie. This is meant to be."

It's true. I knew the moment I finally let myself consider the possibility. Annie and I are destined to become parents together.

She reaches up and frames my face in her hands. "I feel it too," she says with fierce determination. "This. Us. *All* of us. This is right. This is what's meant to be."

I only nod because I still can't believe it. Not one, but two of my impossible dreams are coming true today. How did I ever get this lucky?

"We're actually going to do this, Theo?"

"We're actually going to do this, Annie."

We both shake our heads dazedly at each other. I can tell by Annie's face she's feeling the same emotions as me: equal parts thrilled and excited…with a healthy dose of terror sprinkled in for good measure.

A smile erupts on her face. "Well, since it's all decided, get me back to shore…and quick!" She stabs a finger at the beach. "I want to get started right away!"

CHAPTER THIRTY-THREE

ANNIE

CHARLIE STANDS NEXT to me, looking adorable as always in his signature short-sleeved plaid shirt with the whittle-tipped pencil in his pocket, the few grey hairs left on his head just slightly askew.

"Oh, how Sue would've loved this," he says, smiling wistfully at the chaos unfolding around the room.

Having become ground zero for our wedding preparations, Charlie's sprawling studio is abuzz with activity. Caroline flits cheerfully around the space, alternating between a pottery wheel where she's throwing vases for our table arrangements, to a nearby table to instruct Jack, Theo's nieces, and Lisa's boys how to make tiny pinch pots that will hold sprigs of wildflowers at each of our place settings.

In another corner, Franco and his partner Victor, along with Greta and Wen, stain the wooden bottle stoppers Charlie's been carving on his lathe for weeks. Those will serve as the wedding favors for our guests.

At the table closest to us, Theo's mom and his sister-in-law Sophie work on the seating arrangements. While Rebecca—who just so happens to be a talented calligrapher—painstakingly letters each table card.

Rebecca's help almost makes me forgive her for taking Mom's watercolor painting away from me. I'd been shocked when I'd shown up in her waiting room the other day and found it gone. When I'd questioned her, she'd said she'd taken it home so she could appreciate it more. (Which seemed a little selfish to me since that means I won't be able to appreciate it at all.)

Weaving joyfully throughout all the commotion in the room, little terrier Tully schmoozes each group, racking up head pats and treats like he's the new Mayor of our bustling little wedding town.

Looking around at the beautiful mix of people filling the room, it's hard to believe that only a year ago I was feeling so sad and alone as I prepared to start my job at Camp Boundless.

Now all I feel is gratitude that I have this much love and support in my life.

I glance up at the familiar watercolor painting hanging on the wall and smile.

Yeah Mom, you really knew what you were doing, bringing us all together like this.

Throwing an arm over Charlie's shoulder, I give him an affectionate squeeze. Oh, how I appreciate this man who's become like a surrogate grandpa to all of us in the months since his car 'just so happened' to pull up next to Theo's on that stormy back road.

"Not Sue *would've* loved this, Charlie," I correct him, "Sue *is* loving this right this very minute." I motion skyward, glad Theo's not here to correct my old habit of placing my angels up on high.

"Your angels aren't up above anything, Annie," he's always telling me. "They're everywhere. Most of the time, standing right next to you." And of course I can't argue, since Ewan pretty much backed up his claim with the comment he'd made on the beach just before Theo proposed.

"Mom is loving this commotion too. I can feel it," I tell Charlie. "Although she's probably grumbling about how we need to get those brushes into some water before the paint dries and ruins the bristles." I point to where the kids had been painting parking signs earlier.

"Yeah, and Sue's right next to her moaning about how I better get a window open before we all pass out from the varnish fumes in here."

Charlie and I laugh fondly. Although I know where she is now, my Angel Mom doesn't carry those kinds of grievances anymore. I'm starting to feel firsthand what Theo tried to explain so many months ago. My mom is different now; no longer judging and sorting things into columns of rights and wrongs. No, now she's simply loving it all. Even the fact that I'm getting married.

The door to the workshop opens, and my heart leaps seeing Theo walk in, a groggy Emma snuggled in his arms. He's been walking her around the yard, letting her nap on his shoulder so Caroline can stay focused on keeping the troops in line.

Emma whines as Theo joins Charlie and me, burying her head deeper into the crook of Theo's neck, refusing to look at any of us.

"She's so cute," Theo mouths, both of us having learned the hard way not to speak or make eye contact with a grumpy Emma when she first wakes from her nap.

Seeing us standing together, Theo's mom motions us over to her table.

Charlie waves us off, saying he needs to get back to his lathe to make some more bottle stoppers. "Fifty down and thirty-five more to go!" he cries, raising a determined fist in the air. Before we can stop him, he reaches over to give Emma a tickle on the ribs and is met with a screech so blood-curdling the entire room stops and looks up.

"Sorry! She's cranky when she first wakes up," Theo explains, which only makes Emma scream louder.

"My fault," Charlie teases as he heads off. "I'm lucky I didn't lose any fingers like last time!"

When we get to Maria's table, Theo gently covers Emma's ear before his mom begins talking.

"So what do you think?" Maria asks, pointing to the diagram she and Sophie have been working on all morning. "Does this look good to you, Theo? I mean, it's all pretty cut and dried. I made sure your

Aunt Beatrice isn't next to Uncle Dominik." She rolls her eyes. "We don't want the whole 'I was supposed to get *Babcia*'s stew pot' issue rearing its ugly head again." Tipping her head at me, she goes on, "And you said your family doesn't have any issues, right, Annie?"

"Well, we do have our issues," I say. "But we're more the type to let our grievances silently fester instead of actually speaking them out loud. So it shouldn't affect the seating arrangement. Only our blood pressures."

Maria gives a perfunctory laugh and then barrels on. "I feel kind of bad our family has so many more tables than your side does. Are you sure you don't want to invite anyone else?"

"No, I'm fine… It's fine…don't worry about it."

She holds the paper up to Theo. "What do you think?"

Theo barely glances at it. "Like we said. Whatever you guys decide is fine with us."

It's fine with us. Whatever you decide is good. That's been our familiar refrain these past weeks.

It had started right after Theo had proposed, when he'd whisked me off to his mom's estate where both sides of our families were waiting to celebrate with us.

"But what if I'd said No?" I'd repeated my earlier question when I caught sight of the crowd gathered on the lawn. "Wouldn't this have been awkward for you?"

"No, because I didn't tell them what the party was for," he'd explained. "I just said we had some news to share. So if you'd said No, I would've just switched it from an engagement party to a 'We're Having a Baby' party. One way or another, I knew we'd be celebrating something."

His solid logic surprised me. But before we got out of the car, we both agreed to keep our pregnancy plan to ourselves. Better to not overwhelm our families with too much excitement all at once. Which turned out to be a good call because even though the party was fairly small (only Maria, Nate and his family, and Caroline's family) when we announced our engagement the explosion of joy that erupted from the crowd nearly knocked us right off our feet. Man, those Teodorczyks are loud.

The best part of the night was seeing Maria react to the news. She'd known Theo was going to propose because he'd asked her for his *Babcia*'s ring. But she must have been terrified about what my answer would be because she looked absolutely stunned when Theo told everyone I said Yes. She'd rushed over and cinched me up in a big hug, whispering "Thank you. Thank you," over and over into my ear, like she'd never been more grateful to anyone in her life.

Then she'd hushed the crowd and told us it was dreams like this—of Theo one day being healthy enough to get married—that kept her going during those dark times when he was sick. And now, here she was! Getting to be a part of that happy future in real life. She'd lifted her wineglass and bellowed, "Thank you for making my dreams come true!" Hearing herself she'd gestured to Theo and me and deadpanned, "And your dreams come true too, of course. Wouldn't want to forget about those."

We'd all burst out in laughter, cheering as Maria embraced her blindingly vibrant son. A son who had left her once but had chosen to come back to give her the best gift of all: A bonus round at being his mom.

And that was the moment when I realized I was going to have to adjust my plans.

You see, on the way to the house I'd been planning to suggest Theo and I simply go to the local courthouse and get the legal proceeding done as quickly as possible. Since I'd never expected to get married, I'd never dreamed of my wedding day the way that other girls did. All that pomp and circumstance and churchy stuff? It all seemed so embarrassingly mushy to me. And a huge waste of money too. Besides, the only thing I cared about was getting pregnant quickly so we could spend as much time as possible as a family before Theo had to go. Weddings took so much time and planning. I didn't want to waste what little time we had left worrying about something as frivolous as throwing a fancy party.

But after seeing the excitement in Maria's eyes (and in Theo's too) I knew I couldn't rob them of their dreams. So now here we are, saying "It's fine" and "Whatever" to the people who love us the most. These sweet souls who are determined to make this day special for us. In the way they've deemed as special, that is. (Which according to Maria and Caroline is a morning ceremony at Theo's family church with a reception at a venue down the street, a catered six-course lunch, a place setting I'm going to need a tutor to know how to use properly, a live band, and a horse-drawn carriage to take us to the hotel when the long day is over.)

I cringe every time I think about it.

At least Maria and Caroline have honored the only stipulation Theo and I gave them for the event: It had to happen within two months. When we'd visited the insemination clinic, the doctor told us it would take that long for my cycle to become regular after stopping my birth control pills, so we can't start the first procedure until then. So this super speedy wedding isn't technically delaying the start of our family.

Still, there's something about this wedding that seems off to me. Something I can't quite put into words. It's not about the timing. I'm actually relieved to have something to distract me while we wait for our appointment. And I know, deep down, Theo likes the fact we'll be married before we try to have a baby. And it's not the food, or the four-tiered cake, or the place settings. Yeah, those fancy choices don't match the no-frills vibe of Theo and me. But at least I'm able to add the handmade touches currently being churned out inside this room.

No, Theo and I don't really care *how* we get married. We just care that we do. And since all this hoopla seems to make everyone else happy, we figured we might as well let them have their fun. Besides, it's not like all these tiny details are really going to matter much in the end.

So why do I keep feeling like something's not quite right?

Now as Maria chatters on about head tables and dessert tables and gift tables…and *tables, tables, tables*. And Caroline sweeps over to give her opinion. And Sophie pipes up to give her two cents, a dull ache begins to grow in my temple.

In the commotion, Theo loses focus and forgets to keep his hand pressed to Emma's ear. She sits up, her tiny face scrunched up in fury. "Too much talking!" she shouts.

Everyone at the table laughs loudly, which only makes Emma even angrier. Theo wisely whisks her outside for some quiet. And as I watch them leave, Emma still grumbling "too much talking" into Theo's chest, I smile discreetly to myself. Thinking of how I've never agreed more with a child in my life.

∞

After I assure Maria and Sophie that the seating arrangements they've made are absolutely completely perfect…that I wouldn't change a thing, I slip away to the one place I know I can relax. The bottle stopper table with Greta, Wen, Franco, and Victor.

Plopping down on a stool next to Greta, I heave out a loud sigh. "You guys look like you're having fun." I've been hearing the group laughing together all morning. And I have to admit…I'm a little jealous.

Greta takes a deep sniff of her stain-soaked brush, smiling dreamily. "We're having fun because we're all high on the fumes over here."

"Stop that," I swat the brush away. "You'll give yourself brain damage. And I'll never find another bridesmaid on such short notice. You know I don't have many friends."

Everyone laughs, and I smile, glad to finally be in on one of their jokes. I grab a notched piece of wood and a brush and start dabbing on stain.

"There's quite a few people here today," Victor says, nodding at the room.

"Yeah, I can't believe how everyone's pitching in." This is our third

Saturday meeting at Charlie's, and each time we've filled up the place with a rotating group of eager volunteers.

"We're all really starting to feel like a family," Franco observes.

I couldn't agree more. At the end of our work sessions, everybody usually stays and we cook hot dogs and hamburgers on the grill; then hang out on Charlie's lawn playing croquet and frisbee until it gets dark.

"I know I've said it before," I say. "But thank you all for helping."

"We love it!" Victor pipes up. "It's nice having a mission as romantic as this one."

Greta makes a face. "I don't know. It still feels like a sweatshop to me."

I elbow her in the side and pretend to be mad. But the truth is, Greta's been my saving grace these past few weeks. Her jokes are the only thing that's made this entire crazy endeavor bearable.

Thank goodness she and Honey Bear went wedding dress shopping with me. Maria and Caroline (my matron of honor) were way too flattering about how I looked in the gowns. But as my bridesmaids, Greta and Honey Bear had no problem giving me their no-holds-barred opinions each time I flounced out of the dressing room.

Case in point, Honey Bear's reaction to seeing me in a very full-skirted ballgown: "Well hello, Snow White. What have you got hidden under there? Seven dwarves, the witch and Prince Charming too? Mercy, that dress is big!"

Greta, after I came out in a dress covered with bows: "And now she's Little Bo Peep." Addressing the attendant, "Does this one come with a shepherd's crook and a herd of sheep? Seems like it should if you want to stick with the theme."

Honey Bear, when I twirled around in a dress with a million and six buttons up the back: "Oh, hell no! Theo's not going to like that one. It'll take him forever to get her out of that!" Turning to Maria. "And that's all he cares about, you know. I don't care how sweet and innocent you think your boy is. He's still a man. And all men want their women *naked!*"

Thank God Maria had laughed louder than anyone at that. But even though Maria and Caroline had insisted I looked beautiful in every dress, I agreed with Greta and Honey Bear. The wedding dresses were just too much. And definitely not me.

As the day wore on, I began to lose hope of ever finding something I could tolerate. Waiting for the attendant to bring me another dress, my heart ached, wishing my mom could be with me. Even if she hadn't believed in marriage for herself, when she saw how much I loved Theo, she would've supported me. She would've jumped in and dug through the racks and found a dress that felt more appropriate for a girl like me, who spent most of her life in the woods and looked like it. As I stood there shivering in my bra and underwear, I closed my eyes and prayed that maybe she could still find some kind of simpler dress… even from where she was now.

And lo-and-behold, the next dress the harried shopkeeper slung on the hook was…not perfect (nothing in this shop would ever be perfect for a tomboy like me)…but acceptable. Not quite so poofy. The neckline a little too high, but without so many buttons and baubles. Just a little lace. A tight-fitting bodice and soft flare around my legs. I liked it. And even more shocking, Greta and Honey Bear liked it too.

It was done. I had the dress. Thank God, that ordeal was over.

But what I still haven't told anyone is that last week, when I was shopping downtown, I happened upon a thrift store. In its window was the sweetest wedding dress from the 60s. It had a tea-length skirt made of thin layers of gossamer lace, with cap sleeves, and a band of embroidered daisies around the waist.

I knew it was silly to try it on since I already had my wedding dress, but I did it anyway. And I couldn't believe how light and airy the dress felt on my body, especially compared to the heavy formal wedding dress I'd just bought. In fact, when I'd spun around in the dressing room I felt like something out of a fairytale; a woodland nymph that might dance barefoot under a blanket of stars and a sky full of fireflies. It felt so right that I'd impulsively bought it, even though I knew it was too casual to wear at the wedding being planned for me.

Now, the enchanted wisp of a dress hangs in the back of my closet, as my own little secret. I'll probably never get to wear it. But at least I'll be prepared if the stars and fireflies ever happen to come calling.

CHAPTER THIRTY-FOUR

BACK IN CHARLIE'S studio, Franco asks, "So, are all the out-of-town guests going to make it?" He gives me a pointed look as he dabs varnish on a wood stopper.

"Yeah. Aunt Lydia's going to start driving next week." I shake my head, exasperated. "I swear, that woman will wrestle cows to the ground and go head-to-head with a grizzly bear, but ask her to get on a plane and she turns into a blubbering mess."

When I don't say more, Franco presses further. "I wasn't only asking about Lydia."

"I know who you're asking about, you nosey busybody," I tease, bumping my shoulder into his. "Yes. Dad's coming. All because of you."

Ever since the Treasure Hunt landed us in Franco's office, Theo and I have spent a lot of time at his and Victor's house. On a typical visit, the four of us will gorge ourselves on one of Victor's gourmet meals, then slump in our chairs sipping wine and talking into the wee hours of the night.

Our conversation topics range wildly. One night we could be talking about politics and art and philosophy. The next, reminiscing about the time I threw up from eating too many funnel cakes at the fair. I love how my relationship with my surrogate uncles has changed now that I'm all grown up. It's fun to be seen more as their equal, and not just their best friend's little girl.

One night the conversation had somehow turned to my dad. Franco told a few stories of the early days hanging out with my mom and dad, when they were all at the university together. As he spoke, I realized Franco was the only person I knew (other than a heavily biased Caroline, who for some reason still adores Dad) who had witnessed my parent's relationship firsthand.

"I always liked your dad," Franco had mused, idly swirling his red wine. "He was quiet. But really, really funny in his own subtle way. He'd just sit there saying nothing, then pop out this deadpan one-liner that would have us all rolling on the floor."

I'd made a face at him. Yeah, my dad could be a bit amusing sometimes. If you liked dry humor like that. But still…

Franco continued. "Yeah. I always thought he was the perfect balance for Grace's uh…" He grasped for the right word. "Let's just say more boisterous energy."

My stomach burned, hearing him praise the man I still blamed for everything that was wrong with me. My coldness. My difficulty with commitment. My past proclivity for dating older men.

"Yeah. Dad's a nice enough guy," I grumbled. "But he *did* abandon his children. Let's not forget that little tidbit."

"Why do you always say that?" Franco shot back. "He didn't abandon you! He and your mom made a plan. He was supposed to go ahead to New Haven, get an apartment for you guys, and start the job at Yale. Then, your mom was going to follow with you girls a few months later."

"So I've heard," I'd mumbled contemptuously.

Franco must have been drunk because he kept blabbering away, even though he knew the topic was off limits with me.

"Grace was the one who reneged on her promise," he told Theo, ignoring my huffs. "Once Don got out there, she refused to join him. She told him she'd decided she didn't want to move anymore. That she was going to stay here in Indiana. And when he tried to convince her otherwise, she dug in her heels and broke things off between them.

She said she didn't want to see him anymore. Honestly, she broke the poor man's heart."

"Yeah…but still," I'd sputtered, unable to come up with a good defense for my mom. Of course, I'd heard that story before. But wasn't that all it was? A story? I was only four years old when Dad left, so I didn't really remember many details of that period of our lives. Other than my mom spent a lot of time either in her bed or in her studio, and Caroline suddenly decided she was the boss of me in Mom's absence. As I grew up, I'd put a neat title on the incident: "Dad Left Us." Then I'd made a point of never thinking about it again. It was just easier that way.

It wasn't until I became a teenager and openly bad-mouthed Dad after one of our mandated trips out east that Caroline told me the same story Franco had just repeated. But by then Mom was getting sick, and I didn't have the energy (or guts) to question whether or not that alternate version of my parents' relationship was true.

But that night at Franco's dinner table, hearing the details again, (now as an adult who had seen firsthand how messy relationships can be) I finally allowed myself to consider the possibility that my father might not have been solely at fault for what happened when I was a child.

And because of that, when Caroline and Jonathan made their annual New Year's visit to Connecticut to see my Dad, I decided maybe it would be fun if Theo and I tagged along. Much to the thrill of my father. And his wife Maggie. And her seventeen-year-old daughter Elizabeth. (Who spent the entire weekend following Theo around, making puppy dog eyes at him when she thought I wasn't looking. Which was hilarious because Theo didn't even notice her flirting.)

On that trip, Dad and I had time to talk alone. And since I was no longer overcome with grief and raging teen angst, I actually listened to his side of the story. Being around Theo has smudged up all my black and white thinking. And because of that, I could see my parents break up in a new light. Nobody had set out to hurt me. They'd both merely been young. And naïve. And overwhelmed. And completely human. Lord knows I could relate to that.

The entire experience had once again made me question how many stories I'd made up in the past, then blindly believed simply because I was too afraid (or stubborn) to change my mind.

My dad and I still have a long way to go to re-build a relationship that was pretty scanty in the first place. But after some phone calls and a visit from him this spring, I felt close enough to him to ask him to walk me down the aisle. It's only a first step. But hopefully, there will be many more of those steps to come in our future.

Once again, Mom's little Treasure Hunt—which led me to Franco, which led me to Dad—has made such an unexpected impact on my life. Far beyond what any material treasure could have ever brought me.

Now at the table, Franco bumps my shoulder like I did to him earlier. "I'm glad you forgave him."

"Yeah, me too," I admit. "And I'm also glad he forgave me."

Greta and Wen pretend to be engrossed in their painting, but as the silence at the table stretches I catch them exchanging glances. Wen gives Greta a warning look, which she promptly ignores.

"Soooo, Annie," Greta pipes up. "Are you sure you're all good with these wedding arrangements?"

Her tone is enough to relay her implications. "Yeah. Of course. Why wouldn't I be?"

"No, I agree all this stuff is going to be really cool," Greta gestures around the room. "But I was just wondering if the whole…uh…*church* thing felt right to you?"

Wen placidly paints, but I notice him whack his leg against Greta under the table; then wince because he's unwittingly cracked his knee against her plastic prosthetic. It's clear the two of them have definitely discussed this topic before.

I wave the comment away like it's nothing. "It's fine. It means a lot to Maria. So it doesn't bother me." I don't sound very convincing, even to myself. "Besides, Theo and I don't care about the wedding. All we care about is being married."

"Alright, whatever you say. I just wanted to make sure." She sounds even more unconvinced than I do.

As I furiously dab stain into the grooves of the wood, I realize I'm clenching my jaw. I have to force myself to relax.

My tension only makes what I've been trying to deny even more obvious. Greta (in her infinite bluntness) has just hit upon what's been bothering me about this wedding, but what I've been too afraid to say out loud. The church, the priest, the ceremony—some of which, as a non-member (a.k.a. heathen) I won't be able to participate in—doesn't feel right to me; the girl who broke into a church in high school and stole the communion wine so she and her friends could get drunk in a cow pasture before the Homecoming game. Let's face it. I'm not exactly church material.

But there's only a few weeks left before the ceremony. And Maria has worked so hard with her priest to make the arrangements. I can't disappoint her now. Not with all her dreams on the line. Plus, where else would we get married? Especially on such short notice.

"Just so you know," Victor says, blessedly jarring me back to real life. "A few years ago, when friends of mine were getting married, I became ordained as an officiant in the Unity Church. So if you decide to go wild and change your mind at the last minute, I could conduct the ceremony for you."

I bite my lip to keep from scoffing out loud. *Oh, that's awfully convenient, Mom. You wouldn't happen to be behind that little detail coming to light right now, would you?*

A faint giggle floats in my ear. I send her back an internal growl.

"I'm not going to change my mind!" I say too loudly. All four pairs of eyes around the table shoot to mine. Every one of them looks worried. "It's all going to be fine...completely fine," I repeat determinedly. "We're going to stick to the plan and keep things exactly as they are, and everyone is going to be happy, okay?"

The group stiltedly agrees, looking even more worried than before. I give them all a blinding smile, hoping to ease their fears, as well as my own. Because it's getting harder and harder to ignore the question that keeps whispering inside my head:

Everyone else might be happy. But are you?

CHAPTER THIRTY-FIVE

THAT NIGHT I slip into bed next to Theo, who is already propped up on a pillow, engrossed in his book. Usually, I'd pull out my book too, but tonight I curl on my side and simply watch him, the way I tend to a lot lately. For obvious reasons.

He's shirtless, his hair damp from the shower, the smell of soap and coconut shampoo wafting off him. He got new glasses a few months ago—the lens now crystal clear and the frame dark brown—which makes him look like he should be standing at a lectern teaching a bunch of freshmen the hidden themes of Shakespeare's tragedies, not stretched out next to me half-naked.

He gives me a grin then goes back to his book, idly reaching over to grab my top leg and pull it over his waist as if my body is his personal comforter. Sometimes I don't understand how he can be so nonchalant about everything. How he just goes around acting like everything is normal…as if he's completely forgotten *he's about to die!* Of course, I don't think about dying very often either. But that's different. Unlike me, Theo knows for sure he's leaving this life soon. Why isn't he more panicked about that fact?

Overwhelmed with emotion, I prop up on one elbow and begin planting little kisses from the point of his shoulder all the way down his lovely arm, interrupting his reading when I can't stop myself from kissing the thumb gripping his book.

When I peer up at him, he smiles big, then bends and brushes a soft kiss to my lips.

He scrunches his brow. "You okay?"

I open my mouth to say "Of course," but think better of it. "Actually, I've been feeling a bit…weird lately."

"Really?" He slaps his book shut with a loud *thwack*. He sets it aside, giving me his full attention.

I push myself up to sit cross-legged beside him. I hate admitting what I have to say next. "I got scared again when you left for work on Friday."

He nods, letting that sink in. Lately I've started obsessing again over the phrasing of what his Angels told him in his NDE. *You won't live past twenty-one.* Which means he could go anytime before that. Any. Time. So, I've found myself panicking a bit when Theo leaves my sight. I have this elaborate ritual of hugging him six times and giving him only even numbers of kisses, then following him out to the elevator and saying goodbye the exact same way each time: "I love you so, so, much, Theo. And I will see you again soon." As if my superstitions are an armor that will keep him safe until he comes back home again.

I've told Rebecca about my strange behavior and she's teaching me techniques to help with my anxiety. And with the flurry of plans to keep me occupied these past weeks, I'd returned to simply giving him a normal kiss and a hug goodbye when he left the apartment. But last week, out of nowhere, all my fears came raging back. As the wedding draws closer, I keep having this sense of something big looming ahead. Like we're approaching a crossroads where we'll be forced to make a decision. A decision we won't ever be able to take back.

"I wondered if something was bothering you," Theo says. "That sixteenth kiss goodbye on Friday kind of gave you away." He smiles, but I can feel the tension radiating off his body. If I hurt, he hurts too.

"And I cried for a while after you left," I say.

He bites his lip. I can tell he's surprised. Everything's been good between us lately; both of us nearly delirious with happiness at the prospect of getting married. Truthfully, my odd regression has come as a shock to me too.

"Thanks for telling me." He reaches out, strokes my arm. "Do you want to talk about it?"

I nod, drawing in a deep breath as I try to sort out all my snarled-up emotions. It's all so confusing, I'm not sure I can even put it into words. But I know Theo accepts all of me, not just the happy parts. So I talk, hoping maybe he'll be able to help figure me out.

I tell him about how lately I've felt like I've turned into a walking paradox. One day I'm filled with excitement. The next day, only dread. One second, I feel like everything is perfect. The next second, I feel like something's going terribly wrong.

I feel like I'm ever so slowly being split in two. Like my future could go in one direction or the other. Although why I think that, I can't explain. I try to describe the crossroads I feel creeping closer. This pressure I feel building in my chest…this sense we're being tugged toward this really strong vortex…a kind of otherworldly touchpoint in time that's about to snatch us up and spit us out on the other side. And once there, we'll have no other option but to face the fate we've chosen.

As I talk, I hear how nonsensical it all sounds. And when I finally finish, I'm not surprised to find Theo blinking at me like he's overwhelmed by everything he's just heard.

"Wow, that's a lot," he murmurs. One hand twists the sheet pooled around his waist as he thinks. As the silence stretches, I begin to fear the conclusion he's drawing from my confession.

He opens his mouth to speak, but I cut him off. "This isn't about not wanting to marry you, Theo." I dip my head in front of him so he's forced to look at me. "Believe me, I want to be your wife more than anything in the world. You have to believe that."

A relieved breath escapes his mouth. "I know that…really, I do." The fact that he can say that with such assurance is a testament to how much he's grown in this past year too. He used to barely be able to hear me tell him I love him without doubt clouding his eyes.

"It's just…does everything feel right to you? About the wedding?" I ask. If this strange feeling isn't about marrying Theo, then it must be about the wedding itself.

"I mean, I know it's going to be beautiful. Mom and Caroline are making sure of that."

"Uh huh." I think about how to subtly broach the subject I'm really concerned about. "But do you think the timing of the ceremony is right? The date? The time of day?"

When he nods, my heart speeds up a little. But I can't back down now. "And how about the place? Are you sure the church is the right place for us to get married?" There. It's out. I hold my breath, hoping a dawning will burst across his face. Praying he'll suddenly see things the way I do and question whether the church is where we should get married.

But instead, he seems taken aback. "Yes, of course. Why wouldn't it be?"

"No specific reason." I try to keep my voice light. "I'm just floating different ideas here. Trying to figure things out."

He considers for a second. "Sacred Heart holds a lot of special memories for me. It's the church I grew up in. Where I had my First Communion. Where Nate got married. It's where the entire congregation prayed for me when I was in the hospital."

"I know. You've told me that. I know how special it is to you." I'm starting to regret bringing this up.

"And it's so beautiful. Don't you think?" he says brightly. "With all the spires and stained glass. The place is straight out of a fairy tale. People actually come from all over the state to get married there. We're lucky Father John was able to pull some strings and get us in on such short notice."

"I know. I know. We are so lucky. And you're right. It is one of the most beautiful cathedrals I've ever seen." I don't add, *and it's also dark. And cavernous. And made of cold, heartless stone.* It seems counterintuitive that such a huge space could make me feel so claustrophobic, but

I swear, when Maria took me inside the first time my hands started sweating and my pulse sped up and something inside me kept whispering, "This isn't right," over and over again.

The only highlight of that afternoon had been seeing the huge tapestry hanging behind the altar. The fabric was the same color blue I'd seen in the image of Theo and me standing face to face, wearing white, with flowers and a blue background behind us. The flash of a moment in time that feels like it might hold the key to our entire future.

Now in bed, I recall how the blue of the tapestry matched what I'd seen in that flash. And because of that, I begin to doubt myself. Does my uneasiness about getting married in Theo's church really mean something important like I suspect? Or am I only nervous because I feel uncomfortable in all churches, not only Sacred Heart?

"Look, I know you're not religious," Theo says. "And honestly, after what I saw when I died, I don't believe in the notion that there's only one way of doing things either. I know none of these rules and regulations are what love is truly about. But it means a lot to my family. And since you didn't seem to mind one way or another, I didn't think it was a big deal. But *is* it a big deal, Annie?" His eyes bore into mine. "Because if it is, tell me now."

I struggle to answer him, wondering a bit bitterly why I have to explain this to him. Theo and I were once so in sync that we could read each other's minds. So why doesn't he simply know how I feel? Why can't he remember the image like I can? And worst yet, why does he feel so far away from me right now?

Because this is all part of the plan.

The words send a shock wave of recognition coursing through my body. Yes. That's right. This is all part of the plan. But how?

"What? What's wrong?" Theo asks. I startle back to life. Seeing his dazed expression, I have the sense that he's felt the same shock wave too. Maybe he isn't as far away from me as I think.

"Nothing…it's just…" What am I doing? Theo asks so little of me. Why am I making this hard for him? And for Maria, who has so lovingly welcomed me into her family? Why am I making such a big deal about sweaty palms and strange tugs in my chest and whispers that have no logic to back up their claims? This is probably all just cold feet. Everyone has doubts before they get married, right? I'm not going to blow up all our plans on some random hunch that makes no sense.

The tapestry is blue. The tapestry is blue. I chant in my head. *The church is the right place to get married because the tapestry is blue.*

Sensing my turmoil, Theo pulls me into a hug.

"Listen, I know I can't remember as much about the afterlife as I used to." His voice is low and buttery. The emotion in it makes the thread running between our chests twang like a guitar string.

See, Silly? I scold myself. *Our connection is still there. Stop overreacting.*

Theo continues. "But I can still feel the essence of my time there. I know we're being held and guided by a benevolent force that loves us more than we can even fathom. And that no matter what we do, we can't get it wrong. So just relax, Annie. It's going to be alright. Everything's going to be alright. Where and when we get married doesn't matter. All that matters is that we love each other. That's the only thing we need to focus on right now."

I let out a heavy sigh, feeling suddenly exhausted. Of course. What he's saying makes perfect sense.

"You're right, Theo," I say, trying to placate myself as much as him. "You're always right."

I don't say the rest of the words dancing on the tip of my tongue. *"But what if this time, you're not?"*

CHAPTER THIRTY-SIX

"I SWEAR TO God, if you touch my hair one more time I'm going to scream." I slap Caroline's hand away with a bit more force than is necessary, but she doesn't even complain. I guess brides are allowed a bit of obnoxious behavior on their wedding day.

"It's just…I can't figure out where this one piece looks better," she mumbles, gingerly moving one of my blonde curls to the front of my shoulder…then behind my shoulder…then to the front again. She's been adjusting this one lock of hair for almost twenty minutes now. It's become our odd ritual as we wait in a classroom of the church, only minutes away from the start of the ceremony.

My practice run at the hair salon last week had been a disaster. The hairdresser had curled, teased, pinned, and sprayed my long hair into utter oblivion. When she'd finished blasting my overwrought updo with one final coat of Aqua Net (or wood shellac, I'm not sure which) I'd smiled politely, thanked her, then barely made it to my car before bursting into tears.

"I cannot show up at my wedding looking like this!" I'd wailed to Caroline when I got home, pointing at the pile cemented on top of my head that quite literally defied the laws of gravity. "Theo won't even recognize me when I walk down the aisle! I look like a cross between Dolly Parton and a stick of cotton candy!"

"Hey now! Dolly Parton is a beautiful woman!" Caroline argued, then pointed to my chest, adding wryly. "And believe me, no one's going to mistake you for Dolly with tits like those."

Luckily, the next second Caroline had burst out laughing, agreeing the bird-nest explosion on my head was definitely not me. So this morning, I'd mustered up my courage and firmly told the lady at the salon exactly what I wanted: Nothing fancy or big. Just the sides pulled up and anchored with the gold combs I found in my mom's jewelry box; the rest of my hair hanging long and loosely curled to make me look a little bit special.

Now, Caroline steps back, eyes welling as she takes me in. "I'm sorry," she says, waving a hand in front of her face. "It's just you look so beautiful. And I know Mom—"

"I know," I cut in, choking on my own tears.

"She would've—"

"Oh, she definitely would've."

"I can feel her—"

"Yeah, I can feel her too."

"I just wish—"

"Oh, believe me...I wish the same thing too."

We both lock eyes and burst out laughing at our ridiculous half-conversation.

"I'm so glad we could have this little talk," Caroline jokes, grabbing me and pulling me against her chest. I squeeze her back, thankful that I know this kind of love. The kind that apparently doesn't need full sentences to express itself.

When Caroline gets called away by the church lady in charge of the ceremony, Honey Bear swoops in waving a canister of Secret deodorant at me.

"You sure you don't want another hit of this, Lily Flower?" she asks me. "You don't want people saying, 'That bride sure was pretty, but damn did she stink!'"

I roll my eyes, even though I'm glad for Honey Bear's comic relief. "Listen, I'm happy you're taking your role as bridesmaid seriously,

Honey. But you've already sprayed me from head to toe about twenty times now, so I think I'm good. Besides," I point to my armpit, already sheathed in a long lace sleeve. "I don't think there's any way we can get that shit in there, even if we wanted to."

Honey Bear gives a shrug, shoots a couple of blasts at her own pits "For good measure," then whirls and aims the can at Greta, who takes off running with Honey Bear in hot pursuit. The two of them race around the room, squealing like they're back at camp putting on a show for the kids and not sheathed in high heels and lavender floral Laura Ashley dresses.

I grin at the ruckus, blessing the two of them for the distraction. I was hoping my agitation might calm once this day finally came. But if anything, the looming feeling of unease has only gotten worse. I had the damn dream again last night. The one with Theo in the water. His head going under and not coming back up again. It was so vivid, it almost didn't seem like a dream. I shake my head, trying to force the thought away. No, I can't think like that. It was just a dream. I'm making too much of it. I'm sure it's just my nerves getting the better of me.

But what about the vertigo? Ever since I walked into the church this morning, these episodes keep hitting me out of the blue. All of a sudden I'll feel off balance…like the world is tipping on its side. And with the disorientation comes a loud hum in my ears, like the drone of radio static rising, then falling away. Then, as quickly as an episode comes, it goes away. And I feel completely normal again.

I'm sure it's only because I didn't eat enough for breakfast. I'd forced down some toast and peanut butter. But maybe I shouldn't have had two cups of coffee when I was already so amped up. That must be what's making me feel so strange. It's either that or this damn dress. I squirm, trying to find some space inside the silk cinched like a corset around my rib cage. I don't remember the dress being so tight when I tried it on. Or so itchy. Or so damn claustrophobic. I tug at the neckline, which seems to rise higher and higher, shrinking around my neck like a noose, slowly cutting off my air. God, why is it suddenly so hard to breathe? So much for this being the most beautiful day of my life. All I want is to get this over with.

If only I could see Theo, I'd feel better. I'd stayed at Caroline's last night so we wouldn't see each other until I walked down the aisle. He'd called me early this morning, before he knew I had to leave for the salon. In my bed, I'd curled on my side, twisting the cord around my finger like a lovesick schoolgirl as he'd greeted me in his typical over the top way.

"You ready to do this, Annie?!" he'd shouted through the receiver instead of saying hello.

"More ready than I've ever been for anything in my entire life." It was true. Despite my strange inklings that something is off about the wedding, I have no doubts about marrying Theo. He is the one true thing in my life. And always will be.

"I wish I could see you," I'd complained into the receiver.

"Yeah, I wish I could see you too. Why did we have to give in to this stupid convention of not seeing each other before the wedding, anyway? Have we forgotten there's nothing conventional about us?"

"I guess so," I said, wanting to scream. *That's why we should not be getting married in this church!* But I knew my time for speaking up was long gone.

"Don't worry, even if you can't see me, you'll feel me there with you," he'd assured me.

And he's right. Now standing in this stifling room (did somebody turn on the heat?) I can sense him close by. I imagine him pacing around the room behind the altar, flapping his long arms, flitting here and there, babbling on to Nate and Wen and Leo, his best friend from high school, physically unable to stay still because he's so excited to see me.

Theo's not worried. He doesn't have a nagging sensation that something's off. He doesn't feel some whirling vortex hovering closer and closer. No, Theo is lucky to be oblivious. Unlike me, who currently feels like I'm carrying the weight of the world on my shoulders. Who feels like I need to *do something*. And fast. Before it's too late.

And that's all part of the plan. Mom's words repeat in my ears. But I don't have time to ponder them further because I'm distracted by the sight of Rebecca walking by the doorway, headed to the bathroom down the hall. She lifts her hand in the smallest of waves, still striding like she doesn't want to interrupt whatever's going on in here. (Which apparently is a game of deodorant tag between Greta and Honey Bear and my sister complaining loudly over the placement of one particular flower arrangement on the altar.)

But something on my face makes Rebecca stop dead in her tracks. She points inside and mouths, "Can I come in?" I nod furiously, running to the door to drag her inside.

"My God, you look beautiful!" she gushes, while I fake preen in front of her, flipping that damn lock of hair behind my shoulder, which will probably send Caroline over the edge once again.

Rebecca peppers me with more compliments, but when I tug at my neckline and furiously fan my burning face, her smile fades. "Are you okay?" she asks in her therapist voice.

The concern on her face threatens to undo me, but I work to keep my emotions in check. I guide us behind the full-length mirror for some semblance of privacy, then recount the strange way I've been feeling all day, thankful that I finally have someone to confide in.

She nods along, unperturbed by my odd, world-tilting symptoms. "All the feelings you're having are completely normal," she says when I finish. "You've been under a lot of stress lately, dealing with all these rushed plans, and everyone needing a piece of your time. It's okay. It's all going to be okay," she croons in a soothing voice. "How about we take some deep breaths together? Would you like that?"

I eagerly agree, and the two of us launch into the breathing exercises she taught me in her office. After a few rounds, I begin to feel a little better.

"Just keep things in perspective," she says. "This is all your choice,

Annie. You are in complete control. You are free to do whatever you want. No one is forcing you into anything. You know that, right?"

I nod, more tension loosening in my chest. Rebecca knows feeling trapped can trigger me, so I'm thankful she's reminding me of the real reason I'm here.

"You good?" she asks after a while.

"Yeah. I just want to see Theo. Then I'll feel better." Theo has come to some of my sessions, so Rebecca knows how we feel about each other. In fact, she once told us that she considers our relationship one of the most beautiful love stories she's ever heard.

"Have you seen him yet?" I ask Rebecca.

"Yeah, the guys just came out on the altar."

Only now do I notice the organ music filtering in from the distance; the signal that Theo's mom is taking her seat. My heart races wildly. Oh God, this is really happening. I'm about to walk out there in front of all these people and become Theo's wife.

If I don't keel over first.

Rebecca takes a step to leave, but I grab her arm before she can go, thinking of Theo once again. "How does he look?"

She breaks into a huge smile. "He looks so happy. And excited. And," she lowers her voice conspiratorially, "if I may say without sounding too creepy…very, very handsome." She gives me a playful shove, which surprises me since she's usually so refined. "You're one lucky woman, Annie."

I beam at her, my stomach flipping thinking of seeing Theo in only a few short minutes. I can't believe I still get butterflies when I think about him. Will it always be this way? Will I always feel this visceral thrill whenever I'm near him? I don't know. But I sure as hell can't wait to find out.

Rebecca dashes away as a final rush of activity explodes through the room. The church lady calls for us to line up. Caroline shoves my bouquet in my hands and pulls the damn lock of hair to the front. Greta grabs my shoulders and makes one last joke before we go.

"You do realize that if I could've stomached Theo's sickening belief that all people are inherently good, then it might've been *me* walking down that aisle right now."

"Oh, believe me, I'm well aware I'm only Theo's consolation prize after you turned him down."

Greta cackles loudly. She always says that Theo has been waiting his whole life just to find me. Oh, if she only knew how true that was.

But the next second she grows serious, enveloping me in a rare hug, whispering in my ear, "You know how much I love you, right? Both of you. I wish you guys a long and happy life together. Hell, if anyone can make it through thick and thin, it's the two of you."

My throat constricts as I squeeze her back, thankful when the frantic church lady pulls her away so I don't have to respond. A long and happy life together. Theo and I will get one of those. But we won't get both.

When I get to the doorway, my dad appears out of nowhere, offering the crook of his arm. He looks handsome; his brown hair combed back, his eyes the same pale shade of blue as mine.

He looks so dashing in his dark suit. I can almost imagine my mom standing beside him, looking beautiful in a brightly colored gown with her blonde hair curling along her shoulders, gazing at her husband with shy adoration. The same way she'd gazed at him in a picture I once found of the two of them when they were dating. Oh, what a lovely couple they'd made. Oh, what could have been. If my mom had only had the guts to stay.

Recently, Franco told me that Mom considered my dad the love of her life. He said Mom confessed to him on one of the last days she was alive that pushing my dad away was her only regret in life. But she'd been too scared of how much she loved him to let it grow even more. So she'd ended things to protect herself from getting hurt. I guess Mom did know what it was like to be in love after all. She just wouldn't admit it. Not to us. Or to herself.

Now as I give Dad a kiss on the cheek and think of the boy I adore waiting for me, I whisper to her. *I love you Mom. But I'm not going to make the same mistake as you.*

Dad pats my hand as we wait for the drill sergeant lady to give us permission to move.

"I'm so proud of you, honey," he says in a quivering voice. "And your mother would've been so proud of you, too."

"Dad, stop. You're going to make my mascara run," I complain, even though I bought waterproof mascara especially for this occasion. I squeeze his arm tighter, fighting to speak past the lump in my throat. "Actually, she *is* proud of me, Dad. Right this very minute."

He gives a sharp nod, keeping his eyes trained forward like it's going to take everything he's got to maintain his composure for the next two minutes. That makes two of us.

As we're finally allowed to creep step by agonizing step closer to the door yawning before us, I'm glad to have my Dad's arm to steady me. Watching Honey Bear, then Greta, then Caroline disappear down the aisle, my stomach lurches and my legs go weak. So weak that as we move to stand silhouetted in the doorway, as the organ swells loud with the wedding march and the crowd rises to their feet in synchronized lurch, I wonder if I'm going to be strong enough to make it to Theo standing so far away.

I plaster on a smile, looking around at all the familiar and unfamiliar faces. My family. My friends; some from high school, some from college. All the lovely people we met on the Treasure Hunt. Theo's family. His friends and classmates. Even some of the oncology doctors and nurses who took care of him when he was sick…who brought him back to life when he died. Who understand just how special this day is for him.

Everyone is now standing and smiling and waiting for me to walk down this seemingly endless aisle to start my happily ever after.

But just as I take my first step down the flower-lined path, a horrible thought hits me out of nowhere.

The next time I see all these people will be at Theo's funeral.

CHAPTER THIRTY-SEVEN

I FIRST SAW the bruises two days ago.

When it happened I was making the bed and Theo was toweling himself off in the bathroom after a shower. I'd noticed he'd taken his fresh clothes in there with him, which was odd. Usually after showering, he liked to prance around the bedroom naked, proudly showing off his goods (as well he should, with goods like his) lauding how important it was to air-dry properly before getting dressed.

I'd popped my head inside the door, surprising him. "What? We're getting married and now you're suddenly shy around me?" He'd hurriedly pulled down his shirt, but it was already too late. I'd seen it. The nasty blue-green bruise curving around his ribcage.

Instantly my mouth had gone dry. "How did you get that?" I'd pointed dumbly at his torso, hoping with all my might there was a completely logical explanation for what I'd just seen.

But instead of giving me a reasonable story, Theo had merely shrugged. "I'm not sure. I guess I must have bumped into something at the hospital." His voice, usually so casual, was too casual this time. He refused to look at me, instead busying himself with hanging up his towel, adjusting the shower curtain, wiping the fog off the mirror... anything to avoid meeting my eyes.

"So you don't remember how it happened?" I tried and failed to keep the panic out of my voice. Theo had told me that unexplained bruises and a sudden loss of energy were what first prompted his mom to take him to the doctor when he was fourteen.

Oh, my God. And he'd taken a nap in the middle of the day yesterday, I'd realized with a jolt. *He said it was just because the wedding plans were wearing him out. But he normally works twelve-hour shifts and comes home looking like he could work twelve more. Why hadn't I noticed how tired he seemed?*

Theo had finally stopped moving, reluctantly turning to face me. "No, I don't remember how the bruise happened."

I braced one hand on the sink. A bruise of that size should've come from a very memorable impact. Unless you had a disease that caused a low platelet count. Then, even a glancing blow might cause excessive bleeding beneath your skin. God, I wish Theo hadn't taught me so much about how Acute Myeloid Leukemia works.

"Are there any others?" My voice sounded distant and unfamiliar. Like someone more rational was speaking on my behalf.

He nodded. The action so simple. Just a slight dip of his chin. But that one movement felt like a guillotine slicing through my heart.

Begrudgingly, he tugged at his sleeve and showed me a smaller bruise on the back of his upper arm, pulled his jeans down to reveal another blue-green splotch over his hipbone.

I was barely breathing at that point. "When did they show up?"

"Just in the past few days, actually. I barely even noticed them until this morning."

He'd watched me closely, waiting for my reaction. And I watched him back just as closely. I knew he wasn't outright lying. But I also knew he wasn't telling me the whole truth either. I thought of how he'd been sleeping in a t-shirt the past couple of nights; how when we'd made love he'd wanted to keep the lights off. Which meant he'd suspected something for a while now and hadn't told me.

Theo must've picked up on what I was thinking, because he reached out and held my shoulders, crouching so our faces were close. "Annie, we don't know anything yet. Let's not jump to any conclusions."

I could only blink at him. The pain radiating through my heart was so sharp it was like someone had slammed a hammer into my chest.

"No…no…no…no." I had no idea whether I'd said the words aloud or only inside my head. All I could think of was that this couldn't be happening. Not now. Not when we were about to get married. And have a baby. Not when we were supposed to have more time.

"Listen, I've already made an appointment with my doctor to get checked out," he rushed on. "I'm going to see him right after the wedding."

"The wedding?" I'd repeated half-dazed. My God…it was only a couple of days away. How could I smile and dance and celebrate after what I'd just seen?

"Yes, the wedding," Theo said evenly. "Think about it. There's really nothing we can do before then, so why dwell on it? Let's just take one thing at a time and forget all this for now." He waved a hand over his body. "Instead, let's focus on enjoying this amazing day we have planned."

"Uh huh," I agreed numbly.

"It's going to be okay. We're going to celebrate how much we love each other with all our family and friends and not let a few stupid bruises ruin everything for us, right? Okay?" Desperation shone in his eyes. "Can we please do that, Annie?"

I stood there like a statue, staring into his beautiful face, wondering if this was what had caused the foreboding feeling I'd been having these past weeks. Had I sensed the end was coming sooner than I expected? Is that why things felt so off this whole time?

But that speculation didn't feel right either. No, my agitation seemed to be related to the plan I kept hearing about from my mom. A plan I had agreed to. A plan I somehow knew I was excited about. A plan I alone was in charge of carrying out.

Everything rested on figuring out the details of that plan. If only I could remember what the hell it was.

Think, Annie. You have to think. Everything is up to you.

That day in the bedroom, Theo had mistaken my silence for hesitation. "I know it's scary, Annie. I'm scared too. But this means so much to both of us. Can you please just forget about what you saw for a little while and enjoy our wedding anyway?"

I'd been so distracted by trying to remember the damn plan I'd barely even heard what he'd asked of me. "Yes, of course…of course I can do that, Theo," I'd mumbled, pulling him down and kissing him fiercely so he'd know the truth:

That it wasn't my faith in him that was wavering. What was wavering was my faith in myself.

CHAPTER THIRTY-EIGHT

NOW, AS DAD and I step fully into the cavernous cathedral, I'm determined to keep the promise I made to Theo in our bathroom. I will not think of bruises and funerals and tomorrows. I will follow his lead and stay in the moment and remember what he's taught me over our time together. I can almost hear his voice. "There's only ever this Now, Annie. And this Now is always, *always* enough."

The organ music echoes off the stone walls, slapping against my skin like a harmonic wake-up call. Theo's right once again. This moment is more than enough. In fact, it's heartbreakingly beautiful. The music, the sprays of flowers lining the pews, the smell of the burning candles, all the faces of our loved ones smiling at me. *Everything is perfect. Perfect. Perfect,* I tell myself with each step.

Yet despite how many times I repeat it, my mantra still rings hollow. I hear it for what it is: An attempt to convince myself of something I don't truly believe.

Is everything really *perfect?* The voice in my head presses. *Or is there something you want to change?*

The further I get into the church, the more my body revolts. When I turn my head to scan the crowd, it feels like the world has turned liquid; all the colors and shapes and faces rippling like waves, instead of solid real life. And every few seconds a bright light flashes in my periphery, making my pulse spike in shock. I look around, expecting to see a camera shoved into my face, but the photographer is yards away, already standing at the front of the church. What the hell is going on?

My heart pounds violently, and static roars in my ears as I try to figure out why the world is glitching. Time flashes, then seems to stall, then leaps ahead a few seconds. The vertigo makes me so off balance I have to clutch onto Dad's arm just to stay upright. What is happening to me? Or better question, what is happening to my reality? It's almost like the Universe is trying to get my attention. Flashing like a neon sign, trying to wake me up. Trying to make me stop and listen to what it has to say.

This isn't right. This isn't right. This isn't right.

The words hammer loud and clear in my ears as I ever so slowly progress up the aisle.

Please stop saying that! I scream back in my head, fighting to keep a smile on my face. My mouth is so parched that my lips snag painfully on my teeth. *It's too late. There's nothing I can do now!*

Finally, I'm close enough to see Theo clearly. He's standing with his hands clasped in front of him, smiling so big, I swear he's going to pull a cheek muscle. Rebecca was right. He looks incredibly handsome, filling out his dark suit perfectly, his green eyes twinkling and silky hair tamed to perfect waves, falling to brush his shoulders.

Seeing him, a rush of love explodes through me with such force it feels like my chest is being cracked open from the inside. Being with Theo is right. I know that for sure. That's why I have to keep going. That's why I have to put this nagging voice out of my head.

Yet as I draw closer, I realize the blue tapestry I thought would be behind us during the ceremony is hanging too high. Which means it won't be in the background as we get married. And Theo's suit. The black jacket is wrong. In the vision, we were both wearing white. But why would we both be wearing white? That doesn't make any sense.

This isn't right. This isn't right. This isn't right.

The room continues to ripple and flash and tip to the side, making my stomach lurch sickeningly and sweat pour down my back—despite

Honey Bear's full-body anti-perspirant application earlier. The intensity of the glitches becomes so strong it's hard to pass them off as mere side-effects of my nerves anymore. And as much as it terrifies me, I'm starting to realize I may have no other choice but to listen to what's going on… both around me, and inside me too.

Suddenly I remember what Mom told me on that day in the treehouse. *You already knew what you wanted. You just wouldn't let yourself admit it.*

Next, I see Theo celebrating on Charlie's front porch after we realized I'd led us to the right place. *This girl is amazing! She's brilliant… and knows so much, deep in her heart! She's just too afraid to listen to herself.*

And what Rebecca told me only a few minutes ago. *You're in complete control, Annie. You know that, right?*

I do know that. I know I can change things. But do I really have the guts to speak up now…at the last possible second? Especially when I don't have any proof that I'm right?

You have to decide. Time is running out!

I'm only steps away from Theo. I pray he doesn't notice the ribbon of sweat trickling from my hairline…the tremble in my smile.

Dad turns and kisses me on the cheek before taking his seat, but I can barely enjoy it because I'm too worried that I'm going to collapse the second he lets go of my arm. Luckily, Theo is there, so tall and sturdy, reaching out one blurry hand to me. I lurch for it, grabbing onto his fingers and teetering toward him as if I'm stepping out of a rocking boat. For the first time, Theo's smile falters, brows knitting just slightly with concern. (Which is not the expression a bride hopes for when her groom sees her for the first time.)

"You good?" he whispers as he leads me up the three steps to stand in front of the priest, this horrible dress dragging like a cape of cement behind me. Dear Lord, why do I have to navigate stairs right now?

I nod furiously trying to reassure Theo. But as the music fades and the crowd sits down in a loud *whoosh*…as I look at his black suit jacket and the table of crosses and candles and Catholic doo-hickeys behind us instead of a field of blue, the voice thunders even louder inside my head.

This isn't right! This isn't right! This isn't right!

And for the first time I realize it's not my mom's voice I hear. It's not Theo's voice. It's not some Angel Guide's voice either.

No, this time the voice I hear is my own. And it's sure. And steady. And true. And dammit…I know without a doubt I have to follow it.

Suddenly, a warm calm settles over me and a power ignites in my core that feels like a furnace kicking to life.

And I know exactly what I have to do.

As if in slow motion, I watch as the priest opens his Bible with a crack, then draws in a deep breath, preparing to start the ceremony.

But before he can speak, I turn to my dear, sweet Theo…the man I love as much as life itself…and say the words I know will break his heart.

"I'm sorry, Theo. But I can't do this."

CHAPTER THIRTY-NINE

THEO

ANNIE'S MOUTH MOVES. Her arms wave and her head bobs furiously as she tries to explain what just happened. And yet it feels like someone is holding my head underwater as I stare down at her. Her muffled words now reduced to random rising and falling sounds, none of it making any sense to my panicked brain.

We're alone in the cry room; the little room at the back of the church where parents take their crying babies during the service. Which seems appropriate. Because I'm pretty sure I'm about to burst into tears.

The only thing saving me is the shock of it all. Although I'm not sure why I'm so surprised. I knew I was asking too much of Annie. Especially after she saw the bruises. Which, despite what I told her, I know can only mean one thing. She's right to want to put an end to this before it goes any further. I should be thanking her for having the good sense to speak up and finally say what we've both known all along. It was selfish of me to ask her to commit to me this way.

"Theo! Focus!" Annie claps her hands loudly in front of my face, jarring me back to life. "Are you even listening to me?!"

"I uh…it's just…uh." My tongue feels too fat, and so dry it keeps sticking to the roof of my mouth. "I'm sorry…it's hard for me to think right now, Annie. I'm a little freaked out!"

"Oh Theo, I'm so sorry. I love you so much. Please don't forget that." The cadence of that sentence sounds familiar. I think she's repeated it many times since she shut us in here. Right after she'd told the stunned crowd, "Don't go anywhere…we just need a minute!" then dragged me off the altar, insisting she could explain everything. Although I can't fathom what more she needs to say. "I'm sorry, Theo. But I can't do this" seems pretty self-explanatory to me.

She grabs my shoulders and gives me a hard shake. "Did you hear the part where I said I still want to marry you?!"

I blink. Once. Then twice. I feel my mouth hanging open, but I can't seem to figure out how to close it.

I work hard to respond. "Uh…yes…no…maybe? Ugh, I don't know!" God, why can't I think? Maybe because all my energy is being used up by trying not to cry.

She was so beautiful coming down the aisle. My heart had nearly split in two at the sight of her. I couldn't believe someone like her wanted to be with someone like me. I couldn't believe all my years of waiting had culminated in this moment. I couldn't believe all my dreams were finally coming true.

But then I'd seen her face, and I'd known something was wrong. At first she'd looked scared, but then it was like a switch had been thrown inside her. The set of her jaw, the way she'd blinked around wide-eyed, like she'd just woken up from a dream. Before she even said those awful words, I knew something had changed.

"Take a deep breath and listen to me," she implores gently. "Can you do that?"

I nod. It's funny how much her voice sounds like mine whenever I'm trying to distract her during one of her panic attacks.

She speaks slowly, enunciating each word. "I love you, and we're going to get married." She stops to let that sink in.

"We are?"

"Yes, we are."

My heart soars at the possibility. Then I notice her steeling herself to say more.

"Why do I feel like there's a But coming?"

"Because there is." She reaches down and clasps both of my hands in hers. "We're going to get married, but we can't get married here. In this church."

"Really?!" I'm both giddy—We're still getting married! She still loves me! Nothing has gone wrong!—and confused. "But why not here?"

"Because I can just feel it. This isn't where we're supposed to be right now. We're supposed to get married somewhere else."

I ask her to explain more, and she eagerly goes on. She tells me of her vision again. Of us standing face to face, backed by a field of blue and garlands of flowers. She had mentioned it to me before, but she hadn't brought it up lately, so I thought she had forgotten all about it. But now she's adamant that it means something important. That this church isn't right. That we have to move our wedding…*right now*. And she knows where we need to go.

The implications hit me like a slap in the face. "But, all the plans my mom made. And your sister. They worked so hard to put this together."

"I know, but…"

"And Father John did us a favor, and there's the reception, and the caterers…"

"I know, but…"

"And the band is probably on the way, and the bakers are bringing the cake…and…and…"

Only then do I notice that with each word I speak, Annie shrinks smaller and smaller into herself. The determination pouring forth from her seconds ago has evaporated, leaving only a shell of the former girl behind. My God, did I do that to her? How could I have been so thoughtless? From the day I met her, all I've ever wanted to do was to lift her up. Not drag her down like apparently I'm doing right now.

"I'm sorry, Annie. Forget all of that." I wave my selfish words away. "Explain it to me again."

Hope springs into her eyes and she comes back to life, tripping over her words as she tells me in vivid detail about the voices she's heard in her head, the nagging feeling that's been haunting her, the visceral tug in her gut telling her this church isn't right.

"Please," she reaches up and places her hand against my cheek, blue eyes pleading. "I know it all sounds crazy. I know I don't have any tangible evidence to back up this feeling. But right now, I need you to trust me."

Hearing those words, something inside me clicks into place, like a key sliding into a lock. I lean my cheek into her open palm, feel the soft pillow of her skin against my jaw, holding me up as I once held her up the same way.

I need you to trust me.

My God, how many times over this past year have I asked Annie to trust me?

I'd told her outlandish stories of dying and meeting Angels. Of meeting her before I actually met her and coming back to life. Of fractals and choices and possibilities and intertwined fates. Of telepathy and multiple lives and a Universe that is friendly. And every time she's listened. Every time she's trusted me.

Why would I ever hesitate to do the same for her?

As she waits for my response, the look she'd had when she'd met me in front of the church returns. It's an expression of such power, such ferocious determination it makes me want to drop to my knees and worship at *her* altar instead of the one I was just standing upon.

And with that realization, there's nothing to debate anymore. "Of course, Annie. I'll do whatever you ask of me," I tell her, smiling so big my cheeks hurt. "You're right. You've always been right. Now tell me where you want us to go."

CHAPTER FORTY

ANNIE

EVERYTHING IS FALLING into place perfectly. And I'm not one bit surprised.

My goodness, does this mean I've officially become an optimist? A year ago, the thought would have turned my stomach. Now, I've never felt prouder of myself in my life.

The only tense moments came when we were waiting in Father John's office for Maeve to call us back. When I told Theo I finally knew what my premonition meant—that we had to get married at Bluffpoint Lookout at Camp Boundless—he'd simply said, "Of course! Let's do it, Annie!" Then he'd promptly called the Manor House to get permission from Miles for us to hold our wedding on the grounds.

It was a gamble, of course. There was a 50/50 chance camp was in session this weekend, which would make it impossible to hold our wedding there. But even as the phone was ringing, I had the distinct feeling we had some powerful forces on high pulling the strings on our behalf.

But it seemed even our cosmic connections couldn't make someone answer the phone. After all, it was summer. And Miles was a summer camp director. And summer camp directors were not by their phones in the middle of the day in the summer. So next we tried the dining hall, and luckily Maeve picked up. Only hours ago, I'd been upset to find out she couldn't come to the ceremony because her babysitter bailed out at the last minute. But now, I saw the serendipity of her being exactly where we needed her the most.

While we were talking to Maeve, Tim happened to pass through the kitchen to get a snack. (Surprise, surprise.) So, after Maeve handed us our first bit of good news (it was a changeover weekend so camp was empty) Tim and Rick set off in the golf cart to track down Miles as fast as they could.

While we waited to get confirmation that we could use Camp Boundless, Theo had pulled a flustered Maria and nearly apoplectic Caroline into the office, and with our hands clenched in unity we firmly broke the news to them about our change of plans.

I'd braced myself for their outrage, for the barrage of reasons it was crazy to move an entire wedding after it had already begun, but no arguments came. They both just stared at us in silence for a few beats, then looked at each other and exchanged a solemn nod, as if whatever they saw on our faces was enough to convince them we were right.

"Whatever you want, we'll make it happen, Annie," Caroline assured me.

"Yes, this is about the two of you, not us," Maria said, looking pained, but not for the reason I thought. Afterward, she'd pulled me aside and apologized profusely. "I'm so sorry. Please forgive me if I took over and turned this wedding into something you didn't want. You two kept saying you didn't care about the details, so I was just trying to help. Really. I never meant to ruin things for you!"

I'd vehemently assured her none of this was her fault. That I hadn't known myself what I wanted until only minutes ago. Maria's relief only confirmed what I already knew in my heart. She only cared about what was best for Theo and me. The church, the pageantry, the traditions. All of that meant nothing to her if they didn't make us happy.

Once the phone call came in from Miles giving us permission to use the camp, things started moving fast.

Theo and I rushed to the front of the church to explain what was going to happen next.

"So, new plan!" My voice rang out through the vast space as the crowd murmured in confusion. "We've decided to change locations."

A gasp rolled through the pews. "Yeah, pretty exciting, huh?! We thought so too. Gotta keep you guests on your toes. Wouldn't want you getting too comfortable thinking you were at a normal wedding," I elbowed Theo hard. "Isn't that right, Theo?"

He'd nodded furiously as I barreled on. "But we're going to need a few hours to get set up. So we're going to do this wedding a bit backwards. First, you all are going to have a few appetizers over at the reception hall. And then," I gestured to Jonathan and Caroline passing out scraps of hastily scribbled papers, "we're asking you to meet us at this address for the actual ceremony."

Now as our guests rise and somewhat dazedly move to the doors, Theo and I stand at the front of the church panting as if we've been running up and down the stairs to the choir loft.

Watching my plan being set into motion, the magnitude of what I've done hits me for the first time. I can't believe this is happening. I can't believe I had the power to actually change things. All because I trusted my gut and finally spoke up for what I believed was right.

Theo and I face each other, frozen like wedding cake toppers on the church altar. The world feels like it's swirling in double time around us, yet we remain still, cupped snugly in a pocket of calm untouched by the melee.

I vaguely hear Father John whisper to Maria that he can't officiate a wedding that's not in a church. Then Victor speak up to remind Caroline he has been ordained by the Unity Church and he would be honored to marry us.

I listen as my father huddles with Theo's father, coming up with a plan to ply the various caterers, musicians, and bakers with copious amounts of money to make them move to a new location. (Guess we won't be referring to those two as 'assholes' anymore after this.)

I catch flashes of Greta and Honey Bear dashing around in my periphery, instructing a gaggle of kids to help collect the garlands and bouquets to be transported to camp.

It truly is astounding; how every little detail is being taken care of through no effort of our own.

We got you, Buttercup, Mom says, her voice wrapping around me like a firm hug. *You did good. You did really, really, good.*

I let out a shaky laugh, and when I turn back to Theo he's smiling all goofily at me. I smile just as goofily back, thinking of when I first met him. How I considered him so naïve and immature. I was so damn determined to teach him the harsh truths of the world; that life wasn't fair, so he'd better toughen up or else get hurt the same way I had.

And yet, just the opposite happened. Instead of me making him hard, he's made me soft. He's opened me up. Made me more child-like and tender, just like him. He made me believe in things I couldn't see. Things without proof. Things I could only feel with my heart. And now because of that, we're standing here. And the world isn't tilting anymore. It's solid and steady. And oh, so perfect.

"Thank you," I say to him.

He makes a face. "For what?"

"For not freaking out."

"Well, I did freak out just a little." He lifts a pinched finger and thumb in the air.

"For not doubting my love for you."

He winces. "Well, I did doubt it…just a little."

I smile. "For believing me."

He gives a sharp nod. "Always. But I was only following your lead. Because you believed in me first."

"Only because you taught me how."

He opens his mouth to continue the back and forth, but I interrupt. "How about we admit we're both pretty awesome and leave at that?"

"Sounds good to me." He lifts my hand, kisses the back of it as the outside world whirls around us. Then he repeats his question from our phone call this morning. "So, are you ready to do this, Annie?!"

And this time when I answer, there's no foreboding feeling hanging over my head anymore. "More ready than I've ever been for anything in my entire life!"

CHAPTER FORTY-ONE

A VOLLEY OF slamming car doors echoes off the trees framing the Camp Boundless parking lot.

We'd just driven through the camp gates in a ragtag parade of cars jammed with flower arrangements and garlands; dresses and bouquets; ceramic pots and bottle stoppers. Now our core transition team—basically all those who used to congregate at Charlie's, plus our Dads and their families—step out of their cars and assemble in a circle, waiting for Caroline to tell us what to do next.

There's a giddy buzz in the air. Everyone is feeling the adrenaline surge of both our time crunch and the faint rebellion at having left the strict parameters of the church behind for this new open-air cathedral.

We women have changed out of our restrictive dresses and shoes. I'm now wearing a button-down pink gingham shirt with a pair of frayed denim shorts and flip-flops. An outfit that looks a bit out of place with my makeup and gold-combed hairdo.

The men still wear their suits, although they've abandoned their jackets. I know I should focus on more important issues, but I can't help but feel a flush of desire when I see Theo standing a few feet away with his shirt sleeves rolled up, and the top two buttons of his shirt undone to reveal his smooth tan chest. And I get the distinct impression my stepsister Elizabeth is feeling the same way, because when

Caroline just asked her what assignment she wanted, she'd pointed to Theo and whispered, "I want to be on whatever team *he's* on."

Tim and Rick wait at the trailhead with a golf cart and a four-wheeler with a wagon hitched to the back to carry all our crap to The Lookout. Those sweet, sweet men. Ever since we'd hung up the phone, they've been carting chairs into the woods for the ceremony. Luckily for us, the spring work weekend at Camp Boundless had focused on repairing the rotting wood railings of the platform and patching up the boardwalk path. Which means our guests will have no trouble reaching our destination. Once again, it's crazy how seamlessly all the details are falling into place.

Don't forget, you've got more than just the people in this parking lot on your side.

"Yeah, I know," I whisper back inside my head. "It's nice. Having you all here with me."

Caroline efficiently gives each person their job (pointedly denying Elizabeth's request to shadow Theo) checking tasks off her clipboard as she goes. If this Wedding 2.0 were up to me, we'd all be huddling on a plain, undecorated platform, listening to the bare minimum of niceties, so I could get to the good part: the food and the dancing (and most importantly the wedding night.) But both Maria and Caroline have committed themselves to making sure our new ceremony is even more beautiful than our last.

Caroline tells me my task is to take Theo and check in with Maeve at the dining hall, since she doesn't want me to see The Lookout before the ceremony. As the rowdy group breaks apart with a loud whoop of excitement, I notice my Dad scanning around with an odd look on his face.

"You alright, Dad?" I ask as the others dash away to complete their assignments. Greta is especially thrilled with our change of venue. She's now dancing around the parking lot with a garland of flowers wrapped around her shoulders like a boa, singing to the tune of "Camptown

Races": "This is better than a musty tomb! Doo dah…doo dah! Mother Nature trumps the church! Oh, da doo dah day!"

"Yeah, yeah, I'm fine," Dad assures me, still marveling at the surrounding forest, which is typical for him. Dad is a nature lover like me, and there's no shortage of nature to love at Camp Boundless.

He finally tears his gaze from the treetops to look at me. "I just love how you're making this such a full-circle moment. Having your ceremony here of all places."

I motion to Theo standing beside me. "Right. Because this is where we met."

"Well, that. And also because of your mom."

Theo and I share a confused look. "What about Mom? What does she have to do with Camp Boundless?" As far as I knew, Mom had never been here before.

"Oh, didn't you know? This is where she used to come for her painting retreats. It wasn't called Camp Boundless then. It was just a conference center where they held all kinds of events on the weekends. But I distinctly remember dropping her off here." He tips his head to the direction we drove in. "That winding driveway with the waterfall along the way? That's something you don't easily forget."

Everything inside me goes still as he continues. "Yeah, in fact I remember bringing her here when she was pregnant with you. She was so excited when I picked her up afterwards. She said the retreat had been a great success. That she'd been flooded with all kinds of inspiration and couldn't wait to get back to her easel and get working. She had all these little sketches she'd done of the landscape around here. She ended up using them to make a whole series of paintings. Don't you remember? There were five of them, I think. Each one more beautiful than the last. Although I think she eventually sold them all off…you know, once I left and she was on her own." A flash of guilt shadows his expression.

Theo and I blink at each other, our mouths hanging open.

Dad looks back and forth between us. "What? What's wrong?"

Theo regains his ability to speak first. "No, nothing's wrong, sir. In fact, everything suddenly just became very, *very* right."

At that moment, Caroline barks at Dad to "get your ass in gear, we don't have all day!" and he rushes off before we can question him more.

I turn to Theo. "Oh my God! Mom did the paintings at Camp Boundless! That's why all the scenes looked so familiar!"

"Yeah, because we were literally living inside each one of them all summer!"

I stare off into the distance trying to draw back the paintings in my mind. "Wow. It all makes sense now, doesn't it?"

"Yeah, the one with the lake? That was definitely the view from the center of Lake Henry to the beach."

"And the Indian Caves! Oh my gosh, why didn't we recognize that earlier?"

I rifle through my memory of the other two scenes, but I can't draw back all their details. "Oh man, I wish I could see the paintings right now, so we could figure out exactly where she painted them."

Theo gets a funny look on his face.

"How is this even possible?" I wonder out loud. "How could my mom have been here twenty-some years ago, painting the exact place where I would one day meet you? And fall in love? And get freaking married?!"

Of course, Theo only shrugs, like this unfathomable coincidence is just another ordinary day to him. I go on. "How had she known to send those sketches to you? And to me? How had she known? How had she known any of this?" I'm babbling, but I can't stop. It's impossible to comprehend all this overwhelming information at once.

"I don't think it's something we'll ever be able to understand logically," Theo says gently, as if he's scared I won't like that explanation.

But surprisingly, his words don't annoy me like they once would have. I'm beginning to see the wisdom in what he once said to me. "Maybe we're not meant to understand life, Annie. Maybe we're just meant to live it."

"Come here," Theo says abruptly, motioning me over to his car. "I've got a little surprise for you."

"What? No, Theo, we agreed…" I complain, begrudgingly following him. We'd decided not to get each other presents, even though I secretly got something for him too.

Once at his car, he cryptically instructs me to stand by the hood and not look inside.

"It's just a little something." He swings open the door to his backseat.

After rummaging around for a few seconds, he meets me at the front of the car with a wrapped gift. It's rectangular and looks kind of heavy by the way he's holding it with two hands. "Here," he gives it to me, looking sheepish. "I hope you like it."

As soon as I grip the sides, the colorful paper collapses inward—as if the center of the rectangle is lower than its hard sides. No. It couldn't be.

My heart whirls double time. "No. Theo. You didn't…"

He grins big. "I did."

"But how did you? You shouldn't have."

"Just open it."

I set the gift on the hood of the car and carefully pull the paper away. Even though I already know what's inside, tears spring to my eyes when I get it unwrapped: It's Mom's painting of the birch tree in the center with the two paths diverging around it, one into the darkness and one into the light.

"You bought Rebecca's painting." It's hard to get the words out, I'm so overcome with emotion. So that's why the painting wasn't hanging in her waiting room anymore. She hadn't taken it home like she said. She'd sold it to Theo.

"But this is too extravagant!" I think of the homemade gift I have waiting for him. "It must have cost you a fortune."

He gives me a wink. "Oh, don't worry. I haggled her down to a good price. Besides, what's the use in being rich if you can't use your money to make someone you love happy?"

"Happy is too paltry a word, Theo," I tell him, swallowing the lump in my throat. "Thank you. This is the best gift anyone's ever given me." I reach up on my tiptoes to kiss him, but he pulls away.

"Shouldn't we wait to kiss until we're married? You know, to make it more special on the altar?"

I make a face. "You really think anything can get more special than this?"

He huffs a laugh, but then becomes serious. "Actually yes. Yes, I do."

"Alright, whatever you say, Buster," I grumble, even though I kind of agree with him.

I study the painting more. "So where do you think this fork in the trail is located?"

Theo steps closer, scrutinizing the painting resting on the car hood. "Actually, I'm not sure. But I think I might have seen that tree on the Whippoorwill Trail. I mean, she painted it over twenty years ago, so things might look a lot different now. But it would be fun for us to try to find it."

I smile up at him, pleased by the idea of going on another Treasure Hunt with him. Although we'll have to get to it quickly. Who knows how much time we have left, with his bruises and all.

"But wait!" Theo says, holding up one finger. "There's more!"

"You sound like the man who sells Ginsu knives on those late-night infomercials," I grumble as he dashes back to his open car door.

When he returns with another gift the same size as the last, my mouth drops open. "Theo, no. You didn't."

"It seems that I have."

I tear off the wrapping paper to find Charlie's painting. The one of the lake with the beach in the distance.

Before I can chastise him for spoiling me this way, he pulls another gift out of his backseat. And then another one. By the time I have all four paintings unwrapped and arranged like a mini art gallery on the hood of his car, I'm completely speechless, tears falling freely down my face.

Theo throws an arm around my shoulders, pulling me into his chest. I know I should be worried about getting makeup on his pristine white shirt, but I have a visceral need to feel his body against mine right now.

"Is it okay?" His voice rumbles in the ear I have pressed to his chest. "Did I overstep? Getting them for you before you could get them for yourself?"

I'd told Theo how my dream was to one day buy back the paintings from our Treasure Hunt. Not only were they special because they reminded me of my mom but also because they represented the journey of our love story too. But even though I knew my friends would sell them to me for a good price, I still wasn't sure when I'd ever have enough disposable income to afford them. The old me, full of righteous independence and insular pride, might have been mad at him right now. But I know Theo bought these paintings out of love. And I'm just so damn happy to have them, there's no way I can feel anything but thankful for what he's done for me.

"No, you didn't overstep. On my salary, I would've been eighty years old before I could've ever bought these. So I'm going to accept these with grace and dignity." I elbow him playfully. "Besides, in about an hour from now what's yours is going to be mine, anyway. So technically it was *our* money that bought these, right?"

"Exactly!" he says. "And like I said, sometimes being rich has its perks." He waves a hand at the paintings, not seeing the irony that our new art collection is displayed on the world's most rattletrap car.

A crease suddenly forms between his eyes. "But wait a minute. Didn't your dad just say there were *five* paintings in the series?"

A wave of guilt hits me. I hadn't told him about when Franco mentioned the same number. "Yeah, but Dad said he wasn't sure. It was a long time ago. So who knows if he's remembering right."

Luckily, my excuse is enough to placate him. And after stashing my gifts back in his car, I hurry him off to the dining hall to find Maeve before Caroline puts us in a time-out for lollygagging at our own wedding.

As we walk, I question myself over why I don't want to think about a fifth painting. Maybe it's because everything is so perfect right now. My nerves have calmed. Things are falling into place, piece by poignant piece. Although I still feel something looming close by. (A crux? A turning point? I'm still not sure how to describe it.) But this time I feel aligned…almost eager to meet it. And if there does happen to be a fifth painting? Well then, we'll deal with finding it *after* we become husband and wife.

CHAPTER FORTY-TWO

DAD IS WAITING for me at the curve in the path to The Lookout, right before the boardwalk straightens to become our new wedding aisle.

Tim has chauffeured Caroline and me here in his golf cart. He was so careful on the way up, nervously avoiding bumps and driving painstakingly slowly so I wouldn't mess up my hair. I'm so touched by his thoughtfulness that as soon as the golf cart rolls to a stop, I lean over and give him a big hug.

My uncharacteristic affection flusters him. "Aww, it was nothing," he waves me off with his foot, the same way I might with my arm. "You and Theo. You're good people. Both of you."

His cheeks are red, and he makes a point of not looking directly at me. I guess Tim is more comfortable sharing a toke than sharing his emotions.

"You two are good together. You make cynical old people like me remember that a love like yours is possible. Now get going," he adds gruffly. "You've made your groom wait long enough. You better get your ass up there before he jumps right over the side."

I thank him again, smiling to myself as I step out of his cart. When Dad sees me, he looks even more awestruck than when he was admiring the forest earlier.

I'm no longer wearing my formal wedding gown. Instead, I've

changed into the short vintage dress I'd bought at the thrift store. (And for some reason had thrown in the back of my car this morning thinking maybe, just maybe, I might change into it at the end of the night.)

When I'd emerged from the bathroom at the dining hall wearing the more casual gossamer dress, I'd been nervous about what kind of reaction I'd get. But I still couldn't hold back one quick spin, the sheer layers of the skirt whirling like a feather-light cloud around my legs. God, this dress makes me feel so damn free.

I shouldn't have worried, because upon seeing me, Maeve had gasped out loud. Greta and Honey Bear had whooped in approval. And Caroline had slapped a hand over her mouth and cried for like the fourteenth time today.

"It's so beautiful…you're so beautiful," she'd babbled, gesturing down my body. "It's just so…so…so *you!*" Then, once again we'd both burst out laughing at her rare loss of words.

As the bridal party headed out to be ferried to the starting point by Tim and Rick, I'd lingered behind to talk to Maeve. After putting herself in charge of setting up the dining hall for the reception, she'd spent the last two hours racing around showing the caterers the kitchen, helping the baker set up the wedding cake, making sure the place settings and table arrangements are exactly how we'd talked about on all the Saturdays she and Ewan had helped out at Charlie's house. She'd somehow even managed to whipped up a few batches of my favorite oatmeal cookies in her spare time. Honestly, I don't know how the woman does it.

"Are you sure you don't want to come to the ceremony?" I'd asked, following her around a table as she fussed with one of the pinch pot arrangements.

"You know I'd love to. But I don't think he'd be a very good guest right now." She tipped her head to Ewan revving a dump truck along a windowsill. "This is the time of day we always take our paddle around the lake. And Ewan's a stickler for routine. He'll have a fit if I change things on him at the last minute. Especially after I promised him we could take the canoe out today."

I'd seen Ewan's temper tantrums before, so I understood why Maeve didn't want to risk an explosion during the ceremony. Still, I'd told her we'd miss her.

"Oh, don't worry about me," she'd insisted. "Ewan and I will do our boat trip like always, then we'll meet you back here for the party after that. You'll never even miss us." I hadn't argued. Not because I wouldn't miss her but because I knew it was futile to argue with Maeve once she'd made up her mind.

Now as we line up on the wooden path (all on our own…with absolutely no help from the micromanaging church lady) Dad gestures to my head. "Nice touch."

Just before I ducked into the bathroom to get dressed, Theo's nieces had shyly presented me with a crown of daisies they'd woven for me. The lovely little ringlet matches perfectly with the embroidered daisies on the waist of my dress. (And feels a helluva lot better than the long veil I'd worn in the church.) I swear, everything about this day just keeps getting lighter and lighter. At this rate, I might end up floating down the aisle instead of walking on two feet.

Greta bellows down the trail in her full camp counselor voice, "We're ready!!"

A distant return shout of "Got It!" comes back. (Yeah, this new wedding is definitely going to be *way* less formal than the one before.) The faint sound of guitar music filters through the trees. Victor is not only officiating the wedding but providing all the music too. God, am I ever thankful Franco fell in love with such a multi-talented man on that sabbatical he took to Saint Petersburg years ago.

As we meander down the trail—each of us walking normally, not stiffly processing in measured increments like before—I'm overwhelmed by the beauty of the lush trees curving over us like doting grandmothers, the songbirds chiming in with the strums of the guitar, the breeze moving just enough to stave off the mid-summer heat.

Before me, the bright light of The Lookout shines through the arch of the trees, the same way it did the first time Theo brought me here, back when I still hadn't realized the treasure I'd stumbled upon when I'd nervously offered him a friendship bracelet in the dining hall on that fateful day last May. How many times had we trodden this trail together? Chattering excitedly about our day. Decompressing after a tough night with a camper. Both of us eager to get to the one place we knew would wash all our worries away.

My stomach drops out from under me when my wedding party steps to the side and I finally see Theo standing in the middle of the platform waiting for me. His hair is a little more mussed up, his eyes sparkling an impossible shade of green in the sunlight. To me, he's never looked more handsome in his life.

I let out a shuddering breath. Everything is just like in my vision. The blue sky behind him. The garland of flowers wrapped around the railing. But… wait a minute. My steps falter for a split second. He's still wearing his black jacket. But he's not supposed to be wearing black. He's supposed to be wearing white. Oh my God. After all we've been through. Is there still something wrong with this moment in time?

Just keep going. A voice insists. *It's going to be alright.*

I heed the advice, not knowing for sure if I've just heard cosmic guidance or my own wishful thinking. All I know is I cannot call off this wedding again. I have to go through with this, no matter what. I'm just going to have to trust that, black jacket or not, I've done enough to make this elusive plan I agreed to play out as it should.

I smile at our guests lining the end of the trail. Their chairs are half in the woods, and they probably aren't going to be able to see the ceremony very well. But from the grins on their faces, no one seems to mind. (Which may be because our dads made sure there was an open bar available while they waited for us to get set up here.)

Our immediate family has seats up on the platform. As Maria stands, watching me walk toward her son, she clutches one hand over her heart, her eyes wet with tears. I reach my hand out to her as I pass by, and she squeezes it. When she lets go, she pointedly looks down my dress, then smiles big and gives me a thumbs up, which makes me laugh.

Dad kisses me on the cheek, and as I reach out to once again hold Theo's hand the beautiful lilt of the guitar threatens to undo me. Victor's voice is soft and warm singing "Give Yourself To Love," one of the folk songs we used to sing around the campfire before bedtime. (And in another serendipitous turn, Victor already knew by heart.)

As everyone sits, Theo and I face each other grinning madly as Victor puts his guitar away. I have a funny impulse to lurch forward and kiss Theo before we're actually pronounced husband and wife, so I can win our game from before. His eyebrows shoot up, and he gives just the slightest shake of his head, like he's just read my mind. We both have to look away to keep from cracking up.

"We've gathered together to join Theo and Annie as husband and wife...*again*," Victor quips, and the crowd laughs. Over Theo's shoulder I can just make out Maeve and Ewan in their canoe, paddling around the lake below. I smile big, and Theo turns to see what I'm looking at, and we both give them a little wave, although they're too far away to see us.

We return our focus to Victor, now telling a sweet story of when he'd first met me, back when he and Franco used to hang out with my mom a lot. My chest pangs at the mention of my beloved mom, but the faint pain doesn't scare me anymore. In fact, I like that it's there. Instead of a trigger, it's now a pleasant reminder of how much I once loved her. And how much I still love her now.

I do my best to follow Theo's lead and bask in every detail of the moment. (I know that's what he's doing from the dreamy look on his face right now.) But suddenly, from down below comes a clunking sound, then a splash, then the most blood-curdling scream I've ever heard in my life.

"EWAN!!" The terror in that one word sends a wave of ice rippling through my veins.

Theo and I race to the railing and are met with a horrible sight: An overturned canoe in the middle of the lake, Maeve bobbing helplessly next to an empty child's life jacket, and Ewan way too far away from her, frantically paddling to stay afloat.

A blur whips by the corner of my eye before I can even process what's happening. In one swift motion, Theo hurdles the railing, shouts, "Greta, get a boat!" then disappears down the deer trail to the lake. Instantly, the dense brush swallows him up, leaving only the sounds of crashing branches in his wake.

I sense an explosion of movement behind me as people leap into action. Caroline and Aunt Lydia rush to my side, each grabbling an elbow to steady me. I know I should do something, but I'm frozen in place, watching Maeve paddle in her lifejacket desperately trying to reach her child. Ewan flails valiantly just out of her reach. His little red head goes under. Then comes up. Then goes under again. And this time he doesn't surface again.

"Ewan! No!" Maeve shrieks.

A splash reverberates below me. Seconds later, Theo emerges in the lake wearing only his white shirt and pants with no shoes, swimming faster than is humanly possible, aimed directly at where Ewan just disappeared. Maeve's screams fill the air, raising chill bumps on my skin. I watch in horror as she tries in vain to free herself from her flotation device so she can dive to find her son.

"Oh my God, oh my God, oh my God," Caroline and I chant, hands clutched together, fingernails piercing each other's skin. No. This can't be happening. Ewan can't drown right here in front of us. The world cannot be as cruel as this.

Theo gets to the spot where Ewan was last seen and dives under. He's submerged for a long while. When he finally surfaces, we all gasp in hope. But Ewan isn't with him. Theo dives again. And once again we all stop breathing. But when he breaks the water, he still doesn't have the little boy. Clearly exhausted he gasps for air, then after taking one huge breath goes under for a third time, and as he does a terrible dread clutches at my throat.

Agonizing seconds tick by while he's underwater. Standing frozen in place, watching the scene unfold from up high, unable to help, I suddenly realize why this all feels so familiar: This is my nightmare come to life. The images are so visceral, so *real*. Maybe what I saw was never a nightmare. Maybe it was a premonition of what was to come.

And it was me who made this happen. I forced us to come here to camp today. I thought I was trusting my gut. Doing the right thing. Saving Theo from some tragic fate. But had I instead made a terrible mistake? Had I brought Theo here just to watch him die?

No bubbles rise to the surface where the two disappeared, and Ewan's words on the beach that day flash through my mind. *"My Angels tell me not to be scared when it happens. Because you'll be there to help me."*

My God. Had Ewan known he was going to die? Had he known that Theo would be there with him to usher him into the afterlife? Had he known they were both going to die *together?*

Theo has always been clear with me. *I'm going to die young.*

I knew that. I knew that all along.

Now he's leaving me. And I didn't even get the chance to say goodbye.

A guttural sob echoes out across the vast space, and I'm shocked to realize it's my own voice now blending with Maeve's frantic cries.

No! No! No! This can't be happening. This is NOT the plan!

Just as I think I can't bear the agony of watching the undisturbed surface of the lake for a second longer, something explodes out of the water: It's Theo…gasping for air…and clutched in his arm is a tiny redheaded boy.

My knees buckle. Lydia and Caroline hold me up, the three of us crying out in relief.

"Ewan!" Maeve shrieks. Clearly not a strong swimmer, she struggles to make her way to where Theo and Ewan are now barely afloat. I break away from Lydia to lean over the railing. Out of the corner of my eye, I see two boats full of people rowing swiftly to where Theo floats on his back, fighting to keep Ewan's face out of the water. The little boy is limp and deathly still, but I refuse to think about what that might mean.

Greta is at the helm of one boat, stroking like an Amazonian warrior, her half arm be damned. The silver vessel practically flies over the top of the water, propelled by the sheer determination of its crew. Looking at who is seated inside those boats, my hope lifts. Because those aren't any ordinary people rowing to Ewan's aid. They're nurses. And doctors. And not just any nurses and doctors. They're *pediatric* nurses and doctors. If anyone can save Ewan's life, it's them.

I hold my breath as the first boat finally reaches Theo. As Greta reaches down and plucks Ewan out of his arms and hands him back to his rescuers. As Theo motions for them to forget about him and *GO!* As the second boat with Honey Bear at the helm reaches Maeve, then finally Theo. As Honey Bear hauls Theo out of the water like a limp rag doll, so weak he can't even lift one leg over the side.

And when I know Theo is finally safe inside that boat, I turn toward the path…and I *run*.

CHAPTER FORTY-THREE

BEFORE I EVEN make it to the bottom of the switchback to the lake, I hear Ewan crying. The sheer relief of that sound hits me with such force it brings tears to my eyes. With each slap of my feet, I thank God, my Angels, Ewan's Angels, the friendly Universe, Mother Nature… everyone I can think of for saving that sweet little boy.

I burst out of the forest at a dead run, cursing the sand for slowing my progress to the group now huddled on the beach around Ewan's tiny form. Theo stands along the periphery, bent over with his hands on his knees, his chest still heaving hard. When he sees me barreling toward him, he rises to standing, eyes widening as he takes me in.

I can only imagine what I look like. I lost both my shoes and my daisy crown on the sprint down here, one of my gold combs is about to fall out of my hair, and I'm pretty sure the skirt of my dress has now floated up to encircle my waist. I don't even care. All I care about is getting to Theo. Touching him. Feeling him. Making sure he's okay.

He holds out his arms and I crash into him, wrapping my arms around his torso as he staggers backward.

"Theo, oh my God! Are you okay?" I press my head against his chest, rejoicing in the sound of his beautiful beating heart. "I was so scared. You were there, and then you went under. And I thought…I thought you weren't going to…"

"Yeah," he says, kissing the top of my head. "I thought the same thing for a while there too."

I squeeze him so tightly I hear the air whoosh out of his lips. Then I realize that's probably not the most helpful thing to do to someone already struggling to breathe, and I loosen my grip. Behind me, Maeve is still crying, but in relief this time. I let go of Theo and whirl to see how Ewan is doing.

The doctors and nurses kneeling around him are all breathing hard too but also smiling big at the little boy they've just brought back to life. Honestly, Ewan looks pretty normal to me. His lungs obviously work according to his lusty wails, and his cheeks are pink as he fights against his mom, insisting he "just wants to go home!"

Maeve crouches over him, tears falling down her cheeks as she repeats almost manically, "I always clip his life jacket, I swear. I must have forgotten this time. He leaned over to pick up a leaf. I tried to tell him to sit down, but it was too late. I always clip his life jacket…I swear….I swear…How could I have forgotten this time? I always clip his life jacket. I swear. I always…"

Her words seem directed more at herself than anyone else, and I shudder watching her angst. I can't imagine the range of emotions she's feeling right now. I only hope that in time she'll be able to forgive herself for making such a human mistake.

A siren wails in the distance, and again I bless Camp Boundless for its tried-and-true emergency protocols. Greta hustles around the beachfront, directing Rick to bring back supplies from the nursing office, opening the gate to the access road that will allow the ambulance to pull up at the beach, sending Tim to Maeve's cabin to get what she'll need for the hospital. My jokester friend has transformed into a stunningly efficient nurse in the blink of an eye, and all I can do is marvel at her competence. And think of how useless I was, standing like a statue watching the horror unfold while the rest of the world jumped into action.

With Ewan being taken care of, I turn back to survey Theo. Bloody slash marks stripe his cheeks from his trip through the underbrush. His clothes are soaked, and his shoulders are slumped over like it's taking all his energy just to keep himself upright.

"Are you sure you're okay?" I ask. He nods, refusing to take his eyes off Ewan. "What happened down there?" I whisper.

His gaze darts to Maeve for a split second. "I'll tell you later," he whispers back.

The ambulance arrives, and after an update from the two doctors already attending Ewan, they quickly load the little boy onto the stretcher. Only when she's asked to step aside for a moment, does Maeve look up, blinking around the lakefront like it's the first time she's seen anything other than her son in a long while.

Her eyes land on Theo and she rushes over. I step aside as she wraps him in a hug even fiercer than my own. I guess only grateful moms know how to give a hug like that.

She sobs against his chest as he holds her. "Thank you. Thank you. Thank you," she chants. "You saved my Ewan…you saved my little boy."

Theo rests his head on hers, and the two of them simply hold each other for a long while. Then, Maeve pulls back abruptly. "What would've happened if you hadn't been here?" she asks as if it's the first time she's thought of such a scenario. "What if they hadn't been here?" She gestures to the doctors and nurses. "What if I'd been all alone like I usually am when we take our boat ride? I would've never been able to save him." She shudders at the possibility. And so do I.

"You can't think like that," Theo tells her. "We *were* here. And that's all that matters." He looks over her head at where the ambulance drivers are now preparing to load Ewan into the ambulance. He grabs Maeve's hand, and the two of them go to Ewan's side.

"Bye, Buddy," Theo says, bending close to Ewan's face. "You're going to be alright. Just listen to the doctors and nurses, and I'll be there to see you soon, okay?" He lifts Ewan's tiny hand to his lips and kisses it. "I love you, Ewan. You did good out there. Really, really good. You're a very, very brave boy. You know that?"

I watch Theo, amazed at how he's able to remain so composed after all he's just been through.

Ewan says stoically. "My Angels were right. You were there for me. I knew you would be."

Theo can only nod, his lips a thin line as he watches Ewan and then Maeve load into the back of the ambulance.

He waves and smiles big as they shut the doors, the slam cutting off another litany of Maeve's tear-soaked thank yous.

And it's only after the ambulance has disappeared up the road that Theo finally collapses on his knees in the sand, puts his head in his hands, and cries.

CHAPTER FORTY-FOUR

THEO

ANNIE KNEELS IN the sand, her white dress pooled around her like a mushroom cap, holding me as I cry. She doesn't even seem to care that I'm still soaking wet and most likely ruining her dress. She lets me nestle my face in the crook of her neck, lets my hot tears trickle down the soft skin of her collarbone, and squeezes me tightly; rocking and crooning "it's okay, it's okay" over and over, as she gently strokes my hair.

From the moment I looked over the side of The Lookout and saw that overturned canoe, I've been running on nothing but primal instinct alone; all my rational thoughts cast aside and replaced with clear, unanalyzed action. *Jump, run, swim, dive.* My body had simply responded on its own, as if the person named Theo was no longer in the driver's seat anymore. As if I'd been taken over by something much greater than myself.

But something had happened underneath the weight of that dark water. When I hadn't been able to find Ewan on the first dive. Then the second. When my lungs had burned and my arms had gone weak. That's when my rational mind had swept in again. And with it came the doubt…and the near-paralyzing fear.

All I could think of was Ewan's words on the beach a few months ago. *"My Angels tell me not to be scared when it happens. Because you'll be there to help me.*" Back then I'd assured him he'd never have to be scared if I was around. But what if I'd lied to him? What if I couldn't save him like I'd promised?

My hope had faded further and further away with each passing second I couldn't find him. Clutched with desperation, I'd done the only thing I could think of: I'd silently called out for help. Then I'd let go and turned myself over to that greater force once again. And that's when I saw him.

He was floating in the middle of a glowing bubble, like someone was shining a flashlight on him from up above. He was unconscious, and yet he still had one hand reaching out toward the surface. Toward me. And with one last burst of energy, I dove toward him. Grabbed that little icy hand and *pulled.*

Now on the beach, emptied of tears, I break away from Annie and wipe my eyes. "Sorry. It's just the aftermath of the adrenaline hitting me. I can't help it."

"You don't have to apologize!" she says, gently brushing the tears from my cheeks. "Good grief, that was some next-level heroics you just performed. You can blubber for the rest of the day as far as I'm concerned."

Her eyes dart back and forth between mine as if she can barely believe I'm alive. I can barely believe it either. For a few seconds there underwater, things were a bit touch and go. I truly wondered if my time here was done.

Staring into her awestruck face, she's never looked more beautiful. Her hair is sticking up everywhere and there's sand stuck on the tip of her nose and her cheeks are already pink from the sun. The only thing that would make her even more beautiful is a smile.

"Oh, you call this *blubbering*?" I tease. "Ouch. Talk about kicking a man when he's down."

She gives me a rough shove on the shoulder, grinning big. "You know what I meant." Then she becomes serious again. "I can't believe you saved him."

"You saved him too."

"What? No I didn't. I just stood there like a dunce while everyone else was helping."

"Annie, think about it. What Maeve said is true. What if we hadn't been here? She always takes Ewan out on the boat at this time of day. She would've taken him out today. And the boat would've capsized just like it did. But without us here, she would've been all alone."

Annie listens intently as I go on. "I hate to say it. But I don't think Maeve would've been able to save him. And even if she had, there wouldn't have been a team of pediatric doctors and nurses here to tend to Ewan the second he made it to shore. Don't you get it? None of this would've turned out the way it had if you hadn't insisted we switch the venue and come to Camp Boundless. Annie, if it weren't for you speaking up the way you did, Ewan would've died today."

She clasps a hand over her mouth, eyes wide as she considers my argument. Yes, I'd physically pulled Ewan from the water. But it was Annie who had moved all the chess pieces into place to make the rescue possible. She was the one who had brought me and all the trained medical staff here at this exact moment in time so this disaster could be averted. If she hadn't been so adamant at the church earlier, things here at Camp Boundless would've turned out much differently than they had.

"You said it yourself back at the church," I say. "You said, 'We're not supposed to be here right now. I just know it' And then you knew exactly where we had to be in order to save Ewan."

"Oh my God. You're right." She stares off into the distance, thinking. "Theo, do you think this is what the Angels meant when they said we have a chance to affect many lives? By saving Ewan's life, did we just create a ripple effect that might change a lot of other lives in the future?"

"Yes, Annie! Yes! All because of you!"

I sweep her up in a hug, and she mumbles into my wet shirt. "And also because you listened to my crazy idea and came here with me. Don't forget about that part."

We pull apart and stare at each other in disbelief. While we're kneeling there in silence, Dr. Fletcher, one of my favorite oncologists from when I kid, approaches us.

"Man, that was quite a rescue, Theo." He bends to clap me on the back. "My God, I still don't know how you found him in that lake."

I rise to shake his hand, my spent legs groaning in protest. After I thank him for his part in the rescue, his expression turns serious. "But we probably need to check you now. Make sure you're okay after all you just went through."

Although I tell him I feel fine, he ushers me over to a bench to give me a once-over.

I'm thankful when Greta joins us. Man, am I ever glad she was here today. Greta is the kind of woman who shines in a crisis. Hell, she's the kind of woman who shines all the time. And from the way Wen is looking at her from across the beach, I have a feeling he's thinking the same thing right now.

Greta loops a hand around Annie's waist, the two of them bowing their heads together as they watch Dr. Fletcher examine me. Greta whispers something into Annie's ear, and Annie giggles. She's probably making fun of me, but I don't even care because Annie still looks a little shook up, and clearly needs the distraction.

Dr. Fletcher has me take off my shirt as he listens to my heart and lungs, checks my pulse, and palpates my stomach. We chat back and forth about hospital scuttlebutt, and I assure him that this ceremony will in fact take place at some point today, so nobody should leave quite yet.

"I mean that is, if Annie still wants to marry me," I say with a laugh. When I look up at her, she's staring at me with wide eyes. Uh oh. I hope to hell we're not going to have to move this wedding again.

"What's wrong?" I ask her after Dr. Fletcher pronounces me fit to be wed.

Annie grabs my wrist and drags me off toward the dock while I struggle to get my arm back into my shirt.

She shouts over her shoulder to Greta that we need a minute to ourselves. Then once we're alone, she turns to me with an unreadable expression. "Theo, we need to talk."

CHAPTER FORTY-FIVE

ANNIE

"THEY'RE GONE," I tell Theo.

He cocks his head at me. "What do you mean? Who's gone? You mean Dr. Dean and Andrea? That's okay. They wanted to follow the ambulance to the hospital so they could follow up on Ewan."

"No, not Dr. Dean and Andrea!" I shout, pointing at his torso. "Your bruises. They're gone!"

"What?" he says, looking down at his unbuttoned shirt.

"Look!" I rip open the sides of his shirt, then try to pull it off him, but since it's still soaked it snags on his shoulders. The two of us struggle to release him from the fabric, grunting and tugging until Theo steps back and says with a huff, "Just let me do it!"

He finally shucks the damn thing in the sand, then raises his arms to look down at his ribcage. The same rib cage that had been painted in ugly splotches of greens and browns only yesterday. But now is covered in perfectly tan, unblemished skin.

"Wait. How could this be?" He twists one arm, and the bruise at the top is gone too. As well as the newer one that appeared yesterday near his elbow. He unbuttons his pants, and when he tugs down his underwear we both gasp. The bruise on his hip is gone too. And the bruises haven't merely faded either. It's like they've all been completely erased. Not a trace of yellow or green left behind.

"They were there this morning when I got dressed," Theo whispers in disbelief.

"I know. I saw them yesterday," I whisper back. "What do you think this means?"

"I don't know. But maybe it means…" he hesitates. "That something's changed?"

We both stare wide-eyed at each other, scared to say what we're thinking out loud. That maybe, just maybe…through some crazy twist in fate, Theo isn't sick anymore.

Now, this *was the plan.*

A chill goes through me, and when I look over at Theo, goosebumps pebble his arms too. We nod dumbly at each other, but we still don't say the words out loud. Because we both know we haven't completed all of our promise quite yet.

"Let's go get married, Annie," Theo says, grinning widely.

I give him a determined nod. "Let's go get married, Theo."

But neither of us moves. My eyes land on his perfect, still slightly blue, lips. "God, I can't wait to kiss you."

"Yeah, I can't wait to kiss you too." He collects his dress shirt off the ground, shaking out the sand. Then he abruptly stops, a stricken look on his face. "Shit."

"What? What is it?"

"I lost my jacket in the bushes. And I don't think I'm getting it back." He braces himself, obviously expecting me to be mad.

But believe me, I'm not.

"Oh, don't worry." I say with a laugh. "I think that jacket is exactly where it's supposed to be right now."

∞

"We're gathered together to join Theo and Annie in marriage…*again,*" Victor repeats his one-liner, and everyone laughs. "Hey, I guess third time's a charm, right?"

If there was excitement in the air before, it has now tripled in size. When we finally reassembled at The Lookout a few minutes ago, an impromptu celebration had broken out. Friends, family, strangers all crying and hugging and laughing over the miracle they'd just witnessed. Talk about a magical place. This hilltop precipice is now overflowing with so much love I can literally feel its positive energy vibrating against my skin.

Theo had tried to quietly slip back to his place at the altar, but the crowd was not having it. They'd erupted in applause the moment they saw him. I knew from the pink in his cheeks he wanted to brush off the attention. But after I'd given him a look, he'd graciously accepted the appreciation with his signature shrug and sheepish smile.

Now, we've gone back to our former places, picking up the ceremony where we left off. Theo has somehow squeezed himself back into his white dress shirt—which is a bit crumpled but none the worse for wear. And although he replaced his lost tie with Wen's, he couldn't find his shoes, so he's barefoot. (Along with me, Greta, and Honey Bear, who all lost our shoes in the fray.)

Rebecca and Caroline did an amazing job fixing my hair, and Theo's nieces hurriedly wove a new daisy crown for my head. So aside from a few smudges on the front of my white dress, I look almost the same as before. On the outside. But on the inside, I feel like everything has changed. I can only hope my mom's whisper about this being the plan turns out to be right.

Don't worry. It will all come back to you. Soon.

Victor implores the near-delirious crowd, "How about we forget all the lengthy platitudes? We all just want to get these kids married. And quickly, right?!"

A rowdy cheer explodes around us.

"Then let's do it!" Victor graciously steps aside for us to repeat our simple vows to each other. Vows that aren't the same as the religious ones we'd practiced at the rehearsal last night in the church. No, these are the only vows that make sense to us anymore.

Theo grasps my hands, looking deeply into my eyes. "Annie,"

his voice wobbles sweetly. "I promise to love you across time and distance. Lifetimes and eternities. And I promise we'll always…*always* be together. Forevermore."

I gaze up at his lovely, beat-up face, my heart aching with so many emotions it's impossible to put words to them all. I don't just love this man. I adore him. Marvel at him. Admire him beyond belief. I don't think there will be a day I won't look at him and thank the Lord for bringing him into my life. For whatever time we have left here on Earth. And whatever happens after that.

"Theo," I choke out through the lump in my throat. "I promise to love you across time and distance. Lifetimes and eternities. And I promise we'll always…*always* be together. Forevermore."

Standing there, facing him with my heart bursting with love, I see us as if from a distance. Our white shirts. The flowers in the background. The blue sky filling the frame of the moment.

Yes. This is it. *This* is right.

Suddenly a hummingbird flits in from nowhere and hovers between us. It cocks its head back and forth from Theo to me, then it rises higher, blurred wings outstretched as if offering us a blessing. Then it disappears just as suddenly as it came. The crowd gasps at the seemingly coincidental appearance, but Theo and I can only laugh. We both know who that little bird represents. And we both know its arrival was no coincidence.

"I love you, Mommy," I whisper inside my head.

And I love you too, Buttercup. She says, then laughs. *And I hope you like having me around, because you're not getting rid of me ever again.*

The ceremony continues. Victor says something about nothing ever being able to tear us apart, but despite his heartfelt words, Theo and I can't seem to keep a straight face. We exchange little huffs of laughter back and forth, which quickly grow louder and more out of control the more we fight to stay serious. As our silliness builds, the warm summer air begins to swirl around our bodies; gently at first, then faster and faster the harder we laugh. Theo and I blink at each other, dumbfounded by the tornado we're now standing inside. A tornado that we've somehow created with the sheer force of our conjoined joy.

We look around to find all our friends, our family, the forest itself, blurred into soft pastels, every sharp edge washed and blended as if we're now standing inside a living watercolor painting.

I expect the crowd to gasp or cry out. But everyone acts normally, as if they aren't seeing the same thing that we are.

It's happening. We're inching closer and closer to the moment we've been searching for. I know it. And Theo does too.

We laugh even louder.

Somehow, we muddle through the exchange of rings and some final words that Victor speaks over us in a voice that now sounds very far away. Pressure builds inside my chest, a snapping of electricity looping between where Theo and I touch inside the swirling wind. Its intensity grows where our hands are clasped together. The sensation is pleasant, yet also so strong it feels like every molecule in my body is being altered. The two of us clutch onto each other for dear life as the force builds and builds. It feels like we're teetering on the edge of a precipice about to fall into the vast unknown…an unknown that promises to catch us in its loving arms.

Theo's body begins to glow like there's sunlight bursting out from beneath his skin. And from the warmth I feel, the way his eyes are going wide as he gazes upon me in wonder, I know the same thing is happening to me. By the time we faintly hear Victor say, "You can now kiss the bride," we're both laughing hysterically, like we're high. That's what this feels like. The highest high imaginable. An energy so big it can't stay contain inside one body, so it's leapt the paltry physical barrier between us to now consume two.

Thank goodness Theo has the wherewithal to follow Victor's instructions about kissing me. He lets go of one of my hands and places his palm upon my cheek. Sparks snap and crackle where our skin touches, our glow surging brighter.

Tears now line his eyes. He dips his head, hesitating so his lips hover over mine. We're so close now. I can feel it…our future…waiting to become real.

"Are you ready to go?" he whispers.

"With you, I'll go anywhere," I breathe.

And when our lips finally meet, a white light explodes through my vision, and everything I once knew disappears.

Except for the two of us.

CHAPTER FORTY-SIX

Somewhere *else*...

WHEN THEY ARRIVE, they don't even say hello at first. They're too consumed inside their little whirling bubble of love to even notice where they are. Or notice that I'm here too, standing right in front of them, tapping my foot waiting for them to realize the magnitude of what they've just done.

Soon enough, they break their kiss, blinking around as if they've just woken up from a dream.

"We did it!" Annie shouts in jubilation. Then she hesitates, turning to me with a questioning look. "I mean, we did, didn't we?"

I laugh. It's such a human reaction. Feeling the need to temper hope. Even in a place like this.

"Yes! Yes! You did it!" I pump my fists in the air and dance around wildly. "You two followed your Intertwined Path! You found the one moment in time I showed you and made the jump. You switched your timelines and ended up changing your fates forever!"

Annie dusts her palms together. "Simple, really," she deadpans, and we all crack up.

"Wow!" Theo marvels. "What a rush! That was so much fun. Wasn't it fun, Annie?"

"Yeah, it was fun for you because you were oblivious there at the end. I was the one who had to do all the heavy lifting to get us here."

He hooks an arm around her waist and pulls her to his side. Their forms blur together where they touch. "And you did an amazing job, Annie. I always say no one follows strange dreams, faint memories, and unexplained angelic guidance better than you."

She rolls her eyes, but her smile is as bright as the light illuminating the colors around us.

Noticing the technicolor glare, they turn slow circles, taking in our surroundings. Previously they could only see the trees flanking our sides. But now that they've made it to this point, they're able to see more: The boardwalk trail, the platform we stand upon, the opening that looks out not on a lake, but an endless expanse of blackness filled with countless geometrical facets that represents their conjoined futures.

"So are we here *now*?" Annie asks. "Like in the middle of our wedding? Or is this before? Like when we both first met up? When Theo died and I passed out in the bathroom? Or is this some other time completely?" She looks more confused with every word she speaks

"Again, the questions about time are pointless." I remind her. "Those human brains of yours can never fathom how it really works. How in truth everything happens all at once; time bending and looping and stacking up on itself so that all experience happens simultaneously in a field of never-ending awareness."

Seeing their blank looks I add. "Forget about figuring it out. Just imagine your life as a car. You can go a lot of fun places in a car without ever understanding how it actually works, right?" They nod and I add, "It's the same idea with life."

The two of them grin, seeming satisfied, as if the question suddenly means nothing to them. That's what no one understands until they're fully released into the afterlife. When you get here, you don't suddenly receive all your answers. Instead, you forget all your questions.

"So, do you want to see what you did?" I wave them closer to the edge of the platform. The three of us look out into the darkness. Etched in the black are golden rays of light stretching from point to point, creating millions of diamond-like fractals of decisions that make up their lives.

"See there," I point to the snippet I'd shown them before, of the two of them on their wedding day. "That was the switching point. Like when you throw a switch for a train so the car can jump over to a new set of tracks. You made it to that exact point in time. And now—according to the laws agreed upon in the physical world—instead of following along those routes." I show them all the abbreviated paths they left behind where Theo would've died young. "This is what awaits you."

I sweep a hand at the vast galaxy of possibilities that branch off into their own endless sea of fractals. Where each ray meets another, a scene plays out over and over. Celebrations and hardships and births and achievements. All of them filled with such love and hope and joy. All of them filled with Annie and Theo joined together on their Intertwined Path for a long, long time to come.

They stare into their future in quiet revelry. Neither of them asks if they'll remember all the details from this meeting with me. They already know they won't. Because that's the way they like it. They've always wanted their lives together to be an adventure. And for there to be adventure, there has to be unknowns.

"We really did it," Theo murmurs. They gaze at each other as the space around us swells with nearly blinding light. "I'm going to live a long, long life."

They seem to need a second to let that sink in. Then Annie suddenly remembers something. "And Ewan? Was I right in thinking we altered his timeline too?"

"Yes, of course." I dip my chin at the galaxy before us. In it, Ewan's life has its own solar system. "His life will continue on for a long while too, just like yours. Generations upon generations being born through him; souls that wouldn't have existed if you hadn't saved him on your wedding day. All thanks to two people who learned how to trust each other, trust themselves," I touch a hand to my heart. "And trust us."

"That's why you said we could affect many lives. Not just our own," Annie says. "Man, the implications of this are just so…so… mind-blowing!"

"All decisions have ripple effects," I say. "Most of which you never know about. But it's better that way. We don't want you all taking yourselves too seriously. Especially since this is all supposed to be fun."

Theo laughs, shaking his head in exasperation.

"What?" Annie asks.

"I remember a time when I wanted to stay here in the afterlife and not go back to the physical real. But now all I can think about is how excited I am to get back there." He points at his whirling future. "I can't think of anything better than getting to spend my whole long lifetime with you, Annie."

She gives him a wink. "Are you saying that hanging out with me is even better than being in heaven?"

"I'm saying heaven is wherever *you* are."

"Oh my God! You're such a sap!" She tries to give him a shove but her hands blend right into his chest. She shoots me an imploring look. "You mean I'm going to have to put up with this mushiness for the next sixty years?!"

Theo pipes up. "Sorry, but it's written in the stars." He waves a hand at the blackness. "You aren't getting away from me now!"

With that, Theo starts chasing Annie around the platform. She zigs and zags, squealing in delight. But as they race around, I notice their edges start to blur even more. Uh oh. It looks like this meeting is almost over. They've gotten the confirmation they needed. Now it's time to get them back so they can reap their rewards.

Sensing her departure, Annie stops running and reaches out to me. I firm myself up when I wrap her in an embrace, so she can really feel the sensation of her head resting against my bosom one last time.

"Thank you, Mommy," she says. "For being here for me. For never leaving me, even when I left you." I can feel the human sadness wafting off of her. Such a misunderstanding. And so unnecessary.

"You were always there for me," I tell her. "You just didn't realize it. But I did." I don't need to explain myself any further. No, in time she'll figure it out for herself.

We grin at each other, our one light split into two. But only temporarily.

Annie steps back and weaves her fingers through Theo's again. Seeing them holding onto each other like that, I let out a satisfied sigh. He's got her. And she's got him. And together they're both going to be alright.

CHAPTER FORTY-SEVEN

ANNIE

WHEN I LAND back in my body, my lips are still pressed against Theo's.

We break apart, eyes wild as we take in each other's now very Earthly bodies.

We say three words in unison. "I remember everything." Then we both burst out laughing.

Elation rushes over me. I can't believe it. We did it! We actually freakin' did it!

Hands shaking, I reach up and touch Theo's face, marveling over every beautiful inch of him. My fingertips trace his cheeks, his brow, his jaw; each feature more astonishing than the last. He's here. He's alive. And well. And he's going to remain alive and well for a long, long time.

"You're not going to die young, Theo," I whisper. God, I love the sound of those words. Especially since I can now say them with such confidence.

After everything that happened today, I didn't think it was physically possible for my body to cry any more. But apparently, I was wrong, because tears flow freely down my cheeks.

"I'm not going to die young," Theo repeats softly as if he still can't believe it himself. He's crying too… his hands framing my face and thumbs brushing my teardrops away. "I'm going to live, Annie," he says, sounding so young, so innocent. "I'm going to *live*."

"Yes, you're going to live! You're going to live!" I barely even know what I'm saying anymore…this is all too much. My goodness. Talk about blubbering. We press our foreheads together, ugly crying as we repeat those words over and over again.

It takes us a moment to notice the cheers rising around us. Startled, we pull apart, blinking at the crowd of our loved ones, who only moments ago weren't there. They whoop and holler loudly; probably thinking the reason Theo and I are so emotional is because we finally got married after three tries. Oh, if they only knew the real reason we're such wrecks.

Theo catches my chin and pulls my face back to him. He cups a hand on the back of my head and kisses me with all the passion we usually reserve for behind closed doors. Laughing into his mouth, I melt into him, kissing and crying and clutching onto his shirt like I might never, ever let him go. We're making quite a spectacle of ourselves, but neither of us cares. And the crowd obviously doesn't either because they keep clapping louder and egging us on, like they could stand here and watch us celebrate all day long.

Victor strums our new recessional song: Annie's Song" by John Denver. Hearing the heart-melting lyrics—*you fill up my senses, like a night in the forest*—Theo and I somehow pull ourselves together and with our hands raised triumphantly, we jog down the aisle of our guests and onto the boardwalk path.

Once we clear the chairs, we're supposed to keep walking, leading everyone down to the reception in the dining hall. But only a few steps into the shaded path, we both stop abruptly and turn back, gazing longingly at The Lookout.

"I can't leave it just yet," I say, feeling a familiar tug in my gut: The Lookout silently calling us back.

"Me neither," Theo agrees.

So—in keeping with the day's theme of changing things up at the last minute—we set up an impromptu receiving line right there on the trail. We hug each of our guests as they pass by and assure them we'll join them for the festivities soon. We just need to do one thing first.

Once everyone has drifted away, Theo and I join hands again and step up into our beloved space.

The poignancy of the moment is almost too much to bear. Being here in such glorified beauty, alone with the person I love most in the world after all we've been through…words cannot capture this feeling. So we stay quiet and stand at the edge looking out over the dark water of the lake, thinking of the other, much darker vastness we just gazed upon. A realm of possibilities just gifted to us by the friendliest of all Universes. The loving benevolence that, unbeknownst to me, has been with me all along.

I let out a heavy sigh, nestling into Theo's chest as he wraps his arms around my waist.

"So, what did you see when we were there?" I ask, thinking of the mind-bending time travel trip we just took. The one that, as my Angel Mom suggested, would be futile to try to understand logically.

I can't see Theo's face, but I can sense him smiling above me. "I saw so much joy and happiness and fun."

"Yeah, me too."

He thinks for a little while longer. "And babies. I saw a lot of babies."

I giggle, my heart swelling again. "Yeah, me too. And they were so cute!"

"So, so super cute."

"And we were excellent parents," I chime in.

"The best." His voice is tinged with amusement. We know we're only picking out the good stuff. But who can blame us at a time like this?

"And I saw grandkids too," I add.

"Oh yeah. So many grandkids. Gaggles of them. There were freakin' kids everywhere!"

"And I saw you with gray hair," I say excitedly. My God, just the thought of Theo having enough time for his hair to go gray? Do old people know what a blessing aging really is?

"Yup, and you had gray hair too," he says.

"I was a cute little old lady, wasn't I?" I tease.

"So adorable. With your sweet little wrinkles." He bends and plants little kisses along the corner of my eyes.

He goes on. "And I wasn't half bad myself. Still getting around okay even as I got older." He lets go of me and bounces on the tips of his toes like a boxer. "No one's keeping this guy down." He punches the air, grunting dramatically.

I giggle at his antics. Then pull him back to me. "And you didn't even go completely bald! Did you see that?"

"Yeah. I noticed that too! So I guess I get to keep these luscious locks for a long time." He tosses his hair dramatically.

"You deserve it. You know, since you already did your time as a baldy when you were a kid."

We go on for a while, trying, yet not really trying, to remember everything we saw. As we talk, I can feel the images already slipping away, just as we both knew they would. But it's okay. Like Theo once told me, you don't really want to know your future. Or else life wouldn't be half as much fun.

After a few beats of silence, Theo says. "I think I still die first."

I nod. I wasn't going to mention that part, but I saw a scene of us in bed together saying our final goodbyes. Thank God, it looks like we're both quite old when it happens. But it's clear that I'll be the one left behind.

"It's okay," I tell him cheerfully. "I'm sure after all those years I'll be sick of you. And you know me. I like my alone time, so I'm sure I'll be okay."

"There's no one more capable than you," Theo agrees. "I have no doubt you'll get along just fine without me."

I whirl in front of him. "But that's not going to happen for a very long time, so let's not think about all that sad stuff right now."

He furrows his brow. "Think about what? I've forgotten it already."

I beam at him. Goodness, I love this man. "Kiss me, my husband!"

"Gladly, my wife!"

This time when our lips meet, our kisses are tender and slow. And overflowing with blessed relief. Over these past months we'd done our best to shoulder the weight of losing each other so soon. But who were we kidding? It was so damn hard. There was so much sadness and dread and, let's face it, *anger* over the hand we'd been dealt. Only now, kissing Theo without one shred of worry about impending illnesses or disappearing time, do I realize how heavy that burden was to bear.

When we finally break apart, I try to put that feeling into words. "Hey! Listen up out there!" I shout out over the lake. "We're Theo and Annie! And the world is our damn oyster!"

Theo tips his head up at the sky, laughing hard. I can only imagine all the weight that's just dropped off his poor shoulders too.

"Yes, it is!" Theo shouts back just like I did. Then he turns to me, eyes dancing. "So let's go eat it up!"

∞

We linger just a few moments longer, saying goodbye to The Lookout...at least for now.

I think of how Theo and I always felt so good here. No matter what mood we were in on the walk up, once we stepped up onto this platform, all we ever felt was peace and happiness inside.

We'd attributed our good cheer to the lingering vibrations of happy people from the past. But we'd added our own imprint today, hadn't we? What a celebration we'd had! All those cheers and tears. And whoops and hollers. And heartfelt prayers and blessed sighs of relief. Talk about leaving behind some good vibrations...what happened here today will surely remain etched into this land for centuries to come.

I suddenly remember what my Angel Mom said about time not truly being linear. That everything happens all at once; time bending and looping and stacking up on itself in ways our simple minds can't understand.

Which means today's celebration was never fixed to one point in time. Instead, it's been here all along.

My hand flies to my mouth as all the pieces suddenly fall into place.

"Oh my God!" I yank Theo's arm roughly, jerking him around to me. "Remember how we were always so shocked by how good this place made us feel?"

"Uh, yeah…I guess," he stammers, confused by my sudden vehemence.

"And how we thought it was because we were picking up the emotions of happy people that had been here before us?"

When he nods I go on. "But what if all this time we weren't feeling celebrations from the past… but from *our own* future?"

His gaze darts back and forth between mine as he considers my theory. Then a dawning slowly spreads across his face.

"I see what you're getting at, Annie," he says excitedly. "Good grief! I think you might be right."

"I am…I know I am!"

For what seems like the hundredth time today, we look at each other in wide-eyed wonder.

"What we felt in this space was never about ancient explorers or tribes of Native Americans from long ago…." Theo picks up where I left off.

"No. Every time we came here, we were feeling *this* day," I add. "*This* celebration."

"And who knows." He cocks one brow. "Maybe even some more celebrations to come?"

For a split second the sounds of the forest swell. All the bird chirps and frog galumphs and cricket whirls amplified as if someone has turned up the volume on life. Then the cacophony fades back to normal again.

Theo touches his own ears as if he's heard it too. I'll take that as The Lookout confirming we're right.

I shake my head at him, dumbfounded by my realization. "What we felt here last summer was never about something that happened in the past. Instead, we were feeling our own future… and what would one day happen here." I have to stop and catch my breath before I can say the rest. "All along it was us, Theo. It's always been us. *We* were the happy people."

CHAPTER FORTY-EIGHT

THEO AND I run down the boardwalk, our bare feet slapping the planks and our laughter echoing off the treetops.

I don't even care that one side of my hair is falling down and my Secret deodorant is failing. We're off on our second most thrilling mission of the day: Telling Maria her son is not going to die young. Instead, he's going to live a long and happy life. And have lots of babies and grandbabies. And keep his hair even after it goes gray. And stay married to me the whole damn time. Goodness, I can't wait to see her face when she hears the news.

When we burst out of the forest into the parking lot, I'm surprised to see Aunt Lydia leaning on her car, waiting for us.

She straightens as we approach. Out of breath, I pant, "What's… going…on? Is everything okay?" I should've left the talking to Theo because, true to form, he's not even winded.

"Oh, everything's great! Just peachy, in fact!" She grins in a Cheshire-cat way, like she's hiding some big secret.

"Good, good," I say, then lurch forward and give her a hug. "You're the best, Aunt Lydia!" I feel bad that in all the hullabaloo, I haven't had a chance to properly thank her for all she's done for me lately. I should probably apologize too, because I think I might have inadvertently knocked her down when I took off running to find Theo after he got hauled inside that boat.

I motion to the dining hall. Live music and the low hum of conversation trickle out the open windows. Finally, our guests are getting to eat their meals.

"Ready to go inside?" I don't want to brush Lydia off, but we're really excited to talk to Maria.

"I won't keep you." She turns around and picks up a wrapped gift I hadn't seen resting on the car hood behind her. "I just wanted to give you guys this first."

Theo holds up a palm. "Thanks a lot." He eyes the door to the building like it's taking everything he has not to bolt. "But you can put that on the gift table inside. I think we're going to open gifts later. Right, Annie?"

He gives me a look like, *Do something quick. We need to keep moving!*

Lydia's mouth quirks up. "Oh, I think you're going to want to open this one sooner rather than later."

She lifts the gift higher and, for the first time, Theo and I really look at it. It's a familiar-size rectangle. That she's holding with both hands. Which looks kind of heavy. And has wrapping paper that's solid along four sides, but caves in toward the middle.

Theo and I lock eyes. "No," he says.

"It can't be," I say.

"Oh, it is," Aunt Lydia says.

At that point, Theo and I put our other mission on hold.

"But how?" I say.

"You'll see," Lydia says.

"Let me." Theo gingerly takes the gift from her hands.

He sets it down on the hood of her car, the same way I had with his gifts earlier. I give him a silent nod, asking him to do the unveiling. My heart revs in my chest as Franco's words ring in my ears.

I thought I remembered seeing them all together and there were five.

And my dad's comment. *There were five of them, I think.*

Theo tears the paper away strip by strip. Just as I suspected, it's definitely one of Mom's paintings. But what will the scene be? And will it come with a last clue? And does this mean the Treasure Hunt isn't over quite yet?

Theo is being way too painstaking with the unwrapping, so I reach over him, grab the last chunk of paper and roughly tug it away. We both gasp. Before us sits a heart-achingly beautiful watercolor of Bluffpoint Lookout, painted from the perspective of someone standing on the trail. Curved oak trees frame the edges of the scene, and a cloudless blue sky shines in the background. It's the same vista we've gazed upon so many times. But what makes this rendition so astonishing is my mom has included a garland of brightly colored flowers wrapped around the wooden railings. And clusters of potted wildflowers positioned in the corners, exactly the way Caroline had placed them only hours ago. And the little woven rug where Theo and I had just stood as we'd recited our vows.

It's an exact replica of our wedding altar, brought to life in every tiny, watercolor detail.

That my mom painted twenty-three years ago. Before Theo and I were even born.

Talk about time folding up on itself. If I didn't have a massive brain cramp before seeing this, now I can almost hear my logical mind throwing in the towel and storming off in a huff.

Somehow, in her mind's eye, my mom had seen our wedding day before it ever happened. And painted it. Even though there was a good chance we would never make it to the place where it existed in this version of our lives.

If I didn't believe in miracles before, I certainly do now.

Theo pulls me close. "Now that." He points at the exquisitely detailed painting. "Is a really good clue."

"Yeah, if we'd only gotten that one first, the rest would've certainly been easier," I add, and we both burst out laughing.

We turn to Lydia hoping for some answers and I'm surprised to find my aunt uncharacteristically choked up, holding one hand over her heart, watching us with a tender expression on her face.

When she notices us waiting for her to explain more, she startles back to life. "All I know is, on one of the last days she was alive, Grace told me where to find the painting in her studio and instructed me to take it home with me. She said, and I quote: 'If a very special day comes for Annie and Theo, that's when I want you to give it to them.' Hell, at that point I was so confused I'd given up asking what she meant. I just went along with it and trusted she would help me when I needed it. And boy, did she ever. When you announced your engagement, I knew exactly what I had to do." Lydia shrugs. "Simple, really."

My eyes fly to Theo's and we both laugh. *Simple, really.* Those were the exact words I'd said to Mom when we got sucked through time and space earlier. It feels like a little wink from her, putting my own words in Aunt Lydia's mouth right now.

The next logical question hits Theo and me at the same time. He carefully flips the painting over. Do we need to find the title and give it to Lydia before we can get our last clue?

"Here," Lydia says, holding out an envelope before we can even ask the question out loud. "I'll make it easy on you guys. I'd say by now you've earned it."

Anticipation tickles my throat as I take the envelope. It's exciting to see my mom's handwriting again and imagine what she might have written inside. But unlike when we first started the hunt, I know this clue won't be about finding some material object. No, whatever is inside will be way more valuable than anything I could ever hold in my hand.

Aunt Lydia gives both Theo and me a rough hug. "I'll leave you all to it then." She sketches a bow. "My job here is done."

We wait for her to disappear inside, then face each other, the envelope trembling in my hand as I hold it between us.

"This will finish the poem she wrote through the clues," I say with certainty.

"It's the last line of the message she wanted to leave behind for you," Theo adds.

"For us," I correct him, and he smiles.

I carefully slide my finger along the flap, revealing the paper inside. I pull it out, but don't open it.

"Let's start at the beginning, then add this to the end."

I catch his hand in mine, and in one intertwined voice we recite the lines now etched in both our memories forever.

"Find your center star and follow it North.
Into the dense wooded forest until you can go no more.
Dig beneath the hardened heart,
to find the map at the core.
There you'll find The Hunt was a ruse.
This adventure was only ever about You and You…"

Theo stops, waiting as I shakily read my mom's last line. *"And the real treasure is Life itself."*

Heat blooms across my skin as the meaning of the line settles deep into my soul. The words themselves are so damn simple. Yet, they were written by a dying woman. A woman whose treasure of a life was slipping away. Which makes the message so much more poignant.

When I look up, Theo's eyes are glistening. "We really did it, didn't we?" he says, smile growing wide. "We found the treasure we always dreamed of. "

I reach up on my tiptoes and brush a kiss to his lips. "Yes. And it was beyond anything we could've ever imagined was possible."

Something obvious hits me then, and I huff a laugh. "Even though it was with us all along."

Because it *was* always there, wasn't it? We were smack-dab in the middle of it the whole time. Life, itself. All the joys and heartaches and thrills and sorrows that make up this crazy rollercoaster ride called living. After all Theo had been through, he'd never taken his ticket on this ride for granted. But I had. Now I've been given the chance to see things differently. To have my own bonus life with the man I love. And luckily, I didn't have to almost die in order to wake up and finally recognize the treasure I'd been given.

Out of nowhere, Theo shouts a loud "Woo Hoo!" then grabs me around the waist and spins me around and around, until we get so dizzy we collapse against the car gasping for air.

When the world finally stops reeling, I look down at the paper in my hand again. "Shit," I say, realizing something.

"What's wrong?"

"Oh, it's stupid…it's just that…wait a minute." I dash off to my car and return with the gift I'd made for Theo.

"This is nothing compared to what you gave me." I reluctantly hand the gift bag to him. I'm a little embarrassed when he tosses aside the tissue paper with his typical grand flourish and pulls out another frame. "Seems pretty unoriginal now," I mumble. "Looks like we're going to have to find a hell of a lot of wall space, huh? With all these pictures we now have to hang."

Although my gift isn't really a picture, since it's only made up of words.

"This is amazing, Annie!" Theo marvels down at my little craft project. I'd cut out the clues from the Treasure Hunt, mounted them on colorful cardstock, then framed it for him. I thought having the poem together like that would remind us of our journey. Of all the days we'd spent traversing the countryside of Indiana, falling more and more in love every day.

"Yeah, but now I have to add this," I lift the final clue in the air. "Which means I'm going to have to reframe the whole thing."

Theo traces a finger down the glass, a smile growing as he takes in each sentiment. He chuckles to himself…quietly at first, then louder and louder as he stares at my gift.

I make a face at him. "What's so funny?"

"Oh, it just seems kind of fitting." He looks up, eyes dancing with amusement. "Because these clues aren't the only things we're going to have to reframe, Annie. After what we found out today, we're going to have to reframe our entire lives!"

CHAPTER FORTY-NINE

AS A TURQUOISE wave sneaks up the beach, tickles my toes, then races back into the ocean, I silently commend myself for having the good sense to marry the heir to a vast pierogi fortune.

Our honeymoon trip to an all-inclusive Hawaiian resort was a surprise wedding gift from Maria. Booked when she still believed it would probably be the last time Theo got to travel to such an exotic locale before he died.

I smile to myself thinking of how she'd reacted to our big reveal last week after our wedding ceremony. It had been straight out of a movie: Maria's legs buckling from underneath her; her clutching at Theo's shirt just to stay upright after we'd explained how we'd somehow changed our fates.

Of course it had been hard for her to believe at first, even with how accepting she'd always been of her son's otherworldly connections. But with both of us insisting, and Theo showing her his magical disappearing bruises, it wasn't long before she was jumping up and down alongside us, tears of joy streaming down her face. She told us we'd just given her every mother's dream: a chance to know their child was going to live a long and happy life.

And oh, how we'd all partied after that! In retrospect, I should have trained harder for our wedding reception, because Good Lord, I'd never danced and sang and twirled and shouted for so long in my life. But even though I was gasping for air, clutching my side, I refused to rest for even one moment. Everything was just too perfect…I had to soak in every drop.

At one point, Theo had pulled me off the dance floor and forced me to drink a glass of water, fearing I was on the verge of collapse. We'd stood there, propped against each other like a cockeyed lean-to, surveying the scene: Charlie bopping up and down next to Caroline. Rebecca twirling hand in hand with little Jack. Jonathan bumping butts with Lisa. Franco and Victor performing a perfectly choreographed dance to Madonna's "Vogue." Maria spinning around with Nate and Sophie.

As the lights flickered over their gyrating forms, Theo shook his head in disbelief. "How is this even possible?"

I nestled my cheek against his chest and repeated the words that popped into my head from a certain someone celebrating right alongside us. (Just as she always insisted she was.) "It's possible because we did it together."

Now, wriggling my toes in the pristine white sand, sipping some fruity cocktail with a name I can't remember, I still can't believe I'm here, enjoying such luxury.

It's not surprising Theo and I hadn't planned a honeymoon, since we used to be so careful about not looking too far into the future. (Given that we didn't believe we had one.) The only thing we had planned after our wedding was Theo's appointment with his oncologist. He hadn't told me, but he'd had a preliminary blood test run on himself when he'd first noticed his bruises. And just as he suspected, his platelet level was extremely low. Which is why it was important for him to keep the appointment with the specialist last week. We need those bloodwork results so we finally have empirical proof that our fates had indeed been changed on our wedding day.

I glance over at the empty beach chair beside me. Theo is up in our hotel room right now calling his doctor to get the results. He's been bouncing off the walls, so full of energy these past three days of vacation. And we've seen no bruises since the wedding. (Even though, thanks to Greta and Theo's competitive nature, the dance floor turned into a bit of a mosh pit at the end of the night.) We'd had even further confirmation that we'd switch our future trajectories when, the day after the wedding, we'd pried the back off Mom's fifth painting of The Lookout and seen its title. "The Jump" was penciled in the corner. Oh, how we'd laughed.

But even with all those clues on our side, waiting here alone…with this fragile hope still so new…my old doubts creep back in.

Trying to distract myself, I think of our visit with Maeve after the wedding. Ewan was as rambunctious and carefree as ever, with no signs at all that he'd nearly drowned a couple of days earlier. In fact, Maeve said he spoke of the incident like it was no big deal.

"I fell in the water and played with my Angels until Theo came and got me, that's all," he'd said to her. "Why does that make you cry, Mammy?"

While Ewan commandeered Theo to play trucks with him, Maeve had confided in me that the accident was a wake-up call for her.

"I came to America trying to be so damn independent. Wanting to prove to Ewan's father and my family that I didn't need them." Her eyes welled as she watched Theo and Ewan sprawled on her living room floor. "But I *do* need them. I can't do this all alone. And I now realize there's no shame in asking for help."

I'd choked up, thinking of how I'd learned the same lesson myself on the Treasure Hunt.

"That's why I'm going back to Ireland," she said. "I have so many people there to support me…to support him. It's time I stopped being so stubborn and admit that I can't do this all on my own."

I'd heartily agreed with her. After all the miracles I'd witnessed in my life this past year, I was never going to 'go it alone' ever again.

My mind drifts to the other tiny treasure that came out of our unconventional wedding day. Somehow *The Indianapolis Star* newspaper had caught wind of Theo's heroic rescue and sent a reporter out to meet us at camp for an interview. She and I had hit it off immediately.

She was about my age, with an irreverent sense of humor, and a way of listening that made you feel like you were the most interesting person in the world. After Theo had gotten called away to help Tim with his cabin project, she had lingered, telling me how she once worked at a camp too. And after I'd complimented her hair (a beautiful red-gold color) and she'd complimented mine right back, she'd snapped her notebook shut and the two of us had plopped down at a picnic table and talked for another hour like we were old friends.

It turns out she'd just gotten engaged to her high school sweetheart. (Who is some big-wig, high school basketball coach in Indy, although I'd never heard of him.) They'd reunited last year after spending some time apart to "do some growing up," as she put it. Things were going so well between them they decided they'd wasted enough time being alone and now they couldn't wait to get married. Apparently, her fiancé has some connections at the Colts football team, so she's already invited Theo and me to go to a game with them in the fall. I'm excited to get to know them better. It'll be nice to have another married couple our age to hang out with. Although I've assured a jealous Greta it won't affect our time with her and Wen.

I must doze off in my beach chair, because what seems like only seconds later I wake up to the sound of Theo plopping down beside me. Taking a deep breath, I stare out at the ocean, undulating in beautiful watercolor stripes of green and blue. I want to stay in this place where my happily-ever-after still exists for just a moment longer. Because I know when I turn my head and look at Theo's expression all my hopes and dreams will either be confirmed or shattered. I can only pray that what Mom promised us is true. That Theo and I are going to have a long and happy life together.

He clears his throat loudly, and I know I can't stall any longer. I ever so slowly turn my head.

And see Theo's goofy smile beaming back at me. God, it's the most beautiful sight I've ever seen.

I sit bolt upright. "What did he say?!"

"That my bloodwork came back perfect. That's there's nothing to be concerned about. I'm completely normal." He gives me a wink. "Well, as normal as I can be, considering who I am."

I awkwardly flail out of the chair, heaving myself between his legs and into his open arms. "So it's true then?" I ask, scanning his face, making sure I'm not dreaming. "You're healthy? No cancer?"

"No cancer. I'm healthy as a horse!" Theo lowers his voice. "That was his official diagnosis, by the way. Horse-level vigor demonstrated through perfectly balanced clotters in the red stuff. Dr. Yang always likes to talk real professional like that."

I roll my eyes before I grab his cheeks and kiss him so hard we bash teeth.

When I pull away, he gives me a smirk. "So do you want to reconsider now?"

"Reconsider what?"

"Well, I feel like I pulled the old bait and switch on you. When you agreed to marry me you didn't think I'd be around for very long. So now that you know you're going to be stuck with me for a long, long time, do you want to change your mind?"

I stare over his shoulder, pretending to agonize over his question. "That *was* a little sneaky of you. Luring me in with the promise of freedom after only a year."

He grins big. I sit back on my knees, so I can run my hand down his bare chest. "But you might be handy to keep around for a while longer." My hand drifts lower, fingertips glancing along the waistband of his swim shorts.

He leans forward, catching my mouth with his. "Oh, I promise," he purrs into my lips. "I'll make myself very useful. You'll never regret letting me stay." As he kisses me, his fingertips slide up my bare back, pausing to stroke provocatively along the edge of my bikini top. I lean into him, kissing him deeper, silently thanking Maria for booking us an adults-only resort.

It takes everything I have to pull myself away. He's so damn sexy, with his muscled chest and deep tan and silky wind-blown hair. Not to mention that ineffable quality of his that makes every single woman (and some men too) stop and stare at him when he walks by. And he's all mine. Across time and distance, lifetimes and eternities, always together, forevermore. Yeah, I think I can live with that arrangement.

I tell him I've decided to overlook how he tricked me and let him stick around. Then, I knee-walk back into my beach chair and settle in beside him. We hold hands over our pile of abandoned books and watch the ocean sparkle like a treasure chest poured out at our feet. As the seagulls caw and the sun lazily warms my skin, I'm not sure I've ever felt so peaceful in all my life. This is it. This is what my mom wanted us to notice. Our simple lives. Ebbing and flowing as naturally as these waves. Now, all that's left to do is sit back and enjoy it.

As the relaxing rhythm of the ocean dances in my ears, I think of the one topic we haven't discussed yet.

"Soooo," I start off slowly. I'm pretty sure Theo is on the same page as I am, but this still needs to be discussed out loud. "About the other doctor appointment we have scheduled when we get back...."

"You mean the one at the fertility clinic?"

"Uh huh." I let go of his hand and shift sideways so I can see him better. "I really want to have kids with you...and obviously we *are* going to have them...one day..."

Theo nods. We both agree that the flashes of our futures we saw in the afterlife have gotten fuzzier and fuzzier each day. Now, all that's left are vague notions and the warm essence of lives well-lived and full of love. And that's more than enough for us.

"Yeah...one day," he repeats. Yes. We're thinking the same thing, like always.

"It's just that now that I have you, I'm feeling a little greedy." I trail my fingers down his lovely arm.

He wags his eyebrows, looking down at where I'm touching him. "Oh, greedy...I like the sound of that. And the feel of it too!"

"Yeah, I'm thinking maybe I want you all to myself for a little while longer."

"Hey, I'm all yours!" He holds his hands out, offering himself up to me, the same way he did that day on Charlie's porch. "You can have me whenever you want me. From now until…well, forever!"

I giggle at his puppyish enthusiasm. So far, I'm not sick of it…and honestly, I don't think I ever will be.

"Good. I'm glad we agree." I lift his hand and kiss the back of it. Once, twice, three times. "So maybe we can milk this for a little longer?"

"Mmmm," he says, closing his eyes as I flip his hand over and pepper little kisses all over his palm. Goodness, he tastes so good; both salty and sweet, just the way I like…well, everything. "Yeah, we've got time. I'm all for lingering…and savoring for a little while longer."

"Yeah, just a little while longer," I agree. I press my palm into his and squeeze it tight.

Recognizing my call back to a time when shaking hands wasn't quite so easy, Theo sits up in his chair and leans toward me. He squeezes my hand in a very firm, very Earthly handshake. We smile stupidly at each other; two hearts joined as one for all of eternity.

"We've got time," I repeat.

"Our whole lives ahead of us," Theo adds.

"And knowing that…"

We both give a shrug, then say as one, "What's the rush?"

EPILOGUE

CHAPTER FIFTY

25 Years Later
ANNIE

CHAIRS LINE THE platform at Bluffpoint Lookout. Garlands of flowers snake around the railings. A guitar sits propped next to an arrangement of wildflowers off to one side. And (thanks to all my prayers this week) crystal blue skies shine above the glassy surface of the lake.

"Kind of takes you back in time, huh?" I say to Theo, standing next to me on the trail.

He can only nod, his eyes already filling with tears. I knew he'd be a mess today. All these years of life's ups and downs and my sweet husband has only gotten softer with time.

"Keep it together," I playfully admonish him. "You've got an important job to do today."

"Stop," he chokes out. "You're only making it worse."

We both huff a laugh, mine just as choked as his, despite how I tease. As if this day isn't emotional enough, being here in this place… with it looking so much like that fateful day twenty-five years ago… well, it only serves to make everything so much more heart-wrenching for us. And I wouldn't want it any other way.

Theo's words from that night at our wedding reception flash

back in my mind. "How is this even possible?" he'd marveled as we'd watched all the people we loved celebrating together.

I've stopped counting how many times we've repeated that same line to each other over the years. Stopped noting how many times we've been stopped in our tracks, so stunned by our abundance of good fortune that we've had to bless this friendly Universe right out loud. Gratitude that has swept in during all the big milestones you might expect: the birth of each of our four children, moving to our new house, Theo's promotion to head nurse on the pediatric oncology unit. And in the smaller, more ordinary moments too: During an early morning snuggle on the couch. Laughing with the kids around the dinner table. In the car, with the music playing loud and the wind blowing through our hair and the sunlight slanting at just the right angle off a rain-glittered road.

We've never forgotten how lucky we are. We've never forgotten that this beautiful life we have together almost didn't happen.

Now in the woods, I face him, brushing a fluff of milkweed seed off the shoulder of his black suit. "Try not to lose your jacket this time." I give his lapels a tug for emphasis.

His green eyes dance as he laughs at my jab. I may be biased, but to me Theo is even more handsome now at forty-five years old than he was at nineteen. He's still annoyingly fit—running every day and playing in a basketball league with our boys when he gets the time—his body now more filled out and muscular than the lanky boy I met in the dining hall long ago. The only sign of aging on his tan skin is a few smile lines around his mouth, because of course the man smiles more than anyone I've ever known. And although his chestnut hair is shorter, it's still wavy and streaked from the sun, not a grey strand in sight. Although we both know the gray is eventually coming for us both. Funny how that's one of the few things we still remember from our trip to our future on our wedding day.

"Oh, don't worry," Theo says. "I'll leave the rescuing to the young kids." He lowers his voice conspiratorially. "Although I still think I can probably out-swim them all."

"Hey! Is that a challenge?" Our oldest son, Nick, comes up the trail behind us and playfully punches his dad on the arm. Seeing him, Theo wraps him up in a bear hug, tousling his blonde hair as they rock back and forth.

Nick hugs him back just as hard. Our kids are used to their dad's effusive affection. In fact, the first time our third-born Luke went on a sleepover he came home appalled because his friend's dad only waved goodbye to him on his way to work and didn't do the five minute "kiss 'em, hug 'em, tell 'em how much you love 'em" goodbye ritual that Theo performed every time he left the house.

Theo knows how close he came to never being a father. And because of that, he's never taken that gift for granted.

Once untangled from his dad, Nick throws an arm over my shoulder. "I'll take care of Mom now, Dad." He gestures down the trail. "I've been sent to tell you to get down there and get ready for your big entrance."

Theo hesitates, smiling at the guests streaming up the boardwalk to take their seats. I know he's dying to stay and talk to every one of them. But I assure him he can do that at the reception later; that I'm perfectly capable of welcoming everyone while he's gone.

Although he agrees, he still looks a little fragile as he turns to go. So I follow after him, pulling him to the side of the trail to plant a soft kiss on his lips as reassurance. It astounds me how touching him still sends sparks of electricity coursing through me the same way it did the first time our skin brushed together as I tied a friendship bracelet on him twenty-six years ago. Our bond has never waned. It's only grown stronger with time.

"Can you believe it?" I whisper to him. "Can you believe this is actually happening? And here, of all places? A place that's now all ours?"

Only five years after we were married, when our firstborn daughter

Joya was only three years old, we got the call from Tim that Camp Boundless was slated to be sold. According to Tim's frantic report, developers were ready to sweep in and convert the 2,000 acres into a housing division. An irreversible decision that would not only destroy the natural habitat but close our beloved camp forever.

There was no way we could let that happen. So, with the help of Beato's Pierogies (now the proud benefactors of Camp Boundless), we bought the camp, moved into the Manor House, and never looked back. I've been running the facility year-round since then, my so-called frivolous college degree (as my sister used to call it) being put to all kinds of good use.

Camp Boundless is where we raised our kids (Joya and her three brothers, Nick, Luke, and Antoni). Where I made my dream come true when I'd added special programs for bereaved kids like me. Where countless memories have been made, both for our campers and our family alike. Where Mom's series of painting now hang on display in the dining hall as a tribute to the camp's natural beauty. And where today, our daughter will be married.

Nick darts off to check on his groomsmen brothers, leaving me alone in the shadows of the trail. I scan the guests as they wait for the ceremony to begin. The platform altar isn't the only part of this day that harkens me back in time. Scattered among the younger crowd are many of the same people that were here to witness our "Third Time's A Charm" wedding long ago.

There's my sister and Jonathan sitting with Jack and Emma just behind the front row. My sister found her niche in life when she got her Fine Arts degree when her kids went to elementary school. She now runs her own ceramic studio where she teaches classes and creates her own art, just like our mom used to. Luckily for me (and my campers) she shuts down her studio every summer and becomes the Arts and Craft Director here at Camp Boundless. A job she adores, especially because for the past five years Emma has been her Assistant Director.

Caroline turns to chat with Rebecca, her summer co-worker.

Because yes, I'd also recruited Rebecca onto the staff when I launched my camp for kids battling grief. She started her equine therapy program here fifteen years ago. But Sydney's Gift (named after her beloved horse, who has long since passed) has now grown so big that she has six therapeutic horses, four full-time staff plus tons of volunteers who help her run sessions year-round, which thrills me because I get to see Rebecca almost every day. (The only drawback is I had to get a new therapist because, with Rebecca and I being such good friends, she couldn't be my therapist anymore.)

Sitting next to Caroline, Lisa leans over in her chair to add her two cents to the conversation; the three of them laughing uproariously at whatever brash nugget Lisa's most likely just shared. As I'd hoped, Lisa and Caroline became best friends when they lived in the neighborhood together. In fact, their sons, Jack and Ben, also became so close they now run some kind of online tech company together that none of us really understand, other than it makes them a ton of money.

Unfortunately, Lisa became one of Rebecca's clients last year when her husband was killed in a car accident. It's been hard for Lisa, being so lonely since her kids are out of the house too. But we're all doing our best to look out for her. I just offered her a job as a registrar for camp, which she seems excited about. I hope she takes it. I know what it's like to feel isolated after someone you love dies. And I also know that reaching out for support is the only way to find out that you're never truly alone.

"I'm certainly not alone," I tease inside my head. "Still haven't got rid of you yet, Mom."

And you never will! She volleys back with a soft trill of laughter. I glance around at the woods. There will be a hummingbird appearance here today. We're all sure of that. In fact, my Joya is so sure she put her hand-drawn picture of a hummingbird on the wedding program to honor the grandma she never met. (But swears she still feels as a guiding presence in her life.)

I smile at Maria coming up the boardwalk on Nate's arm. Still spry and active as ever, Maria retired and passed on her position at Beato's to Nate several years ago. She now spends her retirement traveling with a delightfully loud-mouthed pack of girlfriends and heading the fund-raising campaigns for Camp Boundless whenever she's home.

Maria always looked much younger than her years, but I swear ever since she found out she wasn't going to have to watch her beloved son die young, the woman's become so carefree I think she's actually aging backwards.

On the platform, Victor strums beautiful background music on his guitar as we wait for the ceremony to begin. He's officiating today, Joya's sweet homage to both her parents' wedding and her surrogate grandpa. Victor's hair is sparse and gray now, which Franco teases him endlessly about because he still has his thick shock on top. (Although his is totally gray too.) I notice Victor's eyes are wet, and he keeps glancing over at where Franco sits with a tender look on his face. He's probably thinking of their own wedding only a few months ago. They couldn't believe it. Two men in their seventies finally allowed to get married! Neither of them ever thought they'd live to see such a day. Ah, what a poignant wedding that was. And talk about a celebration afterwards! I never would've thought those old guys could still pull off a five-minute synchronized dance to a medley of Cher's greatest hits. But boy, did they prove me wrong.

Aunt Lydia chats with Franco. (A bit too loudly, I notice. The stubborn mule refuses to wear her hearing aids.) She's still on her farm in Montana. But now she has the help of her "man-friend" Dave. (The guy from the feed-store whose appreciation for her truck-driving skills turned romantic years ago.) The kids adore their eccentric great-aunt. Our annual visit to her ranch is always the highlight of their year. Although they could sometimes do without Aunt Lydia's cringey sense of humor. She likes to pretend that she's about to tell them all the details of her love life with Dave just to make them run screaming out of the room. (Although I have to admit, it *is* kind of funny.)

From the front row, Maeve catches my eye and gives me a giddy wave. Next to her is her new husband, Randy. He owns a sheep farm just outside of Galway where Maeve is living her dream: running a bakery aptly called Sweet Dreams in one of the revamped stone outbuildings. I was there a few months ago and can attest firsthand that her treats are indeed dreamy. Especially the gargantuan oatmeal cookies she lovingly named Boundless Oats after the camp where she perfected the recipe for a certain someone named me. I can tell Maeve is as excited about this day as I am, judging by the way she's fidgeting in her seat. And we certainly both have good reason to be.

Just as the ceremony is about to start, Greta and Wen rush up the path, flanked by their two teenage girls, late as always. Greta gives me one of her bone-crushing hugs as Wen sheepishly mouths an apology behind her back.

"Sorry," Greta says in my ear. "Rough delivery at the hospital and I just couldn't get away any sooner."

I tell her not to worry; there's no way we could have started without our two best friends here. Then I make a bad joke about needing them in case we need rowers for a rescue boat. (Thank goodness we can all laugh about that day now. Even Maeve.)

Although Greta and Wen drug their feet on getting married, they finally caved in when Greta got pregnant with Livvy, their oldest. Lila came two years later. Both of their girls are not only stunningly beautiful but also the perfect combination of Greta's fierceness and Wen's quiet confidence. And though they're younger than my boys, that still doesn't mean we parents don't secretly scheme to set them up one day. Who knows? Maybe in the future, our families will be joined by more than just friendship.

Our teenaged son Antoni emerges out of the crowd and proudly offers me his arm. Tall and lithe, with wavy brown hair, he looks so much like a young Theo it makes my heart ache. As we prepare to walk down the aisle together, I think of the one person I wish were still here to celebrate with us: Charlie, who died (or 'went to join Sue' as he preferred to call it in his last days) ten years ago.

Oh, how he would've loved to see this. He'd become such a part of our family in the years after our Treasure Hunt ended. I always liked to believe our "chance" meeting made the last years of his life richer than they might have been if we hadn't met. With our raucous family, combined with Caroline's (who taught pottery classes in his studio for years) we made sure his house was never quiet for too long.

Grandpappy, as my kids called him, taught them woodworking and hosted cookouts and came to every major school event and closing day ceremony at camp that he could. Charlie's death had devastated us all. But at least we gained a great reminder of him when Caroline and Jonathan bought his adorable farmhouse and studio and turned it into Teela Wooket Art Center, now well-known for its low-cost classes, art retreats, and beautiful home decor.

Yes, looking at all these familiar faces, I'm proud to say the intricate web Mom wove in her last days on Earth still thrives to this day. A vast net of beauty and love and connection that encompasses so many lives, and will no doubt continue to expand for years to come.

How is this possible? The question arises again. And I'm happy to admit I don't know the answer. And I'm okay with that.

Victor's guitar music swells sweetly through the summer air as Antoni and I line up behind Maria and Nate, about to be escorted to their seats. My heart threatens to burst right out of my chest. With love. With nostalgia. With hope. And most of all, with awe. Because this wedding has another similarity with the one that took place here twenty-five years ago: Joya and her groom beat billion to one odds to get here today.

CHAPTER FIFTY-ONE

THEO

"SHOULD I BE nervous, Dad?" Joya asks. "Because I'm not nervous. Were you nervous before your wedding? Do you think it's wrong not to be nervous? Or is it good? What do you think, Dad? Do you think I'm being normal or weird right now? Tell me the truth. I can handle it."

I laugh at my precious girl who is currently clutching my arm with such a tight grip I can barely feel my fingers anymore. No, she's not nervous at all. Once again, I see why everyone says she's a lot like me, not just in looks but in spirit too.

"I think you're being exactly perfect just the way you are," I say, bending to kiss her cheek. It's hard to get the words out because she's just so damn beautiful. A bright smile lights her face; her wavy brown hair loosely braided around her head and green eyes dancing with amusement at her own anxious rant. That's one quality Annie and I are proud to have passed on to our kids. None of them take themselves too seriously.

"Yes, sweetheart, I was kind of nervous at my wedding," I tell her. "But only the first time around."

She laughs at that. The kids all know the story of our fateful wedding. Joya keeps pestering Annie to write a book about our magical love story one day. The two of them go back and forth about it endlessly; Annie always making excuses about how she doesn't have the

355

time. But my money is on Joya eventually wearing her mom down. My daughter might have my height, hair, and eyes, but she got all of Annie's stubborn streak. (Which makes it especially funny for me when they butt heads.)

"I was nervous at the church," I clarify. "But once your mom and I got here," I nod to the forest, "everything suddenly felt so right that all I felt was excitement. I couldn't wait to start my life with her."

She considers that, biting her lip the same way Annie always does when she thinks hard about something. "I'm just so excited too, Dad. I can't wait for us to start our lives together."

"I know you are, honey." I pat her hand on the crook of my arm. "As you should be. You're marrying a very special man."

A little over a year ago, Joya called us just before she was leaving to fly home from her summer trip backpacking around Europe. Earlier that spring she'd graduated with her Therapeutic Recreation degree from Indiana University and was slated to come work with us at camp full-time that fall. Like all our kids, Joya had grown up in the woods, tagging along after her mother (and me in the summer when I took time off from the hospital to work at camp), helping with campers during the summer and on weekends in the off season.

Joya had been our trusty assistant since she was a little girl. So we'd decided she deserved a little break and treated her and her best friend to a trip abroad before they had to become real, working adults.

We'd only had sporadic contact with her throughout her trip. A few brief phone calls to let us know she was still alive, but few details other than that. That's why we were so surprised when Joya told us she was bringing a boy home she wanted us to meet. She'd breathlessly explained (so fast neither Annie nor I could get a word in edgewise) that this boy was special. Like no one she had ever met before. That they'd spent the last three months traveling together, and although he was a bit older than her, and although they hadn't known each other very long, she still was *extremely and positively sure* she was in love.

What could Annie or I say to that? Especially since we were the product of a whirlwind summer love ourselves.

Luke had gone to the airport to pick up Joya and "The European Boy," as her brothers had taken to calling their sister's mystery man in the days since the phone call. When they pulled into the driveway of the Manor House Joya had rushed to us before we could even get down the steps, squealing and jumping up and down and smothering us in hugs and kisses the way she always did when she was away from us for too long.

As Luke and The European Boy fished their luggage out of the trunk, Joya quickly briefed us in a hushed tone, clearly desperate for us to like him.

"Oh my God. You guys are going to love him. He's so sweet, and kind, and smart. And he gets along with everyone. And he's so well-traveled."

Annie and I had just nodded, glancing at each other with knowing smiles, thrilled to see our shiny-bright daughter so deliriously in love.

"He even lived in the States when he was little. And get this," Joya rambled on. "He lived in Indiana! Can you believe that coincidence?"

Annie squeezed my arm, a silent warning not to launch into my spiel on how there were no coincidences at that moment. We've accumulated lots of silent warning signals like that over the years. And I have a feeling there will be many more to come.

"In fact, he thinks he might have even been here before," Joya said as Luke slammed the car trunk and we finally got a good look at the boy our daughter had found an entire continent away. "On the drive up here, he said this place looked really familiar."

A rush of heat swept over me as a tall, red-haired man with a smattering of freckles over his nose and a familiar smile walked toward me. Suddenly, he stopped dead in his tracks and stared at me, his mouth hanging open.

He knew. And I did too.

"Mom and Dad," Joya said proudly. "Meet Ewan."

CHAPTER FIFTY-TWO

ANNIE

ONCE AGAIN, HISTORY repeats itself as Theo and I linger hand in hand at The Lookout, the rest of the crowd disappearing down the trail for the reception. But luckily, since we're not the guests of honor this time around, no one really notices us lagging behind.

The ceremony had been simple and yet poignant; so many personal touches added by Ewan and Joya to honor not only their families and their love, but this camp. The place that held the threads of their partnership for so long, then ever so gently tugged those strands together and stitched them into one fabric today.

And the best part was our predictions were right! The hummingbird swooped in just as the couple kissed, its tiny wings spread wide to bless their union. (It seems Mom has become quite a fan of weddings since she turned into an Angel.)

Seeing Joya and Ewan's happiness, all I could think of was walking down that church aisle on my own wedding day and being told so clearly, *This isn't right! This isn't right!* It was no wonder the pull to leave had been so strong that day. Because I now know it wasn't only our futures riding on us moving the ceremony to camp. No, Theo hadn't just saved Ewan that fateful day. He'd saved our daughter's future husband. Our grandchildren's father. Their children's grandfather. And their children's great grandfather…on and on forever.

During our brief time in the afterlife, Theo and I both remember seeing the galaxy of our life choices pouring out into the vast blackness, fractals of future lives expanding out into all of eternity. But we must not have noticed how closely Ewan's own solar system intertwined with our own. Thank God I'd listened to myself that day in the church. And Theo had listened to me. Because if there's one thing I've learned these past years, it's whoever is in charge of this thing called Life, they sure as heck know what they're doing.

"So did I do okay today?" Theo asks, pulling me close, giving me a soft kiss. Then another. Then another.

It takes a while before we're able to pull ourselves apart. When the kids were younger, they used to complain about how affectionate we were with each other. But now that they're older they've grown to admire their parents' special bond.

"You were wonderful," I tell him. "There was only that one glitch when you refused to let go of Joya's hand when Ewan reached for her." I give him a playful poke in the ribs. "But I was probably the only one who noticed that."

"Do we really have to give her away?" he asks with a sad smile. "Ewan's great and all. But she's my one and only baby girl. Can't I keep her forever?"

"Oh, don't worry. She'll always be yours. In fact, I'm a little worried that no man will ever live up to you. You know…since you're perfect and all."

We both laugh at that. Yes, our lives have been blessed. But we've had our share of difficulties. And plenty of fights and disagreements. Neither of us is perfect. We know that. But as it turns out, being imperfect together is what makes this ride so much fun.

That, and the make-up sex. Can't forget about that little perk.

We stroll to the side of the platform, lean our elbows on the railing to gaze down on the lake.

"Can you believe that *that*." Theo points to the sparkling dark water. "Lead to this?" He turns to point to the altar.

As always, he and I are on the same wavelength, thinking about the repercussions of his rescue long ago.

"If I weren't here living it, I wouldn't believe it was possible."

He nods in agreement. "I think we've both given up trying to figure out what is and isn't possible in our lives."

"That's true. I remember a wise man...no, *boy*...once suggesting to me that maybe we aren't meant to understand life. Maybe we're just meant to live it."

"Goodness, that boy was awfully wise, wasn't he? And not annoying at all," Theo jokes.

"Oh, not at all."

"And if I remember correctly, he had great fashion sense?"

"Oh, his clothing choices were impeccable!" The edges of my mouth quirk with humor.

"And he kept his bunk really neat."

"Not a sock out of place."

"And he was *way* too cool to spend the entire summer pestering a girl into loving him."

"The funny thing was, he didn't really have to pester her," I say, squeezing him around the waist. "Her love for him came naturally. As sure and strong as one of these oak trees."

He lets out a heavy sigh as his eyes roam my face, then well with tears once again.

"I love you, Annie. You know that, right?"

"How could I not? You tell me every damn day," I say with fake annoyance. I wait until he's done looking skyward to add, "And I love you too. You know that, right?"

"Well, you don't tell me every day...but yes, I do know that."

We grin stupidly at each other, more in love than one minute ago, another part of my life I'd never believe possible if I wasn't living it right now.

Theo gives a little bow and holds out one chivalrous hand. "May I have this dance, my lovely wife?"

My stomach flips looking at him, standing there offering himself to me once again. He's so dashing in his dark suit, his tall frame looming above me, promising to sweep me off my feet for the millionth time. I can't believe it, but after twenty-five years of marriage, this man still makes me feel like a blushing schoolgirl.

"I'd be honored," I say, as I slap my palm in his.

Theo snugs me tight against his front, one hand strapped across my lower back (a hand that will most likely dip even lower to grab my ass in a few seconds knowing him) the other woven in mine and lifted jauntily in the air. We giggle as we sway around the platform to the music of the forest. The rustling oak leaves providing a faint rhythm. A trio of now oddly synchronized songbirds adding the chorus.

Our hips rub against each other, a promise of things coming later tonight. After a few minutes of slow steps around the wooden planks, Theo increases the tempo, throwing me away from him, then tugging me back; twirling me around while I ham it up pretending to be a ballerina, spinning from the tip of his finger.

We laugh harder as we get more and more silly; breaking apart to gyrate and hop, recreating the dances from our high school years, not minding that the songbirds are no longer keeping the beat. Theo whips his head back and forth, mimicking the heavy metal bands from back in the day as I strum an invisible electric guitar. Thank God no one can see us, or else they might think we've gone mad. (Although they'd be more accurate to think we've gone *happy* instead.)

I finally have to stop to catch my breath. Standing there, clutching the railing, gasping for air, I watch Theo as he thrashes and shakes.

My handsome Muppet.

My clown.

My cross between Steven Tyler and the Roadrunner cartoon.

And best of all...my soulmate, forevermore.

When he notices me staring, he stops and comes to me, slinging an arm over my shoulder, leaning heavily on me as he pants.

"We probably should get to the reception, huh?" he says, beaming one of his sunshine smiles upon my face.

"Yeah. Probably so."

We both let out a deep breath as we gaze out over the expanse before us. I know without asking that we're recalling the same thing again. Reliving the conclusion we came to about this sacred space on our wedding day long ago.

"...*we were feeling this day...this celebration.*" I'd said.

And Theo had added. *"And who knows. Maybe even some more celebrations to come?"*

We'd figured out why The Lookout affected us the way it did then. And why it still affects us the same way now.

"We were right back then, weren't we?" Theo meets my eyes and gives me a wink. I nod in agreement.

Then together we repeat the phrase we've said so often over these past years it's become our family mantra.

"*We* were the happy people."

CHAPTER FIFTY-THREE

40 Years Later
ANNIE

I SHIFT IN my bed, cursing under my breath at the pain that shoots through my body from the simple act.

Then I laugh at myself. My God, this trusty vehicle has carried me through 87 healthy years. (Well, maybe 86 and a half, since I've been going downhill pretty fast these past six months.) What the hell do I have to complain about?

"Mom? You okay?" Joya asks from the chair she's pulled up next to my bed. "What do you need?"

"I need to go see your father," I snap, sounding more like a crotchety old lady than I'd like. "It's been too long, and I'm ready to go."

Joya laughs, now used my familiar refrain. "And I bet he can't wait to see you too. Although I hope you adjust your attitude before you get there. You know Dad never liked hanging around with grumpy people."

I smile, my heart swelling at the thought of seeing Theo again. Just as we glimpsed during our brief peek into our future, Theo did in fact die before me. Five years ago, to be exact. The cancer finally came back for him. But only after we'd had a long life of kids and grandkids and great grandkids. Only after we'd travelled the world. And tried our best to make it a little bit better than we found it. Only after we'd met countless beautiful faces at our camp. Only after Theo had saved even more lives, and I'd tried to save the beautiful natural world I love so dearly.

Maybe we'd made an impact. Maybe we hadn't. All I know is we had a helluva good time trying.

But boy, do I ever miss him. This ride was never quite the same after he left.

He was here at home when he died. We made him as comfortable as possible in a hospital bed we put in the Manor House living room. The home we'd lived in nearly our entire lives. (And where I now rest today.)

His bed looked out on the forest, at the paths he used to run for hours well into his late sixties when a bum knee sent him into the pool and the lake for exercise. That abundance of energy that had bowled me over the first time we met took a long time to wane. I used to tease him that when he got his bonus life, he got an extra shot of life-force too. It served him well right up until the pancreatic cancer landed him in that hospital bed. That's when we knew his extra time had finally run out.

On his last night, I'd sensed him slipping away from me. Desperate to hold on to him for as long as I could, I climbed into his bed and pressed my body alongside his, trying to sear the feel of his skin, the rhythm of his heartbeat, the sound of his breath into my memory forever. He'd murmured a satisfied sigh and pulled my leg over his own just like he used to when we were two (much more flexible) twenty-something-year-olds.

We'd lain there together talking about what a blessing…what a damn *miracle* our lives together had been. Oh, that we'd found each other! And against such odds! Wasn't it amazing? How we pushed past our fears and embraced the unknown and learned to trust in that which could never be proven? It was a wonder; all we'd been given. And looking back, there wasn't much more we could say other than, "Damn, we did good."

"Will we really always be together?" I'd asked, clutching onto his bony frame fiercely, as if I could make him stay with me through sheer determination alone.

He'd nodded, the movement barely perceptible because he was so spent. "Yes, of course. You and me. We'll always be together. Forevermore."

I'd propped up on one arthritic elbow and looked down on him, seeing only the vibrant boy I fell in love with, not the wasting old man in my arms. Then I'd asked him my final question. "You promise, Theo?"

It was the same question I'd asked him when I was a foolish girl thinking of leaving him; so scared of letting myself love that I'd almost missed out on the greatest blessing of my life. Oh Lord, am I ever glad I came to my senses back then.

Theo had given the same answer he had that day when we were young. "I promise, Annie."

I knew he wanted to say more, but he couldn't. So, just like he taught me, I let it be enough. What other choice did I have?

So I held him. And stroked his skin. And thanked him for every loving, crazy, annoying, goofy minute he gave me. I'd fought sleep, but just like the march of time, it had come for me. And when the sunlight tickled my face the next morning, I didn't even have to open my eyes to know my entire world had changed forever. Because Theo was already gone.

∞

Now, in my bedroom at the Manor House, Joya fusses over me, and I let her because I know the busyness soothes her. I don't want her to think she did anything wrong when her mom died, like I once did. Goodness, with all I know now, my worrying back when I was younger seems so silly. But then again, most things seem silly from a long-haul perspective like mine.

In the end, Joya had won. (Just like Theo always said she would.) I finally gave in to her badgering and wrote a book about my love story with Theo. I'd held out a long time, not starting until five years ago, right after he died. I bless my daughter for her persistence because I swear that book saved me during that dark time when all I wanted was to follow my beloved husband to heaven.

I expected writing about our life to be painful. But immersing myself in the memories—being allowed to go back and relive our time together in such a visceral way—actually turned out to be pure bliss. I'd sit down at my desk and start writing, and suddenly I was with Theo again. He was right there beside me…on the trail, in the boat, at the table. And he was just so…so…*real.* I know most people think losing themselves in their imagination is a waste of time. But I'm here to tell you that sometimes, escaping into that space of pure freedom is the most healing place you can go.

The book starts with the scene where Theo and I meet Mom in the afterlife and ends on the beach at our honeymoon when we found out he wasn't going to die young. (With an epilogue thrown in from Joya's wedding, since my goodness, that whole Ewan thing was quite a twist.)

I honestly don't know how I remembered so many details at my "advanced age." (The candy-coated term my doctors use to describe me now.) But with the way my pen flew across the page day after day without me ever getting tired or at a loss for words…I swear it wasn't me telling our story alone.

Who knows what will happen to the book. Joya is determined to publish it. But it looks like I won't live long enough to find out. And that's okay. If our story can help just one person feel less alone…or feel a tiny bit more gratitude for their ordinary life…or heck, simply entertain them for an afternoon or two, that would be one more bonus to come out of our blessed long lives.

Now, resting comfortably in the bed I shared with Theo, my heart warms hearing all the hustle and bustle downstairs. Conversations and laughter and clinking dishes and barking dogs. Along with the occasional hiss of "Be quiet! Grammy's trying to sleep!"

Joya insists on rotating my visitors. There are so many children and grandchildren and great-grandchildren gathered together. (Most of whom wouldn't exist if Theo and I hadn't made the choices we did on our wedding day.) She says she doesn't want to exhaust me with too much activity all at once. I want to say "I've been running camps and raising kids my whole life. I thrive on chaos!" But then I hear the soft classical music Joya is playing in my room. And watch the trees swaying gently outside my window. And enjoy the quiet one-on-one conversations I'm having with each of these gorgeous creatures I'm lucky enough to call my family, and I think, maybe she's right to run a little crowd control.

For the past few months, Antoni and Livvy's youngest daughter, Rose, has been interviewing me. She asks me all kinds of questions about my life and records my answers as if I'm some wise old sage. Which now that I think about it, maybe I am. (Although I've always felt like the same girl who used to push wheelchairs up the switchback from the lake and sing silly songs in front of the dining hall after dinner.) But it's true; I'm the last of my generation in this family. All those I might have deferred to in the past are now already gone.

Months ago, when Rose asked me what lessons I'd learned in my life, I'd blabbered on about all the things Theo had helped me discover. About choosing to believe the Universe is friendly. And embracing this benevolent force dedicated to caring for you throughout your life. And appreciating the simple moments. And how the Now is always enough. I'd told her that learning to trust without proof is the greatest challenge we all face in life. And the most rewarding. And I'd also shared probably the best lesson my sweet, silly husband taught me: Never be afraid to look foolish. Especially if it means you can make someone laugh.

After one of Rose's visits, my mind had drifted to thoughts of what my life would've been like if I'd stuck to my original plan and broken up with Theo when camp ended. What would have happened to me if I had been too scared to commit to loving a dying man?

I would've lived an entirely different life. Married a different man.

Had different children. Experienced a completely different version of this world.

I saw myself in my alternate reality stumbling across the fifth watercolor painting in Aunt Lydia's attic one day. It would've been up there, tucked away, full of cobwebs because she'd never had the occasion to give it to me. How would I have reacted upon seeing it? I imagined myself staring at painting, pulse racing at the unnamable familiarity I sensed looking at the wedding altar in the woods. A hollow ache would tug at my heart; a wave of sadness swallowing me up, making me burst out in tears for reasons I couldn't explain. *I've missed something,* I'd think to myself. *I know that much. But what is it?* I'd never find out for sure. And maybe it would be better that way.

Now my dear Rose sits by my bedside, tears brimming in her hazel eyes, asking if there's anything else I want to say. I think of Theo telling me to let things be easy. And under those parameters, there's only one simple message I want to leave behind. The one piece of advice that trumps all others.

I place my gnarled hand over my granddaughter's porcelain one, and smile at the familiar open-heartedness I feel pouring from deep inside her soul. Oh, there's so much more we pass down to our children than just our eye color and height.

"Just love," I tell her, feeling a chorus of voices speaking through my own. "That's all you have to remember, honey. *Just love.* And the rest will take care of itself."

∞

"Why are you teasing me like this?" I grumble to Theo as I drift off to sleep. These past years since he's been gone, we've kept in touch using our old telepathic connection. But I figured at a time like this, "On my deathbed for Chris's sakes!" he'd make himself seen to me as he prepared to usher me home.

It'll make things more exciting if you wait, he teases back. His voice is so real, it sounds like it's coming from right beside me. But every time I turn to look for him, he's not there. *And I know how much you like things to be exciting*, he adds as if he knows I'm about to complain more.

"Fine. But can you at least hurry up? I'm done with this time around. I'm ready to be with you. Right now!"

Still so impatient. You know I've always loved that about you.

"Mom? Are you okay? What do you want me to hurry with?" Antoni says, leaping to his feet beside me in the dark room.

Whoops. I guess I said all that out loud.

I assure him I'm alright and tell him to go back to sleep, stifling a giggle as he settles back in his chair and closes his eyes. I feel a giddiness bubbling over me as I sense my release coming soon. It's good that Antoni's here. He's more relaxed about this process than the others. As a veterinarian, he's well versed in this whole circle-of-life stuff. Maybe I'm not a dog or a hamster, but as living creatures, aren't we all kind of the same in the end?

All of a sudden, a warmth comes over me, a feeling of being embraced by many arms. I relax into the sensation of being held so tightly, rocked and stroked like I'm the most cherished treasure in the world. I sense my sharp edges blurring, the aches and pains of my physical body dissolving away, drip by blessed drip.

Words can't describe how good I feel. Elation. Freedom. Happiness. Wholeness. These hollow words try their best to point at what this is, but they fall so short of the truth it's comical. I laugh and laugh. Oh, how we've gotten it so wrong! This is unlike anything I learned about death. This isn't sadness and darkness and fear. No, this is just the opposite. In fact, I feel like the lightest, most effervescent cloud in the world… rising up and up…floating and flying and expanding outward until I'm not just a cloud… no, wait…now I'm the sky itself! Stretching wider and wider out into a field of endless joy.

"What's not like they say it is, Mom?" Antoni's voice sounds so far away I can barely make it out.

"Dying," I whisper, as every tension, every worry I've ever had washes away, replaced by an enormous ocean of love. "It's not scary at all, honey. It's…it's…*beautiful.*"

∞

Goodness, this dream feels awfully real.

"More real than anything you've ever felt on Earth," Theo says, his voice still only in my head. "See. I told you so."

"Not this again," I shoot back. "Am I going to have to listen to you be a know-it-all for eternity? Is this really what I signed up for?"

I hear his hearty laugh. In my mind's eye, I see him as he used to be whenever I cracked him up; his head tipped back, eyes all squinty. But when I twirl around to find him, he's still not here.

Although what *is* here is amazing.

I'm on a path in the woods. Not a well-maintained boardwalk, but a dirt path with broken boards every couple of feet and the sides of the trail choked with weeds. A trail that looks exactly as it did that summer long ago, when Theo first took me to The Lookout.

Walking on, I take a deep breath, marveling at how intense everything is…the colors so saturated that the greens and browns and oranges nearly drip off the trees. And the smells. The scents of the pine needles and the loam of the dirt are so rich it feels like they're permeating every molecule of my body.

Body? Do I still have a body? I look down to find that I do. It's a bit fuzzy, but I'm wearing my green Camp Boundless polo and shorts, and damn if I don't have two long blonde braids hanging down the front of my shirt. I twirl them in my fingers. Oh, how I loved having long hair like this.

As I trudge onward, pulled by some powerful force—like a vacuum sucking me toward a whirling vortex—I realize my body doesn't hurt anymore. Yes, Theo told me about this too. All my aches and pains are gone. My body feels so strong and flexible and full of energy. Damn, that's something I should've told Rose. Don't take your youth for granted. Enjoy the hell out of your fresh, healthy body while you can.

Taking my own advice, I break out in a dead run (Ha. Ha. *Dead run.* Isn't that appropriate?!) testing out my newfound perfection. Good gracious. I'm flying! Are my feet even hitting the ground? I feel like a kid again. This is absolute heaven!

I laugh, hearing myself. Theo joins in, the sound swelling not just in my ears but seeming to pass through me and pour like an open faucet out into the beyond. When I slow back to a walk, I notice a light glowing off in the distance. Sunlight dancing through an arch of trees. A wooden platform with a few boards missing along the railings.

A figure stands in the middle of the platform with his back to me, looking out into the glare. Heart soaring, I start running again. As I draw closer, he turns, yellow light streaming in vibrant rays around him, illuminating his long wavy hair, his lanky body, his blinding white smile. He wears bright plaid shorts, a green polo, and striped tube socks pulled all the way up to his knees.

And as I step up onto the platform, all I can do is stare at him in awe. I've never seen such a beautiful sight in all my life. (And apparently in all my death too.) I'm so swept away by the overwrought energy coursing through me…no, not just me, but through *us*…I burst out in hysterical laughter.

"You just had to wear the headband," I wheeze, motioning to Theo's signature red bandana, knotted around his wild hair. "And the glasses!" I blink at the two fashion choices of Theo's I used to complain endlessly about. Now, they just look lovely to me.

"I wanted to remind you of why you fell in love with me." His smile is so radiant, I swear if my body were actually made of flesh and bone and not pulsing energy like this, I might collapse in a heap right now, that's how gorgeous he is to me.

I tease him back, pointing at his garish ensemble. "My goodness, looking like that, how did I ever resist you for so long?!"

We giggle together and I notice him drinking me in, looking a bit stunned by my new (but old, but new?) appearance. Although

I'm not sure why he's surprised, since he's the one who planned this reunion for us.

"Why do we even have all this?" I ask, gesturing back and forth between our bodies. "Do we need these anymore?"

With the mention of bodies, I'm reminded of the old me. Which makes me think of all the loved ones we've left behind. I expect to feel sad about not being with them anymore, but I'm relieved to find that I don't. Because now I truly understand that we haven't left them behind. And just like my mom with me, I have this overwhelming sense I'll be able to do more good for them up here than I ever did down there when I was physical.

Remember, it's not up and down, Mom gently admonishes for the umpteenth time. *It's everywhere and always, all at once.* It's only her voice I hear, but it's so close I know I'll be seeing her again soon too.

Theo answers my question. "Oh, I picked these bodies because I thought it would make this reunion much more..."

"Fun," we finish the sentence together, then laugh at our familiar synchronization.

"God, how I've missed you," I whisper, staring into his dancing green eyes; the one part of him that never changed with time.

"I've missed you too. Although for me it's only been the blink of an eye."

"Well, for me it's been five years, so you got the better end of the deal."

"We'll make sure to switch that up next time around," he says. His expression softens. "But honestly...even the blink of an eye was too long to be away from you."

I nod, surprised I can feel a lump in my throat, when I'm mostly made of mist.

Theo looks over my shoulder back down the trail, eyes wistful. "We did good, didn't we?" he says, as if the bumpy dirt path represents the life we walked side-by-side.

"The best that ever was...at least for now."

Realizing we're still standing a few feet apart, I take a step closer. Being separated from the other half of my intertwined soul just won't do anymore. I need to be back with him again.

Sensing my eagerness, my dear sweet Theo, the love of this life and many more to come, shoots me one last goofy grin. What forms will we take next time? I don't know, but I hope whoever he becomes still has that smile.

"So, are you ready to get started on our next adventure?" he asks, holding out one glowing hand to me.

I take another step closer, a hum swelling in my ears as fate prepares to usher us into the beyond. "With you, I'll go anywhere."

Theo and I are both laughing; our eyes bright and hearts bursting with joy when I place my own glowing hand in his. As our souls bind, a blinding white light erupts around us, the world we once knew dissolving away in an explosion of pure love.

And just like Theo always promised…we are together again.

THE END

(And also, The Beginning.)

ALSO BY KIERSTEN SCHIFFER

The Playlist Diaries Series
Fast Forward My Heart
Rewind My Love
Play My Meant to Be

The Treasured Love Series
Love, Fractally

Dear Reader,

Thank you so much for going along with Annie and Theo on their otherworldly adventure. I hope my story has not only entertained you but made you stop and notice the simple beauty in your own life and opened your heart to the notion that the shedding of our Earthly body might be a transition to more, and not such a final ending.

If this book has touched you in any way I'd love if you could leave a review on Amazon and/or Goodreads so those pesky algorithms will acknowledge that I exist! (Again, I'll leave some prompts below if you need help getting started.)

And, as always, I can't thank you enough for your ongoing support of this romantic daydreamer, who will always see the world through her happily-ever-after glasses.

Love

Kiersten,

Not sure what to write in a review? Here are a few questions to get your ideas flowing!

1. What is an element of this book you won't soon forget?
2. What are some themes and topics addressed in this book?
3. How did you like the characters? The setting?
4. How did you feel as you read it?
5. What kind of readers might like this story?

ACKNOWLEDGMENTS

This story was written as one book, then (after a panicked review of the word count) divided into two, so my thanks to all my family and friends noted in *Love, Fractally* extends to this book as well.

I do have to give a special shout out to my husband Andrew, who not only talked me out of throwing the whole book in the trash multiple times but also edited this series. Your love and support mean the world to me. Wonder Twins forever!

I always knew that I would write a book set at a camp one day. Between the ages of ten and twenty-six, I was either attending, working at, or studying about camps. Yes, I really did get that degree in Outdoor Recreation and it was a helluva lot of fun and I don't regret it one bit! Working with kids in the outdoors changed my life so I thought I'd use this space to thank the camps that made me who I am today.

Camp Na-Wa-Kwa: (The Girl Scout camp I attended throughout my childhood, and where I later got my first paying job as a counselor.) Thank you for showing me the joys of hiking straight down the middle of a creek and coming back covered in mud from head to toe. (No spa can match that treatment!) For teaching me all the best camp songs and how to fold an American flag and that you can actually throw up from eating too much watermelon. And best of all: That sometimes spending a summer away from boys is exactly what a girl needs.

Bradford Woods: (The camp this series is based upon.) Thank you for opening my eyes to the challenges facing those with disabilities. After being a counselor there I never looked at a doorway, sidewalk curb, or bathroom stall the same way again. Thank you for teaching me to slow down and listen. To never underestimate what a healthy dose of determination and resilience can accomplish. And that you can learn so much from those who are different from you.

Frost Valley Y.M.C.A. (The camp where I met my husband.) Thank you for showing me how important it is for city kids to experience nature firsthand. For making me realize you can learn to cross country ski one day, then teach it to six-graders the next because you only have to be a little bit better than them to get through the class. And for teaching me that when you live with the people you work with they become your family. (Through thick and thin and Indian Princess weekends…camp staff sticks together!)

And now I implore you all to *get outside!* For every question in your life, Mother Nature has the answer. That lady sure knows what she's doing.

Raised in a small town in Indiana, Kiersten now lives in Connecticut with her husband. When she's not at her desk, you'll most likely find her unabashedly fan-girling over her latest obsession: usually books, TV, music, or some kitchen contraption she has no space in her cabinets to store.

Always curious about creativity and spirituality and where the two topics intersect, Kiersten writes essays on the topic on her Substack "Thought Bunnies." Blessed with the gift of gab she enjoys connecting with readers and would sincerely love if you reached out to say hello on any of her socials!

 @kierstenschiffer

 @kierstenschiffer.com

 @authorkierstenschiffer

 @kierstenschifferauthor